IT CALLS FROM THE SKY

AN EERIE RIVER PUBLISHING ANTHOLOGY

IT CALLS FROM THE SKY

Paperback ISBN: 978-1-7772750-5-1
Hardcover ISBN: 978-1-7772750-4-4
Digital ISBN: 978-1-7772750-2-0

Edited by Alanna Robertson-Webb
Cover design by Michelle River
Book Formatting by Michelle River
Title page art by Michelle River

When you are finished reading this collection of stories please take a moment and review it on Amazon, Goodreads, and/or BookBub.

ALSO AVAILABLE FROM
EERIE RIVER PUBLISHING

NOVELS
Storming Area 51: Horror At the Gate

SHORT STORY ANTHOLOGIES
Don't Look: 12 Stories of Bite Sized Horror
It Calls From The Forest: Volume I
It Calls From The Forest: Volume II
It Calls From The Sky
Darkness Reclaimed

DRABBLE COLLECTIONS
Forgotten Ones: Drabbles of Myth and Legend

COMING SOON
It Calls From The Sea
With Blood and Ash
Dark Magic: Drabbles of Fantasy and Horror

This book is dedicated to our families and friends, to those who have stood by us and told us never to give up on our dreams.

In these strange times we would also like to dedicate this book to the front line workers that fight to keep us all safe, to the parents that had to make the hard decision to stay home and to the unseen and overlooked heros who make our lives possible. Thank you!

Contents

Foreword

We want to take a moment and thank you for purchasing this book, and for supporting both Eerie River Publishing and the talented authors we've featured.

As humans we rely so much on what the sky provides; we trust in the sun and moon cycles to keep our plant life alive, and to keep the ocean tides at bay. We trust that the clouds will bring rain to nourish the land and our streams, and that storms will eventually pass. But what happens when the sky itself becomes our enemy?

In this collection we challenged our writers to think beyond our safeguards to explore the things we take for granted, and to write about the horrors we pray are not real.

Inside this anthology of the dark and twisted you will read original stories from those brave souls who have dared to look inside the box of "what-if". Let them weave you tales of never ending storms, and of creatures that lurk just beyond our reality. Their stories are born of both beast and human kind, though some are of unspeakable horrors that can befall humanity - should the sky ever turn against us.

May you be forever entertained,
Eerie River Publishing

ASCENSION
R. L. MEZA

*C*limb.

The whisper woke Grease like the warm body of a lover sliding into bed beside him. *Cass,* he thought, and reached for her under the blanket. A car horn blasted in the early dawn, accompanied by the nearby clink and rattle of recyclables and the rustle of plastic garbage bags. Grease blinked, and Cass was gone. He groped for her with rough hands, the memory of clean sheets dissolving as the black crescents of his fingernails skated across the cardboard beneath him.

With a great deal of scuffling Grease forced himself upright, and he felt the press of cold brick at his back. He wiped the crust of sleep from his eyes, the blurred features of the alleyway resolving into depressing detail—dumpsters, their plastic lids thrown wide; broken bottles and reeking piles of excrement; the dark, unmoving lumps of the slumbering homeless with their blankets drawn tight against the wet, chill of dawn in San Francisco. Grease pulled the damp tatters of his own blanket closer. The coarse fabric scratched his nose, causing an eruption of sneezes that wracked his aching bones and startled a stray cat from an overturned garbage can. The cat fled, and someone in the alleyway cursed.

Climb.

It was louder this time. Grease stood, looking around him to find that others were stirring from sleep, their bleary eyes searched their surroundings, their brows knitted in mingled expressions of surprise and confusion. Grease turned to the street and saw people walking past the alleyway. There were always people walking in the city, regardless of the time of day, but these people were differ-ent, somehow—wrong. Frowning, Grease abandoned his pack on the cardboard mat. He stumbled to the alleyway's entrance on feet numbed with cold, ignoring the pins and needles in his extremities as circulation resumed its reluc-tant flow.

A woman rushed past, her neck craned skyward, pink plastic curlers bouncing in her hair. She wore a silk robe and slippers, and it came to him then. Grease stared at the people on the street in disbelief, realizing that most were still clothed in sleep attire or were carrying souvenirs from their morning routines. A man dressed in boxer shorts and socks shuffled around a fire hydrant, his middle-aged paunch protruding from his untied bathrobe. The man's arms hung limp at his sides, the handle of an empty coffee mug gripped in one fist. An old woman splashed barefoot through a puddle without taking notice. She wore a tee shirt that hung to her knees, and the green handle of a toothbrush jutted from between her teeth. Toothpaste foam rimmed her mouth like white parentheses.

There were children too, dressed in nightgowns and brightly-colored pajamas. They trailed behind their parents without complaint, glassy eyes fixed on some distant point above them. Those too young to walk were carried, though the adults hefted toddlers and infants with the dutiful detachment of mail carriers delivering packages.

His pack and cardboard mat forgotten, Grease joined the growing throng on the street. He felt a nagging sense of unease, although it was difficult to focus with the whispered imperative clouding his mind—*Climb, Grease. Climb.* It was not until several minutes later, when Grease turned the corner, that he realized what was bothering him: every man, woman and child on the streets of San Francisco was moving in the same direction.

Traffic within the city had stopped, and vehicles that remained on the road had been abandoned, many with their headlights still shining, their doors left ajar and keys dangling from their ignitions. Streams of people had flooded the streets, some still trickling from the doorways of their apartment buildings, coalescing into a river on the US 101—a procession flowing towards the bay with an unspoken purpose.

Climb.

The Golden Gate Bridge stretched across the bay, International Orange metal shrouded in fog. As those at the head of the procession set foot on the bridge Grease watched the fog at the bridge's center begin to churn. He continued on, caught up in the river of upturned faces, and his scuffed boots left the safety of land to take their first steps onto the bridge. A collective sigh of awe rose from the crowd around him, and Grease heard his own voice join them in wonder. The air above the bridge had cleared, as though an unseen hand had wiped fog from a piece of glass to reveal a brilliant array of clouds in the sky above.

An explosion of neon light emanated from the clouds—flaming oranges, sunrise pinks, glowing purples—colors that Grease had never, in all the fifty-three years of his troubled life, seen displayed with such vivid ferocity. Tears sprang to his eyes, unbidden, as he felt a tug in his chest. It was a physical pull at the core of his being.

Climb, Grease. Climb.

Grease experienced a moment of doubt—he was terrified of heights, and his athletic years were far behind him—but then he reached one of the vertical suspension ropes and placed his hands on the cold steel. A surge of energy flowed into his palms, and Grease felt the graying hairs at his temples stand on end. He looked at the other cables along the bridge's length, saw people of all ages and sizes already engaged in the ascent, and tilted his head up to squint at the cables high above. Several people had completed the climb, and were using the beams and cables to progress higher towards the towers.

Someone pushed Grease aside, and he looked down to find that an eight-year-old girl had taken his place at the suspension rope. The girl hooked her hands into talons and leaped like a monkey, wrapping her legs around the steel rope. Her weight carried her back down several inches, and Grease moved to help her but was rewarded for his efforts with a kick to the jaw as she caught hold and tightened her grasp. Grease saw three of her fingernails tear loose from the force of her grip, and then the girl was gone, shimmying upward with alarming speed.

A second person tried to shove past him—fights were breaking out along the bridge as would-be climbers vied for position at the ropes—and Grease threw an elbow behind him, hearing a muffled snap. It was a woman, her broken nose dribbling blood into the fine, golden hair of the baby clutched at her breast. "Hey, lady," Grease said, "you can't climb with that. Go home."

The woman stared at him with hollow eyes. Her mouth drooped open, and a thin string of saliva trembled on her lower lip. There was a brief spark, an idea in the depths of that vacant stare. Grease watched as the woman turned and began to make her way to the next suspension rope. When she had almost reached the rope the woman stooped and placed her infant on the ground, ignoring the desperate wail that rose from the baby as it extended its pudgy arms towards the breathtaking beauty of the clouds above. The baby's mother shouldered past an elderly woman and began to claw her way skyward.

"Hey," Grease shouted, as the throng of people pressed forward and the infant disappeared from sight. "Hey!"

The wail intensified to a piercing shriek, then cut off.

Climb.

Grease forced himself to look away from the red smears left behind by the climbers on the nearby suspension rope.

Climb, Grease. Climb.

Grease seized the steel rope in his calloused hands, feeling his muscles thrum with strength as he heaved himself upwards. The ease of his ascent was shocking. His feet, in their old, leather boots, found purchase of their own accord. Grease felt buoyant. The weight of his tired bones had vanished, and his body moved like a well-oiled machine. After several minutes Grease realized that he could climb more quickly if he kept his gaze fixed on the sky, and the vibrant colors danced in his vision. They were reflected on the dark surface of his dilated pupils. The clouds throbbed, pulsated and beckoned him closer.

A flutter of movement distracted him, and Grease glanced at the suspension rope to his right where an overweight man had lost his footing, his pale legs thrashing in the air. Grease saw the man's grip on the steel slip, and he slid three feet down—a temporary arrestment that caused the thick folds of his belly to shudder—before his hold failed completely.

The man plunged three-hundred feet to the crowded bridge below in utter silence. Grease watched the people directly under his falling body—a pair of middle-aged men and a family of four, the father and mother guiding their two children to the base of a suspension rope—their eyes fixed on the sky. The distance of the man's fall lent the scene a slow-motion effect, and Grease had time to wonder why the people made no effort to flee. They continued to gaze up, past the man's descent, even as his bulk collided with their upturned faces. Grease heard the sickening crunch from his position, hundreds of feet above the pavement, and winced. The man's body exploded on impact, crushing those beneath him into a compacted mess of broken bones and jellied viscera. It splattered the surrounding crowd with the glistening pulp of his liquefied organs. The crowd shifted, moving around the tangled bodies, eyes staring white from their blood-drenched faces.

Climb.

Grease reached the top of the suspension rope, only aware that his climb was complete when his hand made contact with the thick, metal cable above. With a sigh of angst he looked away from the alluring clouds—where green had begun to appear in bright, emerald flashes—long enough to scrambled atop the cable. He followed the examples of others and proceeded along the cable towards the closest tower. Grease continued to stare at the sky, his arms outstretched, undaunted by the frigid breeze that caused his balance to sway. It was as though the soles of his boots possessed strong magnets, his feet moving along the cable's rounded surface with steady progress as long as his focus did not stray from the clouds.

The population atop the bridge had swelled. When Grease reached the tower, seven-hundred and forty-six feet in the air, he felt a rush of triumph. He had an absurd urge to gloat about his privileged position to those who could no longer squeeze atop the towers, to those who were forced to arrange themselves in a precarious row atop the bridge's sweeping cables. Their balance, like his own, remained steady if they kept looking up. Soon they cluttered the length of the cables like ants. Those who still sought to climb tugged at the legs of those standing on the cables, distracting them from the sky and sending them tumbling to the freezing water below.

The sky above was changing, the colors so bright that they hurt Grease's eyes and left burned after-images on his retinas. New colors boiled from their depths—dark crimson, bruised purple, jaundiced yellow—and the whisper in his mind, the imperative to climb, had gone silent. Grease held his breath and sensed that every person on the bridge was doing the same—waiting, watching the clouds churn and roil overhead, listening.

STEP OFF.

And they did, the population atop the bridge shifting from thousands to none with a single, unified movement. Grease kept his eyes fixed on the clouds above, felt his weight shift forward as his scuffed, leather boot left the hard metal of the tower and stepped into the open air. There was no accompanying pull of gravity in his gut, no sensation of organs rising within his body cavity, no sound of air rushing past his ears. For Grease the anticipated plunge towards the icy strait below, the fatal impact like striking solid pavement rather than water, did not happen, although it did happen to some—those who looked away from the sky in that crucial moment when they stepped from the bridge in unison.

Later, Grease would think of them as the lucky ones.

Doubters, Grease thought, as two-hundred people left the crowded air around him and plummeted, clothes fluttering around their stunned, downturned faces. They did not scream, their simultaneous annihilation marked only by the sound of wet meat smacking the surface of the water. Like discarded bath toys their bodies floated in the strait, turning lazy circles in the current while the survivors above began to ascend.

Grease was borne upwards, weightless, his chest bursting with elation. Others rose with him — true believers ascending to meet the glorious, ethereal clouds — their arms outstretched, fingers groping. Grease smiled, and tears streamed down the leathered creases of his face as the bridge below diminished to thin, orange lines. The air in his lungs grew thin, and very cold.

The clouds were close enough to touch. Grease stared into their vibrant, swirling colors and saw movement there, dark and fleeting. From somewhere in the back of his mind Grease felt a primal instinct stir, and he experienced a faint rush of fear at the sight of the large shapes — contorted, twisting, hulking shadows — shifting behind the curtain of brilliant light. He reached for the clouds, his fingertips caressed by neon shades of fuchsia, the veins on the backs of his hands illuminated by flashes of electric green.

There was a sudden pressure in his gut, and Grease winced. He withdrew his hands to clutch at his stomach, the clouds pulsing violently around him as the pressure intensified into a painful suction that caused him to gasp. Eyes wide he saw that others were doing the same, their o-shaped mouths working at the thin atmosphere, many bent double with their arms wrapped around their midsections. Grease felt an agonizing tear deep within his belly, followed by a spilling warmth down his legs, but he refused to look down—didn't need to—because it was happening all around him.

A young woman floated near Grease, her terrified gaze locked on his face. In a sudden, fluid motion the woman's intestines were sucked outwards through her rectum. They were inverted, the contents of her last meal emptied into the air as she shrieked and raked her cheeks with her fingernails. The purplish-grey of her small intestine gave way to the reddish-brown of the large as an unseen force unraveled the woman's bowels like yarn. The space below her ribs and above her hips collapsed into a horrific depression. A chorus of screams rose around Grease, and he gazed around him in shock, the bodies still rising through clouds of vermillion and bile green, blood red and lemon yellow, intestines trailing like balloon strings.

The shadows in the clouds were black, now grown solid, a malignant presence that Grease felt in his bones like sentient cancer. The clouds were thick, too thick to see the others, and Grease was alone with the shadows. They swallowed the light, and devoured the color. He felt teeth move across his skin; stripping flesh from muscle, rending tissue, grinding bone. Something wet slipped through his hair, trailing slime, and his scalp dissolved into wet flaps that folded over his eyes and obscured his vision.

There was nothing outside of the pain. The shadows enfolded Grease, seized his limbs, clenched tight, and—as he was torn into two pieces, then four, then six—Grease realized that the pain would never stop, that it was everything now, and he began to laugh.

R. L. Meza
About the Author

R. L. Meza lives in a century-old Victorian house on the coast of northern California, with her husband and the host of strange animals that she calls family. When she isn't writing horror, roaming through the forest, or painting fungi, she can be found with a cat in her lap and a book in her hand.

HEADS IN THE CLOUDS
MATTHEW BRADY

There was no pleasure quite like flight, no sincerer sound than the beating of wings through domed lapis, through banks of cool and pallid fleece. Cody Pocock, a charter member in man's enduring dream of flight, knew this, and suspected that everyone else did as well. *Mankind's oldest, yet most childish, dream is a bird's mundanity,* the boy often told himself at night before crawling into his futon in the flophouse room he shared with his older sister. *He counterfeits it with jet planes, with helicopters, with balloons and rockets and other things like that, but he does not* inhabit *it, does not possess it. He only adopted it…and what a rebellious child it is, too.*

That coming-of-spring morning he awoke to the rustle and crinkle of bedsheets somewhere above him. His eyes fluttered open against the sunlight sifting down from the grime-speckled windowpanes, and when he looked up he saw that his sister was already awake. She was sitting cross-legged on the mattress, her lap still under the bedcovers as she bent over her work. She was building her little brother a kite, and was now almost finished, though Cody could see by her wan, translucent face that the task had cost her hours of sleep.

He sat up in rigid alarm, knuckling the grit from his eyes, and said, "Edith, you didn't have to do that. You should be resting! Remember what the doctor said?"

"Don't make such a fuss, Cody," Edith said, smiling slowly, laying aside her crafting materials. "I know I didn't *have* to. But it's finished now, see? I even tied on my hair ribbon to the tail for good luck, like Mom used to do—" She tamped a hand to her mouth as a volley of violent coughs hacked away at her. Cody slid out of his futon and rushed into the connecting bathroom, where he filled a cup with water that tasted of iron from the tap of a chipped basin. He returned to the cramped, drywall room, its walls flaking and crumbling from termites, and gave her the cup. He pretended not to notice the pinheads of blood on the bedsheets as he tenderly patted her back.

"It's getting worse, isn't it..." he said. It wasn't a question.

Edith swallowed the water and wiped her lips. "I'm sorry, Cody. I really am."

"What do you have to be sorry for?" he said, against the sting of anger in his throat. "It's that job of yours, those slave-drivers, that've done this to you..."

"We'll pull through, Cody," she tried to assure him. "We always have, ever since Mom and Dad passed away."

"They didn't *pass* anywhere, Edie," Cody snapped.

"They're dead and under the ground. I'm not going through that again. You just need better treatment, and for that we need more money. So that's what I'll get. You leave it to me." He raided the closet and threw on his clothes in a fervent cyclone.

"Cody, where are you going?" Edith asked in concern.

"I have to get over to the park to register for the contest before it closes," he explained. "You know that."

She shuddered. "You mean New Leaf Park? Oh, Cody, I wish you wouldn't…"

"Huh? Why not?"

"My last shift at the mill," she said, "I heard the other girls talking about all the kids who've gone missing there this month. Some of the women I heard this from were their mothers. I still can't get the looks on their faces out of my head."

"Sis," he said, steadily, "the grand prize for this contest is enough money to set us up for *years*. Think of what we could do, what we could *achieve* with that kind of cash, if I just put in the effort and give it my all! We could move out of this place, we could get you better doctors, better medicine!"

"But, Cody," Edith pleaded, "it's never that simple, and some things aren't worth—"

"Yes, they are," Cody said, firmly. "Now no more arguing. You rest, Edie. An opportunity like this doesn't come around often. I'll be right back."

"You swear?" she said, through her dark-ringed eyes.

"I swear."

After carefully lifting the kite from his sister's bed (a delicate, flat diamond frame of thin paper and bamboo), Cody Pocock left the flophouse and hurried across town, wheeling down sidewalks and cobbled streets. He sailed past high, clangorous factories wreathed in scarves of acrid smoke, past the workhouses inside whose lime-washed walls famished men in gray cotton shirts struck at tar-coated lengths of rope with heavy mallets, where afterward famished women and their children picked the ropes apart, their blackened fingers riddled with sores, into fine fibers for oakum.

Cody did not linger in front of these places. He resented the worn faces he saw in the yards and behind the windows, for he saw his potential future in them.

I won't let that happen to me, the boy thought fiercely, the diamond flier in his arms stoking his dreams. *When I win*, he thought, *we'll finally have enough. We'll finally move up in the world. Just my sister and me.*

He arrived at New Leaf Park and hurried up and down the sloped concrete walkways between the oleander trees until he reached the registration booth set up on the stage of a cream-colored bandshell. Sweating and out of breath, he rushed up the steps and gently laid his kite on the table. The clerk sitting behind the table checked his watch and grinned.

"Here for the Sport of Winds Kite Festival?" he asked.

Cody nodded.

"Cutting it a little fine, aren't we?" he chuckled.

"Am I too late?" Cody asked, out of politeness.

"Not at all," the clerk replied, sliding forward a pen and an entry form pegged to a clipboard. "Just fill this out and you'll be all set. Of course, I'll need to see your kite to make it official." His eyes drifted over the boy's modest aircraft, and Cody could tell from the twitching muscles at the corners of the man's mouth that he was trying not to smile. "Is *that* it?"

"Yeah," Cody said, scribbling down the lines of the form. "Is it a problem?"

"No, not *technically*," the clerk said. "But tell me, sir, how long have you been a kite fighter?"

"For years now," Cody said adamantly as he pushed the clipboard back across the table. "It's a hobby. I learned after my mother taught me how to fly."

"And how many fights have you won?" he asked, with the patient serenity of a cat batting about a crippled mouse.

Cody frowned. "What's that got to do with anything?"

The clerk succumbed to a broad, piano-key smile. "You have a kite, sir," he said, "so I can't bar you from entering. That *is* one of the rules, after all: equal opportunity for all. But you might want to take a look behind this stage on your way out. Have yourself a pleasant afternoon."

Cody took his kite and left the bandshell, standing at the bottom of its steps for a moment. He was a smart enough boy to scent condescension, but far too young to temper curiosity, so he walked to the rear of the bandshell.

He saw the people standing out on the rolling, windblown lawns of open parkland, and felt hope dislodge itself from his now-heavy heart.

The people out there were not just casual park visitors; they were his competition in the Sport of Winds, and each of them was getting in some last-minute practice for the kite fighting contest. They stood with their expensive, magnificent fliers unspooled: colorful, ferocious fishes swimming in the sky with skins of nylon, mylar, polyester, with hard bones of fiberglass or carbon fibre, twitching at the sharp, abrasive strings of their handlers.

Cody turned and ran blindly from New Leaf Park, pursued by the echoing laughter of the clerk from his booth in the bandshell. The laughter nicked at the boy's ears as finely as powdered glass.

⊷—⊶

Exhaustion, and nothing else, made him stop. He stood gasping for air, hands on his knees, in the shadows of an abandoned textile mill. It was identical, like so many of the others, to the one his sister worked in. Tears were lancing his eyes, so he withdrew into the alley beside the mill and grudgingly let them leak. He glared at the kite in his hands, a paper dove competing amid hawks, and cursed. Teeth grinding, he threw the kite to the pavement and stomped it mercilessly, repeatedly, beneath his feet. The torn paper hissed like a startled animal, the bamboo frame cracked and splintered like a ribcage, and by the time the boy's rage diminished the only piece of the kite that remained intact was his sister's hair ribbon.

Cody untied the ribbon from the tail, sullied as it was with dirt and filth from the street, and held it to his breast as he wept freely.

"Poor child, why do you cry?" asked the disembodied voice of a woman.

Cody gasped, and pivoted his head from side-to-side to see where the voice had come from. He followed it to the threshold of a side door leading into the textile mill. Standing behind the opened door was an impossibly tall woman, easily over six feet, Cody estimated; so tall that he could not even see her head, for it disappeared behind the lintel. She wore a black blouse covered at the front with a white apron, bringing to Cody's mind the attire of a maid.

"Who are you?" he said, voice taut.

"The children in my charge affectionately call me Mother Diamante," she answered.

"Why don't you show your face?" he said, suspicious. "Are you afraid?"

There came a pause. "Because if I do, you'll be the one who's afraid. I don't want that."

"Then what *do* you want?" Cody asked, slowly back-pedaling out of the alley.

"To help you, silly boy," said Mother Diamante. "You're in distress, so put your tears in my bottle and come inside."

"I don't think you can help me, miss," Cody said.

"Oh?" said Mother Diamante. "What if I told you that

I can help you win that kite festival tomorrow?"

Cody halted, squeezing his sister's ribbon between his fingers. "How do you know about that?" he asked.

"Why, it's all the children are talking about!" Mother Diamante explained, her voice nursery-sweet. "And so many of them are disadvantaged, much like you, my poor boy. So I *help* them, you see. Their dreams flit so close, yet so far, always out of reach of their small hands. So I *put* them within reach."

"How?"

Mother Diamante chuckled. "Well, not to boast, but I'm quite the able craftswoman. Come inside," she cooed, "and I'll show you the kind of kite that I'll build for you. So what say you, dear boy?"

She held out a spindly hand from an even spindlier arm, beckoning expectantly from the doorway of the mill. Cody stood in the alley, cleaved with hesitation. *What should I do?* he asked himself even as his legs turned traitor and conducted him toward the door, as his own disobedient hand took hold of Mother Diamante's. Her hand was as cold as marble, her long fingers entombing his as he was led into the stale recesses of the mill, through the gloomy halls of spinning rooms where the machinery slumbered in rust. As they walked Cody looked up and tried to see Mother Diamante's face, but all he could make out was the back of her head and thick, ragged curtains of her hair.

"What are you doing in a place like this?" Cody asked.

"It allows me to do my best work," she said, with a smile that he could not see. "Nothing inspires quite like suffering."

"You're talking about the mill workers?" he asked with a shiver.

"Oh yes, dear boy," she said. "Though not a soul has treaded here for years, the air around us is still thick with misery. Can't you smell it?" She pointed into some of the spinning rooms as they passed them. "In that room a girl was scalped after getting her hair caught in one of the belts. The machinery was so loud they couldn't even hear her screams." She pointed to another. "In there a child was crushed to death beneath one of the machines she was trying to oil." They stopped before a room with a closed door. "And in here," she said slowly, twisting the doorknob, "a fire broke out that cooked eight teenage girls alive as they were locked inside. You can still see the scratches their nails gouged in the wood."

"You don't have to teach me about misery," Cody said bitterly. "It's because of places like this that my sister is…" He choked on the last word of his sentence.

"Yes, I know, poor child," Mother Diamante said sadly. "Mill fever. Brown lung disease. From breathing in all that cotton dust…"

For the second time that day he asked, "How do you know that?"

"This land has always called out to dreams," she cryptically intoned, "and has always redeemed them in blood. I only follow."

There was a pit growing in Cody's stomach, but he could not act on it. He felt as though he'd been placed on the rails of a dream, where there was nothing he *could* do but allow Mother Diamante to pull him into the room, a windowless room that was now bare of any machinery and lit by a naked, caged light bulb suspended from the low ceiling. She closed the door behind them and released his hand, and the boy saw, propped against one of the blackened walls, the diamond frame of the largest kite he'd ever laid eyes on. It even dwarfed the extravagant ones he'd seen at New Leaf Park.

He approached the half-finished kite and traced his fingers longingly over the spine and cross-spar. They were smooth, pale and cool to the touch, almost like bone, and studded along the length of the coiled string (a string the same shade of coral pink as a person's gums, and as sharp as piano wire) were wet, glistening fangs that undulated gently…

"All that's missing is the sail," Cody murmured, in little more than an awed whisper.

"That's what you're here for," said Mother Diamante from behind him. She was standing in a corner of the room over a burnt workbench, rummaging through its drawers.

"And will she fly, Mother?" he asked dreamily.

"Of course, my dear child," Mother Diamante cooed, turning to face the boy at last. "I do nothing but give wings to dreams."

Cody turned as well, and saw the woman's face for the first, and last, time. He would've screamed, but he couldn't. All he could do was stand in a trance of terror as an impossibly tall woman advanced toward him across the room, a woman with a deformed head shaped like a kite diamond: all jutting bones and stretched, brittle skin, with crazed, globular eyes and a tender, maternal smile.

In her hand a flaying knife sheened with the light it caught.

⊷――∘――⊶

"You say he went missing yesterday morning," said the impassive policeman, jotting down notes on a pad he carried, "and that this place was his last known location?"

"Yes, that's right," Edith Pocock said, shivering in her sweater on the lawns of New Leaf Park against a coldness that had nothing at all to do with the morning chill. "He was going to be in the kite festival, and he told me he was coming here to register. He never came home."

The policeman pocketed the notepad and almost yawned. "We'll see what we can do, ma'am," he said, glancing at the other park patrons, at the gathered families and kite fliers, "but you should manage your expectations. It's entirely possible the boy's a runaway. We see it all the time, especially with people from your, ah, *station*. People with limited prospects—"

"Cody wouldn't do that!" Edith snapped. "Why won't you listen to me? I told you he's..." But her pleas unraveled into a bout of furious coughing that swiftly doubled her over and left the palm of her hand spotted with blood.

The policeman tipped his hat and said, "We'll see what we can do, ma'am."

He turned to walk away, but Edith seized the crook of his elbow with her stained hand and said, fiercely, "I'm not finished talking to you yet, officer! This is my family we're talking about, the *only* family I have left, so you're going to—"

A ripple of disturbance was swelling among the park goers. A crowd was forming, forefingers were pointing up at the sky like sundials. Little chattering pockets of gasps and murmurs were accumulating in the newly-fallen hush over the park. Kites were hastily reeled in by their owners, stars and birds and octopuses and butterflies and Chinese dragons swiftly dragged back down to earth. The policeman brushed past Edith and joined the gawking crowd, trying to ascertain the source of the commotion, which soon became apparent.

There was a fleet of strange shapes in the sky, drifting lazily down from the clouds. At first they were little more than dark dots against the white banks, but once they reached the treetops, the gasps of the crowd turned to screams, and not without reason. The shapes were actually kites…but kites whose sails were sheets of human flesh, stretched taut over frames of bone. And, dangling at the end of each of their tails was a human head, a child's head. The eyes were sewn shut, as though deep in slumber, and they were wearing an expression of profound pleasure. Little flies caught in the sweetened spider threads of an inescapable dream.

Edith recognized one of the heads as Cody's, and she stumbled forward blankly, uncomprehending, arms outstretched toward what was once her brother as he and the other children floated down inexorably toward the panicking crowd. There wasn't even the faintest breath of wind on the air, yet the kites were still being borne along on some unfathomable current. She never stopped moving toward him, even as the screams of the scattering crowd intensified, even as the fanged tails wrapped themselves around the first hapless victims, shearing, stripping…

"You came back, Cody!" she cried gleefully, manically, tears in her round eyes as her little brother floated toward her. "You came back! I knew you would! You swore, remember? You swore!"

Matthew Brady
About the Author

Matthew Brady is a young writer currently living in Nashville, Tennessee. He attended Belmont University, where he studied writing and literature before earning his bachelor's degree. He is the author of one novelette, *Lovebirds*, with a second to be released in the fall of 2020. In 2018, his short story, "Midnight Oil," was published in the second volume of Nosetouch Press's *The Asterisk Anthology*, where it won first prize in the Southern Gothic genre. You can visit his Amazon Author page at amazon. com/author/writtenwordofmattbrady or follow him on Twitter @Matt_R_Brady.

TENURE

V. A. VAZQUEZ

"What's it doing now?"

Milo Banerjee finished re-reading his teaching statement one final time before clicking *Export to PDF*. An icon popped up on his desktop, and he dragged it into the folder labelled *TENURE*.

"Erm," the voice on the other end of the line said. "It's reaching for something on the kitchen counter."

"The hair?"

"Yes."

Milo started running through the checklist scribbled on his notepad, ticking off each item that'd been completed and saved in the folder: teaching statement, check. Research statement, check. Course syllabi and evaluations, check. List of significant publications, check. CV...

"It's going for a butcher knife."

"Uh-huh..."

"Milo, are you listening? Her hair is picking up a god-damned *butcher knife*, and — oh, shit." The voice dropped to a whisper. "I think it's spotted me. What should I do?"

Had he updated his CV with the new grant from the American Folklife Center?

"*Milo!*" The voice hissed into the microphone. "*Milo! Are you there?*"

"Yeah," he said, turning away from his laptop screen. "A woman's sentient hair picked up a butcher knife, and you think it's seen you?"

Footsteps pounded across the floor, and then the squeak of a door opening and closing. "I'm hiding in a closet right now. I don't know if — " Flesh slapped against flesh, as if the man had muffled his mouth with his hand to keep quiet. For a few seconds there was only the puff of heavy breathing, and then: "Sorry, just saw a tendril wriggle past the door. What should I do?"

"Sounds like a *futakuchi-onna*."

"A what?"

"A two-mouthed woman. You know, one in the front, one in the back?"

The closet door squeaked open again as Lloyd Jennings crept back down the hallway. "When I signed up for this paranormal investigator gig, I thought it'd be easy. Record some EVPs, photograph some orbs. Give the tenants something to post about on Airbnb, you know? I don't get paid enough."

"That makes two of us."

"How am I supposed to beat this thing?"

"Do you have GrubHub on your phone?"

"What?"

"GrubHub. *Futakuchi-onna* are women who've gone hungry. Her family might be food insecure, or maybe she has an eating disorder. Get some large pizzas delivered to the house. Once the mouth in the back has been fed, talk to them about what the underlying problems are; it could be as simple as directing the family to the nearest food bank. The second mouth should disappear once she's properly fed."

"And what am I supposed to do until the pizza arrives? In case you've forgotten she's stalking me around the house with a *butcher knife* and some very stabby tangles."

"Check the bathroom for leave-in conditioner?"

"*Ha*," Lloyd said. "*Ha ha ha ha ha*. Fucking hilarious. Hope you break out punchlines like that at my funeral."

"Sorry, I'm in the middle of something right now."

"Well, don't let me distract you with my little demon problem. I'll just keep dodging this woman's summer beach waves."

And with that, Lloyd hung up the phone.

Milo opened up Adobe Acrobat Pro and started arranging his tenure documents into a single PDF. He'd never been good with technology, especially when working under pressure. His dossier was due tomorrow morning, which wouldn't have been a problem if he could have printed out the documents, stuck them in an envelope, and slid them underneath the department head's door. Unfortunately, academia had decided to join the rest of the world in the twenty-first century, which meant all tenure dossiers needed to be submitted via the University of Lewiston's electronic system.

Good luck with that.

The door creaked open to reveal Edie Walters, skinny as a stick-insect, with her hair half-falling out of a bun as she pushed her way into his office. She was carrying a cardboard tray with two takeaway coffee cups from the university library. "Thought you might need a pick-me-up."

"You're a saint."

"I wouldn't go that far." She set one of the coffee cups down on Milo's desk and took a seat in the armchair reserved for students. "I can't stay long. The retreat's not that far away, but you never know what traffic's going to be like. We still have a spare bunk if you want to come."

"Can't. My tenure dossier's due, and — "

"I know." She waved a hand; the bangle bracelets around her wrist rattled. "Next year you'll be bringing *me* coffee."

"You don't have anything to worry about. Everyone knows you're a shoo-in for tenure."

"There's no such thing as a shoo-in — "

"You have two books published."

"There's still no such thing as a shoo-in. With my luck the department will choose a committee of old, white men who've never even read a graphic novel. They'll spend the entire review commiserating over how I'm not a *real* academic. You research comparative folklore; everyone loves that stuff."

"Are you kidding me?"

Milo pulled out the top drawer, removed an unopened envelope, and tossed it across the desk. "Go ahead. Open it."

She slipped her index finger under the envelope flap and ripped it open, taking out a greeting card. "'Professor Banerjee'," she read. "'How can we even begin to thank you? The information you provided was lifesaving.' See? You're always doing service work in the community— "

"Keep reading."

Edie turned back to the card. "If it hadn't been for you, we would have all been suffocated by that blanket-monster' ..." She stopped reading, and looked up at him from over her thick, plastic glasses.

"See? That's the problem with my tenure application! I'm always getting these calls: *we have a demon haunting one of our toilet stalls. My stuff keeps getting stolen by a dead flying fetus. There's a ghost with a seven-foot tongue that keeps trying to lick me. How can I get rid of it?*" He pointed to the card his colleague was still holding in her hands. "It was an *ittan-momen*, by the way."

"What?"

"The murder-blanket."

"The murder-blanket?"

"Yes."

Edie put the card back on his desk and stood up, smoothing out her sheath dress. "I'd recommend leaving the murder-blanket off your CV."

"Thanks."

"Give me a call if you need anything, and good luck with the tenure dossier."

Edie gave an abrupt little wave before she closed the office door behind her.

They'd originally planned on attending the retreat together; they were even going to share a bedroom. While they'd sworn up-and-down the sleeping arrangements were only because of their meagre salaries, and that nothing untoward would ever happen (*no, of course not, they were both respected professionals*), he'd not-so-secretly hoped that late nights of chapter revisions might give way to something more. He was fairly certain Edie'd been hoping the same thing. When he'd cancelled, tenure dossier looming over his shoulder like a *hidebehind*, it'd been with a heavy heart and a whole lot of bitterness.

He'd finally managed to compile his tenure documents into one PDF (after more than a hundred *fuck!*'s had slipped underneath his office door and into the department hallway) when he realized the service section was missing. He was randomly clicking through folders when his cell phone rang. He considered ignoring the call; whatever it was, he had more pressing problems. But, when he saw Edie's name light up on the caller ID, he picked up immediately.

"Milo?"

"Yeah. Did you get to the cottage?"

"About a half-hour ago. I was worried you'd be too busy to pick up."

"Is something wrong?"

Edie sighed. "Everything's fine with the cottage, but when we went to pick up groceries from Wegmans..."

She didn't finish her sentence. Milo double-checked his phone to make sure the call hadn't been disconnected.

"What happened?"

"All the tires were punctured."

"*All* of them?"

"It's probably just some bored high schoolers," she said, and he could hear her puttering around her bedroom. *Their* bedroom, the one they were supposed to have been sharing. "Nothing to do on a Sunday night, so they head out to the woods to stir up a little trouble. I wouldn't be calling you at all, except the puncture marks looked like... You're going to think I'm ridiculous."

"Trust me," he said, glancing at the thank-you note on his desk. "It takes a lot for me to jump to ridiculous."

"They looked like *teeth marks.*"

"Teeth marks?"

"Like a dog had gotten ahold of the rubber and shredded it. You don't think that's what could have happened, do you? Have you ever heard of anything like that?"

Milo checked on Google. "There was a border collie in Brampton who punctured car tires. Left them leaking so drivers would break down halfway to their destinations."

"These weren't slow leaks; all our tires are flatter than Alabama roadkill."

"Can you call a taxi?"

"A taxi out in *Lewiston*? Are you kidding?" He could hear her smile through the phone: Small and closed-mouth, like she was worried someone would notice her enjoying herself.

"Do you want me to come and get you?"

His stomach flip-flopped at the offer. He really didn't have time, but if something was wrong, if she didn't feel safe out there, he'd get in his car and make the drive.

"No, I'm not going to ask you to come out on the busiest night of the semester just because someone decided to vandalize our cars. We'll get a good night's sleep and call AAA tomorrow morning. We might not have all the snack food we wanted, but we have an entire case of moscato ready to go."

Now it was Milo's turn to smile. He could imagine Edie: swaying on her feet after a few sips of wine, half her bobby pins lying loose on the floor, her high heels kicked into the corner of her bedroom. What he wouldn't give to be at that retreat with her right now.

"Sounds like fun. Wish I could be there."

"I wish you could be here too."

Their unspoken words thrummed through the 4G cell service.

"Well," she finally said. "I'll let you go. Thanks for taking the time to talk."

"No problem. Give me a call if the culprits come back."

And with that, she hung up the call.

Milo couldn't find his service section anywhere, so he decided to quickly redraft the document. As one forum reassured him: *no one was ever denied tenure because of their service section.* While he wanted every sentence in his dossier to be perfect, a credit to his work as an academic, a researcher, and a professor, these five pages were just a list of public lectures he'd organized and hiring committees he'd served on. As long as he didn't mention his off-the-books community service (with the murder-blankets and the stabby-tangles), then he'd be fine.

His phone rang again.

Edie.

"Hey, did your high schoolers come back?"

"Milo, I'm so sorry to bother you again."

"Don't worry about it," he said, pushing his chair away from the desk so he could give her his undivided attention. He heard someone sobbing in the distance: a few nasally snuffles followed by a long, drawn-out wail. "What happened?"

"Everyone came downstairs, and Lauren went to get some glasses for the wine. She was reaching for the kitchen cupboard when something dripped on her."

"Like a busted water pipe?"

"That's what I thought too, but she has these large sores all up and down her forearm now, where the liquid splashed her."

"Can you take a photo?"

"Sure, one second."

A few moments later he received a text message from Edie's phone. He opened it, immediately flinching back into his seat cushion. The sores on Lauren's forearm were more like open ulcers, red and weeping, with globules of pus erupting from the centers. "Did you get it?"

"You guys should call 911."

"We did. They told us they'd send someone as soon as they could."

"Good, and you're sure she didn't accidentally knock over some drain cleaner or bleach?"

"Have you ever heard of bleach causing something like *that*?"

"You never know." But no, Milo couldn't imagine a household cleaning product causing the kinds of corrosive sores he was seeing on his colleague's flesh. "Did Lauren notice anything strange in the kitchen?"

"Let me ask."

He waited while the two women talked in muffled voices, then Edie finally came back on the line.

"She smelled vinegar."

"What?"

"Like the kind you put on french fries."

Vinegar. That didn't sound out-of-place in a kitchen, but strange, dripping acids certainly did. All his inner alarm bells started ringing loud enough to wake the *draugr*.

"Did the EMTs give you an estimated time of arrival?"

"Around twenty minutes."

"Alright. Keep everyone calm, and stay in the living room. Don't let anyone wander off by themselves."

"Why not?"

"Just in case."

"You don't think — "

"No, but it seems like you're having a bit of bad luck over there, and these things seem to come in threes."

"Well, that certainly makes me feel better."

"Thanks. I'm known for my comforting and compassionate demeanor."

As he hung up the phone, Milo couldn't escape the little itch at the back of his brain, the one that seemed to say *you know what this is*. He stared at his laptop, the cursor blinking away on his word document, but then his gaze slid, like raindrops down the windowpane, over to a photograph of Edie on his desk. Well, not of *Edie* per se, but of last year's literature department retreat to Saratoga Springs. She was kneeling behind him on a picnic table, both arms slung over his shoulders and hands knotted together where his tie would've gone. Her eyes looked even bigger behind coke-bottle lenses.

Fuck it, tenure could wait.

Milo pulled down *The Encyclopedia of World Folklore, Vol. 3: Asia* and started flipping through the pages. *Aswang. Tsuchinoko. Manananggal. Gashadokuro. Diao Si Gui.* (That seven-foot tongue ghost that'd tried to lick Lloyd last year, before wrapping her tongue around his throat and almost hanging him with it.) *Pontianak. Penanggalan.*

Penanggalan.

He quickly built a stack of books on his desk all about the Malaysian *penanggalan* and flipped to an illustration: a floating head, jaw distended with tongue curving out of her mouth, spinal column trailing behind her severed head with lungs, stomach and heart still attached, the intestines unravelling like loose threads on a hand-knit scarf.

Women who practice black magic, penanggalans are able to separate head from body by meditating in a ritual bath filled with vinegar. When the head returns to the body at daybreak, the penanggalan will soak her entrails in vinegar to shrink, then insert them back into her body. Penanggalans feed on the blood of women and children, and those who suffer their bite will contract a wasting disease from which there can be no cure. Their organs are also coated with acidic bile; anyone who touches them will be cursed with open sores...

The vinegar. The open sores. The teeth-marks in the tires. He knew they'd all sounded familiar for a reason. He picked up his cell phone and started to dial Edie when his attention flickered back over to the encyclopedia. This was what he did all day, every day; he traveled around the world researching so-called *fictional* monsters and spirits and demons from different cultures. So he was primed to see *penanggalans* where there were only high school hoodlums with X-Acto knives, where there was only a spilled can of Draino, where there was only the heavy scent of vinegar in a *kitchen* for god's sakes.

There was no need to upset Edie if he didn't have to. It was better to wait until the EMTs arrived, until everyone got a lift back into town, and then tell her about his suspicions. He tried to refocus on his tenure dossier. He somehow doubted the committee would accept *chasing down a Malaysian head and entrails combo* as an acceptable reason for his paperwork being late.

Twenty minutes came and went. Edie didn't call back, probably because she was in the backseat of an ambulance headed to Lewiston Memorial with their colleagues. He was on the brink of forgetting all about severed, flying heads when his cell phone rang again.

"Hello?"

"*Milo!* You need to help us. I have no idea what to do, and — "

"Calm down," he said, but he wasn't sure if the words were meant for her or himself. "What happened?"

"I think..." He heard a door thudding closed, her footsteps walking across a hardwood floor with some loose planks. "I think there's something up here with us."

A dread as dark as an unlit suburban street, empty and cold even on a summer night, rushed through him.

"What do you mean? Have the EMTs gotten there yet?"

"The ambulance veered off the road about fifteen miles away from the cottage; ran straight into a tree trunk. They're trying to get another one up here as soon as they can."

Not just one *penanggalan* then. One of them at the cottage, ready to feed on a group of academics, and another guarding the roads, making sure they remained undisturbed.

Two at least.

Or more.

There could be so many more.

"You said something was up there with you?"

"This is going to sound crazy..."

"Go ahead."

"When I was in the living room I looked up at the window, and for a split-second I saw something staring back at me. At first I thought it was a trick of the light, maybe my own reflection distorted in the glass, but this didn't look *anything* like me. Its eyes were so empty, and..."

She trailed off, probably too embarrassed to say what came next.

"It looked like it didn't have a body?" Milo guessed.

The footsteps stopped.

"How did you know?"

"Listen," Milo said, opening up his copy of *Malay Monsters: An Introduction to the Folklore of the Malay Peninsula*. "I don't want to frighten anyone— "

"Then maybe try *not* opening with that sentence?"

"But I think I know what's in the woods with you."

Edie sucked in a breath through her teeth; he could hear a little whistle made by the gap between the two front ones. He almost dropped the book, sprinted downstairs, and jumped into his shitty Ford Fiesta. He almost typed WITMER WOODS into the GPS and broke the speed limit the entire way to the cottage, just so he could rescue Edie Walters.

But that would be useless. Less than useless, actually— it would be detrimental to their chances. If he was stranded on the I-90 with a *penanggalan* nipping at his jugular he wouldn't be able to help them at all. No, he needed to stay in his office and provide them with all the information he could. He needed to keep them alive until the sun rose in three hours.

"What do you think it is?"

"A *penanggalan*. They're women who practice black magic."

"So witchcraft?"

"Yeah."

"That's not so bad, right? I mean, we grew up in the '90s; we all watched *The Craft*. What's the worst they can do?"

"They can detach their heads from their bodies and drink every ounce of blood from your veins."

"Great."

He heard the wooden slide of a drawer being opened and the metallic clink of silverware.

"What's that?"

"A butcher knife. What do you think?" The drawer slid closed again. "Okay, what do we need to know about this thing?"

If Milo had been only half in love with Edie before, this was the moment he fell irrevocably head-over-heels. No *You're talking bullshit*, no *You can't honestly believe that*. Just a skinny, little woman with bones as thin as matchsticks arming herself with a butcher knife and asking for all the information she'd need to pummel a magical, decapitated head until its brains started seeping out its eye-holes.

"Here's the rundown," he said, closing his laptop and

giving her his full attention. "You can't let their organs touch you, or you'll end up with those open sores. You can't let them bite you, or you'll contract a fatal wasting disease. If they don't drain you dry first."

"You keep saying *them*."

"I think there might be more than one."

"Well, you did say bad things come in threes."

"Do you have any barbed wire?"

"There's a shed out back; we can check in there."

Milo didn't mention tha *we can check the shed out back* sounded like a particularly gruesome scene in every horror movie ever.

"Um, maybe send someone else out to check the shed. Like...Is that woman who won the Post-Doc Mentoring Award there? The one who always name-drops her celebrity author friends at dinner parties?"

"Who? Megan?"

"Yeah, send her to the shed. You're also going to need some shattered glass."

"That shouldn't be too hard, although I hate to think what our Airbnb bill is going to look like tomorrow morning."

"That's why you have an expense account. You need to hang the barbed wire around the cottage — across the doors, in the windows, around the surrounding trees if you can. When the *penanggalan* tries to get in, its internal organs should snag on the barbed wire, and it'll be caught. Then all you need to do is force its mouth open and shove the shattered glass down its throat."

Silence at the other end of the line, and then:

"Is there any *other* method for getting rid of these flying heads?"

"Stay alive until morning. As soon as the sun rises the *penanggalans* will be forced to return to their bodies."

"That's all very *From Dusk Till Dawn*."

"I'd recommend the proactive approach, but that's just me. Better to catch them and kill them than beat around the *banshee*, you know?"

The footsteps resumed: *creak-creak-creak* across the floorboards. Finally, Edie said, "I'll send Megan to the shed to see what she can find out there. Let me know if you think of anything else that might be valuable."

"Keep me updated."

"Sure. Thanks, Milo."

He opened his mouth to say *I love you*, but thankfully she'd already hung up. Making himself look like an idiot in the middle of a crisis was really all he needed. Edie had more important things to worry about — like saving their colleagues from bloodthirsty *penanggalans* stalking them from high above the rooftops, dipping down to peer in their windows and hovering in the shadowy corners of their bedrooms. Earlier he would have done anything to avoid being distracted from his tenure dossier; now he found himself using his tenure dossier as nothing more than a distraction.

Service section written.

The phone rang.

FaceTime.

He turned the desk lamp on so Edie could clearly see him, and picked up the call. "How'd Operation Shed go?"

Edie looked more than a little queasy, her face the same color as a ghost slug.

"See for yourself."

She flipped the camera around.

The shed was not what he'd been expecting, probably not what she'd been expecting either. Instead of barbed wire and hatchets and fuel tanks full of gasoline, there were scrapbooking supplies. The walls had been painted with ivory matte, and the hardwood floors had a shag carpet laid over them. Hundreds of drawers contained paper clippings, embellishments, embroidery floss, crochet hooks, rubber stamps, and ink pads. There was even a woodcut sign in the corner that read *LIVE LAUGH LOVE*.

"It's a She-Shed."

"A what?"

"A She-Shed," Edie repeated. "A place where women can get away from their families. Do crafty things."

"A room of one's own."

"That's not what I wanted to show you." She brought the camera over to a corner of the room that looked like it'd been used for painting. It took Milo a second, even with all his consulting experience, to realize the red paint on the wall wasn't paint at all.

Megan sat slumped in the corner, glassy, blue eyes rolled up towards the ceiling. Her throat had been ripped open. Milo'd never realized how many muscles were in the throat before, but he did now. The fibrous cords nestled around the larynx, thyroid and trachea, and since all of those cords had been severed, they fluttered in the nighttime wind like streamers left up after a party.

"You found her like that?"

Edie turned the camera around and nodded.

"It's a *penanggalan,* all right," he said. "You didn't find any barbed wire in that She-Shed, did you?"

Edie held up a ball of knitting yarn, fibers of pink twisted up with metallic silver. "Thought this might do the trick. We could wrap the yarn across all the windows and doors to make a net. Maybe its entrails will get tangled up."

It wasn't the best solution, but he had to give her credit: Edie was making the most of what she had, and she didn't have a lot. "What about the shattered glass?"

Edie held up a wine glass with a little trinket jingling around the stem. She read the message that'd been painted on the bowl: "It's always wine o'clock."

"Classy. Has anyone else seen Megan?"

She shook her head. "I don't want them to flip out."

"Good. Bring the knitting yarn and the wine glasses back to the cottage, and — "

Red paint dripped down the wall behind Edie. He hadn't noticed it at first, since the corner was awash in the stuff, but this wasn't dripping from Megan's torn-out throat or from the gore that'd been splattered against the wall.

This was dripping from the ceiling.

"Edie," he whispered. "Do you have any sharp objects?"

Edie's nose scrunched up for a few seconds before her eyes went as wide and shiny as lodestones. She grabbed the butcher knife from her tote bag, gripping the handle like someone who wasn't afraid to do damage.

"Move to the door. Don't panic."

As Edie started to move, keeping the phone in her hand, he saw something slick flick into the frame. It was akin to spaghetti smothered in too much tomato sauce, coiled up in layers like lasagna.

Intestines.

Followed by organs so raw, so *wet*, he could feel them thudding against the screen of his phone. Kidneys, liver, stomach, lungs that fluttered out with each breath she took, heart that still pumped blood through this impossible mass of tissue. And then a neck and head.

Her eyes had the dull sheen of glass, like marbles you buy at Hobby Lobby and glue into doll-sockets. Her hair was tangled, twigs and leaves knotted into the strands. As she opened her mouth Milo could see the sharp incisors arching out of her jaw.

"*Run.*"

Edie jammed the phone into her pocket and sprinted out of the shed. For a few minutes Milo couldn't see anything, just the stifling blackness of fibers in her dress pocket. There was a loud thump. Something squelched, a wet sound that made him jerk back into his chair, and then a sharp shriek. He couldn't tell if the sound came from Edie or the *penanggalan*.

He wanted to say something, to check and make sure she was okay, but he couldn't take the chance. For all he knew she was tucked away between the tree branches, hiding from the *penanggalan* floating through the woods. If he was the one who gave up her location, all because he was stupid and impatient, he'd never forgive himself. So he held his breath and waited for someone, anyone, to pick up the phone.

A flash of light. The camera adjusting as someone pulled it out of her pocket.

Edie.

She stared into the screen, tiny ribcage heaving with breath, blood splattered across her face. There were even a few specks caught on the lenses of her glasses.

"Are you alright?" he asked.

She nodded.

"What about the *penanggalan*?"

She tipped the camera towards the ground. The *penanggalan* had been pinned to the dirt like a butterfly to a display case, the butcher knife jammed into her open mouth, through the back of her skull, and into the hard-packed dirt below. The *penanggalan*'s jaw cracked on its hinges; its tongue, scraped skinless by the knife-blade, lolled around in its mouth. It wasn't dead then, just trapped.

"How the Hell — ?" Milo stared at the *penanggalan*'s clicking teeth. "How did you get the knife through that thing?"

"I'm stronger than I look."

Edie's throat sounded more wrecked than Megan's.

"Obviously that campus gym membership really paid off."

"Bro," she said, wiping her forehead with the back of her hand. "Do you even lift?"

Milo snorted out a laugh before remembering there was another *penanggalan* who may still be roaming the woods. "Do you have the wine glasses?"

"Yeah." Edie pulled one out of the tote bag and slammed it onto the ground, the glass shattering into a hundred tiny shards. "I'll shove this down her throat and then head back to the cottage."

"Do you want me to stay on the line?"

"No, this is gross enough for one of us." Edie stared at the *penanggalan* for a moment, probably wondering what crushed glass would look like going down its gullet as it shredded the tough fibers of its esophagus and poked out from its entrails like a pincushion. "I'm probably not going to be able to keep my food down, and I'd rather you didn't watch me upchuck in the middle of the woods."

"Call me as soon as you get back to the cottage, and remember there might be another one out there. Maybe more than one."

"Can do."

The phone disconnected.

Milo checked the clock: four in the morning. If the group at the cottage could stay alive for a few hours longer they wouldn't have to worry about the other *penanggalans*. Their disconnected heads would have to return to their bodies; if not they'd sizzle up like bacon grease in a pan.

Maybe this would be as simple as stringing up the doors, grabbing some sharp objects, and hunkering down in the living room.

A text message pinged in his inbox.

Back at the cottage. Going to start pinning the yarn to the doors and windows. I'll check in with you every fifteen minutes just to let you know I'm still alive and everything.

With no other ways to help, he revised and proofread his service statement, the clack of keys splitting the silence that fell over the department offices at night. He was used to being here after-hours, but tonight the stillness felt like a weighted blanket smothering him. He double-checked all his documents and uploaded them to the University of Lewiston's website. Every fifteen minutes his phone pinged with another text message from Edie: photos of windows, yarn knitted across them like spiderwebs, metallic strands shimmering in the light from the patio.

He was just about to press *SUBMIT* when the phone rang.

"Edie?"

"Milo?"

A sharp whisper, more an intake of breath than a word.

"What's wrong?"

"One of them got in the house."

She flipped the camera and panned around the living room.

Blood.

Blood seeping into the couch cushions, so thick that if you sat down on them a fresh flood of liquid would push through the fabric. Blood smeared across the hardwood floors, the soles of Edie's high heels tracked in frantic circles around the room. Blood splattered across the photo frames and coffee table books and fleece blankets from Pier 1 Imports.

"Who's still alive?"

Edie shook her head.

No one.

"How did this happen? *When* did this happen?"

"We finished hanging up the yarn. I went upstairs to the bathroom — I *know* I wasn't supposed to go anywhere alone, but I really needed to pee — and when I came back downstairs..."

She brought the camera over to the door. The yarn had been gnawed through, like a flock of moths had gone on a rampage.

"Guess they didn't get tangled after all."

There was another shriek, like the one he'd heard when Edie'd slammed the butcher knife through the *penanggalan*'s jaw.

"You only have a half-hour before sunrise," he said. "They'll have to leave soon if they want to get back to their bodies in time."

A thumping sound came from the stairs: a lump of intestines being dragged down the steps one-by-one.

"Get out of the house. *Now.*"

Edie didn't have to be told twice. She picked her way through the strands of yarn covering the door, then sprinted into the woods. Milo, meanwhile, muted his phone and picked up the landline in his office. He had 911 on speed dial.

"911, what's your emergency?"

"One of my friends just called me. She's staying at a cottage in Witmer Woods. Someone's broken in, and..."

Milo sputtered to a halt, trying to think of how to phrase the situation without using the word *penanggalan*. He knew from past experiences that would be a major mistake, especially with the police. He remembered early in his career when he'd called 911 about a *shirime*.

Excuse me, sir, the 911 operator had said, *can you describe the suspect again?*

Tall, thin, white. Like really *white.*

Hair color?

No hair, no facial features.

No... What do you mean, sir?

It doesn't have a face. No mouth, no nose, no eyes . .

Well, I mean...

What?

It does have one *eye.*

When he'd told her the location of the *shirime*'s one eye — how if the police saw the creature lifting up its trench coat and bending over, they should look away immediately — the 911 operator had hung up on him. She'd also disconnected every subsequent call he'd made.

"Sir, are you there?"

"Yes. Someone's broken into the cottage, and everyone else's dead. I told her to get out of there; she's running through the woods now, but I believe the suspect's close behind her."

After giving the 911 operator all the relevant details, he hung up the call. By the time the police arrived the *penanggalans* would all be gone, but they might be able to help Edie if she was lost in the woods or, God help him, injured.

"Edie?" he whispered into his cell phone, keeping his voice low to avoid detection. "Are you still there?"

"Yeah."

"Can you see anything?"

"No."

She'd turned the video off, which only made the situation worse. He cranked the volume up as loud as he could, listening for the telltale sounds of snapping branches or rustling leaves, but there was nothing except the strangled panting of Edie's breath against the microphone.

"Still nothing?"

She huffed out a laugh. "Still nothing."

"Hey, Edie?"

"Yeah?"

"I'm sorry I didn't go to the cottage with you this weekend."

"Well, the writing time's been limited, and the company's been *shit*, so you didn't miss much. However, I think there'll be a lot of opportunities opening up in the literature department soon. Great time to be applying for tenure, you know?" A sudden rush of wind through the woods, and then: "I wish you were here too."

"Hey, Edie?"

"Yeah?"

"Everything's going to be fine, but — "

"Hardcore vote of confidence right there."

"If things go wrong, I just want you to know..."

"I know, Milo."

"You know?"

"Yes. I know."

The two of them sat there — Milo in his office at the University of Lewiston, Edie in the middle of Witmer Woods — and let those words stretch between them, like threads pulled tight enough to snap.

Snap.

A branch overhead. "*Shit!*" Edie shouted, and the cell phone dropped to the ground with a dull thud.

"*Edie!*"

Milo couldn't stop her name from wrenching itself out of his throat, couldn't stop the panic that raised his volume fifteen decibels. He listened while high heels scratched against the dirt, while something heavy slammed against a tree trunk, while more shrieks sounded out like car alarms.

The phone disconnected.

Milo called back again and again and again, but no one picked up the phone. He kept pressing redial as the sun broke over the tree-line, the first rays of morning painting the sky the same colors as a bruise. He kept pressing redial as it rose, inch-by-inch, until the alarm went off on his phone.

His tenure dossier.

He'd forgotten to submit his tenure dossier.

Fuck it.

He called every hospital, every police station, but no one could tell him anything. *If you're not her immediate family,* the receptionists all said, *then we can't release that information to you.*

So there is *an Edie Walters there?*

I never said that, sir.

Milo dropped his head down onto his desk, the University of Lewiston's website still open on his computer, the arrow hovering over the *SUBMIT* button — forgotten. It was all his fault. He should've told her about the *penanggalan* earlier, as soon as he'd read the chapter in the encyclopedia. He should've gone to the cottage to pick her up when the tires had been slashed. He never should have backed out of the retreat in the first place. He shouldn't have cared so much about his stupid fucking tenure at this shit-hole university that didn't appreciate him anyway, and *fuck it fuck it fuck it fuck —*

His office door creaked open.

"You still here?"

Milo shot out of his desk-chair. He crossed his office at the speed of light, and yet, when his arms wrapped around Edie, it still felt like getting here had taken most of his adult life. She dropped the paper bag she'd been carrying on the floor and reached up to scrunch her fists in his hair.

"Good to see you too, stranger."

"What happened? I tried calling so many times, and you didn't pick up— "

"That *penanggalan* got the drop on me. Slammed me against a tree, knocked me unconscious. The police stumbled over me during their search. Literally." She lifted up the hem of her T-shirt, revealing a giant bruise on her hipbone. "They still haven't given me back my cell phone. Evidence, you know? I figured the easiest way of reaching you would be to show up for office hours."

"I was terrified."

"I was fine."

She rested her palm against his chest. He wondered if she could feel his heart thumping against his ribcage faster than that little rabbit in *Bambi*.

"Thank you," she said. "For taking care of me."

"I think you took care of yourself."

"Still, it was good not to be alone out there." She reached down and picked up the paper bag. "I brought you brunch. Figured our newest tenured professor would need it."

"About that..."

"What happened?"

"I forgot to submit the dossier."

She pursed her lips together tightly.

"What can I say? I was a little distracted last night."

"Press submit anyway, and I'll talk to the committee. I think they have more important things to worry about than your tenure dossier being late, like replacing half the literature department staff."

"At least you don't have to worry about your application next year."

"No," she said, pushing the paper bag towards his chest. "Looks like we have a bright future ahead of us. Maybe one we should celebrate over dinner?"

Her eyes were the same color as loam, dirty-brown with an amber sheen. He wondered exactly when his heart had taken root in them.

"Yeah, sure."

"I'll pick you up after your last seminar," she said, heading towards the door. As soon as she pulled away, he missed the warmth of her. "Don't forget to press submit."

"I won't."

He slumped back down into his desk-chair, opening up the paper bag. Edie was fine. Whatever mistakes he'd made last night she'd stumbled her way through. She'd been so much stronger, so much sturdier, than he'd expected. The perfect partner-in-crime for a man who spent his life working with murder-blankets and tongue-demons and Stabby McTangles.

He should probably give Lloyd a call and make sure he was still alive.

He reached into the paper bag. It smelled like a char-broiled hamburger with all the fixings, along with a greasy order of fries slathered in vinegar. He grabbed one of the fries and stuffed it into his mouth.

No vinegar.

Salt and grease, but no vinegar.

And yet the scent lingered in his office, right where Edie had been standing.

His lungs constricted, squeezing all the breath out of

him. There was no way. He'd been on the phone with her all night; he'd watched while she'd stuffed crushed glass down a *penanggalan's* throat... But his heart stuttered as he realized that no, he hadn't. She'd gotten him off the line first, claiming she was going to be sick in the middle of the woods. For all he knew the moment the call had disconnected, she'd wrenched the knife out of the *penanggalan's* mouth and let it fly free. For all he knew, she could've been the one to cut the strings protecting the cabin. She could've been the one —

He pressed the back of his hand against his mouth as he remembered what the living room had looked like.

All that blood.

The door to his office creaked open, and he grabbed the plastic fork on his desk. Like cutlery from the campus dining hall would do any good against the forces of darkness. *Stupid Milo.*

Edie's head popped in through the crack, her messy bun flopping to the side.

"Sorry," she said. "I know you have things to do. Just forgot the condiments."

And with that, she crossed the office towards him. He gripped the fork even tighter in his hand, but as he stared at her little smile he knew he wouldn't be able to stab her, even if she was a *penanggalan*. Even if she went straight for his jugular, he would've just stood there and let her gulp down his blood like a 7-11 Slurpee.

But she just held out her hand, and dropped a fistful of packets onto his desk.

Salt.

Pepper.

Ketchup.

Mustard.

. . .

Vinegar.

He stared at the crumpled-up vinegar sachets. None of them looked like they'd been punctured, but that didn't mean anything. One of them probably had burst in her pocket en route from the hospital to his office, and that must've been what left the vinegar smell. He breathed out his relief, dropping the plastic fork onto his desk.

"See you tonight." She headed back for the door. "Don't forget to press submit!"

"I won't. See you later."

And with that, she slipped out of his office.

He felt guilty for having wondered, even just for a moment, if Edie could be a monster. What kind of monster brought you coffee when she knew you were pulling an all-nighter? She never would've harmed their co-workers, even if it did mean the two of them would have no trouble getting their tenure applications approved. Besides, he was one of the world's foremost experts on comparative folklore. He'd dedicated years of his life to learning everything there was to know about *futakuchi-onnas* and *ittan-momens* and *penanggalans*, so of course he would know if his girlfriend was some sort of horrific cryptid.

He stared out the window at Edie's retreating form as she walked across campus. Her strides were brisk and light; you never would've been able to tell she'd been up all night fighting for her life.

He would know.

He would know.

Fingers trembling, he clicked *SUBMIT.*

V. A. Vazquez
About the Author

V. A. Vazquez comes from New York City where she previously worked as a theatre producer and a ghostwriter for famous fashion editors (which you wouldn't be able to tell from looking in her closet). An author of urban fantasy and comedic horror, she specializes in stories that involve women (or men or non-binary folks) romancing monsters, preferably the slimy Lovecraftian kind. She currently lives in Scotland with her husband and their wee doggo. You can find her on Twitter @vavazquezwrites.

www.vavazquez.com
www.facebook.com/vavazquezauthor

Thlush-A-Lum
Rebecca Gomez Farrell

Markella's earliest memories are of the sounds outside her window. At hours when no men moved, the rustling branches and shuffling grasses woke her. A beating pulse like slower, fleshier helicopter blades banished sleep: *thlush-a-lum*. In summers the heat in her attic bedroom was hot enough to incubate, and Markella pushed the window open and dozed to the endless, static drone of cicadas. In winters, when the choking radiator warmth wrapped tight around her, she cracked the window and the low, deep hoots of an owl drifted in with the freezing breeze.

The sounds crept in no matter the season. She did not know then that the noise of a UFO landing might be only the wind whipping through the woods, or that the piercing cries of something caught in a monster's jaws were likely car wheels screeching too fast past the roundabout. The unknowns terrified little Markella, curled up so tight on her bed that she'd spring like a can of snakes if touched.

But no one touched her.

Mother and Father had no patience for tucking her in, or for answering her questions about how winds and teakettles could both whistle. Even the dog, a playful chocolate lab that dug joyfully at every ant hill it encountered, offered no more than a whimper when Markella ventured near.

As she grew older Markella learned to tell the difference between sounds. Wasps buzzed like a kazoo, while carpenter bees plucked a bass. Snow fell quieter than rain, and a pan sizzled differently if there was oil in it rather than water. She took comfort in naming the noises that woke her, in having something to think of until silence and sleep came again. Loud crack like a gun gone off? An ash tree breaking in two. Knocking on the side of the house? A woodpecker looking for an early morning snack. The noises had a purpose, an action they belonged to, unlike Markella. She never quite belonged, was never quite her parents' daughter.

Thlush-a-lum.

Thlush-a-lum.

She never has figured out what makes the noise of the helicopter blades. It wakes her tonight, resonating like leather and bone, not metal. Markella's eyes snap open as she takes in the darkness seeping into her room, reddish-purple like the Chianti Mother gave her at dinner with whispers of "growing up" and "transformation", a rare smile spreading beneath heavy-lidded eyes.

THLUSH-a-lum.

THLUSH-a-lum.

Markella bolts up in bed—it is so loud. She doesn't think it's ever been this loud before, and a breath of relief escapes when the noise stops. But a scratching, then slow scraping, replaces it. *The window—there's something at the window.*

She looks.

Mottled, grey hands grasp the wooden, peeling window sill. Yellowed, cracking fingernails click against the glass as the frame inches higher. Wood grates against wood. Immense wings fill the rectangle of the window— two, no, four of them grouped on the creature's shoulders and hips. Something black as motor oil drips from them.

Markella doesn't want to keep looking, but it is too late. She knows that, yet she watches a sinewy leg, covered in the same slick substance as the wings, push through the opening between frame and sill. The wings begin rotating, each in opposite directions, like gearworks of a clock.

THLUSH-a-lum.

THLUSH-a-lum.

The creature rises high enough to slip the rest of its form inside.

Markella knows in this moment that some noises cannot be explained away, that squealing tires never do sound like screams when she hears them in the light of day. The creature opens its mouth, revealing two rows of teeth as sharp and pointed as the icicles that hang over her window's awning in winter. Those teeth glisten as the dripping wings block out the night sky, and the creature emits a high-pitched shriek that makes the dog bark again and again.

She feels shearing pain at the same time as hearing a sickening *slurtch*. The dimples on her shoulders and lower back—Mother had called them *birthmarks*—split open, and slimy, leathery, skin-covered bones thrust out. Her arms shrink in on themselves, the fat between skin and bone oozing out in minuscule, black droplets. Fingernails lengthen and harden as she twists her hands around and around, completely mesmerized.

Cool air shifts across her back from the wings beginning to rotate and flutter, and Markella stands. The creature's head cocks, eyelids clicking over its pearlescent, oval eyes. Its image divides and multiplies into a million little screens, Markella's vision compounded. Feet curve and toes bind together into a ballet shoe of flesh, and when she lifts off the ground the breeze from the window tickles her soles.

The creature flies outside, moonlight a beacon off its wings. Markella does not hesitate; the desire to propel herself upward, higher and higher, is much stronger than the lingering pain of burst skin. As she jumps out the window and into the open air, she wonders how hurtling through a cloud will sound. The soft noise of untried wings is added to the night sky around her: *thlush-a-lum thlush-a-lum*.

Hidden in the curve of the front alcove, the mother watches her latest charge disappear until it is no more than the speck she wishes it were. She prays it is the last, prays she will not wake to a new larva shaped like the human baby they had bartered for so long ago. Back inside she pulls the cork from another bottle with a soft pop.

"Is it done?" Her husband sits up on the couch in front of a blank, blue television screen. "The dog has stopped barking."

She nods, swishing the wine and watching the film it secretes on the bowl.

"Will they let us go, you think? That's the third one, and they said—"

Her laugh is bitter. "They said that after the first one, too. You can't count on an insect's promises."

The lab comes running, teeth gripping a slobbery rubber ball that squeaks as he drops it at her feet, whining. She tosses the ball, launches it far into the darkened hall. The dog scampers away, cartilage claws scuffing the hardwood floor. The mother sighs, her hand already lowered to take it again. It'll come back, it always does.

Rebecca Gomez Farrell
About the author

Rebecca Gomez Farrell still refuses to say "Bloody Mary" three times into a mirror, though she'll write stories about the people who do. Meerkat Press published her first novel, *Wings Unseen.* Her speculative fiction appears in over twenty outlets, including *Beneath Ceaseless Skies, PULP Literature,* and the *Best Indie Speculative Fiction of 2019.* She co-organizes a local chapter of the national Women Who Submit Lit organization and the East Bay Science Fiction and Fantasy Writers Meetup Group.

For over a decade, Becca has also been blogging on food and drink at http://thegourmez.com

Social Media: @thegourmez.
Website: http://RebeccaGomezFarrell.com

Follow You into the Dark
Christopher Bond

"**M**ake a wish, Darlene."

Bobby took another swig off his beer and held it up to the night sky, toasting the flash of light that streamed in front of the stars like a bottle rocket. Beside him, on the tailgate of his rusted Chevy, Darlene closed her eyes and bowed her head, her lips moving soundlessly.

When she was done she leaned into Bobby and rested her head on his shoulder, taking a drink from her own bottle.

"What'd ya wish for, babe?" he asked. She looked up into his eyes, the brightest emerald-green she'd ever seen, and she smiled.

"Oh, I didn't wish for nothin'," she said. The light from the shooting star twinkled and flashed on the diamond ring Bobby had just put on her finger. It felt like it had always been there. She sighed. "I was just saying a 'thank you' to the universe, ya know…for giving me everything I've ever wanted, right here beside me."

Darlene saw him blush beneath his beard as he pulled the bill of his trucker's hat down, and she felt another layer of her love for him wrap around her. He was everything. Bobby took another drink, trying to hide his face behind the bottle, but then he laughed and tossed it into the trees that bordered the gravel parking lot. He jumped off the tailgate with a yell, and Darlene cried out in mock protest when he lifted her into his arms and swung her around, her long, blonde hair flaring out below her, the warm summer air caressing her like the waves of a tropical ocean. She felt drunk, but it wasn't just the few beers; she was intoxicated by the man who held her. She was enchanted by the night and the stars, and their future that seemed to spread out forever in all directions. She closed her eyes again, and this time she *did* make a wish. She wished that she could hold onto this moment for a lifetime, that this feeling would last for an eternity.

Then it all came crashing down.

Bobby cried out, "Holy shit, it's coming right for us!" He stopped swinging Darlene, his mouth open, his eyes turned up to the sky.

"Wh…what is?" she asked. She lifted her head and then she saw it, too, and the smile wilted on her face like a dying flower. The shooting star was getting bigger, and brighter. It was a ball of roiling flames falling fast, heading for the little lookout at the top of Meadows Hill where the pickup truck was parked.

Heading straight for them.

The air around the burning object howled ferociously

as it fell, whipping the blue and orange flames into chaotic patterns. It sounded like the scream of a wildcat. The last of Darlene's happiness faded, and cold, icy fear rushed in to take its place. Bobby lowered her legs to the ground, never taking his eyes from the burning ball. She hugged him, trying to steady herself, and he hugged her back. He tried to seem brave and unafraid, but he was scared too.

"What is it?" she asked him.

"I don't know," he said. "A meteor or something, I… get down!"

He tackled Darlene to the ground, rocks digging into his palms, knees and even through his blue jeans. The object flew over top of them, just barely clearing the roof of the Chevy as it flew close enough to blister the fading paint. They felt the heat of it press down on them as it passed.

Trees splintered and exploded somewhere behind them, and the ground trembled and shook. Bobby had his arm around Darlene's head, shielding her, and all she could hear was her own rapid breathing and her pulse pumping through her ears.

"Oh, Jesus, that was fucking wild!" Bobby said, after a moment. He stood up. "Holy shit!"

A great swathe of forest had been cut down along the object's trajectory, cleaved as if by a giant scythe. The trees were bowled over, cracked and broken off, jagged stumps sticking up like splintered bones. Flames danced along some of the remaining limbs, casting Bobby and Darlene in flickering oranges and yellows.

Bobby helped Darlene to her feet, brushing the dirt off the front of her shorts. There were small cuts and scrapes on her legs from the gravel. "Damn. You okay, baby? I thought that thing was gonna hit us for sure."

"I'm fine, I'm fine. Really," she said. And she was, physically at least, though she still felt her heart beating in her chest like a war drum. She tried her best to give him a smile. "Who needs a telescope, right?"

"No shit." He went around to the side of the pick-up and reached through the open window. He came back holding two flashlights, and he handed her one.

"What's this for? You're not thinking of going out there, are you?"

"Well, yeah, why wouldn't we? I'll put it on YouTube tonight, and we'll be viral by morning."

She rubbed at her bare arms, the night air seeming less warm and inviting than it had earlier. *I should have worn a jacket,* she thought. *Probably just my nerves.*

"I don't know, Bobby, I…I think I just want to go home, okay? My buzz is gone, and I gotta work in the morning." She gave him her best puppy-dog eyes.

For a moment she thought it worked, then his smile grew wider.

"Oh, c'mon, don't give me that, baby. We almost got creamed by a fuckin' meteor! That don't happen every day. Lemme get a couple minutes of video, then we'll put this place in the rear-view. Deal?"

Darlene sighed. "Alright, Bobby, but just two minutes! It's getting cold out here."

He flipped on his own flashlight and put his other arm around her, guiding her towards the woods. "Don't worry, Darlene baby, Bobby knows how to keep you warm."

"Get me off this hill, and I'll let you prove it to me."

The path of the fallen meteor was easy to follow; it had ripped a tunnel right through the heart of the woods. They climbed around the shattered trunks of fallen pines, some still smoldering and warm to the touch. Trees, their wood blackened and needles singed, towered over them on both sides. Here and there sputtering gouts of flame still clung to some of the branches.

"Makes you feel a bit like Moses, don't it?" Bobby asked her, looking up at the trees that were still standing. "Parting the Red Sea and walking between the waves?"

"I didn't know they let you into church, Bobby Lawson," Darlene said with a smirk. A smile flashed from under his beard.

"Not anymore, maybe, but Sunday school had the best cookies."

They walked on, the stench of charred wood and fresh dirt filling the air. The forest was quiet again, the night calm, though there were no sounds of animals or insects.

"It's awfully quiet," Darlene said, a slight tremor in her voice. "I don't hear nothin' moving around. I don't like it."

Bobby shrugged. "I'd be quiet too if a missile just hit

my fuckin' house."

Even though the land sloped downwards, away from the parking lot, it wasn't an easy hike, and Darlene found herself wishing she had put her foot down more firmly. It wasn't just her emotions or her nerves, it actually *was* a lot colder than it had been, cold enough to see wisps of her breath in the light. Besides, it was dark, and she had never particularly liked the dark. Just off the top of her head she could think of a dozen things she'd rather be doing.

She was counting those things in her mind when a terrible scream pierced the night, coming from somewhere ahead on the comet's path. Bobby and Darlene froze. They swept their flashlight beams over the broken trees and ragged stumps in front of them, seeing nothing.

"Bobby, I – " Darlene began.

"Shhh," Bobby said, one finger to his lips. "Do y'hear that?"

She stayed perfectly still, cocking her head towards where the scream had originated, and then she heard it.

boom–boom–boom–boom

It was a muffled knocking sound; A metallic pounding, almost mechanical, like a rusty piston laboring inside of an archaic engine. It sounded like they were standing outside the engine room of an old steam ship.

BOOM-BOOM-BOOM-BOOM

It was an odd, foreign sound out there in the wilderness. It didn't belong. Darlene didn't feel like they belonged anymore, either. She felt her legs trembling, no longer just from the cold.

BOOMBOOMBOOMBOOMBOOM

The knocking came faster, louder. It was a physical force, pinning them where they stood. Bobby broke free and ran to Darlene's side, grabbing her hand. The pounding reached a maddening pitch, and just when they thought it couldn't possibly get any faster it stopped with a concussive *crunching*. It was metal being folded and rendered, the sound of a head-on collision.

The seconds peeled away slowly as they waited for something else to happen.

Eventually, the silence of the night crept back in.

"OKAY, okay. Whatever the *fuck* that was," Darlene said. Her legs were so weak she felt like she might fall over.

Then they heard the moaning, soft and inarticulate and full of pain, drifting up the path like a black fog. It stopped as quickly as it started.

Darlene heard a whine enter her voice and she hated it, but she couldn't help it. "We shouldn't be here."

Bobby shook his head. "C'mon, don't be like that. Somebody's hurt, don't ya think? We can help them, Darlene." He sighed and shook his head. "I'm going down there."

Darlene sighed, nodded, ignoring the tightening in her stomach.

"Let's get this over with."

They could see the object when they were still twenty feet away from it. It was big and oddly shaped, sort of an upside-down funnel that was half-buried in the dirt and rocks it had dug up when it crashed. Smoke hissed up off of its scorched, silver surface, and between the burnt piec-es there were shiny spots that gleamed in the light of their flashlights. Underneath the soot and grime they could just barely make out the faded colors of the American flag.

Bobby whistled long and low.

"Is that…" Darlene began, but the words wouldn't come.

"A spaceship?" Bobby finished for her. Darlene nod-ded, and he continued, "Yeah, I think so. It's like what the astronauts come down in."

"Well, what's it doin' out here? I thought they landed in the ocean."

"You got me."

The moan came again, softer this time. Bobby stepped towards the capsule, but Darlene grabbed his arm and held him still. Something inside of her was telling her to run, to just turn around and go back to the truck and get the Hell out of these woods.

She clung to his arm, and they approached the craft slowly. It had landed mostly upright, and as they got closer they could see that the metal was dented and pitted. There were porthole windows too, which were circles of cracked, tinted glass hidden under the grime. Darlene reached for the closest one and rubbed the dirt away with her fist.

"I can't see anything," she said. "Something's covering the glass in there."

Bobby knocked on the metal and called out, "Hey! Somebody need help?" Nobody answered. Bobby looked at Darlene and shrugged his shoulders. He rapped the metal a few more times with dull, hollow knocks. It sounded just like the pounding they had heard earlier, and a shiver ran up Darlene's neck. She clutched Bobby's arm a little tighter. They circled the craft, crunching through the dead leaves and broken glass.

Bobby stopped abruptly, pulling Darlene closer to his side.

"Oh my God," Darlene said, covering her mouth with her hand. "Oh my God, oh my God."

A large hole had been ripped outward through the craft's wall, the shiny metal around the edges of the hole shredded and disfigured. It was torn open and peeled back, like the lid of a tin can. Dotted all around the metal and the glass were splashes of blood, and it was dripping down the side in thick layers like melted candle wax as it started to coagulate in the cold. The coppery stench of death wafted out through the hole, poisoning the air.

Bobby knew Darlene was somewhere right beside him, freaking out by the sound of it, but she seemed far away. He barely heard her; He just stood there staring stupidly at the wreckage. His breath steamed out of him, sweat beading on his forehead despite the chill. He didn't say anything, since he didn't know what to say. The smell was strong, and overpowering. His stomach lurched. He tried just breathing through his mouth, but somehow it was worse. He had been hunting nearly his whole life, had strung up dozens of animals so he could drain and gut them, but this…*this* was something worse. Something terrible. *Get it together, man. Get yourself together.* He kept staring at the gaping hole, and the darkness just beyond it. The blood looked fake, almost too red in the beam of their flashlights. Whoever was in there was beyond any help they could offer.

He forced himself to get closer, and Darlene didn't try to stop him. She was already as close as she wanted to be, and he hesitated for a moment right outside of the hole. He felt like a bucket full of termites were running around inside of his stomach as they tried to eat their way out, a million tiny feet scrambling on his insides, a thousand tiny jaws scissoring into the soft tissue.

He stuck his flashlight in first, his hand shaking so bad that the light danced around wildly, then he stuck his head in.

He screamed.

Bobby rocketed backwards, nearly falling on his ass. His light hit the jagged rim of the hole and fell inside the craft, clanging noisily on the floor. He ran to the nearest tree and braced himself against the trunk, gagging and coughing. He fell to his knees and threw up into the weeds, his whole body tremoring. Darlene ran to him, kneeling down behind him and putting her hand on his back.

"Bobby, are you okay? What was it? What did you see?"

He waved a hand, then coughed a few more times.

A thick rivulet of saliva dripped from his mouth, and he wiped it with the back of his hand after he spat on the ground. He looked at Darlene, his emerald-green eyes as wide and terrified as she'd ever seen them.

"We have to go, NOW."

"Bobby, what…what did you se – "

He grabbed both of her shoulders and shook her. His jaw was clenched, and he spoke through his teeth. "Don't look, Darlene. Don't look." Tears were threatening to break out of the corners of his eyes. "We have to go."

"They're dead, aren't they." She said, her voice thin. It wasn't a question.

"We have to go," Bobby was saying, but Darlene wasn't listening anymore. She was looking at the ship, through the hole where Bobby's flashlight had fallen. There were dials and screens and switches, all painted red. And there was a body, she was sure, leaned up against the far wall. She squinted her eyes towards the hole, shrugging Bobby's hands off of her.

"What are you doing, Darlene? No, don't! C'mon, let's move it." Instead she walked toward the torn, metal capsule. She paused just outside of the ragged hole, as Bobby had.

She could see inside of the ship, and now that was all she could see.

Her brain was having a hard time making sense of what her eyes were showing it. There was blood every-where – more blood than a human body could possibly hold, she thought. The astronaut was leaned up against a control panel. A crushed helmet lay discarded at its side, the glass visor shattered. Darlene couldn't tell if it had been a man or a woman. *A man,* she decided, looking at the eyes and nose. They were almost the only things left.

The person's chest had been ripped open like the side of the capsule had been, the ribcage broken and the flesh torn and spread apart like a frog on a dissection board. It was as if someone had jammed a claw hammer inside their ribs and yanked them open, peeling all the skin back. Their lower jaw had been torn off, too. Things were missing, things that weren't supposed to be missing. The chest cavity was almost empty, hollowed out all the way to the arc of grisly spine at the back. No organs, and hardly any blood, were present. It was the same with the neck and throat; no tongue left, hardly any tissue. Steam rose from inside of the corpse; The body was still warm, but was cooling rapidly in the night air.

A wailing moan came from the woods behind Darlene, and as she tried to turn something latched onto the back of her neck and across her mouth.

It was Bobby. He pulled her backwards and whispered into her ear, "Shhh baby, take it easy…something's out there. We gotta go…turn your light off." She nodded, and he let go of her. She clicked the button on the flashlight and the darkness pooled in around them, the only light left that which came from inside the capsule. Bobby took her hand and led her around the edge of the craft. The moaning had stopped, but whatever it was had to be close.

They walked slowly, cautiously, placing each step

carefully as they skirted the crash site. It was hard without the light, and twice Darlene stepped awkwardly on debris and nearly fell. Bobby had to steady her as best he could, and they didn't dare talk, not even a whisper. The night was quiet again – *dead* quiet – and every crunch of their shoes was a gunshot. They got to the backside of the craft and leaned against it. Just by the starlight they could see the path of torn trees that led back to the truck, back to safety.

Bobby took his hat off and wiped his forehead, breathing heavily. He leaned in close to Darlene, his lips nearly kissing her ear, and he said, "Okay baby, that was good. Now, let's just get back up there, okay? Step lightly, and watch out fo – "

A mix between a moan and a howl roared to life, and the brush between the trees exploded violently. A hulking shadow pulled itself away from the other shadows, the wet sounds of its breathing hoarse and ragged. It came running straight at them. Bobby jumped in front of Darlene and she screamed and fell backwards, landing hard in the dirt.

"GO!" Bobby screamed at Darlene, but she was numb. Panic froze her to the ground. She fumbled for the flashlight and flicked it on, washing the trees and Bobby in its light, and they both screamed at the horror in front of them.

The shadow-thing, a nightmare in the flesh.

When the light hit it it stopped, startled, confused or maybe just curious. It stood there gasping, a strangled moan wheezing out with each breath.

It stank of decay, something wild and visceral. It stank of death.

The creature was hunched over and as big as a bear, its black, shiny skin pulled taut over rippling muscle. It was beaded with thousands of red droplets, like it was sweating blood from every pore. Folded wings lay across its back, and if it had a proper head it was hidden somewhere in the folds of gleaming skin. At first Darlene thought the thing was covered in raw meat, with giant chuck roasts plastered across its chest, but the meat was moving. Attached to the front of the creature, somehow entombed within the thing's inky flesh, were the dead astronaut's lungs, inflating and deflating as they steamed in the cold air. Next to the lungs was a still-beating heart. Above the lungs ran a fleshy tube that looked like a roll of packed bratwurst, and the tube ended at the grisly remains of a lower jaw. A gray tongue flapped uselessly above the teeth, slithering around like a blind snake. The tongue wriggled, and a garbled moan came out of the ruined throat.

The thing lunged at Bobby, unfolding its wings and spreading its body out. It wrapped itself around him, and he struggled and screamed and screamed as Darlene fainted.

⬦——◦——⬦

She awoke in a panic on the ground, the back of her head pounding from where she'd had fallen onto a rock. "Bobby," she whispered to the night, but she didn't expect an answer. She knew she was alone. She sat up, her heart instantly galloping. *I gotta get out of here, I gotta get the FUCK out of here.* She scrambled onto her hands and knees, reaching for her fallen flashlight, and then she saw Bobby.

He was lying on the ground just a few feet away, a pool of blood saturating the dirt around him. His clothes had been torn and shredded, the skin underneath ripped open. "No!" Darlene screamed, crawling over to him. "No, my baby, no…what did it do to you…"

Bobby didn't answer. His face was a mass of mangled tissue, and two black craters stared accusingly at Darlene.

His eyes had been gouged out.

She grabbed him and buried her face in his shoulder, never minding the blood and dirt. It had killed him; the fucking thing had killed him. He had wanted to save somebody, and he died for it. She wept, her body spasming as she gasped for air between her sobs. No more wedding. No more kids, no more house by the lake. No more future. No more Bobby.

Darlene didn't want to let him go, didn't want to leave him. She wanted to stay there forever, wanted to die with him. *Till death do us part,* she thought ruefully as she choked out a bitter laugh. She fumbled for her phone, but when she saw there weren't any bars she screamed and threw it into the forest. She collapsed onto what was left of Bobby.

Her forehead was still against his torn shoulder, her tears mixing with his blood, when she heard ragged breathing and a low, choking moan. She lifted her head.

The creature was right in front of her, its stolen lungs wheezing to filter the alien atmosphere.

It was watching her with the brightest emerald-green eyes she had ever seen.

CHRISTOPHER BOND
ABOUT THE AUTHOR

Christopher Bond is the author of dozens of stories encompassing the speculative fiction genre, including tales of high fantasy, urban fantasy, horror, and science-fiction. He has spent most of his adult life living between Hawaii and the Midwest. His work has been included in anthologies from Eerie River Publishing, Hydra Publications, and Corrugated Sky Press. He currently lives in Ohio with his wife, Emily, and their three kids, Kailie, Oliver, and Milo. You can find him on Twitter @CbondKauai

The Forgotten Prince
Elizabeth Nettleton

The child's large, blue eyes followed Pim as she gently pulled the twigs from his hair. He tried to tug his arm free from the bush, but it held firm, chastising him with its sharp branches.

"It won't be long now, I promise," Pim murmured. "You're being very brave. What's your name?"

"Niky." The boy winced as a thorn pricked his forehead, a droplet of blood trickling onto his cheek.

"Oh dear, Niky. How did you manage to get yourself caught like this?"

Those piercing eyes shifted away from Pim's face, and she tried to lighten her question with a smile.

"Well, I hope you were having fun, whatever it was you were doing! There."

The last twig snapped, and Niky scrambled into Pim's arms, his heartbeat racing under his filthy shirt. Pim stroked his back, and a sudden gust of wind cut across their faces.

"Instead of wind, how about sending us a bit of rain?"

Pim joked, turning to the cloudless sky.

It had been weeks since there had been any rain. Even dew had forsaken them, refusing to lay its kisses on the earth when morning drew near. Grass turned brown from the unrelenting heat, and Pim worried her animals were going to die as well if no storms came soon. Her supplies were running out quickly.

Niky stared above him, his blond hair almost golden in the sunlight. "He doesn't care," he said.

"Who, your father? Where is he? And I'm sure that's not true; he must miss you terribly."

The boy didn't answer, and Pim frowned, unsure. Niky's accent was unfamiliar to her - low and lilting, as if he were singing instead of speaking.

"Are you from one of the villages nearby? I haven't seen you around here before," she said, trying again.

"We're travelers. We came here about two months ago, and I got lost. I don't know how to get home again." Tears glistened in Niky's eyes, and Pim folded him back into her arms.

"You've been alone for two months? How have you survived?"

"I found another traveling family, but they were unkind to me, so I ran away."

"Well, I insist that you come home with me until we can find your parents."

Niky nodded eagerly, and Pim led him onto the path towards home.

Pim's house was a flat, wooden building, built by her

father atop the largest hill on the farm. As a child she would wander out before anyone else was awake, her skin prickling under the morning chill, and pretend to be a princess overlooking her kingdom. The sheep were the peasants, the cows and horses her noblemen, and the chickens her soldiers. Her enemies were the foxes and wild cats, of course. When her father asked how she had decided on each animal's role, she hadn't really been able to tell him. It just made sense.

Not much made sense to her anymore. Her father, an industrious man with calloused hands and a kind smile, had passed away two years ago. With no siblings and a mother on the opposite side of the country, the farm was hers. Papa entrusted its care to her, and she had gone about with confidence that she would make him proud.

Each day that confidence waned, as without his guidance she found herself completely inept. The animals seemed to sense her hesitance and shied away from her. She didn't understand what the plants needed, and they produced fewer and fewer crops. Now, *this*. She peered at the sky, desperate for some hint of a cloud.

Nothing.

"Here we are," Pim announced as they approached the porch. Niky inspected the peeling paint and raised his eyebrow in an unspoken question.

"If you were expecting anything fancy, I'm afraid you'll be disappointed," she said with a laugh. Niky smiled and went through the front door, settling himself on one of the lounges.

"Pim!" a voice shouted.

Pim turned to find her neighbor, Kal, riding towards the house. His horse gasped for breath, its flanks slick with sweat.

"Will you ever give that poor girl a break?" Pim asked. She rushed to fill a bucket of water, wincing slightly as the tap spat out more than she could really spare, and placed it in front of the panting mare. The horse gulped it down gratefully.

"Not when it comes to seeing you, Pimmy."

Kal swung his leg over the horse's side, and Pim tried to resist a smile. She and Kal had been friends since childhood, but lately it seemed as if something else was developing between them. She certainly hadn't failed to notice how well Kal suited the stubble inching down his jaw, or the muscles he'd gained from working on his own farm. However, neither of them seemed willing to express their feelings first, so they let their attraction simmer between them, ever-growing.

"Are you listening, Pim?"

"Sure, um…you were talking about the election. I think it's a brilliant idea! The town council needs someone like you."

"Thanks." Kal smiled. "Hey, who's that?"

Pim realized with a start that Niky had walked up behind her. His eyes roved over Kal, and he took Pim's hand.

"This is Niky." She kneeled down and brushed a strand of hair away from Niky's face, revealing the thorn marks. "I found him trapped in one of my shrubs. He's lost, so I told him he could stay here for a little while." She smiled, but Niky's stern expression didn't change.

"How're you doing?" Kal said. "I wish I'd known, Pim, I'd have brought you over some food. What do you like to eat, Niky? If I leave now, I could probably still get back before dark."

Niky frowned. "No."

"Not fond of strangers, hey?" Kal said kindly. "That's okay. Maybe we could hang out tomorrow, get to know one another. I'm Pim's friend."

"No. Pim's my friend now."

Pim chuckled awkwardly. "Hey, hey, Niky. I can be friends with you *and* Kal. Kal's very nice, he's not at all like that family you met. I'll tell you what, why don't we have a picnic tomorrow? We could get some apples from the tree, and…"

"I said NO!"

A bolt of lightning lit the sky, thunder roaring behind it. Kal jumped.

"What the Hell was that?" he asked. He reached for Pim.

"Get away from her!" Niky pushed his hand into the air, and a gust of wind threw Kal backwards, knocking the breath from his body. Pim raced to him.

"Did he push you?" she asked.

Kal brushed the dirt from his pants and rose, his eyes on Niky. "No, he didn't touch me. Not with his hands, anyway. How did you do that, buddy?"

Niky glared at Kal, his teeth bared into a tense smile.

"I'm not telling you anything. I don't like you."

"The wind…"

"Come on Kal, that was just weird timing. He's a little boy!" Pim said.

Dark clouds pulled together over Niky, then erupted in a shower of lightning. Fingers of electricity reached through the sky and swiped above their heads.

"Pim, I think you should come with me," Kal said softly.

"She's not going anywhere."

Wind nudged Pim's side, knocking her against Niky. He wrapped his hands around her arm, and Pim felt a spark of electricity where their skin met. She stared at Kal, her eyes wide.

"Pim…"

"It's okay, Kal. You go on home. I'll be fine," she said. She inclined her head towards the village, and he nodded.

"Alright, Niky. I'm gonna go home now." He fumbled for his horse's reins. "Pim, I'll see you…"

Thunder boomed overhead, rattling Pim's teeth. Kal licked his lips.

"…around. I'll see you around."

Kal mounted his horse. With one last look at Pim he nudged the mare's sides, sending a spray of dust flying into their faces as he took off down the hill. Niky beamed up at Pim, his eyes glistening through his earthen mask. Above him the dark clouds lifted until the sky was clear once more.

"Let's go back inside and have some supper," he instructed.

Pim allowed him to lead her into the house. The wind whistled a warning as she closed the door behind her, and she shivered despite herself.

"What would you like to eat?" she asked. Her voice was strained and tight. "I have some leftover stew we could have."

Niky nodded. Pim made her way to the kitchen, and tried to keep her hands steady as she laid out the cutlery. She cast a sidelong glance at Niky. He stared back, his eyes never leaving hers. Gasping softly she dropped a spoon. It clattered to the floor, and she cursed under her breath.

"Don't swear. It's unbecoming. My stepmother always says so."

"Speaking of your mother…"

"*Step*mother."

"I'm sorry, stepmother. Uh, do you have any idea where she might be now? We should try to find her as quickly as possible. She must miss you."

Niky sat down on one of the dining room chairs and scowled. "She doesn't. They don't care that I'm gone. I've been here for months, and if they wanted to find me, they would have."

"Oh, don't say that. I bet they're looking really hard— "

"It's her fault I ran away, and she knows it. I hate her," Niky snapped. "*She's* the one who banished my mother. *She's* the one who sent me to the Blue Tower. *She's* the one who tells Father not to visit me. I hear their parties at night, the way they laugh with their friends and promise them a prince. Well, they already have a prince. Me!"

"I don't really understand, Niky. You're prince of… what?"

"Everything," he whispered.

Pim breathed a sigh of relief. "Oh, yes. I used to play those games as a child. I pretended to be a qu…"

"This is not pretend!"

Thunder shook the house, and wind beat against the windows until a spiderweb of cracks spun across the glass. Frightened, Pim crawled under the table.

"I am Niky, son of Ukko."

"Ukko? You mean…"

"God of the sky! Thunder and lightning bow before him, and so do you, even if you don't know it. One day you will bow before *me*. I will rule over your Earth, sending rain and drought as I see fit."

"Drought? Are you the reason we haven't had any rain?"

"I'm not allowed to test my powers up there. *She* says so. But I can do whatever I want down here! I am your prince!"

Pim's blood ran cold. "So, you were never really trapped in that bush?"

Niky laughed, a high-pitched squeal of mirth. "Of course not! I've been watching you. I knew you'd be my friend. You're really nice, nicer than *her*."

"Your stepmother?"

Niky brought his fist down upon the table. "*Yes!* She doesn't like me because I'm not her son, but she needs to start respecting me because I'm going to be far more powerful than my father ever was. Father can make it rain, that's true, but my mother is Vellamo, the true goddess of water. Her blood runs through my veins, and I will rain her vengeance upon my enemies."

Lightning parted the sky, crashing down on a nearby tree and setting it alight. Thick tendrils of smoke danced in the blustering wind and fire rose into the air, eager to grasp whatever it could reach.

"Niky, please stop! You'll burn the house down!"

"*Pim!*" Kal's voice carried up the hill. Pim crawled out from under the table.

"You're not going anywhere. You're my friend, not his! Nobody's going to take you away from me. Nobody!"

An arm of wind struck Pim's face. The bones in her nose crunched together, sending a stream of blood running down her chin. Pressing her hand against her nose she scrambled back under the table. Wind circled her, spinning faster and faster until she couldn't move through it. She stared around her helplessly.

"Pim!" Kal called again, closer this time.

"We're coming, Pimmy!" someone else yelled. Pim knew that voice. It belonged to her father's friend, Eljas. He was younger than her papa, but just as strong and kind.

"Let her go!" A chorus sang outside the door. Pim recognized one voice, then another, until she realized that Kal had brought most of the village to her. She closed her eyes and thanked him silently.

Niky's head whipped towards the front door, and an inhuman growl burst from his lips.

"Get away from the house!" he screamed. The wind fell away from the table and Niky grabbed Pim's arm, yanking her to her feet. Pim whimpered as his fingers dug into her skin. "They took my mother away from me, but they won't take you," he hissed.

The front door creaked open. Kal stood in the doorway, his hands held up.

"I can see that you love Pim very much, Niky. So do I. I need to make sure that she's safe."

"She's safe with me."

"You're really strong. I bet you don't even know how strong you are!"

"I *am* very strong. Stronger than you are!"

"I know. You're stronger than Pim, too. Why don't you let go of her arm a little bit? You don't want to accidentally hurt her."

"No…" Niky's eyes darted between Pim and Kal. He loosened his grip slightly. "I didn't mean to hurt your nose, either. They were trying to take you away from me."

"I…um, I know. Thanks, Niky," Pim said.

"Why don't we try and find your parents?" Kal asked.

"I don't want to go home. I like it here."

Kal's gaze fell beyond Pim's shoulder. She shifted slightly and saw through the window that Eljas was at the back door, beckoning her.

"You can stay here with Pim, Niky. We'll put a bed in

the spare room and get you some toys," Kal said.

"Yes! I want a horse, too! A black one."

"We can get you a black horse."

Niky let go of Pim and clasped his hands together. "Pure black, with no markings at all. He needs to be fit for a king!"

"I know just the horse!" Kal said. "He lives on, uh, Mika's farm. Would you like to see him?"

Niky nodded and took a step towards Kal. Pim inched backwards.

"No markings, remember," Niky warned. He took another step.

Pim moved one foot behind her, then the other. *Easy, easy.* Sweat beaded on her forehead. *Nearly there.* She could feel the metal doorknob digging into her back. Kal watched her in his peripheral vision, a smile painted on his lips.

"How big was your horse back home?" he asked Niky.

"Oh, enormous. Bigger than *your* horse, that's for sure."

"I bet!"

"We have lots of horses in the sky. We ride them over the clouds."

"…the sky?" Kal echoed, his brow knotting in confusion. He glanced at Pim. Niky's head turned slowly as he followed Kal's gaze. His eyes met Pim's, and she froze.

"You tricked me."

Niky trembled with rage. He lifted his arm and directed a gale of wind with his fingers. Kal flew into the air, smashing down to the ground with a loud crack.

"You tricked me!" Niky roared. He stood over Kal's body and raised his leg. Kal screamed as the boy stamped down, the bones in his arm splintering.

"Kal!" Pim cried.

Niky snarled. "Don't talk to him! Water, come to me!"

He inhaled deeply. Sweat pooled on Kal's skin, then disappeared into the air. Kal's lips dried and split, followed by the rest of his face. The muscles in his limbs cramped, sending spasms down his body, and his breathing turned to rasps. With a final gasp he was still.

Pim screamed.

"I told you!" Niky said. "All water is at my command. I'm more powerful than my father will ever be. He'll regret ignoring me; they'll all regret it."

"Run, Pim!" Eljas yelled from outside.

Pim wrenched the door open, but a strong blast of wind pushed her back inside. Thunder bellowed overhead, drowning out Eljas as he ran along the house screaming her name. Pim jumped to her feet and tried ineffectively to open the window.

"It's no use, Pim."

The handle rattled, yet would not budge, kept in place by the swirling air outside. Bolts of lightning split the sky, landing on barns throughout the village and setting them on fire.

"Pim!"

Eljas threw his weight against the wall of wind and tumbled into the kitchen. He stared at Kal's body, his face pale, then pulled Pim under his arm.

"I don't know what you are, but you're not keeping her," Eljas said.

Niky's eyes narrowed. "Move aside, old man."

"No, I won't."

"How dare you defy your king!"

Lightning struck the house, and Eljas and Pim huddled together.

"You're no king of mine!" Pim shouted. "Ukko, we're calling on you. Please, come save us!"

Niky charged at Eljas, and their bodies slammed together against the wall. They grabbed at each other, leaving red marks where their fists met skin, until Niky pinned Eljas onto the floor. He held his hand in the air and drew a lightning bolt from one of the dark clouds outside. Grinning, he brought it down upon Eljas.

For a moment the room was still. Niky's hair floated behind him, a golden crown of curls sparking with electricity. Then Eljas' body jolted, and his clothes burst into flames. The room filled with the stench of burning flesh, and Eljas opened his mouth in a scream that never came.

"Am I your king now, Pim?" Niky laughed.

The lightning bolt began to shudder. Niky glanced at it, frowning. Pim seized the opportunity to pour water over Eljas, and the flames died upon his clothes with a hiss. Niky lunged at her, his arm raised, but the lightning jerked out his hand, showering the room with sparks.

"Come back to me!"

The lightning cracked. Niky glared at it, summoning

it, but it would not return to him. Pim pressed her fingers against Eljas's neck. His pulse was weak, but it was there.

"Come back to me. Now!"

Pim glanced out the window and saw a line of lightning bolts hanging in the sky. They were bright against the black clouds, unmoving except for small crackles of electricity at their tails. Niky saw them too, and for a brief moment Pim saw a flicker of fear in his eyes. The lightning moved closer to the house, then the roof exploded.

"No!"

Pim shielded Eljas with her body as wood rained down upon them. Smoke clawed at her eyes, clouding her vision, and heat pricked her back. Somewhere behind her Niky screamed. She lifted her head and saw that the lightning had arranged around him like a cage, locking him inside. Niky tried to shake the bolts, but they burned his skin until purple marks lined his arms.

"Let me go!"

Thunder boomed above them in reply.

"Ukko," Pim whispered.

Niky screamed and stamped his feet, hurling insults at his father. Then he was gone, leaving only a cloud of smoke behind him.

Pim stared through the broken roof into the sky. Lightning bolts threaded through the clouds, chasing each other until all had disappeared back into the heavens.

"Thank you," she whispered.

A raindrop hit her cheek, then another, until water ran down her hair and through her clothes. It fell on the wounded roof, extinguishing the flames and soothing its burns. Pim felt the apology in the gentle breeze, and squeezed her eyes shut to accept it.

"Pim?" a voice croaked.

"Oh, Eljas." Pim buried her face against her friend's shoulder.

"Kal?"

"Gone." The word choked her, resting in her throat until she could barely breathe. She hung her head.

"It's over now, Pimmy. It's over," Eljas murmured.

Is it?

Neighbors ran to them, firing questions at Pim and calling a doctor for Eljas. Someone raised a glass of milk to Pim's lips, and she took a sip.

"What happened? Who did this?" the person asked.

Pim began to shake. The rain was already slowing, their injuries dismissed by a ruler they forgot they had. She drew a breath of ashen dust.

The prince of the skies did this, she thought. She clenched her fists, her fingernails drawing blood upon her palms.

And one day, he will be king.

ELIZABETH NETTLETON
ABOUT THE AUTHOR

Elizabeth Nettleton studied Law at the Queensland University of Technology, Australia, and now lives in England with her family. She enjoys writing dark fiction and horror, and her work has been included in The Sirens Call eZine, Trembling with Fear, Short Fiction Break, and the "Forgotten Ones" and "It Calls From The Forest" anthologies by Eerie River Publishing. Her debut novella, The Price of Gold, is available on Amazon. You can read more about Elizabeth and her work at https://www.elizabethnettleton.com/

Flying Home
Joel R. Hunt

When Emma was a little girl, the idea of flying had been something magical; the realm of angels, pixies and pegasi. She had spent countless hours staring up at the sky in wonder. How far did it go? Would it ripple like the sea? What did clouds taste like? The sky was a land beyond the reach of humanity, and she had fantasized about being the one to finally explore it.

As she grew older, she learned that there were ways for humans to touch the sky, and she begged her parents to take her on a plane so that she could see it with her own eyes.

She had never been so disappointed.

There was nothing mystical about checking in luggage, no whimsy in pat-downs and body scans, no adventure to be had sitting under the stale blast of a broken air vent. With each flight she experienced, the old mystique that the sky had held for Emma's childhood withered further away, until finally, as an adult, it disappeared entirely.

Plane travel became something that she approached with nothing more than weary resignation.

This flight was no different. Without even the meagre consolation of a window seat, Emma found herself sandwiched between a woman whose headphones seemed designed to share the tinniest parts of every song with the entire plane, and a man whose beard alone had more muscles than Emma's entire body. With half an armrest, and a burgeoning headache, Emma settled in for the long journey ahead.

Unable to enjoy the view outside as the plane took off, Emma tried flicking through the in-flight magazine, but she couldn't find a position comfortable enough to read in. She supposed that was just as well, because it looked like a waste of paper. She tucked it away and leaned on the lone armrest available to her.

A few minutes later, Emma's frustration was interrupted by an unpleasant sensation trawling along her neck, like a pair of needles brushing her skin. She reached back with her hand, expecting to find an insect clinging to her body, but found only her own raised neck hairs. Turning to inspect her seat she likewise found nothing there, and Emma was about to shrug it off as her imagination when she spotted the culprit. Five rows back, across the aisle, a man was staring in her direction. His face was slack, his hair limp, but there was a strange intensity about him that Emma couldn't put her finger on. Now that she'd noticed him staring, she waited for some kind of acknowledgement – perhaps a polite smile or a wave, or else the embarrassed shuffling of someone caught in the act – but the man didn't react at all. He simply kept staring.

Emma turned away, shuffling downwards into her seat. A stalker was the last thing that she needed. On the bright side she hadn't ended up sitting next to him; suddenly the music lover and muscular man weren't feeling like such poor companions.

She decided to put the stranger out of her mind, deciding that it might not even be anything untoward. He may have simply thought he recognized her, but in any case he wasn't worth her worrying about. By the time the flight attendant came around to take orders for the in-flight meal Emma had put the man in the back of her mind.

It was some time later that she felt the phantom needles again. Emma bristled; surely the man wasn't still watching her? She didn't want to give him the satisfaction of checking, in case he mistook her discomfort for mutual interest, but she couldn't settle down until she knew. After a moment of consideration Emma turned to the tattooed mountain seated next to her.

"Excuse me," she said.

The man looked down at her, before holding out a hand that must have once belonged to a bear. Emma shook it, grateful that he didn't squeeze too hard.

"Name's Ron," the man said.

"Emma," she replied. "I'm sorry if this is a strange question, but there's a man about five rows back who keeps looking in this direction. Do you know him?"

Ron craned his neck to peer back and grunted.

"Nope."

"But he's still staring?" asked Emma.

"Yeah. Probably just some weirdo."

"Yeah…probably."

"If he's making you uncomfortable I can have a word with him," said Ron. Emma smiled, shaking her head.

"No. It's fine, thanks. I'll just ignore him; he'll get the message sooner or later."

She hoped he would, at least. As strange as the staring man was, Emma didn't want to let him ruin what meagre pleasure she might get from the flight, so she put him out of her mind and tried to get comfortable. The music from her right, with Ron's total domination of the armrest to her left, made a nap all but impossible. Having nothing better to do, and not wanting to risk spotting any other staring strangers, Emma closed her eyes anyway. She only opened them when her food was brought out.

Cold pasta with plastic cutlery: Another reason to lack enthusiasm for flying. She dragged out the meal for as long as her hunger let her, as though if she left it long enough it might turn into something more appetizing. In a few minutes, however, it was gone. She pushed aside the empty tray, and wondered whether it would be worth the inflated prices to wash the meal down with food that didn't hate her taste buds.

Next to her Ron got to his feet, and his seat let out a long, creaking sigh of relief. He looked up and down the plane before turning to Emma and gesturing to either end.

"Toilet?"

"That way," she said.

"Thanks."

In the brief respite that Ron's absence gave her, Emma took full advantage of the vacant armrest. She leaned her elbow across it and leafed through the in-flight magazine. It was as dull as she could have predicted; a cloying introduction from the CEO, glossy images of resorts she'd never go to, and adverts for perfumes and watches that she'd find for a tenth of the price as soon as she left the airport. Still, it was better than pretending to be asleep. As she skimmed over the review section, she absentmindedly scratched at what felt like an insect crawling up the side of her neck.

Emma froze.

Someone had sat down next to her. She hadn't noticed them approach, hadn't heard the creak of the seat as they settled in, but there they were, leaning into the shared armrest. Emma retracted her elbow, keeping her gaze firmly directed towards the magazine while feeling the itching of unfamiliar eyes on her skin. She took in the stranger through the corner of her vision. It definitely wasn't Ron, and she knew in the pit of her stomach who the next most likely candidate was. Fearing the worst, she couldn't help the briefest glance across.

It was him, the creep from five rows back. He was still staring at her.

Unblinking.

"Has anyone ever told you that you have the most wonderful eyes?" he asked. His voice dripped with sleaze, and she could feel it clinging to her.

"I have a boyfriend," said Emma. "He'll be back in a moment. That's his seat that you've taken."

She rankled at how naturally she had resorted to that particular lie; she shouldn't need to pretend to be in a relationship with some burly man in order to keep predators away. Unfortunately, the truth of, 'I recently had a girlfriend, but we're on a break because the long-distance relationship wasn't working out' would be unlikely to yield the desired results.

The creep didn't move, though. He merely offered a lop-sided smile.

"Eyes like yours are very rare," he said. "A beautiful sky blue. They remind me of home."

No doubt he expected her to show interest in that. *'Oh, where are you from? Sounds delightful! Do you come here often?'*

Tough luck - she wasn't going to play his games.

"That is not your seat," she said. "I don't know you. I would like you to please leave."

"Oh, I plan to leave," the creep assured her. "Quite soon, in fact, and I can see in your eyes that you're going to join me."

Emma clenched her fists. She had no desire to get thrown off of a flight for assault, but she wasn't some little lost lamb either. If he kept this up neither of them were going to like where it ended. She took a deep breath and tried to speak with a steady voice.

"I'm not interested. I will never be interested. This

is the last time I will tell you politely to *leave me alone.*"

"Your mouth says one thing," he drawled, "but your eyes scream another. You'd be amazed how often that happens."

Emma opened her mouth, unsure even as she did to whether she was going to rebuke him, scream in his face or bite off his smug nose. Before she reached her decision a tattooed, bearded figure had loomed over the creep.

"You're in my seat," growled Ron.

Emma could have hugged him, if only that hadn't meant moving closer to the insidious creep between them. She kept her fists firmly wrapped around the magazine in her lap, staring straight ahead and silently imploring the creep to lose interest in her - or give Ron an excuse to beat him into a pulp.

Long seconds of silence stretched by. No one moved.

"I said, *you're in my seat*," Ron repeated.

The creep looked him up and down.

"No, I'm not," he said.

The unexpected confidence of his reply shattered Emma's stoic façade. She snapped her head around to glare at the creep, and to her surprise she found Ron frowning at the floor like a child trying to solve a complex equation.

"Your seat is five rows back," the creep said.

Ron's eyes glazed over, and his frown disappeared. He stepped back, raising an apologetic hand.

"My mistake," he said.

Without another word, the bearded giant lumbered off to the back of the plane. By the time Emma's brain caught up with what was happening she called out to him, but he had already disappeared into the creep's original seat.

"There," smiled the creep. "Now it's just the two of us. Much better, don't you think?"

He shuffled as close as the armrest would allow, and his hand slithered its way onto her thigh. Fingers like half-thawed chicken dug into her skin.

"Let go of me!" Emma snapped. Her face burned with fury, and she raised her voice in a rallying cry to her fellow passengers. The woman in the window seat turned and took out a headphone.

"Everything's fine," the creep told her. She paused, her frown softening, and then she nodded and returned to her music. Couldn't she sense Emma's distress? Couldn't she see the creep's wandering fingers?

"Take your hand off of me right now, or I swear to God I will snap it in two," Emma said, half-rising before the creep forced her back down with surprising strength. He reasserted his grip on her leg with his cold, clammy hand, leaning further in.

"Is there a problem here?"

A flight attendant had made her way over, evidently drawn by Emma's outbursts. She had directed her question specifically at Emma, and her eyes spoke of understanding and concern. Emma instinctively knew that she had an ally in this woman.

"Yes, there is a problem," said Emma. "I don't know this man; this isn't his seat. He's been grabbing me, and he refuses to leave me alone."

The flight attendant frowned.

"Sir, I'm going to have to ask you to - "

"We just got married," the creep drawled. "We're on our honeymoon."

"*What?*" Emma spat. Her stomach churned at the audacity of his brazen lie, and a new hatred brewed inside of her. What kind of sick game was he playing? The only reprieve was that it was such an absurd claim that nobody could possibly -

"Congratulations!" chirped the flight attendant, her concern replaced by a startlingly sunny disposition.

"No, he's lying!" cried Emma. "I've never met him before in my life!"

"Yes, we're very happy together," said the creep.

"That's wonderful," said the flight attendant. "Well, if you need anything during the flight please let us know."

With a parting smile, just as Ron had done before her, the flight attendant swallowed the creep's nonsense and marched away. This left him with Emma, his clammy hand still clutching her leg. What was wrong with these people?

Emma was done playing nice. She'd given more chances than a creep like him deserved, and now she no longer cared about the consequences. She snatched the fork from her dinner tray and slammed it as hard as she could into his knuckles. The prongs pierced his skin like old fruit, sinking so deep that the fork stood in place.

Yet, despite the severity of her strike, there was no blood. No scream, not so much as a flinch.

The creep smiled.

"Have you got that out of your system now?" he asked. "I need you to calm down before we go home."

Emma's mouth ran dry. She stared at the fork sticking up effortlessly in his hand, and a sweat as cold as his skin ran down her brow. Emma's head rose and, for the first time, she looked directly into the creep's eyes. As she did, her breath caught in her throat. His eyes were like nothing she had ever seen before. There was no pupil there, no iris, only a roiling, swirling grey like storm clouds before a typhoon. They pulled on her soul, drawing her closer to his unblinking stare until she felt his icy breath on her neck and flinched away.

"You're…not human," said Emma.

The creep's smile grew, as if he was savoring her realization.

"No," he agreed, "I'm not."

"Then what the fuck are you?" Emma snarled.

"You'll find out when you join me," he said.

"I'll never - "

The creep pressed a slimy finger against Emma's lips.

"Let's not have any of that," he said. "You belong to the sky. I can see it in the blue of your eyes."

As he spoke, his own eyes flashed, as if lit for the briefest moment by lightning. There was a power behind them that chilled Emma to her core, but she wasn't going to give in to that power without a fight. She twisted around, spitting in his face. Before it had even reached him, the creep had seized the opening in her mouth and jammed his finger inside, pressing down her tongue and forcing her jaws apart.

"You will come home with me," he said.

Unlikely.

With the snort of a charging bull, Emma snapped her jaw closed as hard as she could. The creep's finger burst between her teeth. She had expected the tang of blood, but the substance that flooded her mouth was like old yoghurt. It seeped across her tongue and coated her teeth, the lumpy, rotten texture causing bile to rise in her throat. Fighting the instinct to retch, Emma spat the appendage into the creep's grinning face and threw her body against him. He tumbled into the aisle, cracking his head against the opposite seat. Emma didn't stop to check the damage. She clambered over his sprawled form and ran to the front of the plane, spitting out the vile, grey fluid that clung to her tongue.

She ran to the nearest uniform she could find, realizing too late that it was the same flight attendant that the creep had somehow fooled minutes earlier. Still, she had to try.

"Please," Emma cried, grasping the woman by the shoulders, "you have to help me! This man is - "

"Oh, your husband."

"He's not my husband!"

"We're so pleased that you chose our airline for your honeymoon," said the attendant. "If there's anything we can do to make your flight more special - "

"You're not listening to me!"

The words dried up in Emma's throat. As she held the attendant's shoulders and stared pleadingly into her eyes, finally beholding the true power of the creep. The whites of the attendant's eyes were drifting across her pupils, blowing like wisps of cloud in a summer breeze. Whatever the creep had done, it was literally changing the way she saw the world.

A figure appeared over Emma's shoulder. She gasped and recoiled, but instead of finding herself facing the creep she saw another passenger, his hand extended in cautious sympathy.

"Are you alright?"

Around him other passengers from the front row were gathering. Whether they believed her, or simply thought she was having a mental breakdown, Emma didn't care. She would rather be surrounded by humans than alone with whatever the creep was.

"No, I'm not alright," she said. "This man has been harassing me, and he's trying to hurt me. He's dangerous, and he needs to be stopped."

She was met with a few scoffs from the small crowd, but mostly there was concern and a willingness to believe. Emma was bombarded with questions that she tried to keep up with, but she knew that the creep could show up at any moment. She needed to steer them in the right direction.

"What happens to dangerous passengers?" she asked. "Is there somewhere to lock them away until we land?"

"We have…a sky marshal," said the attendant, seeming surprised by her own suggestion. The clouds still fogged her eyes, but they were starting to dissipate. The woman was blinking and frowning at her surroundings, as though coming back from a deep sleep.

"Yes!" said Emma. "Can we get the sky marshal?"

"Follow me."

The attendant led Emma and the passengers most invested in her plight down the aisle opposite to where the creep had fallen. Emma's heart beat like a war drum as she tried to spot him between each row of seats, but he had vanished. Her and Ron's seats remained empty, with Ron still sitting in the creep's original place, and both aisles were conspicuously creep-free. At the last row the attendant stopped and leaned in to whisper to one of the passengers. A walrus moustache dominated his face, and he fanned himself with a cowboy hat. The action must have been more habit than necessity, since the cabin was far from warm. In all, the man was a banjo short of being a country music star. When the attendant had finished, he nodded, set his hat aside and rose. He approached Emma with his hand reaching inside his shirt for what she guessed – hoped – was a gun.

"Where's the man who attacked you?" he muttered.

"I don't know, but he - "

Emma froze. Icy breath played along her neck.

"Please stop bothering my wife," said the creep.

Emma lunged for the sky marshal's pocket, but before she could grab his weapon the creep had barked an order:

"Grab her!"

The attendant and two passengers leapt into action, grasping her arms with painful efficiency. Others weren't so eager to comply. Panic and confusion rippled through the other passengers, and the marshal took several steps back, hand still tucked into his shirt.

"Now wait a minute here," he said, "what's this all about?"

"My wife needs help relaxing," said the creep, craning his head to address the entire plane. "Sit her down, she's tired. Everything is fine. This is normal."

"He's lying!" Emma screeched, but she could already see his words taking effect. In every eye in every face she turned to, clouds were beginning to form.

"This is normal?" asked the sky marshal.

"This is normal," said the creep. "Nothing to worry about. Everything is exactly as it should be."

The marshal's hand dropped to his side, and he joined the attendant in forcing Emma into the nearest empty seat. In whatever direction Emma turned, she was greeted with the grinning faces of simpletons. The nearest, an old gentleman whose eyes were almost entirely white, patted her hand as though she were a frightened puppy. That frail tapping was the final crack that burst the dam of her resistance. She slumped into the seat, drained of energy and fury. She was unable to see a way out.

The creep crouched in the aisle next to her.

"You know," he said, "I really didn't want to address the whole lot of them, but now I've done it for you. That's how special you are to me."

"Why?" Emma hissed. "What do you want from me?"

"I want you to come home with me," said the creep.

"Join me in the sky. You'd like that, wouldn't you? I can tell."

Emma scowled, but said nothing. He hadn't answered her question, and she wasn't going to beg. If he wanted her compliance then he'd have to give clearer instructions than that. She let the creep watch in silence, until the slightest flicker of annoyance rippled across his face.

Or was it amusement?

"All you need to do," he said, "is open the door."

Emma's mouth ran dry.

"*Open the door?*" she snapped. "You're mad!"

"Quite," said the creep. "You would be too, if you'd been trapped as long as I have, but now I can go home. *We* can go home. Such perfect eyes...Get us out of this tin prison, and we can ascend together."

Emma didn't know what she'd expected, but it certainly wasn't that. Opening a plane door in mid-flight was suicide, if it was even possible. In the back of her mind she recalled reading that it simply couldn't be done, and she prayed that she was remembering correctly.

"It can't open," she said with infinitely more confidence than she felt. "The pressure at this altitude stops it from - "

"Don't worry about the pressure. I can deal with that."

"Then *you* open it," she spat.

The creep laughed – or rather, he made the sound that was left over after all joy had been drained from laughter.

"I could," he said, "but you wouldn't like me to. This way is kinder."

A shiver ran down Emma's spine. She tried to hide it, but she felt utterly exposed in the glare of his storm cloud eyes. Not trusting herself to speak without her voice quivering, she chose to say nothing. The creep smirked and nodded.

"My wife would like some fresh air," he said. "Lead her to the exit."

The passengers mindlessly obeyed. A dozen hands pulled Emma from her seat, half-leading and half-dragging her to the plane's nearest exit. Emma's fight was futile, her kicks and elbows barely registering with her grinning captors, though she didn't let that stop her. No matter how hard she struggled she was drawn ever closer to the door – her personal gallows.

At the creep's instructions, Emma was forced to her knees just before the exit. Through the tiny window in its center she could see nothing but clouds and empty sky. The plane must have been tens of thousands of feet in the air. Even if she could somehow open the door it would be a death sentence for everyone inside.

The creep's wandering hand crawled onto her shoulder, and his chill breath wormed into her ear.

"Pull the lever," he ordered.

"I can't!"

"It's easy," said the creep. "I've told you, the pressure won't be a problem."

"It'll kill them!" Emma cried.

"But not you."

Across the plane something clunked. Emma, the

creep and every passenger turned as one to the pilot who had emerged from the cockpit. He stared at them all with wild eyes, frozen in the doorway.

"What the Hell's going on here?"

"Help me!" Emma screamed.

"Nothing is wrong, keep flying the plane," said the creep, hastier than his usual drawl.

Too late. The pilot had vanished from view, slamming the cockpit door which muffled the urgent conversation happening within. For a moment Emma dared to believe that the creep might actually be scared, but while his wax-like smile did fade his lazy demeanor remained on full display. He strolled towards the cockpit, seemingly unconcerned about his plot being interrupted.

"Look after my wife," he called over his shoulder. "Don't let her go anywhere."

The crowd pressed in on Emma's sides, dumb grins plastered onto their faces. Hopeless as the situation seemed, Emma realized that this was the first time since he took control of the plane that the creep had actually turned away from her. This was an opportunity she couldn't throw away.

"Please," she whispered to the crowd, hoping to find some semblance of humanity left behind those clouded eyes, "let me go. He's not my husband, he's not human. You're being controlled."

"You're very lucky to have him," said the flight attendant with earnest enthusiasm. "Did you enjoy your honeymoon?"

Emma bit back a scream of rage. She wanted to slap these idiots until they returned to their senses, but by now the creep had reached the cockpit door and was leaning against it, showering the unseen pilots with his mind-altering platitudes. He might turn back around at any moment, and Emma had no desire to bring his attention onto herself any sooner than necessary. She hissed a breath and decided to try a new tactic.

"Ron, dear," she half-sang. The bearded mountain smiled and approached.

"Is everything alright, Emma?" he asked. "Would you like me to get your husband?"

"Oh, please don't worry my husband," she said. Every word felt dirty, but it might be her only way to make them listen. "He was going to give me something, but he forgot. Could you fetch it for me? Only I can't go anywhere myself."

"Of course," said Ron. "What is it?"

Emma pointed to the brightly colored box by the emergency exit.

"That fire extinguisher."

The slightest hint of a frown flickered across Ron's obedient face.

"For my husband," Emma added. "To stop me going anywhere."

He paused to consider this. A bead of sweat trickled down Emma's brow. Her thoughts were racing almost as fast as her heart, but she forced her smile to remain. Ron ran his hand across his beard as his dulled mind processed her request, and at last he reached a decision.

"Alright," he said, and he marched away.

Seconds later the creep pushed his way through the crowd to stand before her. He exuded confidence, and his unblinking stare was once again focused entirely on Emma. For the first time she was glad to have his undivided attention.

"They're sorted now," he said. "Nothing to worry about. Now, I believe before that interruption you were coming to terms with your options. I really do implore you to open the door. I promise you won't fall, neither of us will. Not with eyes like yours."

Ron returned, bearing the fire extinguisher and a simpleton's grin. The creep looked him up and down.

"Who told you to get that?" he asked.

Emma surged forward. In a single motion she hoisted up the extinguisher, swinging it around like a hammer. It collided with the creep's face with a wet smack, flecking Emma with the same grey liquid that had poured from his finger. He stumbled back, and Emma pressed the assault. She slammed the fire extinguisher against his head again and again. His sponge-like skull crumpled, his nose sinking into his face as his lower jaw ripped and flapped loose.

Still he smiled.

"My wife is nervous," he said between blows. "Take her back to her seat."

He shouldn't have been able to speak. His face was a distorted mess, and his mouth no longer formed the words he was using, yet they emerged from his throat with an impossible clarity.

Following his request, a dozen hands grasped Emma and dragged her away from him.

"Let me go!" she cried. "He's not human, I have to kill him! Let me go!"

The hands patted her and stroked her face while their owners cooed vapid reassurances.

"Don't worry dear."

"I used to be a nervous flyer."

"We'll get you a nice, hot drink."

She fought against the crowd with all of her remaining energy, but their sheer numbers soon overpowered her. They plucked the extinguisher from her grasp before forcing her into an empty seat and holding her there. She could only wriggle and kick as the creep stood across the aisle, casually rearranging his face. Some of the damage remained, but that meant nothing to her. The creep had withstood a dozen cracks to the face from the heaviest weapon she could likely find on this aircraft; she couldn't think of any better way to kill him.

Perhaps it was impossible.

When his face was looking almost human again the creep strolled over. He stroked her cheek with his slimy fingers and stared almost wistfully into her eyes.

"This plane will not be landing," he said. "You must come to terms with that. Whatever action you take these humans will not survive their journey; your resistance will not buy them life, it will only sacrifice yours. After all, the only thing I really need is your eyes. If you comply with my wishes I can bring the rest of you home with me as well, but if not…"

He pulled the fork out of his hand with a gut-churning squelch, thrusting the prongs at Emma's face.

"I will gladly take the parts I need."

Emma's lips clamped shut. The creep waited, and when it was clear that she wasn't responding to his threat he sighed. His hand lashed out, and those cold, clammy fingers grasped her hair so tight it nearly tore from her scalp. She cried out and writhed against the passengers holding her limbs, but with no effect. She might as well have been clamped in irons. Even as she pushed her head back to escape the fork's prongs, the creep anticipated her resistance, pushing back to close the gap.

There was nowhere for her to turn, no direction for her to run. The only movement she had left would bring her closer to those impending prongs that threatened to scoop out her eyes. The fork dominated her vision, growing larger with each second, and this was her last chance to decide her own fate.

And she was going to take it.

"Wait!" she cried. "I'll do it! I'll open the door!"

The fork paused inches from her eyeball. The grip on her hair became the slightest bit less painful, though she'd have kept that pain if it would have spared her the suffering of the creep's expression - a victorious smirk blossomed on his face.

"A wise choice," he crooned. "Why throw away eyes as fine as yours?"

So it really was just her eyes that he needed; the rest of her meant nothing to him. That was good to know. It made her decision a lot easier. As the crew and passengers relaxed, along with their master, Emma clamped her teeth tight. She took a steadying breath, then she thrust her face as hard as she could onto the fork.

Agony exploded as the prongs pierced her eye. Fire surged from her ruined eyeball to the back of her skull, threatening to burst out the other side. A scream tore from her mouth, the most raw one she had ever produced, yet it fell infinitely short of conveying her suffering. She doubled over, writhing and twisting, a warm fluid pulsing down her cheek and pooling along her neck. Emma wasn't the only one screaming. As her own lungs emptied, her pained cry withering away, she heard its twin bursting from the throat of the creep. It was the least human thing about him, a mixture of dying animal and hurricane.

Tensing her entire body and forcing the next scream back down into her chest, Emma looked up. Through her undamaged eye she saw the creep staggering away, clutching his own eye as wisps of black mist poured from the wound. He trembled like a leaf in the wind, so that every jolt of agony she felt seemed to strike him twofold.

That thought spurred her on. She groped in front of her face, reaching blindly for the handle of a fork she could no longer see. After a few moments her searching fingers collided with plastic, knocking it further beyond her grip.

The fork spun sideways, bursting from her eyeball with the sound of a popped grape amidst a fresh gush of warm fluids. A lightning bolt of pain punched its way through her skull. Emma cried out, and the creep echoed her.

Collapsing onto her shoulder Emma scrambled along the floor. She cast a desperate, blurring eye for where the fork had landed. After several agonizing moments, she spotted it just beyond arm's reach.

So did the creep.

The pair lunged. Her warm hand crashed into his frigid one. His fingers closed around the plastic, but with a frantic twist she dug into the gap presented by his missing finger and plucked the fork free. She kicked him back, clutching the utensil like a baby.

"Stop her!" the creep shrieked.

A tornado of bodies leapt into action, surging towards her on all sides. Steeling herself, Emma pinned the creep with a determined glare.

The last thing she saw was his look of pure terror.

They both screamed as the fork punctured her second eye. His began as the loudest, but as each heartbeat brought a fresh hammer-blow of agony Emma's cry drowned the creep's out. In a final burst of energy, Emma pulled the fork free, hurling it across the cabin. Then, without the strength to even keep her own head lifted, she collapsed motionless to the floor.

On all sides, hands grasped and plucked at her. Voices rose to fill the gap left by Emma's fading scream.

"Oh God, she's bleeding!"

"Somebody get the captain!"

"What happened? Did anyone see?"

Emma's world was darkness, pain and panic. Yet, as the voices swirled around her head and the floor seemed to spin away, the briefest of chuckles passed through Emma's lips.

She couldn't hear the creep anywhere.

◆──○──◆

Emma woke up in hospital. Before she knew how much time had passed, before she even knew whether she would recover, she vowed to never fly again.

The accounts of her injury, as they trickled in, were confused. None of the passengers proved able to provide a coherent story that led to their discovery of Emma's mutilated body. However, there was one consistency that pleased Emma greatly: Not a single account mentioned the creep at all. It seemed he truly had vanished, along with her eyes. Her sight was a price she was happy to pay to rid the world of him.

She told no one, of course. She was certain that the creep had been real, but she also knew how insane the tale would sound. Being blind was one thing, but being crazy was a label she could do without. Instead she tried to pick up the pieces of her life, satisfied to keep both feet firmly on the ground and confine all thoughts of the sky to her childhood.

And to her nightmares.

It was over a decade later that she broke her vow. A family funeral overseas gave her little room for excuses, and having spent years refusing to use her blindness as an excuse, she was dismayed to find offers of assistance pouring in when she finally tried. So it was that, despite her protests, she was taken to the airport and guided to her gate, where the staff led her to her seat and assured her that they were available if she had any problems at all.

To their credit, there were none. The take-off was about as smooth as could be expected, and it was only after the plane levelled off that it lurched up and down. Emma gasped, gripping the armrests until her knuckles cracked. She felt a frantic pulse behind her damaged eyes.

The plane soon settled. Emma's heart, however, did not.

A gentle hand tapped her shoulder.

"Don't worry," said a woman's voice. "It's only turbulence. It's completely normal."

Emma forced her lips into a smile and settled back into her seat. She reached up to feel for the air vent, hoping to stem the chill that was tickling her shoulders, but it was already off.

Steady breaths, she told herself, *Everything's fine.*

"You seem nervous. Is this your first time flying?"

"No," said Emma, "but I've had a bad experience in the past."

"Well, don't worry. It's perfectly safe. Besides, I'll look after you, and I'm sure your husband will as well."

Emma's heart skipped a beat.

"My…husband?"

Fingers like half-thawed chicken wrapped around Emma's hand.

"Thank you for reassuring my wife," said a voice that dripped with sleaze. "And has anyone ever mentioned that you have the most beautiful sky blue eyes?"

Joel R. Hunt
About the Author

Joel is a writer, proofreader, ex-teacher and part-time human currently residing in the UK. Among his other hobbies of eating, breathing and crouching in dark corners, Joel constantly plans stories and screenplays - a very small number of which actually get written. Most simply languish in his ever-growing 'Unfinished' folder, which is now approaching a mass capable of generating gravitational pull.

Joel's genres of choice are horror and sci-fi, although the odd bit of sentiment does manage to sneak in between the freakishness and disturbing twists. He hopes in time that he might earn a living from putting words on a dead tree in a particular order, or at least earn enough for the occasional cup of tea and vegetarian full English breakfast.

If you are so inclined, you can follow Joel's latest exploits on Twitter, where he also posts daily micro stories. But it might be simpler to cut out the middle-man and seek psychiatric help.

Twitter: https://twitter.com/JoelRHunt1
Website: https://joelrhuntauthor.wordpress.com/
Reddit: https://www.reddit.com/r/JRHEvilInc/
Amazon:https://www.amazon.com/Joel-R.-Hunt/e/
B07SBX6G3W

HATE SKY
JAY SANDLIN

Willard Skye checked again to make sure no one followed him down County Road Seventy-Two. Mardi Gras beads and a plastic set of titties jiggled from his mirror, but he didn't spot a soul in his rear view. Ratcheting the gearshift he switched to four-wheel drive — worn tires kicking up dust and rocks as his truck skidded down an unmarked dirt road. His knuckles tightened on the wheel as the bumpy ride jostled him in his seat. He glanced over his shoulder, concerned over the sensitive equipment concealed by the dingy tarp in the truck bed. *Damn. After all the trouble stealing it, it'd be just my luck if I wrecked it before I could use it.*

Each bump reminded him of the new mayor's empty promises to update the rural county's infrastructure. Scowling, he spit a greasy tobacco glob in the styrofoam cup. *Lying bitch. I never let things get this bad when I was in charge. I took care of things - handled the roads. Kept up the city, even after the worst floods and twisters. His* palm smacked the wheel, and he shook his fist. *How dare they come to my town, try to change things I got perfect for my kind of people. When election time came, did they care? No! Those ungrateful sons of bitches....* However, the neglect of his beloved county's roads suited his purpose. He needed to get away, far away. The more obscure and harder to reach the better. He may have lost his position, but he hadn't lost his youthful zeal for accomplishing his goals. Once he set his mind to something he couldn't be stopped, which was how he'd held on to the mayoral seat for so many terms. He had run unopposed, until social justice liberal eggheads rolled into his town with their socialist agendas. *Damn them all to Hell.*

Thorns and branches smacked against the windshield as his truck stopped a few feet before the so-called road did. Thick brush concealed his vehicle on the off-chance anyone happened to come by, or if patrol cars passed with orders to keep an eye out for the former mayor. Shoving back branches he stumbled out of the cab, trying to avoid getting snagged by thorns. His gut hung over his belt, hairy belly poking through the strained buttons of his plaid shirt. Years of guzzling beers and chili dogs on the golf course had caught up to him in his golden years.

He wrestled the unwieldy metal pole from the truck bed, careful not to bend or break any of the small pieces. Hoisting it over his shoulder he inhaled deeply, praying to the good Lord for strength for the hike ahead. When he was a young boy, with a head full of hair and a body full of spunk, he'd run these trails faster than a jackrabbit addicted to speed. Now, with an overweight body filled with diabetes and emphysema, he was damn lucky to get out of bed each morning without his back aching or knees giving out. Some days it hurt so bad he thought of just giving up; Ending it all. Lots of folks in town, especially the ones down at the radio station and City Hall, would throw a party if he did.

Thinking of those cocky pricks added fuel to his fire, and the antenna's weight felt less like a burden to carry for the benefit it provided. He huffed and wheezed as his trusty Redwings, worn from years of hiking and hunting, carried him down the trails. He hitched up his britches and sucked in the cooler air as he pushed forward. Shade from trees far older than him provided a comforting presence; Leaves turning honey and pumpkin hues drifting to the ground meant Fall was right around the corner. He wasn't concerned with being followed. These hunting trails had been part of his family for years; Known only to him and his pap before he'd passed away. *Oh, Pap. I miss you every day.*

Ole Pap wouldn't recognize Hattiesburg, their beloved, quiet town today. It used to be a one-stoplight town; It never needed more than a grocer, gas station and one church to keep everyone's bellies fed, cars running and spirits full. Every Sunday night, in the summer months after services, everything smelled like donuts and fried chicken. Folks gathered in the square for a potluck, sharing what they had and watching out for their neighbors. He scowled, thinking of the Spanish-speaking trash littering the square now. Days of common decency ruling his county were long gone. Entire neighborhoods of fine, God-fearing Christian folks moved out to be replaced with border-crossing, lazy freeloaders. People used to watch out for each other, but not anymore. He didn't feel safe going out past dark, and nothing looked the same. His hometown didn't even *smell* the same; Beaner restaurants were now on every corner cooking their flour tortilla sandwiches, stinking up Main Street and feeding folks dog meat!

Arriving at his destination he shrugged the antenna off his shoulders. His father's greatest gift to him, besides a fine pedigree and superior genetics, was a beautiful tree house in the woods. Over the years he added to it, shifting it from a kid's play fort to a structure more comfortable than most hovels the illegals cobbled together when they snuck over to squat. Built from solid oak, with enough hardware to stand years of storms, it made the perfect hideaway. He'd poured much time and money coming out here to reinforce the walls, add insulation and even run a generator to really jazz the place up. Every city official used to kiss his ass year-round for an invite when hunting season began; Back when they still dared to speak to him, of course. Looking up he smiled, admiring his handiwork. This was the perfect place to broadcast his message. Hopefully the animal he'd left up there, locked in the crate, hadn't alerted any hunters while he was gone.

He tied a square knot of rope around the base of the antenna, then yanked on the pulley. The metal squealed as he hoisted it to the top of the tree stand, and fighting back a twinge of guilt he bit his bottom lip. Yeah, it was stolen from the local station, but by Hell they deserved it. They cancelled his show because of complaints from bleeding hearts. Those people were lazy, diseased deplorables living off hand-outs from hard working Americans like himself, thinking it's okay to give earned money to those too lazy to work — they wanted to socialize every Goddamn thing until his country fell harder than the USSR. *Who wants to be a socialist? This is the land of the free. The brave! I worked for years to get my retirement, my social security. My pension I earned. Dammit, those people don't need to be given* my *money.* He'd said so for years on his radio show, three hours for five days a week, and Words with Willard was one of the most popular programs in the county until those offended by the truth managed to get the station to pull the plug. *They said it hurt too many feelings. Well, you know what I say to that?* Flipping his middle finger, he shouted at the overcast sky. "Fuck your feelings!"

With the antenna secured he climbed the wooden ladder rungs drilled into the trunk, breathing heavier with every step up. His breath grew shorter, his chest tighter, and he wasn't sure how much more his old heart could take. But it was necessary. They may have taken his mayoral seat, but they wouldn't take away his voice — freedom of speech still meant something in this country, dammit.

Jingling his keys he clicked open the padlock securing the stand. Hinges creaked as he opened the door, and the stale air inside the insulated dwelling reeked with urine and feces. Like any hunter worth his salt he smelled fear mixed with the piss. His eyes darted immediately to the crate in the corner, still draped in dark fabric. He walked over and pulled back the tarp, checking to make sure the animal remained. It cowered in the corner, head tucked between its legs as it shook like a leaf in a blizzard. Willard reared back, kicking the crate with his steel-tipped boot. *Fuck! Little guy pissed and shit all over the place.* Letting out a hearty chuckle he decided a little excrement in his stand was a small price to pay for the satisfaction he received in trapping it.

Trapping came easy, but this target was carefully chosen. He'd watched it for days. Learned its patterns. Where it liked to go, eat, play and bathe. Like a true predator he only made his move when he knew everything there was to know about his prey, so the snatch went down without a hitch. Willard swore he'd remember the terror on its face to his dying day — how it struggled, scratching and biting helplessly against him. It may have put up a fight, but Willard hogtied and gagged it in broad daylight. *Still can't believe how easy I plucked him out of that bitch's yard.*

He delivered another swift kick to the crate. The little critter howled like it'd been shot. Fussing and howling it rushed up to the locked door, rattling the metal bars while it wailed.

Willard's Redwings shut it up. "You hush! I ain't ready for you yet." The varmint retreated to the back of the crate, still whimpering. *Pathetic.* It should be grateful he'd sprung for the extra-large dog breed crate, since it had more room than it needed.

He groaned, snapping his fingers at it to be quiet. When that didn't work he reached for his walking stick leaning against the wall. Slowly he clanged the stick against the cage bars, the animal's brown eyes tracking the stick, tears welling in them. Willard grinned. This walking stick was made of carbon fiber — he'd spared no expense — and was tipped with a steel point almost as sharp as a hunting arrow. It'd been designed for catching one's balance on steep surfaces, but Willard discovered it worked well in teaching unruly critters who was boss.

He slid the pole through the bars, stabbing the animal as it whimpered in the corner. He jabbed the vermin in the sides — not hard enough to impale it, but enough to leave marks. Bloody drops plopped on the floor, staining the carpet he'd laid down just a few seasons back. The more blood he saw the angrier he became. He kept stabbing, but it still didn't take the hint to quiet down. *This thing must be slow, even for its animal family. God dammit!* He hurled his walking stick against the side of the wall. With all this racket he'd never be able to put out his show.

A smile crept up on his face as he spotted his storage chest. Sliding open a plastic drawer, he retrieved his Taurus Judge. "Hello, Baby," he said, greeting the one friend who never let him down. The weapon was technically a pistol, but it looked imposing enough to mount to the side of a tank as artillery. Whenever he squeezed the rubber it was like he held a raging cannon in his palm, and Baby could blow fist-sized holes into full-grown bucks. Pointing it up to the ceiling the gas-powered lights caught the glimmer of the stainless steel hardware, which was mixed with grips black as night. The way it fit in his hand was like it was made for him alone. During his years as mayor every judge in the Hattiesburg Courthouse kept one handy behind the bench. If a prisoner got unruly during sentencing, and the bailiff was a little slow on the uptake, then Baby served out swift justice. Even the most nearsighted judges never missed shooting these. *Thank the Lord and Fiocchi for high velocity .410 shotgun shell ammo*, he thought, flicking his finger and spinning the chamber. The wheel clicked back into place, and he guided it inside the crate bars.

Willard shoved the octagon-shaped barrel against the animal's skull, thumb cocking the gun's hammer. Hearing that click felt better than any orgasm. His dick hardened as he looked into it's fear-filled eyes. At this range a small pull of the trigger would turn its brains into a work of cadmium-colored modern art on the side of his wall, and after a few rounds of target practice with Baby this thing wouldn't be fit to stuff and mount in his rec room. He grinned, raising his eyebrow and daring it to defy him.

It got the point. It retreated to the back of the crate, curling up like a frightened possum on the first day of hunting season. Willard kicked the cage a few more times. The filthy critter soaked silently in blood and tears, not daring to stir; There was nothing like a big gun to send the message to shut the fuck up. He tossed Baby from hand to hand, considering emptying the revolver in the cage then and there. It'd be the humanitarian thing to do, to just put it out of its misery, but not yet. Not until it was time.

Willard's twisted grin grew wider. With the antenna secured to the roof he cranked up his extra power generator. The machine hummed, giving life to his tangled mess of broadcast equipment. Switchboards and dials on his makeshift desk took up much of the room in his fort. His fingers darted from section to section as he adjusted volume levels and accounted for gain and pitch. He dialed up the bass boost to give his voice the extra bit of authority he conveyed so well over the airwaves. Fitting a pair of headphones over his ears he tapped his finger against the mic.

"Check one, check two." Squealing feedback roared, nearly knocking him on his ass. Wheeling back around his fist smacked the table. Adjusting the levels he worked to filter out the background noise as best he could before he went live. Gathering equipment from so many sources resulted in a wiry mess of mismatched junk, which most broadcasters would laugh at. This set up was nothing compared to the studio he'd once had for his show, but trying times called for such measures. No matter the setup, however, he felt the same sense of satisfaction when he flipped the switch. Red lights blazing confirmed he was on the air, and, like any good politician, Willard had learned the strength of words. In many ways a live mic held more power than a gun; Like Moses delivering commandments from Mt. Sinai, or the Savior Himself delivering the Sermon on the Mount. Tonight his voice came down from the sky, sending his message into the ears of listeners. He was the shepherd, and they were *his* flock.

Adjusting his headphones he slid behind the microphone and cleared his throat. "Welcome to another edition of Words with Willard, broadcasting from a hidden location somewhere in Forrest county." Kicking his feet up on the desk he took a long sip of coffee from his thermos, black and strong. The broadcast equipment filled the stand's open area, leaving only a small amount of space between the heavy, wood shutters he could keep open or closed for shooting. Though they remained closed, tonight he fired weapons of a different kind. "It's unfortunate I can't continue broadcasts at the local station. If my constitutional rights were still in effect in this town, I'd still have my show. I'd still have the mayor's chair!"

He grit his teeth. Them stealing the show was the last straw. It was bad enough they kicked him off the air, but banning him from the station because of a minor scuffle with the station manager? Ridiculous! All he did was break the sap's nose when they told him too many advertisers pulled out because of his show. Thin-skinned cowards; Treacherous vipers. The same folks who used to line up just for the pleasure of shaking his hand turned on him as soon as that wetback bitch stole his seat.

Thoughts of the current mayor caused his blood to boil, and he leaned in closer to the mic. "Of course, very few constitutional freedoms remain intact since her *honor* Mayor Garcia won that sham election. Did we even check the citizenship of everyone who voted? I'm sure the caravan of illegals bussed in on election day had absolutely nothing to do with her upset victory over a longtime incumbent." He wiped coffee residue from his mouth, tasting the bitterness of the beans. "My attempts to investigate the obvious, widespread voter fraud were stonewalled at every turn, even when I called the Goddamn Attorney General at his house!" His fist pounded the wooden desk, causing the little animal in the crate behind him to yelp. "I tell you, this conspiracy to replace conservative, Bible-believing politicians with pants-wearing women spouting their New Age Marxism is wide-ranging. There's no telling how deep the corruption goes." He counted off on his fingers. "City council's as impotent as a Jew on Saturday. Senorita Mayor's got the police in her pocket, state troopers too. She won't stop harassing ICE. How are they supposed to do their damn jobs? How deep does this go? It's like rot in a condemned house. Rot starts at the foundation, and I suspect the rot in our county spreads all the way to the damn governor's office. It has to, right? Every day more illegals slip into our borders. Who's lettin' em in? Why isn't anyone stopping them? I tried, and look what happened to me! If they can take my job, you think they can't take yours too?!"

Rising, with mic in hand, he paced as he spoke. Sparks flew in his voice. "They *want* your jobs, your land, your women, your freedoms! It's no question that they're coming to take 'em, my friends..." on the last word he bit down on his lower lip, a slight trickle of blood dripped down his chin. "...my only question is: What will you *do* about it?"

Willard let the question hang out in space. There was no way to know how many listeners tuned in, or how many more he gained with the boost from the antenna, but tonight Willard felt something during his broadcast—a presence accompanying his words. He heard it in the night; It disturbed the trees and fluttered through the leaves. Peeking behind the window shade he saw the hours of twilight had passed him by. Darkness fell over the woods, accompanied by stars and cricket songs.

And high-pitched chirping, *loud* chirping.

Peculiar, he thought. For years his family shared these grounds with large nests of vampire bats. The winged rats filled several caves over the acres, only coming out at night to hunt the smallest prey. The cretins got ornery enough during mating season, but tonight they were unusually active. They were flapping and screeching, riled up like a herd of rabid wolverines.

Willard dabbed his forehead with a handkerchief. *Can't let more varmints distract me from my mission.* "Because, as the Good Book says," he spoke into the microphone, "faith without works is dead. What are your works? What are you doing to restore Hattiesburg to the paradise it once was?" His voice dropped an octave, his tone growing melancholy. Closing his eyes he thought of days long past: Spinning on a stool in the local ice cream parlor, the smell of a fresh banana split in the big bowl in front of him. His parents never worried where he went, not when reputable businesses displayed signs for white-only clientele. Those days when businesses had actual freedom

—freedom to refuse service to *whomever* they damn well pleased.

"We used to watch out for each other in this town. We were small, and isolated, but that's just the way we liked it. Neighbors knew one another by name, and we went to bed with doors unlocked and windows open." To make his point he pulled open the hunting shutters, letting in a rush of cold night air. "Those days are long gone. I can't remember the last time I walked main street at night. My home has a security system, and bars on the window. That's the way it has to be, all because of those Goddamn foreigners."

Willard paused, inhaling the crisp, fall air. His heart pounded, his mind flailing slightly as there was a sudden hint of light-headedness. Reaching into his Carhartt jacket he fumbled for his heart pills. Finding his thermos empty he dry-swallowed the horse-sized pill in one hard gulp.

His fingers groped for the sound board's mute button. Exhaling he hacked out a cough so wet it sounded like the ocean came to life from his lungs. *Dammit.* It'd be harder to swallow the pills, but he needed the pill to work now! Leaning out the window he struggled to catch his breath.

That's when he saw them: A whirling dervish of a tornado approaching — not one made of wind and water, but a congregation of swirling vampire bats. Their almost-deafening screeches surrounded him, the stench nearly suffocating. The night seemed like a scene from a horror movie as the bats outnumbered the population of Hattiesburg by several hundred, maybe more. Tree branches snapped and cracked from the sheer weight of bats, and a cacophony of wails accompanied the swarm's descent from the sky.

His hand raced to close the window shutters, but tiny fangs bore into his wrist. They broke skin; Even drew blood. "Yeoow!" He wrenched his hand back, sucking the blood with his tightly-drawn lips. *Little fuckers bit right into the meat. The bats must be crazy!* They'd always called these woods home, but he'd never see them act so aggressive, so ravenous.

So wild.

The mammalian vortex of swirling blackness swarmed inside his fortress. Willard cupped his ears, the high-pitched squeals of the flying critters joining together in a glass-cracking agony on his inner lobes. It threw him off balance. Rotting smells of blood, death, and feces from the tiny scavengers traveled the air.

A rush of furry creatures swept past his cheeks, scratching exposed skin. With a scream he flipped up his hood, but fangs bit the skin of his eyelids. He opened his mouth to scream again, but a bat flew down deep. He spit it out like wet tobacco chaw. Crawling on his hands and knees he reached up to the switchboard and flipped the switch, re-opening the channel. Tugging the microphone to the ground by the cord he shouted for his flock to listen. "Help me! I'm being overrun! Invaders! Toxic! Full of disease! Help! Oh God, HELP!"

The mic fell out of his hands and bounced out of

sight, lost in the sea of black, chirping filth. He coughed and sputtered. The machinery sizzled, his generator going off-line from the overflow of bats attracted to the warmth. Bats humped in every corner, little furry shits with foaming mouths and fangs bared. Hundreds more came from the sky, eating through the ceiling and devouring his expensive insulation like hungry kids inhaling cotton candy at a carnival. The ones not humping each other were chomping on every bit of flesh they could find on Willard. Gashes opened, and blood flowed from his body freer than a stuck pig on the Fourth of July.

The chomping continued. Chunks of pale flesh were ripped away by ravenous jaws. The putrid scent of the swarm vanished after several dozen bats bit off his nose, fighting over the meat in a corner. A few of the critters found their way down his pants, tearing his pubic hairs as their teeth gnawed his ballsack. Willard's bloody fingers struggled through the flapping menaces to retrieve his gun. Baby fired deafening shots in the enclosed space, but it was like trying to fight a fire with an eyedropper.

After four rounds the last shell in the chamber looked mighty friendly...

Willard shot a glance back at the dog crate. Covered by the tarp still, he imagined it was only a matter of time before the bats found their way inside. *Damn.* He wanted to put down the animal himself, preferably live on air, but at least he could die knowing the bats carried out his job.

He fought against the swarm and raised the gun to

his head. When he fired he smiled, knowing at least the animal's mother would feel the same pain he did when she found his sorry carcass.

◆━━◆

The officers stepped carefully around the shambles of the hunting post. It was almost impossible not to trip over the circuits and radio equipment, which were showered in blood and bat shit. Detective Hernandez kept a handkerchief to his nose; He'd probably burn these clothes after today.

The CSI, Diaz, came up the ladder, entering dressed in full hazmat suit and a mask. "You really shouldn't be in here without equipment, it's a biohazard."

Hernandez waved his concerns away. "What do you make of this shit-show?"

Diaz shook his head. "Nothing like I've ever seen, Sir." He held up the garbled remains of metal wire he'd carried up the ladder. "This is the broadcast antenna reported stolen from the local station; Apparently he stole it, then brought it out here to boost his signal."

Hernandez nodded. "Makes sense. He couldn't handle losing the election *and* his show, so he was desperate to continue getting his message of hate out there."

Diaz studied the metal remains. "I can't be sure, but I believe that's what backfired on him. The working theory from the techs down at the lab is that the frequency he pirated attracted a swarm of bats, basically causing them to attack his location in full numbers." His eyes darted, examining the countless blood splatters and dark fur around the shack. "We're still examining the evidence, but as near as we can tell the majority of Willard Skye is inside thousands of vampire bats."

Hernandez shuddered. He nudged his neck towards the mangled pet crate in the corner. "What about the little guy we found in there?"

Diaz grinned. "Perfectly healthy, at least physically. It's going to take a lot of therapy, but as near as we can tell none of the bats touched him. Doesn't really make sense."

Hernandez put his hands on his hips, clicking his tongue as he stared at the floor. "Thank Heaven for small miracles." He bit back rising vile in his esophagus, the smell sending a rank taste down his throat. "I think you're right, I'm going to need to come back with the right equipment." He pointed back to the pet crate. "In the meantime, make sure someone contacts the Mayor. She needs to know her son is alright."

Jay Sandlin
About the Author

From a young age, Jay Sandlin wrote short stories and comics to entertain himself and friends. From age 8 onward, theatre was his main storytelling passion and he appeared in over fifty productions from 8-23, including a selection of short plays written from Ray Bradbury stories. Jay met Ray in person at one of these performances and never forgot the interaction.

In 2015, he shifted to writing regularly. In 2018, he won the Mad Cave Studios talent search, leading to publishing his first comic books. *Over the Ropes* was his first comic series, followed by *Hellfighter Quin* all available in trade paperback. More comics are coming in 2021. He's also published a short story collection of his own, *Space Police Files*, which has been described as COPS meets the Twilight Zone.

There's more stories, comics and books to come from Jay. To keep up, visit www.JaySandlin.com and sign up for his newsletter.

Follow him on twitter or Instagram @JaySandlin_. You can also get the latest episodes of his podcast, GeekOPedia on his website or any app hosting podcasts.

https://amzn.to/32Debmm

Thorn in My Side
Chris Hewitt

Mila Yakhontov glided across the command module and deftly spun herself around to view the bank of display panels nestled into the bulkhead. Hooking her feet into the Velcro footholds, she steadied herself and slid on a headset.

"I can see my house from here," crackled mission specialist Karl Turner's voice over the radio.

Mila turned on each of the displays and selected the best views of Karl's progress, reserving the central panel for the live-feed from his helmet camera. The feed showed Karl looking down at a stunning, blue vista of the Earth. "You live in the Pacific Ocean then?"

Karl laughed. "It'll be along in a minute."

"More like forty minutes. How about you get on with some work in the meantime?" said Mila, switching radio channels. "Houston, we're good to go for EVA."

"Roger that, Commander," came the response from Ground Control.

"Party time," said Karl, stepping from the airlock. With well-practiced dexterity, he slid along the side of the International Space Station, his safety tether snaking behind him.

Mila switched one of her displays to show a wide-angle view of the science module's access panel. In the distance, she could see Karl approaching. "Okay, twenty feet. Slow it down."

"It's beautiful out here, Mila. When was the last time you got out of that tin can?" goaded Karl, slowing his progress.

"Oy! Less of the tin can," hissed Mila. They both knew exactly how long she'd been on the ISS: four hundred and seven days. A month short of the record, which would secure her name in the history books. Patting the bulkhead, she smiled. "Don't you listen to him, little bird."

"Tell me you're not stroking it again," joked Karl.

"Nyet, get on with your repair. And be gentle this time."

Mila felt embarrassed, both by her predictability and her growing fondness for the inanimate station. She watched Karl twist into position, securing his tether before unscrewing the bolts that held the science module's access panel in place.

"Okay, first bolt removed. At least something's getting screwed around here."

Mila laughed. He wasn't wrong.

A few seconds later, the radio crackled. "ISS, please be advised we've got a bunch of VIPs from the Capstone

Elementary school here today, and although the kids might have enjoyed that last comment, the headteacher did not. Please confirm."

The radio channel burst into laughter.

"Sorry, Houston, confirm that. We seem to have picked up some erm…radio interference on our end," lied Mila.

"Status check, Karl," said Mila, trying to sound every part the professional.

"One…one bolt to go," replied Karl. Mila could see his helmet feed shaking with laughter. "Give me a minute."

Mila pushed the spherical tears away from her eyes and regained her composure.

"Okay, last bolt removed," Karl managed, pulling the panel free. "A special message to our VIP's today. Stay in school, ki-"

Mila saw Karl's camera jerk left to face the inky blackness of space.

"Did you see that?" Karl asked.

Mila checked her displays. "See what?"

"I don't know. Something shot past."

Mila pulled up the ISS status display, searching for any anomalies. Everything appeared normal. Switching back to Karl's feed she saw him tumble, the tether snapping him hard against the station. "Karl!"

"Fuck, I'm hit," cried Karl. He was breathing hard, moaning, clearly in pain.

Mila watched Karl steady himself, before staring down at his arm. Close to his elbow, a fist-sized object resembling a spiky sea urchin protruded from his suit. Black, and glinting like polished onyx, its countless purple-tipped spines shimmered. Mila gasped as she watched Karl turn his arm to reveal two long, bloody spines protruding from his suit. A stream of red droplets boiled in the vacuum.

"Mila!"

Before she could answer, a large urchin struck Karl in the shoulder, foot-long spines exploding through his chest, its momentum pinning his ragdoll body against the station.

"Karl!" Mila screamed. A spiraling nebula of blood threatened to obscure the view from his camera. There was another explosion of crimson as a third urchin tore into Karl, leaving a long, bloody smear along the length of the science module. Karl and his video feed died.

Mila stared at the black screen in shock, listening to the scraping, skittering sounds of things peppering the station. The lights flickered, and one by one, the remaining video feeds went dark. With a shuddering groan, the station lurched, ripping Mila from her Velcro bindings and throwing her against the bulkhead. Rebounding off the wall, she flew across the cabin, her arms flailing as she scrabbled for a handhold. The station's master alarm rang out as her ears popped. It was Mila's worst nightmare; the station was compromised.

"Houston, come in Houston, we have a problem."

Pushing off of the ceiling, she twisted herself towards the far end of the module. The air was thinning as she reached the round hatch and wrestling it closed, with a clunk and hiss, she stared through the small porthole.

Through the strobing lights, and rapidly forming ice, she saw a crisscross of purple spines shredding the habitat module.

"Houston, come in control."

"We see it, Commander," crackled the radio. "We're working on the problem. Give us a minute."

She took comfort in the reassuring voice, a reminder that she wasn't alone. Mila gave a thumbs up, knowing they'd be watching in Ground Control. Gliding back to the display panels, she pulled up a schematic of the station. Normally green, the complex diagram was now a swirling jigsaw of flashing orange and red. All the while, she could hear and feel the screech of twisting metal, and the terrifying clangs of urchins bombarding the station.

"Okay, Commander. Here's what we're going to do..."

Mila's world exploded as a monstrous purple needle sliced through the station, ripping the command module apart as if it was tin foil. Mila spun in the hard vacuum of space, feeling the instant bite of cold as the air exploded from her lungs. She looked down at the Earth, knowing it would be the last thing she'd see, and as her eyes turned to ice, she tried to find some solace in the glorious view.

But damn, she'd wanted that record.

◄——►

"Ouch," cried Ava as a rose thorn pricked her finger. She shook her hand and licked away the blood. Rubbing the cut with her thumb, she pulled the vibrating pager from her back pocket. "Bloody thing."

In the midday sun, she couldn't read its scratched display. It didn't matter; Whatever it said, her day off was canceled. Throwing the clippers into the basket, she stormed off into the house looking for her phone.

It wasn't any cooler in the house. Nowhere in Alice Springs would be cool in January, but at least in the shade she could read the cryptic message.

"Code sixty-nine. What the hell is code…"

She rolled her eyes, remembering the childlike glee with which Dan had published the alert codes. Sixty-nine had one meaning: They were fucked. The shit was hitting the fan.

In the nine years she'd worked at the ultra-secret Pine Gap facility she'd been paged three times, and one of those was to pick up coffee. That was code twenty-two on Dan's cryptic code system. Ava loved working at the Joint Defense Facility, if only for the looks people would give her when she told them, and after a couple of drinks, she loved to tell everyone. Mention Pine Gap and the locals assumed she was a spy, which was fine by Ava. 'Technician' didn't quite have the same impact. Usually, by the time she'd explained orbital mechanics, she'd be talking to an empty barstool. Best to stick with the Jason Bourne persona. Whatever was happening, it was serious, or at least it had bloody well better be to interrupt her day off.

"Shit!" hissed Ava, hunting around for her phone. Her father used to say she'd have lost her head if it wasn't attached, and he had a point. Another five minutes of wild searching and Ava found the errant phone in the pocket of a pair of jeans, which were buried amongst her neglected washing. Unlocking the display, she stared at twenty-seven missed calls and a dozen text messages from Dan. They were increasingly urgent and blunt suggestions to get in touch, while the last two comprised of one-word, auto-corrected cryptic expletives.

She hit redial on Dan's missed call and sniffed the jeans while the phone rang. Switching to speakerphone, she threw the phone down, quickly changing into the skanky jeans and selecting a matching T-shirt that stank slightly less than the sweat-soaked one she was wearing. The phone dropped the unanswered call.

"Fuck it!" Snatching up the device, she wrestled on her boots, grabbed her rucksack and bolted out the front door. Twenty seconds later she burst back into the house hunting for the pager. "Oh, for God's sake." A buzzing from the kitchen counter put her out of misery, and she leaped at the pager. Code sixty-nine, sixty-nine, double fucked!

Jumping into her rusting Toyota Hilux, she launched the rucksack into the passenger seat and slotted her phone into the crude mount on the dashboard. The engine sputtered as Ava turned the key, and she closed her eyes and prayed. "Not now. Please!"

In a cloud of black smoke, gears grinding, the truck burst into life as did the radio. "Next up is a classic eighties track, Thorn in My Side, by the Eurythmics. Enjoy."

"You are taking the piss," moaned Ava. Even the universe mocked her misfortune. She turned the radio down with her throbbing finger. Slipping the truck into reverse, she backed out of the driveway, and with tires squealing, gunned the old Toyota down the road.

❖

"Pick up, pick up!" Ava screamed as she reached the highway and headed south. Pine Gap was a thirty-minute commute at the best of times, but she aimed to be there in twenty-five. The phone rang off again, and she punched the roof. Nursing her aching fist, Ava could just hear the words "breaking news" from the muted radio and turned up the volume. The DJ was announcing, "Terrible news, people. We have reports coming in that the International Space Station has suffered a catastrophic failure. Early indications suggest the crew may be dead."

Ava narrowly avoided a slowing car and slamming on the brakes, veered to the side of the road. The truck skidded to a stop in a cloud of red dust, its engine stalling, as the radio cut out. Cursing her luck, and still reeling from the news, Ava grabbed her phone and jumped out of the truck. She opened the bonnet to a cloud of steam and redialed Dan.

"Ava, finally. Didn't you get my messages?"

"Didn't you get my calls? Dan, is it true? Is the ISS gone?"

"It's not just the ISS, it's everything."

"What?"

"The station, the satellites, everything in Low Earth Orbit."

"You're not making any sense," said Ava. Staring off into the distance, she saw a flash of fire in the sky. Then another and another, until the heavens were full of fiery meteors streaking across the firmament. "Dan?"

No signal flashed on the phone display.

Ava stared up at the chaos, trying to make sense of what she was seeing. What could take down every satellite and the space station? She needed to get to Pine Gap. Turning her attention to the stalled truck, it didn't take her long to find the problem. The lead to the battery had detached, and not for the first time. The rusted bracket did a poor job of holding the battery, which was one of a dozen reasons she should have scrapped the truck ages ago, but she was finding it hard to let go of her father's pride and joy. When she was a kid, they'd work on the truck together every weekend, and it had been a big part of why she'd pursued the career she had.

Jumping back into the cab, she turned over the engine, and the old truck burst into life. She went to call Dan, but her phone still reported no signal. Whatever was happening, it wasn't just the satellites.

Tearing down the road, she'd almost convinced herself it was a solar flare, except for the satellites. The damn satellites. A flare might knock them out, but something else had pushed them into the atmosphere. "All of them?" she hissed under her breath.

Pulling up at the entrance to the Pine Gap facility, Ava could already see the base was on lockdown. Several guards in full combat gear pointed M16's squarely at her head, as one of the guards walked over and signaled for her to roll down her window. Rummaging through her rucksack she found her ID, holding it out as non-threateningly as she could. The guard took her ID and scanned it. "Doctor Ava Lee."

Ava nodded.

"Thought that was you," smiled the guard. He tilted back his helmet so she could see his face. "You look… different…"

With a dawning recognition, Ava tried to hide the stain on her T-shirt. "Hey!"

The young marine had been far less threatening in the bar last month, from what little she could remember. "Mike, what's going on?"

There was a snigger amongst the other guards, and Mike handed her back her ID. "No idea. We've got a Code Red to lock down the place. Lucky for you, you're on the list."

He nodded to his squad, and Ava breathed a sigh of relief as they lowered their rifles. Mike waved his hand. The barrier rose, and he banged on the truck for her to go. "Best you get up there. Whatever is going down, it's all happening up there."

"Thanks, Mike."

"It's Nick," said the embarrassed marine, eliciting a round of laughter from his squad.

"Shit, sorry Nick," Ava blushed and drove through the checkpoint, trying not to make eye contact. When she looked in the rear-view mirror, she could see the barrier lowering and Nick getting a ribbing from his mates.

◆───◦───◆

Upon entering the command complex Ava faced another threatening security check. Another scan of her ID by another disturbingly familiar guard and she was sure of two things: The shit was definitely hitting the fan and going ahead she'd need to look beyond the bars of Alice Springs for signs of life.

Through the last checkpoint she stepped into the packed command-and-control center. She'd never seen it so busy. The C&C usually ran three shifts, but not today. Everyone was here, including the top brass and more spooks than a funfair ghost train. Buried in the heart of the Australian outback Pine Gap was a US-led operation, and the C&C operated a clear pecking order. The military ran the show, easily identifiable by their snazzy matching uniforms. Then there were the spooks, a.k.a. the spies. The boys from Langley wore business suits and didn't answer questions, ever. Last there were the technicians, like herself and Dan. Contractors mostly, or those that couldn't be trusted with guns and secrets.

Dan was sitting at Ava's workstation, looking worried. She tapped him on the shoulder. "What's going on?"

"You took your time!" screamed Dan, garnering several stares.

"Traffic was a bitch. You want to fill me in?"

"We've lost almost everything in orbit."

"I saw. Is there anything left up there?"

"I don't know, it's a mess. We've lost contact with most of the relay stations. That's why you're here," said Dan, nervously nodding towards General Hackett. The four-star General had a fearsome reputation; He even scared the spooks. He ran a tight ship at Pine Gap, and was rarely, if ever, to be found in the C&C.

"Okay," said Ava, tying back her hair and waving to Dan to move. "Scoot!"

Ava jumped into the rapidly-vacated seat and started typing. She knew the satellite relay and control systems like a spider knows its web, as she'd been responsible for spinning many of its threads. What she found terrified her: Something had punched a hole right through the middle of her precious web. "Fuck!"

"Is that your technical opinion, Miss?" said General Hackett, appearing behind her. The old man was light on his feet.

Ava stared up at the General's unblinking, stern gaze. "Technician Lee, Sir!"

"Well, Ms. Lee?"

"We're under attack, Sir."

"Thank you for that analysis, but I knew that thirty minutes ago when I stepped into this radio shack."

The general turned and glared at Dan. "The best we've got, eh?"

"It's not a military attack," Ava said, resuming her typing.

The general turned back. "I'm sorry?"

"It's not a military attack," said Ava, pulling up a diagram on one of the large central screens. It showed the Earth, and around it hundreds of flashing dots falling into the blue disc. "Do you see?"

"Shit, she's right," said Dan, quickly realizing he'd used his outside voice.

"One of you'd better start making some sense," said the General.

"The satellites are falling to Earth,"

"Even I know what goes up-" said the General.

"No!"

"Newton got it wrong, Ms. Lee?"

"No, Newton was right. These satellites will all fall back to earth, eventually! Months, years from now. But that's not what's happening."

The General raised an eyebrow. He didn't look like a man used to being lectured, but Ava was on a roll now and she couldn't help herself.

"Newton's first law. An object in motion will stay in motion unless-"

"Acted upon by an external force," completed Dan, covering his mouth. It seemed he couldn't help himself either.

Ava nodded. "Exactly!"

"Someone get me a gun!" said the General, only half joking.

"General, if someone disabled the satellites using say a laser, missile or EMP they would continue in their orbits. They wouldn't fall, not that quickly. Something is pushing the satellites into the atmosphere."

"What?"

"I don't know, I've just gotten here. I'm going to need ten minutes."

An uncomfortable silence descended over the C&C, only broken by the General laughing. "Well, Ms. Lee, I see the apple hasn't fallen far from the tree."

Ava looked at him quizzically.

"I knew your father. He liked to run his mouth as well. Luckily what came out of his was usually useful, unless he'd been on the sauce. How about I give you five minutes, Ms. Lee? Cause you know I'm a busy man, what with the sky falling in." Walking away, he bellowed. "What've I got to do to get a coffee around here?"

"Christ, Ava," said Dan. "Rein it in, he's a four-star General."

Ava didn't hear him. Her fingers were dancing across the keyboard as she reached out into what remained of the tattered web of military networks and satellites. It was a mess, and she was having to jump from server to server, satellite to satellite to piece together what was happening. Dan watched in awe. No one knew the systems like Ava. Her father had been instrumental in the design of many of the critical systems, and for Ava they'd been her playground. That was before the military had taken over and everything became hush, hush, top secret. Even now many of her father's original threads still held firm, and bouncing from a relay station in Brazil she accessed a polar satellite. One of a pair. This one monitored the southern ice cap. It didn't have a name; It didn't even officially exist. It was a watcher in the night, waiting for a Cold War attack that thankfully never came. Its optical systems might have been forty years old, Cold War budgets being what they were, but it could still put most modern commercial satellites to shame. Ava stopped typing and looked up.

"What?" asked Dan.

Ava was weighing up her choices. With the damage she'd seen across the global systems it was clear something apocalyptic was happening, and they were in the blind. Desperate times called for desperate measures, career-ending measures. "Screw it!"

"Ava!" said Dan. Things never went well when she used that tone.

◆━━◦━━◆

Ava issued a sequence of commands to the satellite. Thirty-six thousand kilometers above the South Pole the ancient hardware tilted from its view of the ice cap towards the equator, and using the last of its propellant raised itself into a higher orbit. It would be the death throes of the billion-dollar satellite, but before its demise Ava hoped it might provide some insight into the unfolding catastrophe.

She pulled up the satellite's live feed onto the C&C's large, central display.

"Now that's more like it," shouted the General. Pointing a mug of coffee towards the screen. "What am I looking at?"

"It's one of our southern satellites, Sir," said Ava.

"You didn't," hissed Dan.

"What's up with the picture?" asked the General. Australia was sliding into view, but the top of the image seemed to have a black band of static.

Ava tilted her head and frowned. It could be anything, since just moving the archaic lump of iron could have damaged it. Ava sent another set of commands, and the camera zoomed into the shimmering, black static. Slowly the image resolved from a band of black into its constituent parts, revealing countless spiked structures.

"What happened to the satellite view? What's this National Geographic shit?" barked the General.

Ava rose from her seat slowly without taking her eyes from the screen.

"Ms. Lee," hollered the General. "What happened to my-"

The General stopped mid-sentence as the coastline of the Northern Territories loomed into view through the sea of black.

Ava enabled the real-time image processing filters, and the central display was awash with statistics measuring and cataloguing everything they saw. She struggled to process all of the data, but the conclusion was clear. "If you ever wondered what first contact would look like, this is it and they don't look friendly."

There was a flurry of activity around the general. Military and intelligence officers went into a huddle trying to determine what the playbook was for an alien invasion.

"Look at the size of some of these," said Dan.

The statement snapped Ava from her thoughts, and she scanned the geometry metrics. "Twelve kilometers!"

"I'm sorry Ms. Lee, what was that?" asked the General, staring past the throng that surrounded him.

"Some of them are the size of a city."

"We're going down like the dinosaurs," said Dan, abandoning all efforts to use his inside voice. "Something that large is an extinction-level event. Game over, man!"

Ava shook her head and double checked the numbers, desperately trying to come up with another conclusion. There was no way of escaping the fact that anything that large must have enormous mass. The impact of one would probably do the job; A dozen would seal the deal. As the urchins glowed orange, she set to calculating the first impact points. "Darwin will get hit first. I'll try to find some live feeds."

Reaching out across military and public networks she quickly located a dozen live feeds, ranging from civil and military security cameras to beach cams giving surfers a heads-up of wave conditions. All revealed a beautiful day in Darwin. The locals were going about their business, blissfully unaware of what was about to hit them.

"Any minute now," said Ava. At least it would be

quick, she thought. The last thing she expected to see was the video feeds growing dark, as if a monstrous hand had stretched across the heavens. A second later the first small urchins struck the water on the beach camera. Towards the horizon larger urchins exploded into the sea, and she could see the surfers on the beach watching the spectacle. "Run!" she pleaded, even though she knew there'd be nowhere they could hide. The water boiled now, countless impacts frothing the sea to foam, and here and there larger urchins splashed down, sending immense columns of water into the sky. The surfers finally saw the danger and ran, but it was too late.

Ava watched in horror as the first surfer fell, a mist of blood spraying into the air from the impact. Another was eviscerated by an urchin not much larger than the volley-ball they'd held. The beach turned into a massacre under the alien hail, and no one made it off of the blood-soaked sands. A moment later the beach feed died, the C&C going deathly silent except for sobbing.

Ava couldn't understand what she'd seen. "There's something wrong."

"Very wrong, did you see that slaughter!?" exclaimed Dan.

Ava shook her head. "That's just it, we shouldn't have seen it. There should've been an explosion?"

Ava retrieved the footage from the beach and selecting the last frame. "Look at the ocean."

Dan's jaw dropped. "They're floating!"

In the background, beyond the carnage of the beach,

it was possible to make out thousands of urchins afloat in the water. There was little time to absorb what they were seeing as one of the security cameras caught the first thorny invaders crashing onto the Darwin dock.

What started with one or two rapidly turned into a torrential downpour of horrors. Far from being destroyed on impact, the things piled on top of each other. Even a car-sized urchin failed to make a crater, its spines not penetrating the concrete. The security camera cut out a few seconds later, and Ava looked eagerly to the next display. The screen showed a street bustling with weekend shoppers, only a kilometer from the waterfront.

Ava's blood turned to ice. Among the shoppers was a stroller being pushed along, three birthday balloons trailing in its wake. Ava felt sick to her stomach. She had to warn them, but how? Then it came to her: there had to be a civil alarm siren. Were they even online? A flurry of typing and she had her answer. She wasn't sure which siren to activate, so she activated them all right across the country. On the screen she could see people stopping and looking up. She'd done it; Surely, they'd see the danger. The crowd on the street were joined by people flooding out of the shops and cafes, all eager to know what all the commotion was about.

"Noooo, get inside," screamed Ava.

"What have you done?" asked Dan.

There was a commotion at the far end of the street, and a visible ripple of fear snaked up the concourse. When the shopper started to run Ava had to turn away. She couldn't watch. The gasps and cries in the C&C, and the revulsion on Dan's face, left little to her imagination. As Dan steadied himself against a desk Ava hesitantly looked back at the screen. The packed street was now a gory mess of alien spines and human mincemeat, and in the bloody detritus three familiar balloons floated into the air. Ava's world twisted. She tried to stand, tried to run, but fell to the floor. An unstoppable wave of nausea washing over her, as she retched into the wastepaper bin. Her world spun, then blacked out.

◆━━◦━━◆

The next thing Ava knew was General Hackett yanking her arm and pulling her to her feet. "Steady, soldier."

With Dan's help the General eased her back into her seat.

"I'm going to need you to keep it together," said the General.

"General!" a spook shouted, pointing to one of the video feeds. The remaining feeds showed a blur of urchins raining down all over Darwin. The aid pointed at a grainy home security feed showing what appeared to be a cul-de-sac in the suburbs. A handful of smaller horrors were already bouncing off the street, but what was of more interest was the monstrous urchin crashing to Earth in the background. It was impossible to gauge its size until it slowly rolled over, revealing a dozen people skewered like ants on its purple-tipped needles.

With a groan Ava grabbed the wastepaper bin.

"It's moving!" gasped the General. The humongous urchin was slowly rolling in the direction of the cul-de-sac leaving a wide trail of carnage in its wake.

"I…I think it might be being blown? Look at the trees," cried Dan. The trees shook in the increasingly strong coastal winds. "They must have almost no mass."

The whole C&C watched in stunned silence as the ball of purple-tipped thorns rolled into the cul-de-sac. The last frame before the camera's destruction captured a close-up of a skewered, but still living victim, hitting the camera. Another sickening sight which had Ava plumbing new depths of despair, as she continued to fill the bin.

As the last of the video feeds from Darwin failed the general handed Ava a bottle of water. "Just when you think you've seen everything, eh?"

Ava tried to wipe away the remains of her breakfast from her chin. "I killed them."

The General nodded. "Probably."

Ava shot the General an incredulous look. "Thanks!"

"You made a call. It didn't pan out, but a lot more people are going to die before this is over. Best to save the waterworks for later and see if you can balance the scales."

"Fuck you…Sir!"

The General smiled. "That's the spirit."

"Sir!" said a military officer, running up to the General. Leaning in close he whispered, and by the General's reaction it wasn't good news. For a moment the General stared up at the screens, slowly shaking his head.

"Change of plans, people. We're bugging out!"

"I can't leave," implored Ava. "I've got work to do. The satellite-"

The General nodded to a new image on the main display and Ava could make out a handful of inky shadows bouncing off of an all-too-familiar gatehouse.

"Ten minutes, people. Move it! We're in the firing line," barked the General as he headed off with his entourage.

Ava wiped her face and slid the fetid trash bin under the desk before reviewing the latest satellite imagery. The black band was still there, but on closer inspection it was apparent it didn't account for all of the aliens.

Aliens!

The word gave her pause, though the historic moment had almost passed her by. This was it; First contact, validation for every tin foil cap wearing nut. Zooming the satellite feed in on what remained of Darwin, she could see a band of creeping darkness heading south.

◆——◆

Ava threw her rucksack over her shoulder and followed Dan past the empty security desk and out into the bright, midday sun. The heat radiated off of the tarmac in the busy parking lot where a dozen military vehicles were being loaded up with people and equipment. Several people were already speeding out of the gates in their cars.

There was a swoosh, followed by a scream, and Ava

saw one of the marines hit the floor dead, spines protruding from the top of their crushed helmet. A few seconds later, with a sound like an unfolding switchblade, the marine's head exploded as the urchin spasmed, extending its needle-like spines out.

"Run!" Dan screamed, pushing Ava towards a nearby Humvee. Ava couldn't take her eyes from the twitching corpse with a ball of spikes for a head. The marine's brain and face impaled on the shimmering barbs.

The armored doors slammed closed as they reached the Humvee, and the driver rudely gestured to the next vehicle as he pulled away. It was utter chaos in the parking lot. Most had given up waiting for the military and were running for their own cars. Ava was pulling Dan towards her truck when a screech of tortured metal proceeded an explosive blast which threw everyone to the ground. Ava felt her scratched face and turned to look at the Humvee. An urchin, twenty feet across, sat balanced precariously on the burning wreckage. Several marines approached the black structure, unloading all the ammo they could into the body of the intruder. The bullets sparked across the urchin's surface with no effect.

Watching the marines near their target the hairs on Ava's neck bristled as some part of her realized the danger and scrabbling to her feet she tried to pull Dan away. "Run!"

She'd gotten a few yards before she heard a noise like a thousand shears being closed at once, and the urchin extended its appendages like a diabolical blowfish. The marines didn't stand a chance. Purple-tipped spears tore through them, leaving their lifeless, limp bodies hanging. The urchin began to retract its spines, dragging several corpses towards it.

Ava's instincts kicked in. Adrenaline kept her moving now as her mind reeled at the unfolding horror. She reached out to Dan, but he wasn't there. Twisting around she saw fear in his eyes, and a barb buried in his leg. His fingers clawed at the ground as the urchin continued to retract its weapons, and no matter how hard Ava tugged Dan's hands she couldn't stop the diabolical progress towards the alien monstrosity. He begged her for help, but there was nothing she could do. The convoy moved out all around her, cars and trucks racing to get away from the slaughter. There was no one left to help.

Ava was in danger of being impaled herself as she fought to save Dan, and as more spines slid into his legs he screamed. It was hopeless. "I'm sorry Dan, I can't…"

Ava stared into his desperate eyes as he slipped from her grasp and his screams were replaced by a muted gurgling. His body spasmodically jerked as the relentless needles sliced through his torso and sprouted from his face. The sight of Dan staring cross-eyed at the spine emerging from his mouth, still alive - still conscious - was the final straw.

Ava was up and running. Every instinct demanded flight. Slamming into her truck she fumbled for her keys, trying to hold them still long enough to unlock the truck. Using both hands she managed to get the key in the lock and jumped in, starting the engine.

The convoy was gone; She could make out its dust in the distance on the long access road. They'd left her behind, just like she'd left Dan behind. The compound was a graveyard now. At its center was the large, alien urchin, slick with blood, wearing its trophies. An almighty crash startled Ava and she stared up at the impossibly sharp tips of several needles that had narrowly missed her head. She screamed and jammed the accelerator, terrified that the spines would reach out for her as they had the marines.

Scrunched down, her face pressed against the driver's window, she tried to steer the truck towards the exit, but she misjudged one of the bollards at the guard gate. The truck crunched into the concrete post throwing Ava against the steering wheel and launching the abomination on the roof onto the tarmac. Dazed, Ava touched the fresh cut above her eye. "Ow!"

A loud thud and Ava screamed before spotting the familiar face, imploring her to open the door.

"Mike!" she cried, throwing open the door. "I'm so glad- " she looked down at his arm and saw he was hurt. He looked pale. "Are you okay, Mike?"

Running around to the passenger's side he jumped in. "Drive!"

Ava tried the engine, and to her amazement it spluttered into life on the first attempt. Putting the truck into reverse she left a rusted, chrome bumper wrapped around the bollard as she set off in pursuit of the convoy. All around them small urchins crashed into the scrub, throwing up plumes of dust.

"Do you know where the convoy went, Mike?" asked Ava.

"For fuck's sake, it's Nick! My name is Nick!"

Ava swallowed hard. She couldn't believe she had any more room for emotion, but on top of the terror, guilt and grief she could add embarrassment. "Sorry. Sorry Nick, I'm having a bad day."

Nick laughed, wincing at the pain in his arm. "Yeah, you and me both."

Ava couldn't help but laugh. In the midst of the apocalypse, with all she'd seen and done, she could still find ways to fuck up the little things.

"The last I heard the convoy was going south; I'd guess down to Adelaide," said Nick.

"Can you drive?"

"Sure, it's a scratch."

Ava slammed the brakes on, and they swapped sides. As Nick accelerated off after the convoy Ava fished out her laptop and a few other items she'd grabbed for the road trip. Key among them was a military-grade radio transmitter and receiver. It took her a few minutes to wire everything together and establish a connection.

"I'm not sure updating your Facebook page is a priority," joked Nick, steering out the way of a large urchin sitting in the road. "You got Google Maps on that thing?"

Ava was busy hopping around the military networks trying to find a route to the satellite. The Brazilian relay station was gone, White Sands died as she was using it, which left her trying to repurpose a commercial satellite relay in Greenland. Connection re-established, she twisted her laptop around so Nick could see it and pulled up the real-time view of them driving along the road, red dust visible in their wake. "Who needs Google Maps when I've got my own billion-dollar military satellite?"

"Whoa! Cool." said Nick, veering the truck across the road and watching it on the satellite view.

Ava turned the laptop back and started searching for the convoy. "Found them! You're right, they're heading south down Stuart Highway, about six miles ahead."

"Good," said Nick, rubbing his arm.

"You sure you're okay? I can take a look."

"I'll be okay," Nick assured her.

Ava returned to her laptop and the satellite imagery. Zooming in on Darwin the screen went blank. No, not blank, black. She scrolled the display south, and only the latitude numbers ticking over gave any indication of the distance. The sea of urchins extended hundreds of miles beyond Darwin. When she found its edge, she gasped.

"What?" Asked Nick.

"There's a wave of these things being blown towards us, and not just the small ones we've seen."

"Small ones!? How big do they get?"

"Big, think Godzilla sized."

"Bullshit! You need your eyes tested."

"I've got the best eyes on the planet," said Ava, pointing a finger upwards. "There are millions of these bastards heading our way, and you won't be able to drive around them."

As if to prove a point Nick almost lost control of the truck as he swerved around an urchin rolling across the road.

"Can we outrun them?"

Ava was trying to do the math. "I don't know. I don't understand how they're moving south so fast; The wind would have to be hundreds of miles an hour. Have you seen any of them move? On their own, I mean?"

"Only that shrug thing they do," said Nick, shivering.

"What else do we know? They're incredibly light."

"Bulletproof and razor sharp," added Nick, rubbing his arm.

"Heat-resistant. Otherwise they'd have burned up on entry."

"They're cold to the touch too."

"Cold?"

"Yeah," said Nick, pulling his sleeve back to reveal a long, red gash along his forearm. "That isn't a burn, that's frostbite. It brushed me for maybe a second."

"That's it!" said Ava, tapping away. Sure enough, the satellite's thermal camera revealed the band wasn't just black, it was cold, freezing cold. "Cold enough to affect the weather. They're creating the wind just by sheer numbers. Warm air is rushing in, and they're riding the storm front."

"Christ! It really is an alien invasion."

"Guess so."

"I thought it was meant to be little green men. Or

Greys? I'd take killer tripods at this point, but bloody space urchins? Are they even alive?"

Ava hadn't considered the question. What were they? Animal, vegetable, mineral...or something else altogether? Ava shook her head. Did it matter when they rolled over you? She put the image out of her mind. "Let's catch up with the convoy. Safety in numbers, and all that."

⊷⸺⸺⸲

They'd been on the highway for twenty minutes chasing the convoy, and Nick had expertly steered the truck around the urchins that blew across the road like deadly tumbleweeds.

"Shouldn't we be able to see them by now?" asked Nick.

Ava could see the convoy on the satellite view, but they were still two miles ahead of them. Squinting at the horizon she couldn't see them through the heat haze radiating from the scorching tarmac. The latest satellite image showed the dark wave picking up speed, and a sense of dread entered Ava's calculations. She doubted they'd catch the convoy, let alone outrun the shadowy tsunami.

Ava stared out the window despondently as they passed a wrecked car, a large urchin impaled on the hood. She went to turn away when her gaze met that of a young girl sitting on the back seat of the car. She could see the tracks of tears on her terrified face.

"Pull over!"

"What!?"

"Pull over!"

"You're joking! We-"

Ava grabbed the wheel and forced Nick to slam the brakes on. Jumping from the truck she ran up the road, and she didn't need to see the driver's seat to know the fate of anyone in the front.

Nearing the vehicle, she slowed, inching towards the rear of the car and slowly, carefully, she opened the passenger door. A snarling flurry of teeth sent her scrambling as a Border Collie leaped at her, barking, its tail wagging furiously.

"Hey, boy!" Ava cried.

"Down, Blue," said the girl climbing from the car. The dog sat down obediently, tail whipping back and forth. "Can you help my mum? She's stuck." pleaded the girl, looking back towards the front passenger seat.

Ava stared back down the road, where she could see Nick disappearing into the heat haze with her truck.

Bastard!

"Let me take a look. Why don't you and Blue stand over there, off of the road?"

Ava could see and hear small urchins crashing into the scrubland, so she needed to be quick. Leaning through the door she saw a large, spine sticking through the back of the driver's seat. Blood had pooled under it, and the girl had been lucky. A few more inches... It didn't bear thinking about. Ava couldn't hear anything from the front passenger seat, and part of her hoped the girl's mother was dead. A bloody hand hitting the roof filled her with guilt and dread.

"Hello? Are you okay?" asked Ava, realizing how stupid her question sounded. "Can I help?"

"Suzy! Where's my Suzy?" croaked a voice.

"She's safe. She's over there," Ava said, pointing to the girl playing with her dog.

"Can you…" the woman spluttered. "Can you take care of her?"

"Hey! You can take her of yourself. Let's get you out of here," said Ava, leaning forward. Cheek-to-cheek with the woman Ava reached down to her seatbelt and froze. Three blood-slick spines ensured the woman wouldn't be going anywhere. It was a miracle she was alive.

Ava stared out at the window at Suzy and flinched as another urchin impacted yards from her. Blue barked at the intruder but was wise enough to keep his distance. There was a screech of tires, and Ava was surprised to see her truck and Nick.

"Get in! We're running out of time," hollered Nick.

"Please!" the woman begged, straining to look Ava in the eye. Ava knew she couldn't save the woman, just as she'd known she couldn't save Dan. She wasn't even sure she could save herself let alone Suzy. "I'll take care of her. I promise."

The woman smiled, and a rivulet of blood trickled from the corner of her mouth as she slumped in her seat. Exiting the car, Ava shouted over to the girl. "Suzy, we have to go."

"My Mum?"

Ava didn't know what to say. She had no words, so she just shook her head.

Suzy understood, and stared at her feet as Blue nestled against her leg.

"I'm sorry Suzy, but we can't stay here, it's dangerous," said Ava, sprinting over and putting an arm around the shellshocked girl. Ava led her to the truck and helped her in, and without saying a word she curled up next to Nick. Ava banged on the back of the truck and Blue jumped in, tail still wagging, ready for his next adventure.

Five minutes later they were back chasing the convoy.

"Don't ever do that again," said Nick, shaking his head. "Next time I won't be coming back."

"There isn't going to be a next time," said Ava, staring at her laptop. The convoy was miles ahead. They were never going to catch up, but that was the least of their problems. The real problem was chasing them, and it was catching up.

Ava looked back at Blue sitting on the bed of the speeding truck, his tongue lapping in the breeze as he seemed to enjoy life. In the distance Ava thought she could see the first signs of the impending darkness, but she put the thought out of her head. They had to make it.

She'd promised.

⊷——◦——⊶

The sunset was as spectacular as any Ava could recall, and

she watched it knowing it was likely to be her last. She'd closed her laptop when she saw it was hopeless. Staring back through the window even Blue looked worried, panting hard as his eyes scanned the approaching storm. Purple flashes of lightning silhouetted unearthly shapes, titanic monsters that couldn't be outrun.

Suzy hadn't moved, she just stared straight ahead unblinkingly. Ava caught Nick's eye, and biting her lip shook her head. He understood, nodding slowly. His eyes had hardly left the rear-view mirror in the last few miles, and he could see what was coming.

"We need to find somewhere safe." said Nick.

Safe? What would be safe from a rolling city of thorns? "We're in the middle of nowhere. I don't think there's anywhere safe."

"I know somewhere," whispered Suzy.

The poor girl was clearly still in shock, and Ava pulled her close. "You do?"

"Just up here on the right," said Suzy, pointing the way.

Ava looked along the road, but there were no signs of any exit. Opening her laptop, it took a moment for the connection to establish, with Pine Gap no longer being a routing option. Ava pulled up the map and searched the highway for exits, but there was nothing except a dirt track.

A dirt track to where?

"Suzy, what were you doing out here before the accident?"

"My Pa was taking opals to market."

"Opal stones?"

"Yes, from our mine."

"Mine?!" said Ava.

Suzy nodded, and Nick glanced at Ava. Maybe there was a chance, if the mine was deep enough and they could get there in time.

"It's a better option than staying on the road," said Ava.

"Honey, do you know how to get there?"

The girl nodded.

⊶──⊷

The dirt track would have been treacherous in daylight. In the dark, at high speeds, it was a twisting, rocky roller-coaster that threatened to destroy the truck at every turn. The wind was howling now, buffeting the vehicle, and urchins were shooting past like leaves in a hurricane.

"This is madness," cried Nick.

"How far?" Ava asked Suzy.

"Just up ahead."

"You've been saying that for ten minutes," cried Nick.

"Hey!" berated Ava.

"We're out of time."

A jarring crash lifted the truck off its axles and onto its side. It slid along the dirt road, coming to rest upside-down in a ditch. Ava found herself against the truck's ceiling, with Suzy laid awkwardly across her. Nick was hanging by his seat belt, and with a groan he unfastened it, falling on top of Ava and Suzy.

"Ow!" screamed Suzy.

"Everyone okay?" said Ava.

Suzy scrambled towards the rear window. "Where's Blue?"

Ava couldn't see how the dog could have survived; he wasn't her priority. She needed to get out from under this crazy game of Twister and find the mine. Nick kicked open the door and climbed out, followed by Suzy. Ava found her smashed laptop, noting that the radio transmitter still worked, and it still had power. She flipped a switch, and a pulsing red light illuminated the cab as she headed out into the raging storm.

Purple lightning flashes gave terrible glimpses of the surrounding maelstrom. That's when she saw it, saw what had clipped the truck: A skyscraper of darkness rolled south, and Ava shuddered at both the bodies stuck to its many spines and the realization of how close they'd come to disaster.

"Honey, where's the mine?"

"Just up ahead."

"She's going to get us killed," yelled Nick.

"No, she's going to get us to the mine," she hollered back, "Come on Suzy!"

Suzy led the way along the ditch, and Ava held her hand tight. Overhead urchins shot past like bullets, forcing them to keep low. Approaching the end of the ditch Suzy pointed to a dark entrance in the hill's side beyond. "There!"

Nick and Ava looked at each other. It was so close, but it might as well have been a mile away. It was a suicidal game of Frogger with countless urchins rushing past like speeding traffic, and the chances of making it across the exposed ground were slim.

With a howl Blue came sprinting down the ditch, shooting straight past them and barking madly as he went.

"Blue!" screamed Suzy, yanking free of Ava's grip and rushing off after the suicidal mutt.

"Wait!" bellowed Ava and took off in pursuit.

Ava stumbled on the uneven ground, and when she wasn't falling over, she was having to duck and dive around the larger urchins that rolled past. Out ahead Blue was having the time of his life, barking incessantly.

Ava saw Suzy trip, and feared the worst. Catching up with her ward, Ava found she'd twisted her ankle. "Put your arms around my neck and hold on!" screamed Ava over the howling wind.

Suzy threw her arms around Ava's neck and climbed onto her back. With Suzy secured she set off in the direction of Blue's frenzied barking. She'd got a dozen yards before she stumbled, and Suzy when flying. Face down in the dirt Ava watched Suzy clamber back to her feet and then in in terrible slow motion saw an urchin bearing down on her. She screamed at Suzy to duck as she desperately tried to get to her.

With death inches from the child's head, Nick launched himself into the path of the urchin and they hit the ground hard. Ava rushed over and helped Suzy crawl out from under Nick's motionless body. Clutching Suzy close Ava looked down at the fist-sized urchin buried between Nick's shoulder blades. "Nick!"

Nick turned his dirt-covered face to look at her, and with trembling lips grinned. "There you go. I knew you'd remember my name."

Ava chuckled as Nick's eyes rolled back into his head. "Nick!" She nudged him again, but this time he didn't move. "Nick!" Ava's heart sank.

With a cough Nick's eyes blinked open, and he looked up at her. "Fuck's sake, don't wear it out!"

"You bastard!" cried Ava.

A sickening scissor-like noise tore through the night as a warm, red mist exploded in Ada's face. Wiping her eyes, she looked down at what remained of Nick. The sounds of chaos fading to silence as Ava's world slowed, and she stared at her blood-soaked hands. All about them purple chain-lightning leapt and danced between black monoliths. A wall of skewered bodies reached up into the heavens as far as she could see, and she imagined that each one screamed out to her in their pain and anguish. Part of her longed to join them, if only to end her suffering. Maybe she could find peace if she rose to Heaven on one of those diabolical spines. Defeated, Ava stared at into the unnatural storm and waited for the end.

Suzy's small hand slipped into Ava's palm, and Ava looked into the face of an angel. For a moment she wasn't sure if she was alive or dead. Was this it? Would there really be a dog barking? Ava shook her head, regaining her senses. She was alive. Suzy was alive, and somewhere in the darkness Blue was alive resolute in his incessant, excited yapping. Gritting her teeth, and snatching up Suzy, Ava sprinted with every ounce of strength she had left. Reaching the mine entrance, the girl in her arms, she ran into the impenetrable gloom of the tunnel, stumbling as she dragged her way along the walls. She'd rather face the perils of the mine than the horrors that lay outside. Suzy's breath was warm in her ear, and somewhere ahead Blue kept up his noisy vigil.

Ava could see nothing. She had no idea how far they'd run into the mine, or whether it was far enough. A low, base rumble echoed down the tunnel as the ground shook. It seemed as if the urchins were chasing them into the mine. A gust of putrid wind blasted through the tunnel, knocking them to the floor and for a moment Ava thought they'd suffocate in its toxic, rotting stench. The thunder reached a crescendo, and Ava wrapped herself around Suzy in the darkness and hugged her tight.

<<——o——>>

Ava had held Suzy close throughout the long night. When the storm had passed, and the mine was silent, Suzy had slept, and Ava had drifted in and out of nightmares, her mind unable to process the horrors she'd seen. Ava awoke to the sound of Blue barking and staring down the tunnel saw a sliver of light. Carefully picking up Suzy, trying not to wake her, Ava stiffly carried the girl out into the first light of a new dawn. A fresh breeze blew across Ava's face as she scanned the devastation. It was as if a tornado had blown through a city, but there'd never been a city here in the outback. Smashed fishing boats offered a clue to the debris' distant origins.

After the nightmare of the previous day the thing that struck Ava, was the lack of gore. There was not one body, not even Nick's. Horizon to horizon the trappings of humanity littered the landscape, but not a single corpse. It seemed as if humanity had been harvested, plucked from the earth and Ava wondered if there could be other survivors? As if to answer her doubts, the eerie silence of the wasteland was broken by a distant, rhythmic thumping that grew louder with each passing minute.

Ava held Suzy tighter and braced herself for the worst.

When she saw the helicopter swoop in low, she fell to her knees, jolting Suzy from her slumber. "Shh, it's okay. We're safe. It's going to be okay."

They watched the chopper bank in low and land in a whirlwind of dust. Half-blinded Ava climbed to her feet and grabbing Blue by his collar, squinted at the figure running towards them.

"Ah, Ms. Lee. Glad to see you're still with us," yelled General Hackett, over the helicopters din. "We got your distress signal. Clever, very clever."

With a big hand he ruffled Suzy's hair and patted Blue before turning back to stare at Ava's dirty tear-streaked face. "If you're quite finished with your little road trip. You've still got work to do."

Chris Hewitt
About the Author

Chris lives in the beautiful garden of England and in the odd moments that he's not walking the dog, he pursues his passion for writing fiction. Chris' background is in software development, which means he's well-versed in writing horror, fantasy and science-fiction. Keep an eye out for several short stories being published throughout 2020.

Storm Clouds
Sarah Jane Justice

The thunder from the incoming storm howled like the voice of an angry god. When Lydia heard that sound she knew it was coming.

Her eyes snapped open from sleep, replaced by a rush of hurried breath. With shaking hands she pulled herself up, struggling to fight against the force of her own panic. She knew that taking a moment to slow her breathing stole valuable seconds away from any attempt at escape, but without it she was sure to fall with the rest of them.

"Come on, Cider," she urged the dog whimpering at her feet, "We have to run."

On the horizon the clouds were shifting into a shade of green that was both dazzling and sickly at the same time. It provided a captivating display, but Lydia knew better than to fall into the trap of watching it. As soon as the thunder announced its booming presence every second became a precious commodity, and Lydia wasn't about to waste any time watching the shapes of the clouds when they started rolling towards her.

Cider howled at the discomfort of being woken up too soon, but even he seemed to realise the importance of urgency at the current moment. Lydia clapped her hands several times in an effort to push them both into vigilance, cursing the remnants of sleep that still clouded her eyes. As soon as she and Cider were both ready Lydia began to run.

The storm moved too quickly to allow anyone the luxury of choosing their shelter. Under the appearance of dark clouds, which cracked with neon lightning, the survivors were the ones who weren't afraid to use force. The first roars of thunder would always be followed by desperate voices shouting into the nearest closed door, and fists hammering windows in the hopes of breaking them open.

Lydia never allowed herself to stray too far from shelter. She had seen how suddenly the clouds could set in, and how fast they could speed across open sky. More importantly she had seen the consequences of not running fast enough away from them. The strongest of men had collapsed in front of her eyes, struck down with a pain they couldn't withstand. Lydia couldn't erase those images from her mind, but she could at least be thankful that they kept her running.

Since the storms had first started cracking through the sky communication had become more challenging. Radios fizzled into static, while phone lines burned with noxious smoke. Those who lived in the path of the storm knew only that they needed to escape, and the specifics of planning any further had proven impossible. Lydia needed to believe that safety was hiding somewhere, but she was stuck with no way of knowing where to look for it.

Gasping, Lydia forced her aching legs into a dive as the clouds began to close in behind her. She landed under the low awning of an abandoned store with scratched knees and burning joints, but the relief of prolonged survival was worth any temporary pain. She looked down to see that Cider was still with her, and she pulled him to her chest as her relief began to muddle with fear. In the crack of a sudden instant, heavy rain began splashing onto the roof.

Struggling to pull herself together, Lydia steeled her mind for the screams she knew would hit any minute now. Despite her best efforts no amount of preparation had so far succeeded in dulling their impact. She bit her lip as voices cried out in garbled tongues, sounds of anguish that bled through the storm in every direction. She pushed herself against the front wall of the store, but her survival instincts wouldn't allow her eyes to stay shut. Under a brow that was dripping with sweat, she looked out into the rain.

No more than a few feet in front of her a man had fallen to his knees. As streaming rivulets of murky liquid began to drip down his face, he looked up at Lydia with a helpless expression that chilled her to the bone. Feeling the shadow of the man's inescapable pain, Lydia shivered as he silently begged in her direction. She felt cruel, standing in her small patch of dry land, but refused to let herself fall into the trap of moving. She had learned long enough ago that there was nothing she could do to help this man, or any of the others. With his eyes firmly locked on hers she saw the exact moment when they glazed into madness, leaving his body to fall to the ground in a heap.

Lydia felt herself sob as she watched the man writhing through his own screams. Doing what she could to pull her attention back to her own survival, she took a moment to focus on the sound of rain pouring onto the roof. She scratched Cider behind the ear, slowly feeling her senses return to her enough to plan her next movements.

"What does it do to them?"

The voice seemed to spring out from nowhere, causing Lydia to spin around in a fighting stance. Crouching in the dirt behind her, a woman in a dark, torn jacket was recoiling at Lydia's sudden movement. As the woman put up her hands to suggest surrender, she appeared so weak that Lydia wondered how she had survived this long. Lydia let her stance drop, but kept the woman in the centre of her vision. She knew that the greatest threat to her survival wasn't currently to be found in any other person, but she also knew human nature well enough to be wary.

"It gets into their brain," Lydia answered the woman's question, "The best explanation I've heard is that the water contains some kind of chemical, like a drug, I guess. It falls in the rain and seeps through their skin. It gives them visions."

As she walked through the explanation, Cider let out a whine and nuzzled against her hand. In front of them the man on the ground wailed in sounds that were too far removed from words to recognise.

"What do you think they see?" The woman in the coat stammered, tightening her hood with shaking hands.

"Enough to destroy them," Lydia spat out the words with blunt force.

She shook her head, not wanting to waste another second on conversation. With the rain still pounding onto the roof above them she spun around to begin examining the window that faced into the abandoned shop.

"Hey," the other woman ventured, "I'm Danni."

"I don't care," Lydia snapped.

With hands that were cut and bruised, Lydia managed to get enough of a hold on the decaying window frame to pull out the pane of glass. It was rough, with sharp blades jutting out along its edges, but it provided enough of a gap to get inside. Moving as quickly as she could Lydia lifted Cider up high enough to get him through unscathed. She aimed a slow, cautionary glance around the area before jumping up and manoeuvring herself through the gap behind him. She considered her actions carefully before reluctantly gesturing for Danni to follow.

The room was dark and cold, littered with the frames of broken mannequins. As Cider began sniffing around Lydia wasted no time in checking every patch of flooring for any signs of a leak. Danni hung back in a corner, holding her own arms with gripping tightness.

"Some people are saying that we're part of an experiment," Danni muttered across the room, "I've heard them say that this is the work of the government, that they're testing some new kind of weapon."

"On their own people," Lydia grumbled back, kicking a patch of debris with a cautious foot.

"Well, it's either that, or we're cursed," Danni frowned, her voice wavering on the edge of tears, "Suffering in the absence of God."

Lydia responded only with a gruff sigh, glancing back towards the window to see that the rain was still pouring onto the ground outside.

"What do you think?" Danni muttered, awkward in the frame of one-sided conversation.

"I think we should focus on surviving," Lydia snapped, "We can start looking for the cause if we make it out alive."

Trembling slightly at Lydia's blunt tone Danni nodded, pulling herself down to sit on the dirt-encrusted floor. Lydia ignored the terror on the other woman's face as she continued working to assess the state of their shelter. When she was satisfied enough she strode back to the window with an air of grim determination.

"It's coming down harder than it was yesterday," she frowned, "I haven't seen the clouds this thick before."

Danni snapped her head up in a startled motion. Still feeling the need to avoid letting the other woman out of her sight, Lydia watched carefully as she bit her lip in silence. Danni opened her mouth, looking like she was struggling to find a response, but her efforts were immediately stifled by a roar of thunder that shook the walls. Both women flinched when they heard the overwhelming boom bleed into the sound of a siren that blared through the streets.

"Oh God," Danni cried, "What's that?"

The drifting noise seemed somehow familiar, and Lydia strained her ears trying to recognise it. She felt a cold shudder rip through her body when she realised the sound was being dulled under the splatter of thickening rain. Falling faster by the minute the dripping water was growing into a heavy sheet, drowning out the cries of anyone who still had the ability to scream.

With her survival instincts surging through her chest Lydia's eyes darted around the room, before settling on the roof. Her stomach lurched when she noticed that their fragile shelter was shaking under raindrops, which pounded against it with the strength of hammers.

"Shit!" she hissed at Danni, "Get away from the wall!"

Danni jumped up as quickly as her legs would allow, narrowly missing the pouring gush of water that slipped suddenly through a widening hole in the roof. The siren that continued to wail through the streets felt like a distant memory as spitting raindrops began to punch holes into the roof. Lydia pulled Cider into her arms, desperately spinning around to try and figure out a plan of escape.

Clutching the whining dog as tightly as she could, Lydia's head snapped up as she heard a roar that didn't sound like it belonged to thunder. As the sound grew louder she tried desperately to kick her brain into gear well enough to figure out what was happening. Still staring at the roof her jaw fell open when she realised that the seeping rain was zipping over them in horizontal lines.

"Wh- what-" Danni stuttered, taking a hesitant step forward.

"The alarm," Lydia gasped, "It's the tornado alarm."

Without stopping to check that Danni was following suit Lydia dove under the first piece of furniture she could see, gripping Cider in her arms. She could barely hear herself scream as the crumbling roof was ripped away from the walls, flying towards the whirling beast of wind that had appeared near the town centre.

In the face of the new danger, which seemed to be escalating beyond the possibility of escape, Lydia buried her face in Cider's fur, unable to hear her own sobs over the rising noise of battling storms. With a deep breath she waited for the rain to hit her, and although she couldn't measure how many seconds were rushing by her she could tell when too long had passed. Feeling only the biting cold of wind on her face, Lydia looked up.

With little more than bare walls left to surround her, she could see the tornado spinning in violent motions. As her thoughts caught up with the vision before her eyes, she realised why the rain had started streaming across the sky above them instead of falling to the ground.

"I don't- I-" Lydia stuttered, lacking the energy to turn syllables into words.

"Oh, my God," Danni gasped, standing up behind her, "Maybe God hasn't left us."

Lydia barely heard the comment as she continued to stare at the scene unfolding before her eyes. The tornado was pulling every drop of rain into its core, sucking the clouds along with it. The spinning roar of wind grew to a deafening volume as blue sky started appearing above them in patches. Still gripping Cider with every ounce of strength she could gather, Lydia watched as the tornado pulled away towards the horizon.

"Or maybe they were right about it being an experiment," Danni breathed, "and that's just another part of it."

Lydia snapped back to her senses, checking over Cider before placing him back on the ground.

"Doesn't matter. It's gone, that's all I care about," Lydia shook her head, "At least for now."

As exhaustion finally hit her Lydia collapsed onto her knees. Breathing through sobs of sheer relief she let Cider lick the drying patches of blood from her hands.

"What if it comes back?" Danni asked, still staring out towards the horizon, her eyes glazing over with fatigue.

Lydia took in a deep breath, pushing herself to avoid losing the biting presence of survival instinct. She looked out across the lingering devastation that surrounded her, taking in the sight of walls crumbling around bodies that quivered in desperate madness.

"If it comes back," Lydia frowned, slowly collecting her thoughts, "If it comes back…"

She paused, taking a moment to feel her own pain. Looking at the state of the landscape, she let out a breath that she hadn't realised she was holding.

"If it comes back," she repeated, "We'll know there's something out there that can stop it."

Without another moment given to hesitation, Lydia

whistled to Cider. The dog scrambled to her side, looking up at her with eyes that told her he would follow her anywhere. Frowning at the realisation that she no longer knew what escape meant to her, Lydia closed her eyes and pulled in a deep breath of dry air.

"Come on, Cider," she muttered over her shoulder, "Let's go."

With her dog by her side the only thing she could remember how to do was walk away.

Sarah Jane Justice
About the Author

Sarah Jane Justice is a South Australian writer whose work has been commended across a wide variety of fields. Her poetry and prose have been published on four continents, including in releases from Caustic Frolic, The Blue Nib, and Black Hare Press. As a spoken word artist, she has won a tidy number of awards, and competed as a National Finalist at the Australian Poetry Slam. Her other achievements include writing and performing an original one-woman cabaret show, creating four studio releases of original music, and curating the mixed-media exhibition 'Cracks in our Shadows'.

sarahjanejusticewriting.com
facebook.com/sarahjanejusticewriting
instagram.com/sarahjanejusticewriting

FLASH
C.A. McDonald

"**S**ergeant, if you're making those cinnamon rolls of yours tomorrow morning, you best share them with me! I don't care if it's your day off." The dispatcher's best cajoling tone crackled as the radio signal struggled for clarity. "Otherwise I might decide to send you some choice calls when you're back Wednesday. We clear, over?"

Carlos laughed and shook his head. Outside his windshield the forested night seemed a little less dark with Vera to banter with, even if she was almost twice his age, and on her third husband. "Vera, it sounds like you're making criminal threats over there. Gonna make me arrest you?"

"God, can you two quit it?" The Captain's voice cut over the CB, grouchy as ever. "I'm gonna write you both up. Sergeant Fernandez, you're 10-10, so get off the damn radio and get home."

Carlos' smile didn't fade. "Roger that, Captain." He heard Vera acknowledge, even fainter now that he was nearing the limits of his radio's ability to cope with the mountainous terrain. His home and destination was Silver Falls, a tiny town in the Siskiyou Mountains of California, so small Google maps had yet to document it's handful of streets. The Sheriff's office was a good thirty miles away from town, and with the trees, elevation gain, and ever-present hills, his radio usually gave up the ghost of maintaining a signal about now on his drive home.

He glanced at the clock on the dash and wished he could just teleport himself directly from the car to bed. He'd worked a twelve hour shift which, although it brought a nice boost of overtime, also meant he was exhausted. It was nearly midnight. His ass hurt from sitting in the car all day when he was on patrol, and his neck hurt from the paperwork that had followed in the office. Vera had been right when she'd chastised him this morning; he did need a new chair, or he was going to end up retiring at thirty-five with a busted spine.

The engine on his car groaned as it fought to make one of the final ascents of the evening. There was no one else on the road, which was no surprise, but he felt lonely nonetheless. It was just him and the endless sea of darkness passing coldly by his window, and above was the clear sky with stars, like thousands of eyes, staring down on him. When he got home it was honestly going to be more of the same; being single in a small town sometimes was like slowly bleeding to death.

A flash of light made him jerk and tap the break, suddenly terrified he was about to crash into a parked car he didn't see. When he didn't immediately eat someone's bumper, he slowed. There was nothing there, just empty road. He felt stupid. Had he imagined it?

Another flash erupted in his vision, and he could see it was coming from somewhere above and ahead of him. It steadied as the road turned toward the right, and finally he saw the source. It was a wreck, half-hidden by the curve of the road and thick bodies of foxtail pines. Thankfully it was tucked off the shoulder, and out of the path of any potential traffic.

"This is Sergeant Fernandez to base."

"Go ahead Serg," Vera sounded all business now.

"I've got a wreck here about five miles outside of Silver Falls, on I5. Code 2, possible 11-44. I'm going to stop."

"You want us to send an ambulance?"

"Yes, please." He pulled up near the wreck and pointed his headlights at the debris. "It looks real bad." The whole front of the older, rusted Ford Escort was crumpled on the driver's side, looking as if it had taken the brunt of the impact from the collision. Smoke billowed from the crushed engine, and there was glass everywhere on the street.

"Ten-four, 11-78 confirmed. Please keep us advised."

Carlos tried to move as quickly as he could while still maintaining calm. He got out his flashlight and ran toward the vehicle. The passenger's side door was open, and the automated alert was pathetically pinging to notify the passengers. There was blood on the asphalt, and the whole windshield was destroyed. A single figure was slumped over the steering wheel, a man. Carlos immediately checked for a pulse, but as he did the man's head flopped limply to the side. A wedge of glass, thicker than two of Carlos' thumbs, jutted from the left side of his skull. There were bits of bone and mashed brain on the dashboard.

"Base, this is Fernandez, I've got a deceased man in here—"

A flash. Not from the car. He jerked toward where he thought he saw it was coming from, across the road between the trees and a little up a hill. It had looked like a lightning strike.

"Sorry, and I—"

There was another flash, and a scream, like someone in pain. He stared out at the hill, saw the blood on the glass, the passenger door open…

"Get the ambulance here right away, I think I have another crash victim who may have wandered out into the woods; I'm going to go after them."

"Do you need back up, Fernandez?"

"No, I think we've just got someone in shock." He'd seen it before, people wandering away from accidents, not knowing what they were doing or where they were going, particularly if they were injured. He started to run for the hill.

"10-4, ambulance is fifteen minutes away from you."

"Roger."

The hill took up off from the main road, too steep and grassy to drive his car on. He trudged up, calves burning. The beam of his light showed blood on the grass, and footsteps where the soft ground had given way. He suddenly regretted not going to the gym as much as he should have. Another flash lit up the sky, followed by the shrill jolt of another scream, this time closer and…definitely female. His lungs burned and his chest ached, and he was gulping for air by the time the ground evened out again.

"Ma'am!" He shouted. "Ma'am, do you need help?"

He didn't see her. The trees began again, deepening the shadows to near-perfect black. The air was cooler too, and smelled like something wild and alien. He could feel the chill air creep against his skin. Everything was so quiet, and the woods at night were never quiet. There was always the hum of insects or night calling birds. It went beyond a physical silence and became something else, a soundlessness he couldn't find the bottom of. The silence of a void.

"Ma'am?"

A moan made him turn his head. He saw her, curled up into a ball, hands sprawled strangely in the dirt like she had been clawing at it. There was sweat and blood on her face. Something shiny jutted from the skin on her shoulder, and he realized it was shards of the windshield embedded in her body.

"Don't come near me!" She shouted. "It won't stay away for long!"

He held up his hands as a calming gesture. Yes, he'd seen them like this before. Temporarily insane by the shock of what had happened. "Ma'am, I'm with the Sheriff's department. I saw your wreck and I came to help you. There is an ambulance on the way, okay?"

"No. No. No." She shook her head, but her gaze wasn't fixed on him. She was looking up, toward the tops of the trees where they were lost in darkness. "He'll get you, too."

Carlos didn't listen. Carefully, like he was handling a child, he crept toward her and took her by the hand. Human contact was important to bring people back to themselves in a moment of trauma. It seemed to work - she let him pull her to her feet. This close he could smell the fear on her, mixed with something herbaceous and a little rotten, like roses past their prime. She had tattoos on her arms of strange symbols he didn't know specifically, but they reminded him of something occult. Lines within lines, crossing each other to make flowing over circles along her arms and chest.

"Come on, this way. What is your name?"

"Amy Benoit," she said, staring through him. "My brother is Brian. Oh God, Brian. Oh God, I told him not to do it, and he wouldn't listen!"

"Is Brian the one in the car?"

"Yes. It was just him and me. Just us left. The others are gone, he made sure of that. We were so stupid, thinking we could..." She went stiff in his hands and looked up again at the sky, terrified. "He's coming back. I can't stop him."

"Ma'am, I need you to calm down. We need to get you some help."

The wind picked up, and it was cold. Her face drained

of all color. "We're dead. There is nothing we can do."

"You're safe with me. I promise you there is no one here who can hurt you." Carlos was beginning to feel a little desperate. Amy was not like the other cases he had seen; she was having a complete psychotic break, or she was schizophrenic and having an episode. "Let's just go back to my car, and we can wait for help."

The wind was picking up, tugging at his clothes, at his hair. There were no clouds in the sky, and yet the trees shuddered in it.

"Your car?" Her gaze settled on him and focused. "Yes. Yes. Okay."

Like she'd suddenly come to life, she took his arm and tried to hurry him down the hillside. His shoes dug ruts in the soft damp earth as he tried to slow them. He didn't want to threaten her out of fear she'd decide to run back into the woods, and then he'd be forced to hurt her to get her to comply. He used his sternest voice instead.

"Ma'am, please let go of my hand."

Amy released him, but it only made her run faster down the hill. She was going to get herself killed. The wind behind him howled, and he tried to focus on just keeping upright as he followed her down the incline.

They hit the flat ground and Amy fell to her knees, breathless. He could see now, nearer to the light of his headlights, that she was bleeding from her feet - her shoes were missing, and there were scratches on her neck and back. He helped her stand and she leaned a little on him, clearly reaching the end of her strength.

"Can you tell me what happened?" He asked softly, as he walked her towards his car.

"Pazuzu," she said.

"Pardon?"

"Brian and his friends did it as a joke, three days ago. They didn't believe anything bad would happen." The wind jerked at her clothes and her sweat-slicked hair. "He never believed. Thought it would be harmless. A prank just to freak me out, because he knows I have more experience in stuff like this." She looked defeated, her eyes haunted. "But then they paid the price."

The skin on his arms had risen to gooseflesh. She didn't seem insane right now. "Can you explain all that in detail? I am not sure what you mean."

"Do you believe in demons, Officer?"

He had a flash of a memory of his grandmother from when he was about twelve. She was seated on a porch with a shawl over her legs in the summer heat, a Bible in her hands as she warned him of evil spirits. He had ignored her. He wasn't particularly religious, despite the best efforts of his parents. It wasn't that he didn't believe in anything at all, he just had trouble believing anything in particular.

Amy's belief was so strong that it was breaking her sanity.

"Miss Benoit, are you telling me you believe a demon caused this car crash?"

"Our car was hit by a gust of wind so strong it pushed the car off the road and killed my brother. Then it chased me up the hill. I only got away because I hurt it, but it's temporary. It will come back, and it will demand blood - that is the only way you satisfy Pazuzu for good. He is old, and he is angry that we were stupid enough to wake him up."

He didn't believe for two seconds that a demon was involved in this, strange wind be damned. They were almost to his car now, but there was one thing that bothered him.

"What were you doing to make that flash of light?" He asked. "Did you have a camera or a phone or something with you on the hill?"

"That was him. His lightning."

A chill ran down his arms again. That wasn't possible. She had to be lying, or maybe, just maybe, there was a freak storm afoot that had caused a discharge of lightning.

The wind blasted him from behind as he touched the door of his car. Amy turned from him, staring toward it. It rushed at them down the hill, bringing with it dust, leaves and grit. He held up a hand to protect his eyes as it grew stronger, strong enough to lift some of the smaller shards of glass and roll them against the concrete.

"Don't you see, Officer?" Amy said. "He's coming. He demands payment."

The trees were starting to bend. A branch detached from a tree and crashed against the roof of the Escort, big enough to have seriously injured either of them.

"Get in the car!" He yelled, and reached for her, but Amy was walking toward where her dead brother lay. "Miss Benoit, *Amy*, get back here!"

The trees groaned and whipped in the impossible gale. He leaned against it, his eyes beginning to sting. This couldn't be happening, couldn't be possible. He had never seen a storm grow in strength like this before, without a single drop of rain or a cloud in the sky. Amy had reached her brother and was doing something with him. The wind was near deafening now, and Carlos had to get the both of them somewhere safe.

He was going to have to use force if necessary; they couldn't delay further.

"Amy—"

She turned to him and sank a wedge of glass into his stomach. He gasped and tried to push her away, but she pushed it deeper with her frenzied strength. The pain was blinding. He'd never been shot, never been knifed. His arms felt heavy. He reached for his gun, but his fingers felt like fat, dead worms. His legs wobbled and gave way. She had hit something bad, an artery or his heart. He felt dizzy. Carlos knew whatever she'd done was fatal.

"I'm sorry," she said, and turned to face the wailing gale. "Pazuzu! King of the demon wind! I offer you blood. Your price is paid!" She dropped the glass and held her arms up high toward the shrieking gale. "Take his life and spare my own!"

The wind did not heed her. He could feel it still, somehow, even as the world was growing fuzzy and dimming all around him. There was blood in a river around his useless legs, studded with diamond archipelagos of shattered glass.

The storm became something else, like a living thing, ripping and clawing at all it touched. Still Amy kept her arms raised. Blood was seeping from her skin where it scoured her with grit.

"Mercy, my King!"

Carlos heard the voice then, like something out of a nightmare. Inhuman, like a giant exhalation of destruction.

"No mercy."

"No!"

The glass and stone it had toyed with before lifted from the ground and soared around Amy. He saw her try to collapse into a ball and protect her face, but it was no use. The wind eroded her skin like she was made of soft clay, smearing flesh from bone in the blink of an eye. Blood and bits of hair splattered against his face. He wanted to look away, but he didn't have the strength anymore.

Amy stopped screaming. He could see part of her arm, flayed down to the bone. It trembled for a moment and then ceased, utterly still.

He waited his turn, for the wind to murder him. It roared, then the air stilled violently, sending every piece of grit and debris in motion careening off on its own trajectory. Then there was nothing. No movement, no sound save for his ears ringing.

Flash.

No, not ringing. The sound of sirens, and the flash of ambulance lights as they pulled up toward the wreck.

Flash.

He had to hold on.

Flash.

Just a little longer.

Flash.

Just a little.

Flash.

C.A. McDonald
About the Author

The works of CA McDonald have appeared in several horror and sci-fi anthologies from across the globe. In her spare time she indulges in a billion hobbies, including running, yoga, cooking, gaming and other miscellaneous inanities. She lives in Portland, OR with her daughter, husband, two dogs and too many plants to count.
camcdonald.com

https://www.facebook.com/CA-McDonald-111584803526185

THE DAY THE ANGELS FELL
MCKENZIE RICHARDSON

The sky wept silver tears the day the angels fell. The clouds had been gathering for hours, as if drawn by gargantuan magnets over the rural town of Megiddo. Throughout the day careful eyes were cast overhead, anticipatingly attentive to the awakening of the storm.

By midday the sky was dark. It was eerie in its pewter glow, as though the sun were doing its best to send its rays to Earth, yet found itself overpowered by those unnatural clouds.

When the clouds finally broke the rain started as a drizzle, a little sprinkle that sent the townspeople rushing indoors. It was odd, the color of the drops, but they thought nothing of it. Surely it was some strange, meteorological phenomenon that modern science could easily explain if any of them had an inclination to search for an answer.

As the afternoon crept on, the intensity of the drops grew more severe. They pinged against drainpipes and banged on rooftops, as though demanding to be let inside.

The drops grew so heavy and forceful that they left little divots in the soft grass. Flowers lost their heads, sliced clean off by the fierce droplets as they flashed like blades in the streetlights. Even the *Welcome to Megiddo* sign, which boasted of a steady population of 1,289 residents, was not safe from the rain. It burrowed holes into the surface, obscuring its friendly message.

Always there was the strange color of the drops, metallic and shining with glints of wicked light like daggers poised to strike.

As night fell the little town was plunged deeper into darkness, and the first figure appeared.

Catharine McFee saw it as she dreamily watched the rain splash outside the window. She was gazing out in fear and wonder, half lost in her own thoughts, when suddenly it appeared. It was a dark shape that certainly hadn't been there before. The person was tall, taller than her father, so tall it could easily have been mistaken for a small tree. It stood in the middle of the yard, dressed in a long robe even blacker than the surrounding night. It was like looking at a piece of obsidian drenched in oil.

The figure stood motionless as Catharine's eyes widened. Her mind raced with countless explanations. After a moment of staring, of trying to comprehend, the person looked up at her as though it had heard her thoughts. Its eyes flashed under its midnight hood with an animalistic light, and her stomach heaved as she felt the person's gaze bore into her soul.

Catharine screamed, and the world crashed down.

As if the piercing shriek had summoned them many figures smashed to Earth, like space junk called home once again. All over town the figures appeared; in yards, on sidewalks, outside windows, in driveways, at storefronts, on top of cars, in the middle of roads.

They came like meteorites, marring the surface of the little town as their forceful descent gouged deep craters into whatever they'd landed on. They cracked sidewalks, smashed into grassy lawns and collapsed car roofs. There they stood, wherever they'd landed, absolutely still.

The people of the town looked out at the things, hearts pounding as if to the same beat. They watched, waiting expectantly for whatever chaos was surely to come, yet none approached the strangers. There was no peaceful rest, or soothing dreams, that night for the many minds awake in the darkness.

When the sun rose the next morning, bathing the town in a pale light through the tattered remains of the previous day's clouds, the figures still stood at their posts, immobile and silent.

Stores remained closed that day. No pedestrians strolled the sidewalks, and no cars rolled down the main roads. An unspoken agreement had been made that no one would leave their homes. Outside even the wind did not dare rustle leaves or bend grass, and it was as if time stood still.

The people tried to go about their business from the safety of their homes, but were unable to shake the continuous sensation of being watched. Even behind closed curtains and deadbolts it was impossible to ignore the waiting strangers on the other side of doors, windows, and walls.

Aside from that there was the strangeness of the noise. Throughout the day no one could say exactly when it first began. It wasn't a simple matter of it not being there one moment, and then suddenly there the next. It must have been more gradual; perhaps it started soft and slowly got louder over time, with such incremental change that it was impossible to notice until it was blaringly loud.

By midmorning every person was painfully aware of the ticking noise. Sasha Phillips was sure it was her grandfather clock possessed by spirits, and Jack Smith had the pragmatic idea that it was something wrong with the pipes. Fawn Glenis thought it came from outside, maybe even from the sky itself. Whatever it was, it was loud. It cracked through the air like the mechanisms of a clock, ticking consistently as though counting down the seconds. It was almost like a metronome, providing a dreadful rhythm for some unknown purpose.

Tension rose, and all through town eyes watched, ears strained, shoulders tensed, and teeth nervously nibbled the skin of lower lips. No one knew what to expect, or what was coming.

Marvin Thesis was nearly driven mad by the ticking. His wife Theodora was already a nervous woman, and she sat unresponsively in her armchair, one leg bouncing erratically. She'd been that way for hours. Marvin wanted the ticking to end, hoping silence would calm his wife, but at the same time he feared the event to which the ticking surely counted down.

It was nearly noon when he gave into his anger, so enraged by the ticking, the strangers and the weirdness of it all. He loaded his shotgun and stormed out the front door.

"Hey, you!" he called to the black-swathed figure still standing inert on the lawn. "Don't pretend you can't hear me. Move along, you."

He waved the shotgun vaguely, hoping it would be enough to scare the person away, that this was all some sort of elaborate practical joke.

The figure didn't budge. Marvin stepped closer, raising the gun and taking aim at the immobile patch of black. He'd never fired at anyone, and had never even pointed a gun at another human before. As a child he'd been trained to never point a gun at someone you weren't willing to shoot, but now the situation was different; this was one he'd never imagined he'd be faced with.

A fleeting thought crept into his mind that perhaps the figure wasn't even human. As quickly as it had come he shook it away, then addressed the figure once more. "I mean it. It's time for you to leave."

No movement. Not even the wind blew across the scene, and the air was stagnant and thick.

From the large, bay window in the living room Marvin's son Tad peered out at what occurred on the front lawn. To his right his mother still sat in her armchair, foot tapping. He watched as anxious minutes ticked by, the only sound inside the squeak of his mother's chair that was nearly drowned out by that dreadful ticking.

The gun remained fixed on the figure, clenched in Marvin's hands. Sweat beaded on his forehead, unleashed from his pores and dribbling down his face in nervous torrents. Periodically he yelled half-hearted threats at the person, hoping each time it would be enough to convince them to leave, to remind them that they had no business here.

The ticking went on and on, droning in the background and plaguing his thoughts. It was difficult to think with all that noise.

Finally, Marvin made a decision. He gave one last warning, then pulled the trigger.

He saw the bullet hit; if he hadn't he would have assumed he'd missed. Where the bullet struck the mound of the figure's left shoulder a swirling vortex appeared, even blacker than the shrouding cloak surrounding it. It sucked the bullet up and disappeared, leaving no trace behind. The figure didn't even flinch at the ear-ringing blast, or the definite impact.

Marvin considered firing a second shot, but the image of that spinning black hole had startled him. He began questioning his sanity.

He nearly jumped out of his skin when the chimes started.

Not until the third ring did he identify them as the bells of the church at the end of the road. They clanged loudly, mercifully replacing the incessant ticking that had brought him out in the first place.

Inside Tad counted the chimes as they erupted, splitting the tense air into chasms of uncertainty. He never took his eyes from the unmoving figure and the pale shape of his father, still standing with his gun raised. His father was now as unresponsive as the figure, and if the bells hadn't been ringing Tad might have thought that Earth had stopped spinning, or that time had simply ceased.

On the twelfth chime there was momentary silence before the air crackled with electricity. Even inside Tad could feel the change; it was like dragging your feet along the carpet, but magnified to the extreme. Tad could almost taste it on his tongue, and he could see the fringe of hair circling his father's balding head lift slightly with the static.

Just when the charge in the air felt unbearable the sky burst into flame. Snakes of fire slithered overhead, glowing fiercely against the iron-gray clouds. Tad's father nearly dropped the gun, mouth gaping open as he observed the sky. He took a step back, then another, slowly retreating toward the door.

Overhead a fiery burst thundered down with an audible boom that shook the house's frame. The flashing string of fire shot earthward, striking the dark figure. As it did the person's shoulders jutted back violently, chest exposed to take the full force of the blast. Other lines of flames sparked down from the sky, presumably hitting other figures where they stood throughout the town.

Watching in horror Tad noted that the figure did not appear pained by the shock, but rather as if it were absorbing it and being energized by it like a battery.

When Marvin reached the front porch, one hand on the banister to guide his blind retreat, the fire overhead smoldered out. As it did the streams branching from it died in a chain reaction, like a power outage sweeping over town.

It was then the figure moved.

Marvin stood stationary, shocked, as it tilted its head to the left, then the right, cracking its neck beneath its hood.

Two black wings unfurled and stretched behind it, as dark as onyx, the feathers gleaming in the faint, residual light of the fiery sky.

What happened next occurred so quickly that Tad hardly perceived it, even though his eyes remained fixed on the scene. One moment the figure was at its post as though standing guard, and the next it was inches from his father. The new silence was shattered by another crackling shot of the gun. It was impossible to tell where the bullet flew, but it did nothing to stop the black-clad figure.

Tad heard his father shout, another gunshot, and then pounding. He smashed his face against the window, trying to get a better view of what occurred outside the front door, but he couldn't see the struggle obscured at the front of the house.

Still pressed against the glass, he was shocked when an alarming splash of scarlet spewed onto the window. Tad was so confused by all he'd witnessed that it took him a movement to discern what it was. When it clicked into place he hurled himself back, staggering further into the room.

Tad grabbed his mother, still perched in her chair, and shook her. "Mom, come on! We have to go." Her leg continued its crazed jiggling, but other than that she made no movements. She didn't even look at him as he practically screamed in her face.

"We need to leave, now!" he insisted.

In the silence the front door clicked, unlatching. Tad's ears prickled, waiting for the familiar squeak of hinges that his father kept meaning to oil. With that reminder he glanced at the red spatters on the window, shaking the thought from his head. That didn't matter now.

He dropped his tone to a harsh whisper, pressing urgency into his plea. "Mother, please! We have to get out of here now!"

It was no use. His mother stared straight ahead, leg bouncing and chair squeaking quietly.

Hastily Tad looked around the room; he needed a weapon. There was a heavy lamp on the end table next to a hardback book, but his eyes settled on the sturdy fire poker. He took it up in his hand, though he wasn't confident of his chances. After all, he was only a high-schooler. If a grown man with a gun couldn't beat the thing then what chance did he have? Still, he had to try.

He quickly draped a quilt over his mother, then shut off the overhead light. The corner where the armchair sat was dim. If you looked closely you could still see his mother's leg bobbing beneath the blanket, but he hoped it would conceal her enough to convince whoever was at the door to move on.

When he'd finished Tad stooped behind the couch, which rested a few feet in front of the doorway that led into the kitchen. His grip on the fire poker tightened as the front door squeaked open. He waited for footsteps, but none came. Instead there was a sound that was not quite silence, but so like silence that it was barely a sound at all. It was reminiscent of snow falling, lace slipping from a table or feathers twitching.

The next thing he heard was his mother's voice.

"Oh, you're here," she said. She sounded so calm, so serene, as though she were relieved. It was as if what she'd been waiting for had finally arrived. Then there was a popping noise, followed by a wet splash, before the silence resumed.

Bile rose in Tad's throat as the smell of fresh blood assaulted his senses. It was so strong he could almost picture it before his closed eyes as it saturated the armchair. He pressed his lips together tightly, sweat slickening his grip on his weapon.

His heart thumped in his head, and he was sure the person who'd just murdered his parents could hear it give away his position.

He heard the quiet, feathery sound again, like a hawk on a breeze, and his ears strained to discern which direction they moved. It was impossible to tell.

As if in answer to his silent prayers there was the faint rustle of something brushing against the doorframe on the other side of the room. It led to the office, which circled along the far side of the house, and to the central stairway to the bedrooms.

After a moment of complete stillness Tad let out his breath, then tentatively stood. The dim room was empty as far as he could tell, although he dared not look too closely at the corner where his mother's armchair rested.

Gripping the fire poker he tiptoed into the kitchen, his ears alert for any indication that the intruder was near.

It was darker at the back of the house, where the trees overlooking the backyard blocked out most of the sunshine. Only a few rays found their way through the small windows. Tad inched quietly across the floor, slowly making his way to the garage door. He'd just need to slip through the short hallway, then into the garage. He hoped the shadow person had gone upstairs to continue its search. He knew it was hunting him; he could feel his status as prey, and his resulting desperation to escape.

He kept fear from clouding his mind by focusing on his goal. He just needed to make it to the door, and from there it was easy. He walked so slowly along the tiled floor it was as if he were barely moving. Yet, before he knew it, his foot found the rug that stretched into the entryway. He was almost there, almost out.

Behind him came a slithering sound, as gentle as a whisper. He froze like a deer, alert to the presence of a predator. His mind raced as he debated whether to turn around, or to continue his path. He bit his lip, trying to convince himself that there was nothing there, that he should just keep walking.

Curiosity won out. He snuck a quick glance over his left shoulder, just a tiny peek. A hulking mass blocked the doorframe from the office, and from the corner of his eye he could just make it out. The figure had slunk around the other side of the house, silently sneaking up on him. It was too late: He'd already looked. There was no turning back now.

As though a string were attached to his chin he slowly turned his head further, and he saw the shape clearly.

It was a coat lazily hung over the office door.

He almost cried out with relief, but choked it back. He calmed his breathing, then took a step into the hallway.

The sound of a single beat of massive wings erupted behind him. Tad spun around to find the shadowy figure a few feet behind him, hovering with its feathers fluttering slightly in the breeze they created.

Tad hardly had time to think as he took in the tall figure. It was cloaked in dark coverings, its obsidian wings looming above as it intensified its menacing size.

A scream burst from his throat as he hurled the fire poker at the figure, then hurried toward the door. Behind him there was a clang as the poker smacked against the kitchen island before crashing to the floor. His mother had loved those tiles with their navy-blue, flowery swirls. No doubt the impact had chipped at least one of them. Tad upbraided himself from the momentary distraction, pushing his mother from his mind.

He was at the door, the knob slipping in his sweaty

palm. He wiped his hand inelegantly against the stomach of his shirt, and on his next try he flung the door open. He lunged through it, and didn't look back. He ran as fast as he could through the garage to the backdoor that opened out to the yard, then he raced across the grass.

He didn't know where he was going. He was just running, relieved that he was out of the house and away from that creature. As he ran he was haunted by the image he'd seen in the kitchen. His heart pounded as he tried to piece together what the thing had looked like.

It wore a hood, but beneath it, where the face should have been, was a black smudge like an inky fingerprint. It was as though someone had tried to scribble out its features, and the fact that he couldn't identify it only made the hair raise up on his arms and the back of his neck. Whatever it was it was decidedly not human, at least not fully.

Sprinting through the town he'd lived in all his life, Tad was vaguely aware of the world around him. There were bloody patches along his impromptu path, as if others had tried his father's method with similar results. Here and there he heard screams or crashing, doors slamming, things being thrown as though some were fighting their way out of their homes.

He didn't stop. His heart hurt at the idea of leaving behind neighbors, friends, classmates and acquaintances. The town wasn't very big; he knew most people by name, even knew the names of their children, parents and grandparents, but he couldn't stop. If he stopped he was dead.

He needed to put as much distance between himself and that thing as possible.

He fled, aimless, in whatever direction his feet took him. Everywhere he looked was chaos: Impact holes on every surface, bloody spatters and carnage. Strangely enough he didn't see any bodies, just gory puddles. It was as if everyone had simply popped where they stood, exploding into tiny fragments.

Just above the treetops he caught a glimpse of the bell tower of the church, and he thought of the thick doors and stone walls. If he could make it there then perhaps he could hide, assuming the church was empty.

Tad made his way through the tiny copse of trees that separated his street from the church. His pace slowed as much as he dared in order to safely traverse the tangled ground, sticks and rocks stabbing at the soles of his bare feet. All he needed was one fall; a broken leg meant he wouldn't stand a chance.

He'd be as good as dead.

Emerging on the other side he scanned his surroundings. Nothing moved as far as he could see, and there was less activity here than near the houses.

Approaching the church he kept a watchful eye out for anything creeping about, but all was quiet and still; no life dared move, if it were present at all. For the first time he felt the ache in his thighs from his mad dash. The adrenalin had masked the pain before, but now it was agonizingly noticeable just how far he'd run. Gym class had not prepared him for this.

His hands shook as he came off the high of his flight response. His mouth was uncomfortably dry, like he'd swallowed a desert, and his skin felt clammy and cold despite the sweat. He shifted his gaze, careful not to let his guard down even though the church was in sight. He was not safe yet; he could not forget that.

A movement at the front of the church nearly made him cry out, and he stopped dead in his tracks. He quickly clamped his mouth shut, gnashing his teeth against his lower lip. He tasted metallic blood as his bottom teeth cut into the skin on the inside of his mouth.

It took him a moment to piece together the motion. The front door of the church had opened, and from inside someone beckoned to him. Someone with a face, definitely human. He shook his head, snapping himself out of his daze, then he hurried toward the entrance.

When he was within arm's reach the person pulled him inside, closing and bolting the thick door behind him.

Once inside Tad got a good look at the person. The man was tall, with olive-toned skin. His face was friendly, but lined with worry. It took Tad's slow mind a few seconds to work out who it was: Father Naomh.

The man gathered Tad into his arms, and it was only then that Tad realized how much he was shaking. His mind had been on one thing at a time for so long: Get through the garage door, get away from the monster, get to the church. Now that he was finally here everything he'd seen, heard and felt came rushing at him simultaneously.

Held by the priest, Tad broke down into heaving sobs.

Tears streamed down his face and dripped from his chin. He cried so hard he choked on his own clumsy attempts to pull air into his lungs. He cried for his murdered father, he cried for his slain mother, he cried because of the thing that chased him and he cried because of pain, fear and hopelessness.

But he also cried in relief. He had made it to the church, and now he could breath.

An abrupt thump pounded against the door.

Tad bolted upright, but the priest held him tightly. Father Naomh met his eyes, shook his head once, then raised his index finger to his lips. Tad obeyed the signal, but could not keep the panic from his eyes or the tremble from his limbs. The kindly priest released him. He approached the door, shooing Tad further behind him.

Then he opened it a crack, and peered out.

As Tad waited anxiously he heard a few hushed whispers exchanged behind the thick wood. The priest obstructed his view, so he couldn't clearly see who was at the door, but the whispers were a good sign. The strange figures hadn't spoken as far as he could tell.

Father Naomh thanked the person, then quietly closed the door. He turned back to Tad, the wrinkles in his forehead less severe now. He took Tad's arm and led him deeper into the church.

"That was Malcom Luaidhe," the priest explained. "He's an usher here." The name sounded familiar to Tad, but in his tingling relief he had a difficult time picturing the face.

"You're Tad Thesis?" he went on. "Marvin's boy? Your father–"

Subconsciously Tad flinched at the memory his father's name stirred. The priest stopped; he'd spent decades picking up on other's silent emotions, and he let out a deep sigh. "I figured as much. I'm sorry, son." He put a reassuring hand on Tad's shoulder. "You're safe here. Malcom has been keeping watch around the church, and he's the one who alerted me that you were close. He just came to check in, to make sure you made it okay. He says he hasn't seen any of those creatures nearby."

Warmth washed over Tad's heart, easing some of the ache.

"What are those things?" Tad asked, his voice hoarse from running.

Father Naomh didn't answer for a long time, so long that Tad didn't think he would. Finally he spoke, his voice so soft it was almost a whisper. "I don't know. They almost look like angels with those great wings, but they dress in death garb and clearly mean us harm. Perhaps they're those who have fallen from Heaven, as they did appear to fall from the sky, but in all honesty I couldn't say. There are things in this world we aren't meant to understand."

The answer itself was not reassuring, but Tad felt a little better knowing he was not alone in his lack of knowledge. It was soothing to be around another human, away from the frightening, bloodthirsty creatures.

The priest led Tad to a small room further in the silent church, a storeroom of sorts, and directed him to a small chair in the corner. From a cabinet he pulled out a glass bottle, along with a paper cup with blue flowers printed on it. He uncorked the bottle, pouring a tiny amount of red liquid into the cup before handing it to Tad.

Tad took it, peered inside, then glanced back to the priest. A look of concern passed over his face, as though this were some sort of test.

Father Naomh grinned good-naturedly. "Don't worry, it's only used for communion once it's been blessed. Even still, I think God would understand. Go ahead, sip it slowly and it'll calm your nerves."

Tad brought the cup to his lips, breathing in the heady aroma, then took a tentative sip. It was slightly bitter on his tongue. With his eyes closed he tried visualizing the tension easing out of every muscle in his body, taking periodic sips of the liquid.

When he'd swallowed the last drop Father Naomh poured him a little more. They sat for a long time in silence, minutes slowly slipping away in the stream of time. They didn't speak, but the priest's presence was comforting. Father Naomh had always been a constant in Tad's life, there every Sunday to speak of the Lord and His mysterious ways.

After a while the priest excused himself to check for an update from the usher.

Tad's heartbeat had finally resumed its normal rhythm when he was startled by the door slamming forcefully. He leapt to his feet, clenching the cup tightly in his hand as a bit of liquid splashed out and onto his foot.

He waited for what felt like an eternity.

"Father Naomh?" he called in his raspy voice as he took a hesitant step toward the door. He paused, listening intently. Not hearing anything he took another step, then another. When he'd reached the threshold of the backroom he peered around the corner.

Something wet caressed his foot. Before he could look down to investigate a red hand slammed into the doorframe with a sloppy slap, gripping the wood loosely. It slid against the surface, leaving a messy trail of crimson stains.

The priest's face came into view. Surprised, Tad yelped and fumbled backward.

Father Naomh's eyes were wide as they stared into Tad's with a horrified sense of urgency.

"Run," the priest whispered.

A movement behind the priest caught Tad's eye. Tearing his gaze from the priest he saw the black-clad figure who was halfway across the main room of the church. The reddening light of the dipping sun slipped through the stained-glass windows overhead, illuminating the stranger and casting it in an eerie glow. Its wings spread behind it, emphasizing its massive size. Its black hood was pulled up over the obscure smudge of a face, and Tad's heart beat furiously in his chest. He had to get away, had to flee.

He dropped the paper cup he still clenched in his hand. It fell to the floor with the barest of sounds, sloshing its red contents onto the tiled floor. They merged with a thicker puddle of scarlet.

Beside him Father Naomh grabbed his sleeve. "Run!" he yelled, his voice echoing against the domed ceiling.

This time Tad spun around and took off. In his haste he didn't hear what happened behind him, but felt the loss of Father Naomh in his racing heart. Without conscious effort his mind brought forth images of the kindly old priest popping like a bloody grape, just as his father and mother had. A single tear slid down his face as he ran. His only hope was violently crushed by the arrival of the newcomer, and his savior was reduced to a puddle of murky liquid on the floor of the church.

Tad stumbled through a long hallway he'd never been in before. At the end was an old, wooden door with black, iron hinges like a portal to a dungeon. He rushed toward it, doing his best not to think of what was behind him or how closely his pursuer followed. When he reached the door he had the fleeting fear that it may be locked, but when he pulled it opened easily.

He sprang through it, closing it as quickly and quietly as he could manage. Pressing his back against the door he observed his new surroundings. There was a series of narrow steps that steeply climbed up a slim column.

The bell tower.

He shambled up the stairs. His heavy feet stumbled on the awkward steps clearly not meant for public use, but thankfully he caught himself each time. He was halfway up when a burst of wind swept through the stairwell, nearly making him lose his balance.

The door to the bell tower flew open.

As Tad resumed his climb up the long staircase the toe of his foot slammed against the riser of one of the steps. Pain shot up his leg, and he sank to one knee. As quickly as he'd fallen he was up and moving, continuing his ascent. With each step shots and sparks raced through his lower body. He did his best to ignore it, focusing his whole mind on reaching the top.

From there he could see a hatch in the ceiling, with a little ladder leading up to it. He pushed himself forward, focusing on his goal.

When he reached the ladder his hand gripped one of the rungs, the tower filling with the sound of beating wings.

In a moment Tad was up the ladder and bursting through the double doors. He slammed them shut behind him, applying all his weight as he prepared for the imminent attempt to break through from below. He waited, but all he heard was his own rushed breathing.

As his breaths slowed he closed his eyes, listening in the darkness of the rapidly-approaching dusk. He knew the thing was just below him on the other side of the door; he could feel it in the marrow of his bones.

For one hopeful minute of silence he thought perhaps it had been enough, that perhaps he'd gotten away and the creature had given up. Then something thumped against the doors with such force that they opened an inch before closing again, lifting Tad up momentarily.

As the doors banged down solidly into their frame Tad clenched his fists around the door handles, the tips of his nails biting into his palms. With the thing so close he felt like crying again, like releasing all the pent-up pain and emotion. His foot still throbbed, but his fear distracted him from the pain.

There was another thump, less forceful than the first, which was quickly followed by a third.

Tad squeezed his eyes shut so hard that he saw fiery red rush past his eyelids, then there was an ominous quiet.

He waited through tension-filled seconds with no further sound from below.

A shout came from down on the ground. Tentatively Tad rose, keeping his eyes glued to the doors. There was a coil of rope in one corner of the tiny space that he quickly looped through the handles, effectively sealing the hatch closed.

Then he firmly rattled the doors. When they didn't open he crawled to the edge of the tower, careful not to hit his head on the large bell in the center.

Peering over the edge the ground appeared dramatically far away. By the light of the brightening moon Tad could see the green grass, as well as the gravel path that led to the front door of the church. There was the small garden, and the patch of fruit trees that were decorated every Christmas with strings of twinkling lights.

For a moment all was still, and Tad could almost pretend that none of this had happened. He could pretend that he was simply up on top of the church admiring the countryside.

Then the figure of Malcom Luaidhe came into view,

interrupting the delusion. Tad watched from overhead, an observer perched at the top of the world. Malcom streaked across the lawn. A dark figure appeared from under the eaves of the church, gently flapping its oily wings. It pursued Malcom at a pace that was easy and slow, yet somehow covered more ground than the desperate Malcom. With its fluttering movements the figure's hood swept back.

Its back was to Tad, so he couldn't see its face, but there was a long appendage coming from it. It was narrow, jutting out sharply like the masks worn by plague doctors that Tad had seen in one of his school books.

Before long the figure was upon Malcom. Tad opened his mouth, but his voice dried up in his throat.

Sensing its presence Malcom turned and came face-to-face with the thing. As soon as he did his feet stopped running, and he looked as if he were hypnotized. He stared into the face of the figure, his body relaxing, the tension melting from it.

For a second Malcom came out of the trance. He looked upon the person, as if for the first time, then opened his mouth to let out a blood-curdling scream. The figure spread its great, towering wings, momentarily blocking Malcom from view. The scream did not come.

The wings lowered slightly as the shadowy person planted both pale palms firmly on each of Malcom's shoulders, holding him in place.

Then, with abrupt violence, the thing thrashed its face forward, like a charging boar or a striking snake. The sharp thing that protruded from its face pierced Malcom's cheek.

Then it pressed further inward, seemingly sliding down his throat.

Even from up in the belfry Tad could hear the sucking sound the figure produced. It slurped Malcom's insides as though through a giant straw, and liquid as dark as the wine the priest had given Tad oozed out of the hole in Malcom's cheek as the figure continued to feed.

It was so unlike how he'd pictured his father's death. He thought back to the splatter of blood against the window. Even his mother's death had been silent, not accompanied by these messy sounds of feasting. Perhaps the first wave of creatures had simply killed to thin out the herd, and now that the population had been reduced they'd begun to feed. Tad shuddered at the thought.

He could not take his eyes from the disgusting scene below him, as fascinated as he was sickened. The whole process was done with such precision, such practiced care, that it was almost an art.

When the figure had finished its meal it retracted the needle-like protrusion, allowing Malcom's body to slump to the grass. The body did not bleed, and was thoroughly sucked dry of all fluids.

The thing beat its wings once, pulling the hood back over its head before twisting toward the belfry. From the depths of the hood Tad felt its watchful gaze upon him, as if it were examining his soul.

A cold shock rushed through his entire body, and his heart seemed to stop beating. He'd heard of dying of fear, but it was not until this moment that he believed it could ever actually happen.

Just as suddenly the creature broke its stare and slowly floated off in search of another meal as night fell and darkness took over.

Before Tad could bask in his relief the world was filled with heavy wing beats, and in an instant a large mass rocketed from the ground up into the darkened sky. Tad looked out from the belfry at the thing, sure it was the same creature who'd pursued him before. It flew straight upward with unfathomable speed, disappearing against the blackness.

Tad leaned over the edge of the tower, peering out from under the tiny roof. At the highest point in the sky the moon loomed overhead, its large, pale face watching unfeelingly at the horrors that filled the night. Its surface was dimpled with blemishes, scars from its own traumas which made it cold to the suffering of others.

A dark shape appeared in front of the moon, wings spread fully. For the first time Tad took in just how large the strangers were. The tips of its shadowy wings brushed the edges of the moon on either side, the hem of its cloak flowing down the moon's length and colliding with the darkness of the sky below.

The stark image, so massive and awful, against the pale moon sent a shiver through him. Tad was so filled with fear that it was almost transcendent, as if all the world clicked into place at once. It was like understanding the meaning of life, or like beholding the face of God. He knew then what he was seeing, that dark angel from the

Heavens, knew the fate its arrival promised.

When the figure pulled its wings back and down, diving toward the church like some giant bird of prey, Tad went scrambling. Despite his newfound understanding his will to survive still pushed him on.

Fleeing blindly he stupidly bumped into the heavy bell, banging his head against its curve. The clang of the metal ricocheted through Tad's skull. He fell to his knees and crawled toward the trapdoor, feeling his way along in the darkness. Only when he'd reached it did he remember the tangle of knots meant to protect him, which now ironically prevented his escape.

He spun around, sure the figure was just behind him, but there was only darkness.

To his left he noticed a thin ladder. Following it with his eyes he saw that it led to another trapdoor, smaller than the first, which was probably an attic.

In a dash he was up the ladder and trying the door, which was thankfully unlocked. He pushed his way through, nearly crying in relief at having solid walls between him and the creature. He lay on the floor, panting heavily in the near blackness.

At the other end of the minuscule room was a small opening covered with vertical slats, a vent of some sort.

All was quiet as Tad crept toward the hole. Wedging his index finger between two of the slats he opened the vent slightly, just enough to peek through. Outside it was fully dark. Everything was still, almost peaceful.

A flash of light against the inky sky alerted him to

movement. Two glowing stars burned more brightly than the others, but as he watched Tad knew that wasn't quite right. The stars were coming closer and growing larger as they neared.

It was then he knew they were not stars at all, but eyes reflecting the moonlight. Around them he could just make out the slight outline of the creature as it plunged directly toward him.

Tad jumped backward, but he was too late. With a quick sweep the winged creature tore the roof from the bell tower with the same ferocity as a child ripping paper from a birthday present. The remains of the roof crumbled down the length of the tower, scratching shingles loose before slamming to the ground.

Without the roof the room was brighter, and Tad could clearly see his pursuer. It fluttered over his fumbled hiding place, wings beating softly behind it. It stared down at Tad, inspecting its prize.

During its flight the dark hood had fallen back, and its face was no longer hidden behind the safety of the smudge. No longer were its features blocked out by blackness, as though Tad's own fear had sheltered him from the dreadful sight. The face was horrifyingly clear.

The skin was pale like moonlight, contrasting sharply with the wings that framed it. Where the eyes should have been were two blank holes, like the empty sockets of a freshly-cleaned skull. Below the gaping holes was a long, pointed nose that tapered at the end. It stuck out about a foot from the face, narrowing to the size of a pinhead. It gave the impression of a massive mosquito, straw-like and hungry. Below the nose there was no mouth.

Tad scurried up the ruined remains of the attic wall, unable to stop himself from sneaking a glance down below. His stomach lurched at the sight of the drop.

He looked back at the creature, then to the drop once again. His options were quickly diminishing, and there was only one thing he could think to do. One step, two steps, then he was hurling through the air in a desperate leap. His legs cycled as they left solid footing and hovered in the black sky.

For a moment he felt like he was flying, as though he were truly free.

Then, with a whoosh of feathers, the dark figure snatched him from the air, like a bird catching a bug.

In its grasp it rotated Tad so he was facing it. Tad looked into the empty sockets boring into him, and immediately a sense of calm eased over his body and mind. He didn't even feel it when the creature's nose slithered its way down his throat. In midair the creature sucked the life out of Tad, feasting on his innards.

When it had finished it released the limp body, which fell to the grass as a dry husk.

Having finally made its catch the creature flew on to join its brethren in their pursuits. Together they bled the town dry, consuming the essence of the townspeople.

When they were done nothing remained but the empty shell of a town. As quickly as they'd come they flew back up into the sky, disappearing through the gray clouds.

When the last of them had vanished a break formed in the overcast sky, allowing a few slips of morning sunshine to sneak through.

They fell on an empty town and shimmered against the *Welcome to Megiddo* sign. It was pocked with holes from the rain, and bore notice of a population that was significantly out-of-date. In its emptiness the place held infinite possibilities, like it was ready for a new start.

The sun rose slowly in the sky, bringing a close to the chaos of the past few days, which began with a silver rainstorm and ended with a haunting silence, the day the angels fell.

McKenzie Richardson
About the Author

McKenzie Richardson lives in Milwaukee, WI. A lifelong explorer of imagined worlds on the written page, over the last few years she has been finding homes for her own creations. Most recently, her work will be published in Eerie River Publishing's With Blood and Ash, coming 2021. Her stories and poetry are also featured in anthologies from Black Hare Press, Iron Faerie Publishing, and Dragon Soul Press. In addition, she has published a poetry collaboration with Casey Renee Kiser, 433 Lighted Way, and her middle-grade fantasy novel, Heartstrings, is available on Amazon.

McKenzie loves all things books and is currently working towards a master's degree in Library and Information Sciences. When not writing, she can usually be found in her book hoard, reading or just looking at her shelves longingly.

For more on her writing, follow her on:

Facebook: http://www.facebook.com/mckenzielrichardson/

Instagram: http://www.instagram.com/mckenzielrichardson/

Blog: http://www.craft-cycle.com

On A Wing And A Prayer
Tim Mendees

October 29th 1940 - Somewhere Over The North Sea:

The rain came from out of nowhere. It pelted the cockpit of Flight Sergeant Mike Warren's Hurricane in fat globs, making the already poor visibility much worse. Lining up the ring and bead sight on the incoming Messerschmidt, he squeezed the triggers. The roar of the guns was deafening, and his vision danced as the reverberation shook him to his standard-issue boots.

All was clear and bright when the Number Seventeen Squadron scrambled from RAF Castletown. But, as everyone knows, the weather in the Scottish highlands moves faster than the ruddy Luftwaffe, and it wasn't long before they were flying in conditions akin to pea soup.

Radar had picked up German bombers flanked by a squadron of fighters crossing the North Sea. This wasn't surprising; What was surprising was that they were this far north, though the rising winds could probably account for them being slightly off course.

His volley of machine-gun fire peppered the wing of his opponent. It should have been a direct hit, but the wing-mounted machine-guns were never all that accurate. Sometimes Mike thought he would do better poking his arm out of the cockpit and firing with his trusty service revolver.

The Messerschmidt returned fire, so Mike yanked the throttle and climbed sharply. The rain of lead caught his rear fuselage a glancing blow, but nothing too drastic. The poor blighter next to him wasn't so lucky. Bullets punctured his fuel tank and his cockpit erupted into flame, roasting him alive.

Mike cursed. The dead man had been a friend; All of the dead men had been friends.

Glancing around at the melee his mouth went dry with fear. It wasn't looking good. The Luftwaffe had superior numbers, and seemed to have luck on their side. He was one of the last Allied birds in the sky.

Mike's father had flown during the great war, and the plucky old bugger had narrowly survived being shot down on three separate occasions. When he was young Mike asked if he had God on his side. Mr Warren Senior had smiled and looked wistful, but never answered.

More bullets raked in his direction. He banked to the right, nearly colliding with one of the bombers that they were there to shoot down. It would have made his mission a success, but he would rather have found a less fatal way to do it.

He unloaded the four 20mm cannons on his wings, and they punched huge holes in the grey skin of the bomber. None of his hits were critical, but with a bit of luck it wouldn't make it to land.

Mike gave himself a pat on the back and climbed out of its path. As he rose above the target he looked at his handiwork: Yes, it looked like he had done it.

His momentary lapse in concentration nearly proved fatal, however. One of the Messerschmidt's had him in its sights, and it raked his left wing.

Now his manoeuvrability was severely compromised. The only way he would have survived the skirmish is if he could have kept moving, but he was now a sitting duck.

When war broke out Mike told his father that he was joining the RAF to follow in his jet stream, so to speak. His father was proud, of course, but he knew that his son's chances of going the distance were slim. After all, he wouldn't have gone the distance if he hadn't had a little help.

A father's duty is to guide and teach a son how to be the best man he could be, so he couldn't very well object to his desire to fight for king and country. There were other things he could do, though, to aid his only heir's survival. When Mike went off for training his father gave him a good luck charm and a special prayer.

As another burst of fire slammed into his plane, Mike reached for the charm that he kept around his neck on an old bootlace. He pressed it tightly against his chest, where it felt like a shard of ice.

Flames erupted behind him, the wood and fabric fuselage burning up like kindling. It was too late to bail, and he was miles out to sea so a crash-landing was out of the question. His number was up.

Mike muttered the words his father taught him all those years ago...

The wind gathered in strength, and a freak storm battered the combatants. Lightning flashed; Hailstones rattled off their wings like someone had emptied a sack of ball-bearings in the stratosphere. Two of the Messerschmidt's were blown into each other. They burst into a fireball, sending debris in all directions. A chunk of grey metal slammed into Mike's one good wing, taking a huge bite out of it. If he wasn't already done for then he certainly was now.

Mike went into a nosedive.

Death was inevitable.

The plummeting plane produced a huge roar as it rocketed towards the waves far below.

The charm hadn't worked. He ripped it off his neck and tossed it aside in frustration, yet still he kept on muttering the strange prayer as the sea rose up to meet him.

November 6th 1940 - Killimster, Caithness, Scotland:

Algernon MacTavish looked up at the sky and shivered. Even for a hardened Scott it was bleak, and since the freak storm just over a week ago the weather had been even more savage than usual. In the forty-odd years he had run the moderately-sized sheep farm at Killimster for he had never seen weather like it. Still, it meant that there had been fewer German bombers in the sky than normal.

Placing two frozen fingers in the dark slit between his bushy, ginger beard, he blew out a series of sharp whistles. His faithful sheepdog, Bonnie, answered with a bark and proceeded to try and round up the frenzied sheep. The poor creatures had been driven half-demented by the fierce winds and horizontal hailstones.

At first the strange noise sounded like a particularly persistent mosquito: A low, continuous whine. Al looked around, cap in hand, but there was nothing to swat at. Besides, it was the wrong time of year for the little devils.

Then the whine started to get louder.

"Och, Christ!" Al panicked. "A sodding bomb!"

But there were no planes in the sky. He looked around in confusion as the whine built into a roar. It was the sort of noise usually attributed to a downed plane, but there was nothing that he could see.

Boom!

The ground in the adjacent field erupted, soil bursting high into the air. Al swore oaths in pure, Scottish Gaelic as he dropped to the floor with his hands over his head. He awaited the coming explosion, but nothing happened.

Bonnie barked in a wild frenzy and jumped at the fence. Al looked up, thanking the Lord, and looked over at his dog. She was snarling at something in the next field.

Pulling himself up and, brushing sheep droppings off his tweed overcoat, Al made his way carefully towards his dog.

"Hush now, girl." He whispered in calming tones. Bonnie looked at him. He had never seen a look like the one in his dog's eyes before: It was a look of sheer terror. "What's got ye so spooked, lass?"

Al approached the fence and peered over. About fifty yards away something large and rectangular had slammed into the ground, half-burying itself.

When something hits the ground at such velocity, you expect a fire. Al scratched his head, as the object wasn't even hot. In fact, it was freezing cold. He hopped over the fence with his eyes fixated on whatever the Hell had just landed in his field. So rapt with attention was he that he nearly entangled himself on the barbed wire.

The ground steamed and hissed. The object was evidently much colder than the frozen ground he walked upon, which in itself was a mystery.

The ground was chillier than his mother-in-law.

Finally reaching the object he knelt down to get a better look. What was inside nearly turned his ginger locks the purest white, and a second later, he was charging across the field with Bonnie at his heels.

Climbing into his tractor he turned the ignition and headed towards the nearest centre of civilisation, the town of Wick. He needed to get in touch with the RAF at the airbase there pronto, though he didn't expect them to believe him for a second when he would say that one of their pilots, glowing orange and encased in a perfectly rectangular block of ice, had just landed in his field and scared his sheep. No, he expected them to check his breath for whiskey.

◆—○—◆

November 9th 1940, RAF Wick, Caithness, Scotland:

Group Captain Blake's buttocks were numb. The hard seat of the Austin K4 troop transport vehicle had turned the long journey from RAF Sutton on Hull to the far end of Scotland into an exercise in endurance. He was the only passenger, yet the tell-tale aroma of sweat, boot polish, machine oil and fear from hundreds of national service-men still lingered like a dark cloud. Blake was more ac-customed to upgraded vehicles, but none were available to ferry him up to RAF Wick at such short notice.

He must have read the report on the strange events that had taken place since the sixth about a hundred times by now. Even when he knew the document back to front it was either that, or share banalities with his driver, Evans. He was a nice enough chap, but there was only so much conversation to be had with a man with a lower IQ than a mug of mess-hall tea.

The main issue with Evans was that he didn't seem to understand the word 'classified.' No matter how many times Blake changed the subject the talkative Welshman kept on asking him why, in all that is sacred, did he have to go to Wick so urgently. It wasn't exactly the hub of the war effort. Blake was saying nothing, as 'loose lips sink ships' and all that.

Even if he did want to reveal his mission he was almost certain that his driver would think he was pulling his leg, for nobody would give credence to such a wild story. Hell, he wouldn't believe it fully until he saw the chap with his own two eyes.

It was beyond belief. A pilot who was shot down over the North Sea, believed KIA, turns up a week later in a farmers field and is glowing orange and encased in ice. If that wasn't unbelievable enough the fact that the man subsequently defrosted, and is now alive and well in a makeshift quarantine, pushed it firmly into the realms of fantasy.

As the rattling vehicle neared its final destination he was treated to first-hand evidence that something weird was indeed happening. It had been reported that, since the seventh, the base and its surrounding area had been pummelled by a freak snowstorm. Blake got the driver to pull over and jumped out of the cab.

"Bugger me," Blake muttered to himself. They had stopped at a perfect vantage point to witness the anomaly for themselves. Below them, covering the windswept, heather-blanketed land, was a perfect circle of deep snow. It radiated for what looked to be a mile in diameter, with Wick at the epicentre.

A brutal storm raged and lightning flashed.

Blake walked a couple of hundred yards down the

road, with Evans tagging along behind him. Eventually he reached the threshold of the storm; It was uncanny. It went from a perfectly clear road to a fifteen-inch drift without so much as a spray of powder.

"Well, will you look at that?" Evans said with his mouth agape in wonder. "It looks like a bloody snow-globe."

"Hmm?" Blake was miles away. In all his years as a pilot he had never seen such bizarre weather.

"I were just sayin' that it looks like a snow-globe, sir." Replied Evans.

"Quite right," Blake said distractedly. "Do you think we can get through this lot?" He swept his blue-coated arm dramatically over the frigid landscape.

"Oh, no problem, boyo...Um...Sir!" Evans stumbled, turning red in the face for such a rank faux pas.

It was okay. Blake didn't notice, or if he did he decided to let it slide. "Right, shall we press on, then?"

"Yes, sir. I'll have you there in no time." Evans grinned.

✦

Driver Evans was wrong, very wrong. Less than five-hundred yards down the road they became bogged down, and had to dig the front left wheel out of a pot-hole. It took them several hours to make it to Wick, and in the end they left the vehicle at Algernon McTavish's farm and trudged on foot the rest of the way.

By the time Blake arrived it was dark, and he was frozen to the core. It appeared that the storm raged with increasing ferocity the closer they got to the epicentre, where the block housing Flight Sergeant Warren was. The guards on the gate let them inside after a brief check of credentials, and they ushered them into the mess hall where they were to be met by Doctor Blythe. He was the man who had been the sole person tasked with looking after Warren since his miraculous resurrection.

Since it looked like they would be stuck in Wick for some time Blake gave Evans leave to go to the NAFFI for a couple of well-earned pints, and Evans could have kissed him. It also fulfilled a secondary motive: getting the nosy devil out of earshot.

Since Blake had read the report ad nauseam Doctor Blythe got straight down to business.

"I don't know what to tell you, sir. I have never seen anything like it. When he was brought in we had him thawed out using paraffin heaters. I thought I was to be conducting an autopsy, but..." Blythe shrugged then buffed his wire-rim spectacles on his tunic.

"Did he just wake up there and then?" Blake was scribbling notes on the back of one of the papers in his file.

"No, not right away. We had him on the slab when it happened." Blythe replied.

Doctor Blythe had just finished his evening rations, and was scrubbed up and ready to cut Warren open to examine the orange glow that seemed to pulse and radiate from the cadaver. He had his scalpel in hand, ready to make the first incision from neck to navel, when Warren's eyes snapped open and swivelled wildly in their sockets.

"Blimey," Blake said after hearing the tale. "I bet that scared the bejesus out of you?"

"Not half, sir. I nearly jumped out of my skin." Blythe continued. "After crying out in apparent agony he sat bolt upright, then started asking where he was and how he got there. I was dumbfounded, for the man had been stone dead."

"Could there have been some kind of mistake, doctor?" Blake cocked an eyebrow.

"No," Blythe replied flatly. "There was no mistake. The man hadn't breathed, and his heart hadn't pumped since he was defrosted. He was dead, I'll stake my reputation on it."

"Very well." Blake smiled. "What did he say after he came to his senses?"

"Ahh," the doctor sighed and pinched the bridge of his nose with his thumb and forefinger. "He told me a wild tale indeed. We recorded it on reel-to-reel, which you are welcome to listen to at your leisure. But I'll give you the bare bones..."

As the doctor paused and licked his lips, a young airman came charging into the room calling doctor Blythe's name. "Doctor, come quick!"

"What is it, airman?" Blake asked with authority.

"It's Warren, sir. He's dead!"

Blake and Blythe looked at each other, then followed the youngster out of the mess and across the courtyard to the main building. The storm had risen to an almost apocalyptic level, snow and hail swirling in a chaotic dance. The troops had taken cover under tent-flaps and other structures, their poor faces whipped red-raw by the onslaught.

Warren was indeed dead; He had cut his own throat with a pen-knife.

According to the man who found him Warren had been ranting and raving for the previous hour. He had been screaming to be allowed free. He bellowed at the top of his voice that "He comes for me!"

Apparently the rising storm was the source of his agitation. Doctor Blythe nodded, as though he had heard him say such things before. For the time being Blake was in the dark.

The guard in the hastily-outfitted quarantine room said that he was alerted when it became suddenly quiet. Blake asked him why he didn't check on the man when he was carrying on, to which the airman replied that he had been instructed by Blythe not to have any contact with him - a fact that Blythe backed up, as he wasn't sure that the odd, orange glow wasn't contagious.

Once Warren had been stretchered out Blythe decided that he would conduct the autopsy in the morning. Blake agreed, as he was shattered from his journey. In the meantime he had one of the men kit him out with a room that had a bed, a desk and the reel-to-reel machine.

Blake was very interested to hear what Warren had to say.

Blake sat in the hastily-converted store cupboard by the dim light of an oil lamp. He had, in front of him, a stack of paper and a pencil stub. Blythe had warned him that Warren spun a wild story, so in preparation he had poured himself a large Scotch. Once he had sat back and lit a cigarette he hit play.

The tape crackled and hissed before settling down and becoming audible. Doctor Blythe introduced himself and gave the date and time, before asking Warren how he felt."

"Not good, doc," Warren answered in a raspy Cornish burr.

"I understand that you keep burning up and keep having to be placed in ice-baths?" Blythe asked.

"That's right. I feel like me fingers are on fire. Why is it so hot in here?"

"It isn't. Look, you can see my breath."

"Oh." Warren sounded sullen.

"Could you tell me what happened before you were found in Mr. McTavish's field?"

"I'll try, but I'm not completely sure myself." Blake could hear the chair under Warren creak as he fidgeted uncomfortably. "My father flew in the last war, did you know that?"

"Yes, we have spoken to your CO and he gave us a run-down of your background." Blythe shifted some papers that rustled and crackled on the recording.

"He survived several times when it looked like his

number was up. He put it down to the protection of 'he who walks on the winds'. I didn't believe a word of it, until..."

"Go on." Blythe prompted after a short pause.

"My plane was done for. Before I left to join up, he gave me this charm, see? It looked like a kind of wonky star. I kept it around my neck. He also taught me a kind of prayer...God, I wish he hadn't. Anyway, when I was going down I grabbed the star and said the prayer. I didn't think it had worked, so I ripped off the charm and threw it down in anger. What a fool." Warren suddenly became agitated. "Have you recovered my plane? I must get the star back!"

"There is no chance of that, I'm afraid. Your Hawker will be at the bottom of the sea by now." Blyth stated without emotion. Blake could tell by the tone of his voice that he wasn't swallowing Warren's story.

"Then I am doomed..."

"Can you tell me how you got from crashing into the North Sea to winding up a week later in a farmer's field?"

"You won't believe me." Warren sniffed.

"Try me."

"Okay doc, if you insist. *He* came for me."

"Who did?"

"The wind-walker. A storm, the likes you have never seen, slammed into us. All the German planes were slapped out of the sky, like someone swatting flies. All around me was chaos, but it was like I was suspended in a bubble of calm. Like the eye of the storm. *Something* lifted me from the cockpit. I thought it was a guardian angel...Boy, was

I wrong. The storm moulded into this awful shape with glowing eyes."

"Glowing?"

"Yeah, the same colour as my skin. They were like two hot coals in the sky, but gave off no heat. It laughed at me. It was such a horrible sound. It told me, well, not so much *told* as put the knowledge in my head, that I had made a mistake. To call him without protection was to give your very soul to him. I struggled and fought, but it was no good. My arms and legs were bound by wispy ropes of vapour. The *thing* took me in its clutches and raced off into the atmosphere. I don't know how I breathed; He must have done something to me. For what seemed like an eternity we raced through distant skies and lightless voids. He laughed while I screamed. I saw things that no human eyes should see. Horrible, horrible things. I saw creatures that shouldn't be. I saw atrocities committed in the creature's unholy name. I saw..."

The silence in the room hung heavy on the tape, and only the faint tick of a clock could be discerned.

"Eventually I managed to escape. I don't know how, maybe he let me go. Maybe all this is part of his scheme..."

"Scheme? What scheme?" Blythe sounded like his mouth was dry.

Warren laughed humourlessly. "I dread to imagine. I can hear the storm outside, and I think he has come back for me. Anyway, next thing I know, I was falling. Then I woke up with you waving a scalpel in my face."

"You said the creature had a name?"

"Yes, doctor. Ithaqua."

"Ithaqua?"

"Have you ever heard of the Wendigo, doctor?"

Click!

Blake turned off the machine, his head spinning. What he heard sounded like the ravings of a madman, but what other explanation was there? Clearly something very strange had occurred to the poor man, though unfortunately it looked like he had taken the truth to his grave.

The strong alcohol plus the long journey had taken their toll, and his eyelids grew heavy. After extinguishing the lamp he fell onto the cot and into a fitful slumber.

Evans had partaken of more than just a couple of pints. The rough-looking chap was as pissed as a newt. He wandered the corridors of the barracks, swaying wildly, singing 'The Green Green Grass Of Home' at the top of his voice, so the base had kindly given him a temporary bed in one of the auxiliary dorms.

The storm had nearly blown him to Orkney as he crossed the yard. He was glad of being given a bed, as the last thing he wanted was to have been stuck out in that lot.

The dorm was plunged into darkness, since the weather had taken out most of the electricity earlier in the day. He had been given a lamp, but in his drunkenness he had left the wretched thing in the NAAFI. There was no way in hell he was going back to get it.

Nobody was using the dorm at that moment, as the auxiliary unit was unable to get back to base and was staying in Inverness until the storm passed. This meant he had the place to himself, and he recalled being given the bed in the far corner. Evans figured that he would head in that direction, then fall on whatever bed he made it to. As long as he was close what did it matter?

Taking a box of matches from out of his pocket he struck one, bathing the room in dim light. He spotted his kit-bag, pointed his feet towards it and started weaving.

The match burned down quickly, and burnt his fingers. Evans cursed, blowing on his singed digits, and it took a while before he realised that the dim glow hadn't died with the match.

He spun around unsteadily, and came face to face with the corpse of Flight Sergeant Warren.

Evans screamed.

Warren reached out an icy hand and grabbed him by the hair. His touch burned, and Evans could feel the frostbite eating into his flesh. As the driver struggled Warren held out his other hand, where a miniature storm played in his palm before growing into a mountainous icicle.

Evans was powerless as the frigid weapon slammed through his eyeball and into his brain.

✦──◦──✦

The sound of an alarm bell jolted Blake awake. Before he could question what the bloody Hell was going on the young airman, the one who had found Warren's corpse, came bounding into the room.

"Sir! Sir! Come quickly, sir." He yelped hysterically.

"What the devil is going on, airman? And don't you bloody knock?" Blake snapped.

"Yes, sir. Sorry, sir. It's Evans, sir. Some bugger's killed him, sir!"

"What?" Blake boomed, the haze of sleep finally lifting.

Before he could answer something large and heavy slammed into the wall of the room from outside, plaster crashing to the floor as the wall buckled.

"What the bloody Hell was that?" Blake yelled.

"I dunno, sir." Airman Jones stammered. "Should I go and find out?"

Blake thought for a second, "Yes, on the double. I'll see to Evans. Where did it happen?"

Jones started to take off at a run down the corridor after informing him that Evans was in the barracks.

Blake headed towards the murder site. More objects slammed into the building, and the ground itself was shaking. Brick-dust and filth rained down from the ceiling in torrents, and what lights were still functioning on the backup generator flickered and sizzled.

He rounded the corner, stepping into the area that was completely without light. He whipped his flashlight from his inside pocket and pointed it into the gloom. It wasn't far to the barracks, so he broke into a steady jog.

He was nearing a crossroads when a noise stopped

him dead in his tracks. It was the sound of gunfire.

"What the Hell is going on?" He said to himself.

As he looked around a figure came shambling around the corner. Blake shone the light in their face as he reached for his revolver.

"Doctor Blythe? What the devil is going on? You nearly gave me a bally heart attack!" Blake panted.

"Sorry." Blythe wheezed. "We need to get the Hell out of here!"

"Why? What's happening, man?"

As Doctor Blythe opened his mouth to speak a shard of wickedly-sharp ice burst through the front of his head. Blake bellowed in shock as he was showered in blood, brains and fragments of skull.

A blanket of frost started to engulf the corridor. The growth cracked and hissed as black veins of ice spread along the wall, advancing towards him.

Blake drew his revolver and backed away. Blythe froze where he stood, like some grotesque sculpture, and from behind him stumbled the reanimated body of Warren. His eyes were blank, and his mouth hung slack. Each step he made crunched and ground.

Sensing that it was of no use to talk to the man, Blake didn't hesitate in pumping all six rounds into the walking cadaver...None of them stopped it coming.

Blake backed away as he reloaded. Warren kept advancing, and so did the encroaching ice. It was taking over the base, and with each second the ice grew in thickness. It was like being chased by a glacier.

Blake figured his bullets would be of no use, and he turned and sprinted back down the corridor. Another colossal impact shook the building, nearly sending him sprawling.

Using the wall to steady himself he carried on running. After turning the corner he nearly collided with Jones and a small group of panicked-looking airmen.

"Thank God, sir!" Jones breathed. "Outside, sir, there's this thing..."

Blake had doubled over to catch his breath; He wasn't as young as he once was. Before he could say anything one of the other men called out in alarm.

Warren was coming around the corner, with the ice still following.

Jones grabbed Blake by the lapel and started to run. He screamed at the others to follow, but they decided to put their faith in bullets...A very foolish choice.

Each man fired off a burst of rounds. They slammed into Warren, but didn't even make him flinch. Blake and Jones looked around just in time to see Warren open his mouth and belch forth a gale of ice shards.

The knife-like objects tore huge chunks of flesh from the brave airmen as they smashed bones and severed limbs. In seconds the men looked like they had been minced.

A shard slammed into Jones' back, and he flew forward with such force that his ribs cracked from slamming into the wall at the end of the corridor. Blake flung the lad's arm over his shoulder, hauling him through the double doors and into the storm.

What Blake saw as he stepped outside was a nightmare. A huge cyclone of ice and snow had formed itself into a massive, insect-like shape. It had spindly legs and burning, orange eyes. Planes and trucks were sent flying through the air as it swept its enormous claws back and forth.

With the last vestiges of his sanity he dragged Jones into the nearest shelter, the medical tent, and lay him on the bed. It was no good. Jones' lungs had been punctured. He coughed up thick, black blood, then lay still.

Blake cried.

Laughter made him peek around the door-flap. Warren had walked outside and approached the creature, his arms raised in worship and his head tilted back. The beast took him up in one of its hands and the next second, they exploded in a plume of snow.

The wind dropped almost instantly. The clouds dispersed and the stars came out. Blake curled up into a ball and gibbered.

❦

The RAF Wick tragedy was never made public, and the top brass passed it off as the result of German bombs. There was a full enquiry, but the findings were suppressed.

As for Group Captain Blake, he was given a Section Eight discharge and was sent to live out the rest of the war in a sanatorium. He perished a year later during an uncommonly cold winter.

Tim Mendees
About the Author

Tim Mendees is a horror writer from Macclesfield in the North-West of England that specialises in cosmic horror and weird fiction. He has had over fifty stories accepted for publication in anthologies and magazines with publishers all over the world and has two novellas, Miracle Growth (Black Hare Press) and Burning Reflection (Mannison Press), coming soon.

When he is not arguing with the spellchecker, Tim is a goth DJ, crustacean and cephalopod enthusiast, and the presenter of a popular web series of live video readings of his material. He currently lives in Brighton & Hove with his pet crab, Gerald, and an army of stuffed octopods.

https://timmendeeswriter.wordpress.com/
https://tinyurl.com/timmendeesyoutube
https://www.facebook.com/goatinthemachine

The Traveler
G. Allen Wilbanks

No air, no food, no warmth. The traveler slept, remaining dormant and conserving what little reserves it had remaining. Its cocoon of rock hurtled through the black void, shielding the flagging life force within as it sought a new home, or oblivion.

Whichever came first.

The traveler was not afraid. Too tiny to hold enough consciousness to be self-aware, it merely hibernated as its fate was decided for it, blissfully unaware of time or distance during its journey.

A flare of white light and heat aroused the traveler, even as its protective encasement of rock was consumed around it. It was suddenly free and awake as it landed on its new home, with an impact that would have destroyed any less-resilient creature. Having no shell to crack, and no bones to break, the traveler spattered like a tiny puddle, then pulled itself back together.

Warmth, oxygen, and light suffused the traveler with

energy, bringing it fully alert. It moved along the ground, extending a narrow pseudopod, then dragging the rest of itself along behind. The traveler did not move with any urgency; it remained too tiny to effectively think or act with initiative. It was hungry, however, and it understood there was no food to be had where it currently sat. Instinct dictated that, if it wished to feed, it needed to move away from where there was no food to wherever food might await its arrival.

Direction had no meaning, either. One path was as good as another, so it crawled, if not with thoughtful determination, then at least with purpose.

The traveler touched an upright green spike with its extended foot. The spike rose from the ground, firmly rooted below the surface. As the new arrival to this unfamiliar place explored the anomaly it brushed more of its body against the spike, and it could feel that there was a life force within. Many living things provided nourishment, so this obstacle in its path was potential food.

Tasting the item by encircling it, the traveler tried to digest a small portion. Immediately it pushed away, repulsed. This life-form was unpleasant to ingest. Also, insufficient. The traveler slipped away and encountered more of the same stalks in its path. They were numerous and covered the ground in patches, but it now knew better than to try to eat any of them and paid them no further attention.

Something new and unexpected made its presence known moments later. Tentative touches along the traveler's sensitive surface drew its attention. The inquisitive thing touching it held much more life force within it than did the inedible spikes in the ground, but the traveler did not know yet if it would taste much better. A tendril extended from the traveler, spreading along the hard, outer layer of the creature. The maybe-food startled and tried to back away from the traveler's exploring pseudopod, but its retreat came too late. The traveler held fast; dragged along behind the creature as it made its frantic attempts at escape.

Pulling more of itself around the fleeing thing, the traveler realized this life-form was precisely what it had been seeking. It encircled its prey. Internal acids formed and went to work, liquifying the creature's softer organs and incorporating them into the traveler's own body. The hard shell encasing the traveler's victim remained intact, inedible, but rather than discard it the traveler chose to hold onto the rigid structure.

Legs could be useful. Walking would allow it to move faster than it had previously been able, creeping along the ground. The self-awareness of the creature the traveler consumed, though limited, suffused its own consciousness. There wasn't much to ingest from this one paltry being, but the mind of its tiny meal told the traveler there were many more like it. Thousands, in fact. An entire colony waiting for the traveler to find it and feed upon it. Using the now lifeless shell as a framework, the traveler shaped itself to best utilize its new legs, then scurried in the direction of more food.

A crack in the ground acted as an entrance to the underground hive. The traveler slipped inside and was identified immediately as an unwelcome trespasser. It began to feed as the inhabitants of the underground den reacted to the intrusion and attacked. Their tiny jaws offered no threat to an entity like the traveler, and there was nothing for their mandibles to grab or damage. Each would-be warrior was simply absorbed and consumed as it attempted to defend its home.

Minutes later the traveler oozed from the crack, dragging itself and thousands of its victims' lifeless bodies to the surface. It was much larger now; too large to form itself around any one of the tiny shapes. Instead, it arranged thousands of individual carcasses into a greater structure that mimicked the smaller design; a tri-segmented body supported above six slender legs. The traveler had become much more massive, and with its physical size its hunger also grew.

In addition to the growing hunger, the traveler felt a new urge developing deep within itself. Something tugged from the middle of its essence, encouraging it to pull apart; to replicate itself and form others. It resisted the pull. The desire to propagate was primal, deeply rooted, but the traveler's ability to reason increased with each conscious being that it consumed, and reason dictated that remaining intact right now was the proper course.

The hive-mind of the creatures it had recently consumed informed it that larger life-forms existed nearby. These would serve as much better prey, but in order to capture them the traveler could not be small and many. It must remain one, and continue to grow large enough to take full advantage of the greater resources.

Firming itself around its artificial internal structure, the traveler rose on its fabricated legs and moved onward, seeking larger game to satisfy its cravings.

At first it fed primarily on the smaller, furry animals unlucky enough to cross its path. The traveler was an opportunistic hunter, waiting for the unwary to stumble upon it rather than seek them out directly. As it consumed creatures containing more self-awareness, more intelligence, its own consciousness expanded. For the first time since arriving in this environment, it began to act with clear direction. The minds it absorbed all feared the larger animals in the area. They had spent their entire lives running and hiding from teeth and claws that would rend them into no more than bloody meat and fur.

The traveler felt the inherent fear and, at first, avoided these same larger animals, but as it continued to feed and grow it realized there was nothing to fear from these beasts. The traveler was not prey, not to anything it had so far encountered, and therefore it chose not to behave like prey. It was the ultimate predator in this environment, and would not shy from any confrontation.

Over the next several days the traveler captured and consumed all manner of beings that ran, crawled and flew. The collection of miniature outer shells was discarded in favor of larger, more sturdy internal structures collected from its new food sources. Six legs had become eight, then ten in order to support its growing mass. Eyes, ears, noses, and a pseudo-armor appeared over its surface, taking in the stimuli of its surroundings while similarly warding against any potential attacks. With the greater awareness of the world around it, nothing escaped the traveler's notice.

The traveler also enjoyed a new array of weapons it garnered from its victims. Long, sharp claws protruded from extended appendages along its body length, and several skulls containing jaws full of pointed teeth appeared in random locations to provide vicious, biting mouths whenever needed. It was a patchwork collection of undigested animal bones, and its own flesh shaped to mimic the creatures the skeletons had once supported. The traveler was a composite of all its meals, yet, overall, it appeared like nothing that had ever previously existed on the planet.

Three times since arriving on this new world the traveler had, at last, succumbed to its internal urge to divide. It had reached what it considered in its limited experience to be an optimal size. Before each split it had emptied itself of all unincorporated bits of the creatures it had absorbed, depositing the bones and teeth and claws on the ground and crawling away from the resulting pile. During each division the traveler flattened itself and shuddered in increasingly more violent waves; ripples rolled out from its center toward the edges of its mass until a hole formed in the middle. The opening widened and elongated, until it evenly divided the traveler into two equal halves.

There was no pain. Similarly, there was no pleasure or satisfaction in the act. It was merely an urge that needed to be acknowledged. Where there had once been only itself, there was now itself and an "other." When the division was completed the traveler pulled its remaining mass together and returned to its pile of treasures, gathering up discarded teeth, claws, and other supporting structures. At half its previous size the traveler did not need all the items it had collected, so it took only what it immediately desired and left the rest of the debris where it lay. The "other" was welcome to gather up what had been left behind.

In time food in the surrounding areas grew scarce, slowing its endless growth. The traveler consumed all that it found, and the surviving animals learned to be wary and avoid the new predator in their midst whenever possible. It was forced to expand the boundaries of its hunting grounds in order to continue to find viable prey, covering more distance each day yet finding less to eat.

Then came an encounter that would forever change the way it hunted.

While circling a small body of water in search of animals that might come to drink, the traveler encountered a creature it had never before come across.

The animal appeared from out of the dense brush surrounding the water. Snapping twigs and leaves crushed underfoot announced its presence long before the traveler saw it. This creature clearly considered itself a dominant predator, as it made no effort to conceal its presence from the other animals. It walked on two legs, but was not one of the flying things. It had no feathers. It wrapped itself in dead things, as it appeared to have no fur or scales of its own to protect its flesh.

The traveler watched as the unfamiliar animal walked to the pond and began pacing along the water's edge, looking for tracks or depressions in the mud. It was hunting. The traveler recognized the behavior, as it had been doing much the same thing only moments earlier. This was intolerable. There was little enough food in the area to sustain itself without having to share with this odd, two-legged predator. The thing must be confronted. Eaten, if possible, but if not then at least driven away.

The traveler rushed toward the new creature, its claws slashing through the air, its mouths snapping in anticipation of taking down this intruder.

The two-legged animal did not flee. It rose to its full height, raising up some sort of stick. It placed the stick to its shoulder and pointed the opposite end toward the traveler. Yes, this was a predator, and predators did not run. That was acceptable to the traveler. It had consumed many predators recently, many of them too foolish to run away.

A loud explosion sounded, and a flash of light emanated from the end of the stick. Something impacted the traveler's body. A heavy, metal pellet pierced its flesh, launched at incredible speed from the unknown predator's stick. Soft tissues parted from the impact, and one of the many, carefully collected bones broke into fragments as the pellet passed through it. The damage was surprising, coming so suddenly and from such a distance, but the injury did not slow the traveler. Nothing was injured that could not be replaced, and the malleable substance of its true body reformed as quickly as the metal ball tore it open.

The traveler continued its charge, unhindered, and crashed into the unwelcome hunter, bearing it to the ground. The stick emitted another roar of noise as the two enemies tumbled in the dirt, but the ejected metal ball flew harmlessly away.

Not that the traveler cared. It could have been a direct hit and it would not have changed the outcome of this struggle.

The traveler spread itself over the hunter, moving with the speed of flowing liquid as it engulfed its opponent. The creature tried to scream, but the traveler covered its face, oozing into the openings of its nose and mouth. It could feel the creature beginning to panic as it realized it could not breath, and could not escape.

Suffocation was not the goal, however. The corrosive digestive acids inside the traveler went to work on the creature now enclosed within its body. Flesh dissolved quickly under the assault, and in a matter of moments the two-legged predator's struggles faded to nothing as it succumbed to the inevitable. The traveler digested the creature, incorporating the flesh into itself, keeping the bones to be sorted through later, and discarding the dead wrappings that had covered the body.

The thing – the "man" it called itself – was intelligent, and the traveler felt its own consciousness expanding as it consumed the new lifeforce. The primal cunning, the hunger and instinct that had driven the traveler up to this point, resolved into true thought and reason. For the first time the traveler began to think beyond its immediate needs; for the first time it considered the future, and what its purpose on this planet might be.

This thing that walked on two legs, this "human," had been sentient, fully self-aware. Now, thanks to the consciousness it had ingested, so was the traveler. It looked around at its surroundings with new understanding of what it had so recently experienced. The growth surrounding the traveler was called a "forest," comprised of trees, bushes, and creeping vines. Beneath its feet was a carpet of the small spikes, "grass," that had been so unpleasant to eat when it first arrived. It had fed upon the "ants" that swarmed beneath the ground, then moved on to larger food such as mice and squirrels, before finally graduating to the greater predators in these woods: wolves and large cats.

Today, it had consumed the dominant predator here on "Earth." It liked the taste, and it reveled in the knowledge that thousands – no, millions! – more were available at its leisure. The foolish creatures congregated in large gatherings, called "cities." At least the ants had the common sense to build their homes underground. These "humans" were helpless, out in the open, waiting to be taken.

The traveler, using its newly acquired ability to plan and prepare, decided it would remain in this forest a little while longer. It would not be wise to simply march into the city and begin eating. The humans would band together, and it was possible they would figure out how to hurt the traveler. Perhaps even kill it. It was strong, but not invulnerable.

Going into the city alone would be foolish. It needed enough time to grow a bit larger, a bit stronger, then it would need to make others. The humans would work together, so the traveler must create others like itself and they must also work together if they were to thrive on this planet. When the time came, and the traveler was certain that it could comfortably face anything the humans might have to defend themselves, it would go to the city and take the others with it. They would eat. They would grow. They would multiply.

And when the city was empty, they would move on to the next one.

Then the next.

G. Allen Wilbanks
About the Author

G. Allen Wilbanks is a retired police officer living in Northern California. For twenty-five years he wrote collision and crime reports during the day to pay the bills and, during his time-off, he wrote short fiction to stay sane.

From an early age, he was drawn to dark fantasy and horror stories in movies, books, and every other form of media he could find. His childhood was relatively normal, so it is unknown just what emotional trauma led to his love of all things macabre.

He is a member of the Horror Writers Association (HWA) and his work has appeared in over 200 print and electronic publications all over the world. In the past two years, his short stories have featured in several internationally best-selling anthologies, including Worlds, Blaze, and Eerie Christmas, as well as Eerie River Publishing's own It Calls From the Forest and It Calls From the Sky. He is the author of two short story collections, and his most recent novel, A Life Of Adventure, was just released in

July of 2020. In addition to his fiction writing, he writes a weekly humor blog entitled, Deep Dark Thoughts, where he ponders life and why it apparently seems to hate him.

Website: www.gallenwilbanks.com
Blog: www.deepdarkthoughts.com
Amazon: www.amazon.com/author/gallenwilbanks
Facebook: www.facebook.com/gallenwilbanks/
Twitter: https://twitter.com/gallenwilbanks

FLICKERING
G.A. ALEXANDER

The video was already flickering as Alice expanded it to full-screen. It was something she had seen a million times over in different variations: A shaky handheld camera phone, filming a residential house as the screen filled with distortion and glitching.

Another one of these. She thought to herself as a short, distorted screech burst from her computer speakers, like some sort of digital bird cry.

In her three years working as a content moderator for Fly Night Media she'd learned to pick out the telltale signs of fraud. The scam was a clever one: certain cheap brands of mobile phones have cameras with variable light sensitivity, so drastic variations in the light being filmed (say, for example, someone off-camera flipping a light switch on and off) could cause digital distortions on video as it focused and unfocused. Instant 'glitch effects' were much less predictable than the After Effects templates she'd seen time and time again, but easily identified if you knew what to look for.

This camera's autofocus was in overdrive as the lights were strobing. As the image reached clarity for Alice could see that it was filming in what looked like a small kitchen. The light, coming from a fixture she could see overhead, was flickering on and off. As this continued she heard the shouting of several gruff voices, voices so loud that they were clipping the camera's audio.

"Hey! Hey, Mark! Mark!"

The camera, and camera operator, shuffled quickly through the off-white kitchen and into what looked like a living room. Within the center of the room stood three men.

No, stood two men.

The third was floating.

The floating man, presumably 'Mark', was a skinny, pale guy with a trucker cap and a Chevrolet t-shirt. He hung in the air and twitched slightly as the other two men, one a well built, sandy-haired guy in a jean jacket and the other a slightly portly man with a large, black beard, yelled at him. As the cameraman focused on his face the bearded man turned to the camera.

"The fuck you doing? We need help here, man!"

'Mark' shrieked, closing his eyes tight before suddenly opening them to reveal deep, black pupils. They began to leak, and streams of black fluid dripped from his cold, empty eyes. He began moving his lips, mumbling something Alice couldn't make out. He grinned as more black fluid began dripping from his lips, flowing past his chin and onto his t-shirt.

That's where the video ended.

Alice took a moment to grab a sip of her coffee, then hit "Play" again. The filename, *secret.mov*, faded out and back in as the video started over.

Fly Night Media got its start in the late 1970s as *Fly Night Radio*, a late-night AM dial talk show hosted by the legendary broadcaster Carl Phillips, who would go on to mainstream success later in his career as a Top 40 announcer. Fly Night Radio was a talk show for a discussion of the supernatural - ghosts, demons, UFOs, conspiracies and the various combinations of the above. Carl cut his teeth fielding calls from youth pastors to truck drivers to self-proclaimed 'occultists', each hoping for a precious few minutes live on the air to tell the world about their experiences with the unexplainable.

While Fly Night Radio was officially canceled when it lost its last affiliate in 1998, and Carl Philips himself had passed away in 2008 of pneumonia, the Fly Night Media company had lived on. As extremely early adopters of the internet they were in a unique position to pivot to modern web content. They did, taking advantage of the blog explosion of the early 2000s as the internet landscape turned more to socially-driven content curation.

That's where Alice found herself in her 28th year on Earth, in a fairly thankless job approving or deleting videos submitted by Fly Night audience members. Sifting through hour upon hour of airplane footage submitted under the auspices of being *A UFO, finally caught on film,* deleting video after video of rubber goblins, bad camera tricks, and Slender Man after Slender Man after Slender Man.

Alice watched the video three times in a row, attempting to figure out the trick. Normally 'floating' effects were somewhat easy to do: Some wire, a concealed harness and a little Final Cut magic made all the difference, but this was different. The camera work was so shaky and erratic that it would have taken hours, days even, of work to fix in post-production. It seemed like a lot of work for an untagged video submitted on a blank throwaway account.

After the third watch-through Alice glanced at the clock on her laptop. 4:45 pm.

I'll deal with this next week. She thought to herself.

⟡——⟡

5pm was always a busy time at Flanagan's Bar, and 5pm on a Friday afternoon was even crazier. Alice was surprised to find that, despite the Happy Hour rush, Kelsey had managed to save her a bar stool. Alice had always thought that Kelsey was a little too cool to be hanging out with her, but ever since they had met in a college literature class years earlier they had remained close.

"Heyyyy, happy Friday!" Kelsey exclaimed as Alice stepped into the bar. Kelsey's cheery and chipper nature was part of her personal, and professional, brand at this point.

"How's it going, babe?" Alice asked, pulling up to the bar stool Kelsey nodded at.

"Can't complain. You?"

"Same here, another day in paradise."

"Ooh, another vampire sighting in Spokane?" She joked. Kelsey was always a fan of the stories that came out of Fly Night Media.

"I wish. Just more fake-out videos. We always get a lot, but submissions have *really* gone up lately."

"Aren't they all fake, though?" Kelsey asked with a half-smirk on her face, pouring an IPA for the older man sat two seats down.

"Kinda? Some are fake, but some are regular things that people CONFUSE for supernatural. Then one or two end up being so weird they HAVE to be fake, but you can't figure out how." She paused. "There's this one I saw earlier today…absolutely crazy looking."

✦—◦—✦

Hours later Flanagan's was clearing out. It was a popular after-work spot, but was never really the center of nightlife in town. People came, drank a couple of beers and then shuffled off home. With only a couple of people dotted around the bar Kelsey's signature mischievous grin appeared.

"Okay, show me." She muttered.

"What?" Alice replied.

"Show me the video, the one you mentioned earlier."

Alice groaned. She ALWAYS did this.

"I can't do that again."

"Aww, c'mon."

"They're REALLY cracking down on us. There's all kinds of privacy…"

Alice was stopped in her tracks by Kelsey's second patented move: The sad puppy-face. Alice absolutely hated it, but being a few drinks deep she was in a particularly vulnerable mood.

"Okay, fine. Quickly." She mumbled, pulling her work phone out of her clutch.

◆━━◆

"Weird." Kelsey agreed after watching it.

"Yeah, and it was submitted anonymously so we've gotta make sure it's not copyrighted, or a clip from some indie movie no-one's ever seen. Or even some sort of prank."

"Some guys from a special effects school *doin' it for the 'gram*?"

"Ugh." Alice groaned, "We get something like that every other week at this point."

"I can imagine…Hold on, can you rewind it a bit?" Kelsey asked. Alice nodded, dragging her finger back across the play bar on the video app. She got to the part where all three men were visible in front of the camera.

"Stop."

"What?"

"See the guy with the beard."

"That guy?" Alice asked, pointing at the stocky,

bearded man.

"I know him. That's Mitchell Downing. He's been a regular here for years."

Alice stared at Kelsey.

"You know these guys?"

"Just that one, but…"

"What?"

"He's not the kind of guy that would make a video like this. Y'know, the fake-floating thing. He's an old-fashioned good-ol'-boy. All 'Yes Ma'am, No Ma'am', Jesus-freak who loves his mama type."

"Well, here he is. Maybe his friends are running the show, and he's just tagging along?"

"Maybe." Kelsey breathed, lost in thought for a second. "You wanna try asking him if it's fake?"

Alice pondered this for a second. It was a more personal investigation than she had ever put into someone's submission to Fly Night before, and certainly violated some of the many security agreements she signed before being onboarded. At the same time the mild curiosity she had experienced watching the video before had now exploded into something much stronger. Alice felt like she needed to know.

"You have his number?"

"Guy tried to ask me out once. Not my type though." Kelsey gave Alice a wink as she said it. "I keep a little collection around here somewhere." She pulled a stack of paper scraps and post-it notes out from a compartment under the bar and started flipping through them.

The phone rang three times, then went to voicemail. Mitchell's mailbox was full, according to the electronic voice on the other end of the phone.

Kelsey tried the number one more time and received the same result.

"Sorry." She offered.

Alice shrugged, unsure what to do.

◈──◦──◈

Alice knew she was dreaming, but unlike other moments, when she caught herself in the midst of a dream, she was not able to wake up or affect it in any way.

She stood in the kitchen, and it looked halfway between her own kitchen and the one from the video. On the sink sat three small crows, who were staring at her. One of the crows cawed, but the sound was distorted. Above her the light flickered slightly, the bright fluorescent color turning black. There was a metallic *thud* sound that repeated over and over again in a rhythm.

She stepped away from the crows and walked to the end of the kitchen, which, in the video, had connected to the living room. Instead of the living room she stood in Flanagan's Bar. Tall, featureless people stood around the room, their skin grey and their eyes were cold, black and empty.

A woman who looked like Kelsey, but was not Kelsey, was behind the bar. The woman was silently pouring beers into glasses, pouring those glasses into the sink, and then repeating the action. In the center of the room Mark floated, barely a half-foot off the ground, his eyes were bleeding black fluid and a noise escaped from his lips. Alice's stomach churned when she realized what Mark was muttering:

It was a secret.

He was whispering a secret over and over again, and if she wanted to be sure what it was Alice knew she would need to walk up to him and listen. Slowly, step by step, she made her way to Mark and leaned in to hear him. Mark, barely registering her approach, kept mumbling.

◆—◦—◆

Alice woke in a cold sweat. She pulled her phone off the charger dock and glanced at the time: 2:42am. She had only been asleep for three or four hours.

What was I just dreaming about? She wondered. There was something at the back of her mind…*something about crows? Whispers?* But it was gone, and her stomach felt queasy.

Alice's phone burst into life as her ringtone went off, and she glanced at the caller ID.

KELSEY

"Yo." She grumbled sleepily.

"Are you awake?" Kelsey replied, her voice dripping with excitement.

Alice pondered the question for a moment, then decided to disregard it.

"What?"

"I found Mitch's address. One of the other bartenders knows him."

"Oh." Alice paused, still trying to collect her thoughts and come to terms with the waking world. "You want to go now?"

"Fuck no, I've got an hour or so cleaning up this place before I can get out of here. What are you doing tomorrow?"

Alice thought for a moment. She had no plans at all for Saturday, so she told Kelsey as much.

"Great! Figure it'll be better to barge into some dude's home in broad daylight rather than three in the morning, right?"

"Sure."

"Awesome! Pick you up at eleven or so?"

Alice tried, but couldn't get back to sleep for the rest of the night. She booted up Netflix, watching episode after episode of The Office. She stared at the screen until light peered through the blinds on her bedroom window.

Her weary eyes were not quite ready for Kelsey's happy-go-lucky demeanor, which had somehow spilled out of the workplace and into the real world. Alice had no idea how she did it - working at a bar, working around alcohol, working around alcoholics, working till 4:00 am and still somehow showing up fresh-faced and happy to greet the world.

"Heya!" Kelsey waved at her from her car as Alice descended the three flights of stairs on the outside of the apartment.

"Hrmm." Alice managed as she reached Kelsey's car. If Kelsey was put off by Alice's demeanor she didn't show it at all.

◆──◇──◆

"Is this it?" Alice managed between swigs of the Americano she had purchased on the way. She was pointing at a small, nondescript house in a row of small, nondescript houses they were passing. Mitchell's neighborhood had been a housing development by a local real estate agency, who had kept every house on-model. While variations in paint and gardens existed, almost every house looked identical.

"147," Kelsey muttered, noting the house number. "Looks like it."

Parking on the street outside, the women made their way to the front door. It was as non-descript as the rest of the house: Off-white with a little chipping paint, a matching door frame and a plate near the top of the door stating the house number.

Alice rang the doorbell.

No answer.

"Of course." She sighed.

She rang again, adding a loud knock afterward for punctuation.

No answer.

They stood there for a moment in the beating midday sun. Alice felt an equal amount of relief and disappointment. There was a feeling of dread, deep in the pit of her stomach, but her curiosity about this situation had gotten the better of her.

"Well, what do you want to do now?" Alice asked Kelsey after a short pause.

Kelsey got that mischievous smile on her face again.

Thanks to a rock Kelsey found in the garden, the back bedroom window to Mitch's house was now a collection of glass shards littered across the carpet. Alice was horrified; she knew Kelsey was impulsive, but didn't realize that breaking and entering would be something she'd be so willingly up for.

"Y'know, Omelettes. Eggs." She had shrugged at Alice's open-mouthed shock before pulling herself into the house, narrowly avoiding the jagged shards still sticking out of the window frame. After some encouragement Alice followed.

The back bedroom was empty. The bed had been stripped down to a bare mattress, and the sheets were thrown on the floor. The dresser's top drawer was open, and an empty, black box was visibly poking out from a pile of socks. There were noticeable shoe prints on the carpet in the bedroom, which led out to the hallway outside. They followed them quietly, just in case someone else was in the house, but found no-one.

The house had an unhealthy feeling to it that made

Alice's skin crawl. Each light in the house was on, revealing that Mitchell's residence was dirty, very dirty. *Green wallpaper in EVERY room?* Alice wondered to herself. While his choice in decor was already suspect, the dirt and filth that caked every surface made it so much worse.

They soon found themselves in the kitchen, the one from the video. She paused for a second before looking around.

"I think…"

"Yup." Kelsey replied, knowing what she was about to say.

"What do you think actually happened?"

"I don't know. We could check out the living room where that floating scene was shot, I think it's just around the…" Kelsey's voice trailed off.

"What?"

"Wasn't it daytime when we came inside?"

Alice furrowed her brow. She didn't know what Kelsey meant. It WAS daytime, shortly before noon to be more specific.

She glanced out the kitchen window. The night and the stars glanced back.

"Fuck." Alice said.

"What's happening?"

A noise came from outside, the same static, digital bird cry she had heard from the video.

Above them the kitchen lights flickered.

"Let's get out of here."

Kelsey and Alice turned tail and hurried back. The

hallway seemed longer than before, and the dirty footprints on the carpet seemed to have been joined by more, of different sizes and shoe types. Every light they passed seemed to flicker and strobe in their presence, as if reacting to their proximity.

Finally they reached the bedroom from where they had entered, but it wasn't empty this time. Mitchell was there, sitting on the bed in the dark.

The stocky, bearded man stared at the two women. The light from the hallway didn't reveal much, but they could see that his face was twisted into an ecstatic smile.

"Mitch?"

Mitchell allowed his jaw to hang open, revealing the empty gape of his mouth. A single noise emerged from him: That same distorted bird call. It echoed from his mouth as his throat shook violently. The bedroom light flickered on by itself, revealing the man's form in full. Mitch's shirt hung in rags at either side of his torso. His chest had been torn open, and the ragged shreds of his flesh hung bloodlessly on either side of his torso among the fabric of his ripped shirt. Within his ribcage nested four small crows. They stared at Alice and Kelsey with black, empty eyes.

Mitchell stood up from the bed.

Alice and Kelsey ran.

Mitchell followed.

The halls outside the bedroom didn't resemble the ones they had just explored. Sure, they had the same carpet and dirty, green wallpaper, but the turns didn't match. The doors they passed didn't have the same molding or paint colors.

Mitchell was behind them, moving jerkily as if every muscle in his body was acting independently. The crows within his ribcage, disturbed by the movement of their host, were flapping their wings and screaming.

The lights were flickering constantly now. Alice and Kelsey turned a corner in the hallway, which should have led them back to the kitchen, but found only another hallway. As they ran down it, Alice looked back again. Mitchell had been close behind them, but she saw that he was gone now. The lights flickered again, and suddenly something else was there, just behind them. A tall, thin grey thing that barely resembled a person. Its eyes were black, and it watched as they ran.

They ran down the hallway as fast as they could. Alice knew she had to get them away from this place.

How could the hall be this long? She thought to herself. *This seems longer than the house could be.*

At the end of the long, twisting hallway they finally found themselves in the living room. Amy shuddered as she remembered the video: The two men shouting at the third, and the silent videographer who seemed more interested in capturing the moment than assisting. They had seen Mitchell in the bedroom and in the hallway, so it was possible the other men were somewhere in the house. She wondered if Mark was still there, hovering inches off the floor as he whispered unknowable things to his friends.

She turned to Kelsey, looking for some sort of reassurance from her, but there was none to be found.

Kelsey hovered slightly above the ground, deep, black

ooze trickling from her face. Her eyes sank into her head and turned black as pitch, while her lips began moving as black bile-smelling liquid ejected itself from her mouth.

Alice wanted to scream and scream and scream and scream.

She couldn't though; She could only make one noise.

The distorted call of a crow shrieked from her lips.

⟨⊷—∘—⊶⟩

Outside of Mitchell's house, Alice stood in the garden staring upward. The sky flickered like a broken lightbulb as something black and metallic congealed overhead.

They're arriving.

They've been arriving for some time now.

She glanced around. She looked at the trees, every branch now covered in crows. She looked at the tall, grey, misshapen things moving around in the shadows behind the house. Behind EVERY house.

I KNOW.

Her lips began to twist in that ecstatic smile she had seen on Mitchell back in the house. She could feel a stirring in her chest, like little wings beating in her heart. She felt such joy, the same joy Mitchell must have felt, the same joy Kelsey must be feeling.

The same joy she was sure everyone would soon feel.

THE SECRET IS:

THE LIGHT IS ALWAYS FLICKERING

AS WE CALL THEM HOME.

G.A. Alexander
About the Author

G.A. Alexander is a British-American writer based out of Seattle, WA. He is the author of the comic book Keepsakes, released in 2019. Along with writing, he has performed in bands such as Golden Gardens, The Vera Violets, and Push Button Press. You can follow him at @ ritual_83 on Twitter or his website at http://ritual83.rip

Raindance
Kimberly Rei

"Tropical storm Odalys looks to build into a hurricane over the next two days. If you haven't started yet you're going to want to board up, or plan to head out, folks. This one could get nasty."

Kara reached for the remote and muted the news without glancing up from the scattering of papers before her. It was the same thing every year; Each hurricane "could get nasty", and each one fizzled out once it made landfall. It wasn't that Kara didn't trust the weather experts - she just trusted the duplicitous nature of hurricanes more.

Maybe this time she'd get lucky, and it would strike while Greg was out. Storms always put him in a foul mood, so the bartender or the latest flavour-of-the-month could put up with him for a night. She could use the sleep.

She shuffled the papers around again, heart heavy as her fingers brushed the ashen edges. Pieces of her fell away with the crumbling of her work. There was enough to be salvaged, but Greg's latest tantrum was going to set her back weeks. She considered emailing her professor to ask for more time, immediately dismissing the notion. He'd scold her for not backing everything up digitally. He was a kind, generous teacher, but he couldn't grasp Kara's need to set pen to paper - to feel the words flow from her in ways a keyboard would never accommodate.

And she was ashamed to tell him what happened.

Rain spattered against the window, drawing her attention and raising hope. There was an emotion she didn't indulge in often. She let it snuggle into a warm blanket and tucked it into the back of her heart; There was no time for any of that. If Greg came home and found her sorting through this "waste of fucking time" he'd finish the job he started, and then he'd turn on her to vent what was left of his insatiable rage.

Shaking fingers tucked what was left of her final project into their folders and hid them in the laundry room, the one place he was guaranteed to never explore.

She had just settled onto the couch with a large mug of cocoa, complete with marshmallows and whipped cream, when the winds began to pick up. Tension Kara was all too used to carrying eased, and she burrowed deeper into the overstuffed pillows. Her gaze slid to the obnoxious painting over the fireplace. Traditional and ostentatious, just as Greg liked it, just as she had once dreamt of. He sat in a leather, wing-backed chair, his legs properly and quite masculinely crossed. She stood behind him in a tailored skirt and prim top, complete with pearls and one loving, supportive hand on his shoulder. The very image of an up-

and-coming politician.

Kara sipped at the cocoa and considered adding a spike of amaretto, but opted not to. He'd smell it on her.

The first time he came home and found her enjoying a drink wasn't the first time he'd hit her. It was, however, the first time he broke something. Her lip, to be precise. She'd needed five stitches, and something a good deal stronger than the glass of wine that caused the fuss. She had been surprised how much a split lip could hurt, and even more surprised at the variety of foods she suddenly had no interest in eating.

Her lack of calling for police assistance or running home to her mother emboldened him, so suddenly any perceived slight brought waves of fury.

Kara had loved storms for as long as she could remember. Her mother told her tales of her dancing in utero every time the sky roared. "It was your music, which was, of course, lovely. Unless I was trying to sleep." This was always with a warm smile and a hand to her belly, as if she could still feel her baby shift.

Storms took on a new meaning when Greg was in a mood. No rain, just the thunder of his voice and the lightning that came with blinding pain. Never to the face, though, not after that first time. Greg was running for office, and needed a wife who appeared perfect in all ways. He did apologize each time he lost his temper, and if he managed to send her to the hospital he'd hire a maid for the week and bring her lovely gifts. The longer it took her to heal the more luxurious his apology; She couldn't remember the night that won her a long-coveted trip to Italy.

Kara uncurled and wandered to the kitchen to refresh her cocoa. Her gaze slid to the double pantry doors. She couldn't walk into the room without at least glancing at those doors, which is exactly how Greg wanted it. More than one interview had been done in the house, but he wouldn't let journalists into the kitchen. They weren't allowed to film anywhere but the living room, a pristine island in a house full of reminders.

The doors stared back at her, dispassionate and silent. They were a shade of cream, a rich, deep colour that played nicely off the greys of the cabinets and the gunmetal of the appliances. He'd been amused at her choice of decor, leaning on the "gun" part of the style. It was early enough that she'd dismissed such odd quirks, as they lived in Texas. One door was crisp and clean while the other played a continuous role in her nightmares.

Dark browns, with streaked hints of red, were smeared up and down the wood. Part of the center was splintered and dented. A single handprint taunted, reminding her of the night she burned his dinner. It was so cliche, and so pedantic, that every mournful movie about an abused woman involved a ruined meal. Her hand tightened on her mug, cheek pulsing with remembered agony. The door handle was knocked loose, but he wouldn't let her fix it.

When he was in a particularly nasty mood he'd follow her into the kitchen, leaning against the wall and eyeing the handle until she followed his stare. He stayed until she needed something from the pantry so he could watch her shaking hand reach out. At that point he would chuckle and stroll out, content he'd ensured dinner would be up to his standards. It was a macabre scene, and she knew how to play her role.

She had returned to her cozy spot when the winds started howling. She closed her eyes to listen, savouring the rise and fall. There was a growing rhythm to it, a pounding that lulled her into a soft place. Not quite asleep, not quite awake, she lingered somewhere in between. The wind's relentless pulse became hooves landing on the wet shore. The thunder melded into growling voices, calling out to each other as they rode hard for...

Her phone rang, and she nearly threw her mug. His voice purred in her ear, and for a moment she remembered why she fell so hard and fast for him.

"Hello, my beautiful girl. Looks like I'm not going to make it home tonight. You good?"

Kara put a loving smile in her voice, tampering down the glee she couldn't let him hear, "Oh yes, I'm fine. Curled up with a mug of cocoa, listening to the rain."

"I know how much you hate storms. Get to bed early and sleep through it. I don't imagine it will amount to much," there was a pause and her back spasmed, dreading her next line "What are you?"

There it was.

"Your good girl."

"Of course you are." He clicked off without another word, but Kara kept her phone close.

Two minutes passed before it rang again.

"Tell me."

"I love you, Greg."

"Of course you do."

She sighed and set her phone on the coffee table. The urge to jump up and dance was overwhelming. She'd have an entire night to herself, free of fear. For a moment Kara considered running. She'd thought of it before, of course, but Greg not only had every part of her life and identity locked down, he had her mother fooled. Running would either destroy that relationship or destroy her mother; Or both. The idea threatened to crush what little joy she had in that moment, so she pushed it aside.

Instead she pulled out her folders and once more spread them on the dining room table. She smiled as her fingers stroked the title page. *The Wild Hunt and Its Place Throughout History and Culture.*

Her professor had raised a brow when she submitted her idea. He warned her that it was a huge topic, one with few truly scholarly works. There were so many variations that she could get bogged down in all of it and lose her focus, but it was a chance she was willing to take.

Kara opened her notebook and began transcribing the pages Greg had thrown in the fire. Rage stirred within her, but she set it aside and kept her mind on her work. Two hours passed before she looked up; Two hours, then a sudden loss of power. The house went momentarily dark, and then the back-up lighting kicked in. Not enough to work by, but enough to not run into anything.

The rain was pounding at the house now, trying to

tear siding away and punch through windows. She had just finished stacking her pages, ready to hide them away again, when she heard his voice. It was faint at first, and she couldn't be sure what she was hearing.

And then it was all too clear.

"KARA! KARAAAAAAA!"

Greg.

She twitched the curtains aside just enough to look out the window. He stood in the middle of the front lawn, swaying and soaked. One hand clutched a familiar bottle as he bellowed her name again. She reached for the door handle, that small voice in the back of her mind begging her to stop.

"Kara, baby, come dance in the rain with me!"

She stood in the open doorway, "Greg, what're you doing?"

She ducked as he hurled the bottle at her. When it struck the side of the house and exploded, the skies flashed black. Her ears were ringing, but the sound of hooves returned. It was louder, and growing more so.

Greg was shouting again, but she only heard random words. He wanted her to dance. He wanted to fuck her on the lawn. He was angry and ecstatic at once, drunk and out of his mind on cocaine. The question of what he'd been up to rose, swiftly followed by survival instinct. She was frozen in place, sure that if she didn't move he wouldn't either.

Thunder shook the world again, and rational thought stirred. Thunder was rare in a hurricane; So was lightning, but the sky was frenzied with flashes of blinding light. She could taste the ozone, and an underlying tang of freshly-turned earth.

Her head began to pound. There was too much happening at once, too much demanding her attention, too many threats from too many directions. Going into the house wasn't an option: It wasn't smart to run from a predator.

Kara took her eyes off her maddened husband and stared into the boiling clouds. One hand fumbled for the door frame for balance. There was movement up there, too, orchestrated and pure to the storm. She couldn't pull away from the cadence as it began to gel, and her mind skittered in terror.

The thunder wasn't thunder at all; It was the slamming of hooves. The lightning too was a false translation, and each crack was a weapon glowing in the light they wrought.

Horses, larger than sanity allowed, hammered down from the storm, following their own path and heading straight for the house. Crimson eyes glowed in skulls bare of flesh, and powerful bodies covered in tattered, torn hide showed bone and fire peeking through. Where flaming hooves struck an invisible trail shadow and smoke followed.

If the horses threatened reality then their riders broke it entirely. Clad in armour, neither matching nor complete, they rode with one hand on their mount's neck. They needed no reigns, and their other hand swung an axe or mace. Kara watched one draw back a bowstring. The rider turned to look at her, nodding once as he loosed an arrow the size of a lance. It landed on her lawn, precisely halfway between her and Greg.

A line in the sand.

Greg's ranting stopped, and he shook his head in confusion. He looked to her, then up, and even through the cacophony she could hear him squeak.

The Wild Hunt. She was watching the Wild Hunt tear past her home, and elation warred with desperation. They were real, and she would spend the rest of her life carrying the memory of their terrifying glory. But they were leaving, and when they were gone Greg would find a way to blame her. To hurt her; To maybe end her this time.

Except they weren't leaving, not all of them. Three broke away and slowed enough to whirl a circle around Greg, keeping him in place. He had begun to chatter, waving his hands at them as if to drive them off. A fourth rider stepped into the circle. The horse halted, shadow pouring from nostrils as it stomped at the ground.

Greg cringed back.

The storm raged on, destroying his words even as they left his lips. The woman who slid from the back of the stallion had no such problem.

"Gregory Brocken, you have been judged."

Her voice didn't so much rise above the thunder as cut through it. Even-toned, lyrical, mythic. From the porch Kara felt the pull, and she took one step forward.

White hair whipped around the woman's face as she

turned her gaze toward the house, and where there should be eyes vast depths called. The face danced between youth, maturity, and age, over and over. Maiden, Mother, Crone. She wore a sheer, white gown and what must have once been a heavy winter cloak. Empty eyes returned to Greg.

"Kings bow before me,
Death turns away.
I have always been,
And shall always be."

The remaining riders raced above, echoing the circle shredding her lawn. As they drew closer Kara could see dogs, saliva running down their jaws, and there were fierce, bare-chested women among the Hunt. They howled in victory, driving the storm higher. At the back of the infernal parade, the lost and condemned reached out from spiked cages, their arms shredded from wounds that would never heal. They were criminals the Hunt had collected as they tore through history. Their bodies were gaunt, caught in eternal starvation. A few of the wraithed faces looked familiar, but it was hard to be sure in the driving rain.

One finger, taloned and malicious, raised, drawing her attention back.

"But you, Gregory Brocken, you are no longer."

She pointed at him, and dread swept over Kara. She was still frozen in place, but for far different reasons now. The Crone snapped her fingers and four riders, all women, descended. Whips snapped out, each ending in a glistening, sharp hook. Wet leather lashed around Greg's wrists, the hooks driving through his flesh. His ankles followed.

He screeched, yanking on each limb with a panic only the doomed understand. The pain had yet to register, so ragged and overwhelming was the terror.

The Maiden turned to Kara, her voice the only sound, "Be worthy."

The Mother climbed onto the deathly-still stallion. The beast leapt into the air, taking the lead of the Hunt.

Greg lifted off the ground, screaming Kara's name as the viragos spiraled upward. Kara met his gaze. She was staring at him, trying to remember why she'd ever loved him, when the women broke in four separate directions.

The man who brutalized her vanished, leaving behind the young and vibrant boy she'd fallen for. Fear glazed his eyes and made him slack-jawed; Pain twisted his forehead as he hung from the hooks. Ghosts and spectres swirled around him, jabbing out with glowing spears, and his joints were starting to split under the pressure. He was sobbing, the sounds carried away in the wind, but the torment was clear in every line of his body. The four warriors raised a fist, and called a command to their mounts.

Kara clenched her hands together and forced herself to watch. This was happening for her, so she could do no less than honour the Hunt by bearing witness.

The moment Greg split apart, into precise quarters, the rain turned to hot blood and the sky echoed his despair. Wet pieces of him landed on the lawn, but the quarters themselves hung from the hooks, waving behind their riders. For the fleeting space between one heartbeat and the next, Greg's revenant lingered. It was a twisted, ugly creature. It hissed and lunged, features breaking to madness as it was ripped away and shoved in a cage. Her last image as the Hunt took to the storm was that of his soul, reaching like the others, savage and desperate.

Kara stepped back into the house. In moments the storm had blown itself out, leaving behind a soothing calm.

KIMBERLY REI
ABOUT THE AUTHOR

When Kimberly Rei was five years old, her parents gifted her with a set of Children's Classics that she had no hope of reading. Yet. Sitting at the Christmas tree, surrounded by dozens of beautiful hardcovers, she was giddy with the potential of one day diving into the pages. That love of words and hunger for stories has never wavered.

Kimberly has been featured in more than a dozen anthologies. Her tales lean creepy and aim to leave you with an unsettling urge to look over your shoulder. She is, like most authors, working on a novel, but an addiction to micro-fiction is keeping her on her literary toes, chasing paper dragons.

Always seeking new ways to make words dance, she has taught workshops and edited novels for Authors You May Recognize.

Kimberly currently lives in Tampa Bay, Florida, with her bladesmith wife, a circle of creative friends, and an abundance of gorgeous beaches to explore. Life is good!

http://tales.studiorei.org/

https://www.facebook.com/ReiTales/

https://twitter.com/SeersDaughter

https://www.instagram.com/theseersdaughter/

GODSPORE
MARC SORONDO

It was late at night when the light exploded in the north sky and then shot across the heavens, leaving a luminous green trail behind. It seemed almost to growl as it passed overhead, and to roar when it hit the Earth over the southern horizon.

The small band of Aurignacian hunter-gatherers watched it with their mouths open, their hearts full of fear and confusion. They knew the sky and the stars; comets and meteors were nothing new to them, but this was something else.

They went to the elder.

<+————+>

The old man stayed deep in the cave, where it was warmest, lit by a small fire and surrounded by images of animals rubbed onto the walls with colored clay and ground-up beetles.

His long hair was white as the freshly fallen snow, and his face was brown and weathered, lined with wrinkles and crevasses like the side of an ancient mountain.

By the dim light of the fire his eyes seemed to glow with wisdom. The old man was revered, for the tribe knew his immense importance: though the body deteriorates, the mind grows more powerful.

They went to him and asked him about the roaring light in the sky.

The elder shook his head. He closed his eyes for a moment. "I have a memory," the old man started. "I was a young boy, too small to be a part of it, but old enough to remember."

He opened his eyes and scanned the people gathered around him: brave hunters who wore their scars like ornaments, mothers with bellies curved like that of the first goddess, little children destined to keep this memory for their descendents the way the old man had.

"I was old enough to remember the stories and the bodies of dead brothers that returned. I was old enough to know that the hunters had saved us all that day, even you who were not yet born. Light flashed across the sky like a star fallen to Earth, but the light roared like the cave lion and growled like the wolf pack. The light hides the pod. It is the Godspore, sent from above to seed this world with new deities, dark deities."

The mothers gasped, the hunters grunted, and the children watched the old man in awe.

"The hunters went to face the newborn god, to kill it

while it was still weak. Many died at the hands of the dark one, but the hunters fought bravely, pleasing the first goddess, and she smiled upon them and gave them strength."

There was a moment of complete silence in the cave.

"Now the Godspore falls again, and hunters must be sent. The new god cannot be allowed to grow into power, or it will be the end of us all."

The elder paused and considered the darkness at the mouth of the cave.

"Four must be sent, one for each of the four winds. Some of you will die, but your death will be that of the great bear in winter, destined to wake at some distant thaw."

All of the tribe's hunters stepped forward. Ten men stood before the elder, and he looked each one over. "He of the hair like hot embers…" A young man, his hair a brilliant shade of red, stepped forward, separating himself from the other hunters. "He of the bear claw…" Another man, this one older and marked by long, thick scars across his chest, stepped forward. "He of the stone axe…" Another man, the youngest of all the hunters, stepped forward.

The old man examined the remaining choices by the dancing light of the fire. "He of the eyes like water…" The final hunter stepped forward, his blue eyes shining in the firelight.

"Journey south, and find the seed. The infant god must die. You hunt now to protect your families, your people, and even the first goddess. Fight for her, and she will smile upon you."

The chosen four looked at each other. The elder had not chosen the most experienced or biggest, nor had he chosen he of the hair like night, the best hunter in the tribe.

◆━━◆

Red Hair and Bear Claw went armed with wooden spears and antler daggers. Blue Eyes had a bone dagger and a wooden club. Stone Axe carried his namesake weapon, a hand axe made of chipped stone that was strong and sharp.

They left that night and headed south by the light of a crescent moon. The wolves, thinking the hunters were off to kill a mammoth and would leave tasty scraps of flesh behind, followed them.

"How do we kill a god?" Blue Eyes asked.

"The way you kill a deer," Bear Claw answered. "Draw its blood, pierce its hide."

Stone Axe shook his head. He had seen most animals, and he'd seen pictures drawn of others, but he had never seen a god, not even a picture of one. He doubted killing a god was like killing a deer.

◆━━◆

They walked until the sun began crawling up out of the sea. Then they laid down in a small circle, just beside the dozing pack of wolves, and slept for a few hours.

Once the sun had reached the very top of the sky, Blue Eyes woke. He looked around, expecting to see the inside of the cave system that had sheltered their tribe for generations. Once the shock of open space had worn off, he roused the other hunters.

Their grumbles of displeasure caused the ears of the wolves to prick up, followed quickly by their heads, which followed the hunters as they headed off again.

The alpha male stood and trotted after the hunters, and the other wolves followed.

They saw the smoke just as the sky began to split into reds and pinks and purples. There was a large fire ahead.

"The wolves are upset," Bear Claw said.

"How do you know?" Stone Axe asked.

"Look at how they move, weaving back and forth amongst each other, snapping at each other if they get too close."

Stone Axe nodded.

As they approached the smoke they found a forested stretch of land, running up between a craggy mountain on one side and a shallow stream on the other. The smoke was rising from deep within the wood, and the air was filled with the scent of burning trees.

The wolves whined and howled, falling behind the hunters with their tails between their legs and their backs arched.

As the hunters entered the wood the wolves turned and ran back the way they had come.

Bear Claw turned to watch the animals sprint away. "They know better," he said.

"They are afraid," Red Hair said.

"As am I," Blue Eyes said.

There was a moment of silence before Bear Claw cleared his throat and said, "I am the oldest here. I have seen the most, and there is no place for fear in the hunt. A fearful hunter is dead. Only the fearless can become great."

"Some of us will die," Stone Axe said.

"To wake again refreshed, like the great bear after a winter slumber," Red Hair said.

Bear Claw nodded in agreement. "The first goddess, she who gave birth to the earth and the sky and to all of the other gods, she will care for us as a mother for her children…in victory or in death."

Blue Eyes grunted and nodded.

Stone Axe held up his weapon. "May our ancestors give us strength, may the animal spirits give us power…"

"May the gods hunt with us today," they finished in unison.

Stone Axe had considered the prayer for the dead, but had chosen the prayer for the hunt instead. It did them all good. Empowered, they advanced towards the infant god.

⊷—⊶

Amidst the flames, surrounded by broken trees and half buried in the earth, they found the seed. It was round and smooth as a river stone, the color of slate, and big enough to house a tribe.

Bear Claw moved around it, and the flames, in a wide arch. "It has already hatched," he said, pointing at it.

When the others joined him they found an opening in the smoothness of the seed.

Blue Eyes fell to the ground, examining the dirt and the leaves of the ferns. He moved around without direction for a bit before grunting, crawling towards the east for a few feet, and then pointing. "It's moving towards the east."

They moved slowly then, Blue Eyes in front, following a subtle trail that the others could not discern. They crossed the stream, and on the far side Blue Eyes found the trail again.

◆━━━◆

They saw the dark god in the distance. It was making its way across a field, heading away from them at a slow pace.

"Now we hunt," Bear Claw said.

They sped up, running on the balls of their feet, Bear Claw in the lead. They moved like a pack of wolves, of one mind and one purpose.

The new god stopped and turned, as if it had heard them. It was armored like a black crab, its plates glistening in the light of the rising moon. It was as tall as a bear, and stood on two legs like a man. Its hands ended in three-fingered claws. Eyes the color of jade glowed above a mouth full of thin teeth, like bone sewing needles.

"Fear nothing, brothers!" Bear Claw yelled as he lifted his wooden spear.

The dark god responded unintelligibly. It's voice was like the screeching of the bat, the howl of the wolf, and the roar of the lion all at once.

Bear Claw threw his spear. It flew through the air, straight and strong, and all of the hunters could see that the strength of Bear Claw's ancestors was in that throw. Truly the first goddess had smiled on them.

The spear struck, hitting the god in its armored chest. It fell to the ground.

Then the dark god stood, and it came towards them.

◂—○—▸

The hunters found that their spears could not penetrate the armored hide of the new god, and that their arms could not force their dagger points through the black plates.

The god reached out and grabbed Red Hair by the face, wrapping its three long, clawed fingers around his head. The hunter screamed, and beat against the god's arm with his fist. Then, feeling a soft spot at the wrist, a joint between two plates of obsidian shell, Red Hair stabbed his antler dagger into it.

Though his vision was blocked by the clawed hand Red Hair felt the tip of his weapon penetrate, and heard the cry of the dark god; it was a sound like thunder and wailing.

Red Hair smiled, expecting the injured god to drop him. He was smiling still when the three fingers closed into a fist, crushing his skull.

Bear Claw, Blue Eyes, and Stone Axe watched the dark god drop Red Hair's body, and they knew that the hunter's spirit had left.

The dagger still protruded from the black wrist. The wound oozed a thick slime, dark and flecked with iridescence.

"Strike where it is weak," Bear Claw said as he dashed towards the creature, Blue Eyes and Stone Axe following close behind.

The dark god caught Bear Claw, and the experienced hunter attacked with his dagger, seeking another weak point.

Stone Axe threw himself at the infant god and swung his weapon with all of his strength. The heavy ax hit the armor and broke through it, with an explosive crack like a lightning bolt.

The god screamed again. It lashed out at Stone Axe, but Blue Eyes got in its way, taking the blow meant for the younger man.

"Kill it," Blue Eyes said. He coughed, and blood splashed out onto his lips and chin. He reached down and held on to the arm that had been plunged into his abdomen.

Stone Axe brought his blade down on the dark god's arm, hitting the soft spot at the elbow and severing it completely.

Blue Eyes smiled at Stone Axe and said, "Until

spring." He fell back, the god's claw still buried in his belly, and died.

Bear Claw stumbled back when the infant god let go.

It reached out for Stone Axe, a deep rumbling erupting from its throat.

Bear Claw jumped onto the god's back, wrapping his free arm around its neck, and stabbed his dagger deep into its right eye.

The god bellowed and shook, tossing Bear Claw into the tall grass.

The god's leftover eye went back and forth between Bear Claw and Stone Axe. The dark god reached up with its remaining hand and plucked the dagger from its eye.

Bear Claw and Stone Axe ran at the god at the same time.

The clawed hand lashed out and the dark god shoved two of its talons into Bear Claw's eyes, just as Stone Axe brought his blade down on the center of its face.

Bear Claw and the dark god fell in unison, one still in the grasp of the other. Stone Axe let go of his weapon, accepting that it was too stuck in the hard exterior of the face to free it.

He looked around at the bodies of his tribesmen, and at the strange shape of the infant god of evil.

He took a long look at the god, committing its features to memory. He would go back and draw it on the wall of the caves, noting the weak points and the effectiveness of heavy stone weapons. He would make sure that the tales of the dark god would be passed down, that his descendents knew what it was and how to kill it.

Stone Axe turned and headed back to his tribe, alone and empty-handed, his mind full of horrors for the cave walls.

Marc Sorondo
About the Author

Marc Sorondo lives with his wife and children in New York. He loves to read, and his interests range from fiction to comic books, physics to history, oceanography to cryptozoology, and just about everything in between. He's a perpetual student and occasional teacher. For more information, go to MarcSorondo.com.

FAITHLESS
M. A. HOYLER

Elias Ober didn't believe his daughter Molly when she came back from the forest, jabbering about hearing a strange sound and seeing something moving in the trees. She already had an overactive imagination, and the fact that her mother, Faithful Ober, hadn't fully cooled in the grave yet didn't help. Instead Elias scolded Molly for leaving the babe by itself in the yard while she chased her fantasy into the surrounding woods, reminding her that, without his mama, Baby Abner would need his sister to take care of him while Elias worked the rocky fields. It was nearly harvest time, and the loss of Faithful came as a blow that Elias did not have time to truly consider.

Not that he was a man given to sitting and thinking, for he knew that idle hands are the Devil's playground. The itinerant preacher wasn't due to pass through for another few weeks, so Elias had buried Faithful himself in the round clearing in the trees where nothing else would grow, and said a few words and what prayers he remembered at the wooden cross that marked the grave. He intended that, if he had his work done before the daylight ended, he'd go and sit awhile next to the grave. So far there had been too much work to do.

In just a few more months the Ober family would have lived on their land long enough, and Mr. Erwin would sign it over to Elias. Until then the harvest had to come in, and preparations for winter had to be made.

"But Papa, there's something out there!" Molly cried. "I saw it."

"You saw some kind of animal, Molly," he replied. "Probably nothing more than a squirrel."

Molly rubbed her ear where his fingers had pinched. "I know what a squirrel looks like, Papa!"

He growled, "Go, there's chores to do, child!"

Molly fled to the lean-to where their ox, goats, and few chickens rested.

Elias stood from the knee he'd rested on the ground and ran a hand through his thinning hair. Baby Abner sat on a blanket his mother had sewn together from scraps when she'd made winter dresses for herself and Molly, and Elias watched Molly's retreating back. At eight winters she was getting older and taller, and soon he'd need to think about how he was going to get clothing for her.

As far out as the Ober land was from the nearest town (and in truth, Elias and Faithful had planned it that way), Elias knew his odds of finding another wife before the hard winter winds blew were not good. As it was he wasn't sure he could trust the babe to Molly long enough to make the three-day journey and sell the extra harvest.

Sighing, he picked up Baby Abner and carried him back into the one-room cabin he'd built with the help of his distant neighbors.

At supper that night Molly kept her peace, but her silence had become a constant companion. Before her mother's death Molly had been fond of singing, not loudly, but just to herself or her brother. Elias found that he missed it as he balanced Abner on his lap, feeding the babe and himself in equal measure. Molly gobbled down everything on her plate before beginning the task of cleaning up without being reminded.

The babe was, thankfully, a solid sleeper. When he'd been alive no more than a month he'd already been sleeping through most of the night, so once Elias laid him in the hand-carved cradle, which Abner was already outgrowing, he knew the child wouldn't stir until morning. Molly climbed up the ladder to her sleeping platform, while Elias sat by the banked fire and stared into the shifting embers. After a while he also crawled into bed, but found himself unable to sleep, instead rolling over to watch the flames once more.

Abner stirred once or twice, and a night bird called outside. Something rustled through the trees that reached over the cabin, then thumped onto the roof, more loudly than the usual squirrel or racoon.

Elias rolled to his back, the ropes creaking beneath him as his eyes followed the soft scratching of whatever night-time animal crawled above him. It stopped moving just above where he reckoned Molly was sleeping, and the sounds changed from scratching to an insistent scraping sound.

When the noise changed again, this time to the shredding of the shingles, Elias slid out of bed and climbed the ladder. He'd been right about where the animal clawed at the roof. Just below the shriek of the wood, Molly lay curled into a tiny ball underneath her mother's dress. Balling up his fist Elias struck the spot on the inside of the roof, and the digging noises stopped. Something large crawled to the eastern edge, and then it was gone.

Elias gathered Molly in his arms and made his way carefully down the ladder. She stirred only slightly as he lay her in the bed that he and Faithful had once shared.

Before going into the field the next morning, Elias leaned the ladder against the side of the house and climbed up, the scent of burned bread from Molly's attempt at breakfast drifting through the roof to his nose. He found the animal's tracks quickly — shallow gouges in the soft wooden shingles, from underneath that odd tree to where it had been trying to claw through the roof. Elias considered himself a practical man, and not given to flights of fancy, but he couldn't help imagining that whatever animal had been on top of his home that night had known exactly what it was after. He observed the neat cross-hatch of claw marks that ran straight through layers of the roof. In fact, now that he looked closely, Elias saw how near the animal had come to breaking through.

Before going back inside for breakfast Elias used a

few of his remaining, precious nails to attach new shingles over the hole.

"I had a dream last night," Molly said as she poured his cup of coffee and set it on the table.

"You did?" Elias asked, wanting to humor the girl a bit, after his vitriol of the day before.

"I dreamed about Mama," Molly said, her voice barely louder than the hiss of the fire.

Baby Abner sat on the floor, chewing happily on a piece of dried apple. Elias grunted at this, his thoughts still on whatever creature had tried to invade their house.

"It's getting colder," he announced. "You can sleep downstairs with me, from now until spring."

"Yes, Papa," Molly said, a bit of disappointment leaking into her voice.

❖──○──❖

He took both children out to the fields with him that day, Molly to work and Abner strapped to his back. Their nearest neighbor, William, arrived with his sons Arthur and Benjamin. He nodded once to Elias before they began to work.

The field was rocky, and wasn't good for the wheat Elias had wanted to grow, but the corn had done very well. At the recommendation of the innkeeper Faithful had insisted that they plant squash, which had also prospered.

With William, Arthur, and Benjamin's help, the corn crib Elias had built that summer filled with ears of corn.

They placed the squash on the floor.

"I was hoping to get a root cellar dug," Elias said to William.

"Plenty of time for that still," William replied. "There's some space in ours, if you need it."

"And walk a mile and a half to get our supper?"

The men shared what might have passed for a laugh between friends.

"How's the little one?" William asked, meaning Abner.

"Too small to even notice the difference," Elias replied, hoping it was true.

William looked up and called to his sons. "We'd best be headed back before those clouds burst," he said, indicating the gathering dark clouds above them.

"Thank you for your help," Elias said.

They shook hands.

The rain arrived about an hour later, while Elias was chopping firewood. He paused, hearing the oncoming rush before the deluge began. Cold rain ran down his neck, soaking Elias to the skin. The animal lean-to was closer than the closed door of the house, and he stepped into its shelter. The goats *maa'd* at the intrusion, but the chickens seemed not to care. In the back the ox mooed softly.

Stomping his feet Elias held his axe down by his side, staring through the gray curtain of rain that hid the entrance of the cabin. The pounding of raindrops on the roof drowned out any sound. A shadow of light showed where Molly had opened the door to the house, her small silhouette barely visible against it. She may have called to him, but he could not hear. The light and her shadow disappeared a moment later.

Elias sat on the edge of the food trough, hands tucked into his armpits while watching the rainfall. He was shivering by the time it lessened enough for him to see the shape of the cabin in the shadows.

He bent, wrapping his hand around the worn handle of his axe, and stood slowly. The late afternoon sun cut through the slow rain, revealing the familiar shapes of the small yard, the woodpile, and the newly built corn-crib. Something moved in the space between him and the house, something that jerked like the hands of a broken clock.

Elias squinted, his grip tightening around the wooden handle.

A sunbeam cut through the clouds, lighting up the yard in a warm glow. Something that might have been a person lurched ungainly across the yard, moving on stiff legs. The light flashed off its shimmering skin.

As it reached the cabin door Elias broke free from whatever spell had paralyzed him.

He shouted, lunging out into the rain. The creature turned slowly towards him, bringing a too-long arm to deflect his ax blade. Metal struck metal, and the intruder half fell away from Elias, already turning to retreat to the woods.

The smell of deep earth and rotting meat hit Elias's nose, and he stumbled back. Swallowing down bile he swung the axe over his head, bringing it down onto the creature.

Matted and tangled hair ripped as the axe took it, part of it falling away to the ground while the rest stayed on the bleached, white skull his blow had revealed. The animal stumbled, screamed, and spun. A clawed paw caught Elias across the cheek, sending him sprawling against the wall of the cabin.

Claws grasped either side of his face, twisting it upward. The falling raindrops blinded Elias as pain dragged down to the sides of his nose. One of the fingers stabbed towards his eyes, and he closed them instinctively. Axe gone, he tried to pry the thing's grip off. The awful scream sounded again, this time drawn out from a wordless shriek into something that might have been his name.

He couldn't grip the cold, slippery limbs, so Elias reached for the eyes he couldn't see. His fingers slid across skin as smooth and hard as stone, then there was the sticky touch of wet flesh. The creature released its grip and moved its head back, out of his reach, and Elias fell into the mud.

"Papa!" Molly's frantic shout brought him out of a daze. Elias sat, spitting water and mud. The axe was only a few inches from his hand and he snatched it up. He couldn't stand upright, instead falling onto one knee, his grip on the smooth, wooden handle the only thing that kept his face out of the dirt.

Molly's small hands were on him, pulling him into the house and pressing a wet rag against the side of his face. It came away bloody, her face pale and eyes wide. She said something, taking another cloth and shoving it into the blind spot that had formed on his left side. The axe was worked from his hands and dragged across the dirt floor.

He shuddered, finally coming back to awareness in bed to the scent of burning food, vomit and Abner's wailing.

"The babe is crying," he said, grabbing Molly before she could put another cloth against his face.

"You're bleeding, Papa," she replied. Her face was pale and serious, and it reminded him so much of Faithful.

"Quiet the babe," he ordered, taking the cloth from her hand and pressing it against the searing lines of pain. Elias tried to sit up, the bed creaking in protest. There was no sunlight under the cabin door, or through the shutters of the small window.

"What time of day is it?" he asked, bracing himself against the wall.

"It's almost night, Papa," Molly answered. Baby Abner looked large in her arms. "Papa, what are you doing?"

Elias had gotten his feet under him. Ignoring his children he lifted the musket down from its pegs above the door and retrieved his powder horn, his awareness of the surrounding cabin fading as he loaded the lead ball.

"Papa!" Molly's hand on his interrupted his practiced routine, and black powder fell across her and the floor.

"Let go of me, child!" he roared, throwing her back.

She stumbled, falling onto the dirt floor. She fell out of his vision sooner than she should have, and Elias raised his left hand to his face. As he reached toward his left eye his hand vanished from sight well before his fingers found a blood-stiffened cloth. He pulled this out, tearing the scabs around it, and his fingers explored the hollow left behind.

"Papa?" Molly's voice was small.

"My eye?" he asked.

Molly refused to look at him. "I don't know where it is." she said.

"Stay in the house," he ordered, opening the door and stumbling out. The rain had lightened enough, and he could see the dark edges of the forest that surrounded the homestead in the deep, gray light. Trying to step away from the house was a mistake, and he fell to his knees.

"Stay away from my family!" he roared into the growing night, aiming his cry at a suspicious-looking shadow under the spreading oak. "Do you hear me? Stay away!" The final echoes of his shout faded out, leaving only the soft sound of the rain on the leaves.

Satisfied with his effort Elias stumbled back into the house, closing the door and blocking it with the heavy oak chest he had argued against bringing.

"Don't go outside," he ordered Molly. Her blue eyes flicked past him to the chest, then back to his face. He ignored her concerned look, crawling back into bed and pressing his bleeding face against the pillow that still smelled faintly of his wife.

There were sounds on the roof again that night. Abner snored softly in the center of the bed, and Molly was curled around the babe, her small back to Elias. Sitting up he grabbed the loaded musket where it leaned against the wall, and listened.

At first it was the same scratching he'd heard the night before, but then there was a heavy thump that startled Molly awake.

She sat up, eyes wide in the faint light of the fire. Elias raised the rifle to his shoulder, keeping the barrel aimed downward. If he'd regained his balance he would have followed the movements underneath, but settled on watching. He joined his child in staring anxiously up at the exposed beams as the distinct sound of footfalls moved across the roof.

"Papa," Molly said in a whisper.

"Shh," Elias silenced her with a quick hand wave.

The steps continued to right above Molly's bed, and it treated them to the screech of nails being dragged out of wood. Molly's sleep loft blocked any certain shot Elias had, and reloading would take too long. Elias opened his mouth to shout a warning, but his dry throat allowed nothing.

Another shingle was ripped out and Molly screamed, pressing her hands against her head. The large animal scrambled across the roof and over the peak, to just above where Elias and his children were.

Raising his gun to his shoulder Elias fired, gun smoke filling the cabin as the lead ball bounced off the ceiling and into the opposite wall. The same shriek he'd heard earlier split the air, and the creature leaped off the roof. After a tense heartbeat a clatter came from the door, gently at first, then hard enough that the wood creaked. Molly screamed again, diving under the blankets. Elias pressed his teeth together, hands shaking as he tried to hurry through reloading the musket.

Abner woke and began to cry.

Whatever was outside shrieked again, and the door rattled.

"Molly, where's the axe?" he demanded, repeating himself when she didn't answer him. "My axe, Molly, where is it!?"

"By the fire, Papa," Molly answered. She wrapped her arms around Abner, gripping him against her small chest.

Elias left his musket on the bed, lurching across the small room to the wooden handle resting against the fireplace. He kept his balance, fear compensating for whatever he had lost when the blow had struck.

The door went silent. Elias limped back to the foot of the bed, staring at the now silent boards.

"Papa, beside you!" Molly whispered. Elias followed her pointing finger. Too poor by far to purchase window glass, the single hole in the wall was covered with thick, wooden shutters. Six long talons glinted in the firelight, three facing the other three as they pressed the shutters inward, all bending unnaturally towards the latch.

Elias found his voice, screaming as he brought the axe downward.

The limb fell to the floor, and the broken shutter clattered as the shriek sounded again, loud enough to be heard over the sound of his and both children's cries.

Elias froze where he stood, trying to hear if the creature continued to stalk, or if it had moved on.

Only Abner slept that night, curled up in the corner furthest from the window or door. Molly sat upright the entire time, hands pressed together as though in prayer, tears falling silently down her face.

When the vertigo wouldn't let Elias pace he sat, and when the pounding in his chest wouldn't let him sit he paced. Molly was the one who pointed out that the sunrise was showing, and after listening a moment Elias shoved the chest aside and unbarred the door, balancing both the musket and the axe.

The rain had erased most tracks, but he found two underneath the eaves, just outside the window. Like the claw he'd thrown into the fire they featured six toes, three facing one direction, three facing the other.

Elias went back inside. "Pack up what you and the babe will need for the next few days," he ordered.

"Why, Papa?" Molly asked.

"You're going to stay with the Laurence family until I rid us of this beast," Elias explained.

Abner woke on the bumpy wagon ride to the neighbor's settlement, crying until Molly gave him the tip of her finger to suck.

Abigail stood in the doorway of her cabin, graying hair covered with a cap as Elias explained the situation to her and her husband.

"I'll pay you," he said. "As soon as I take a load to market."

"You needn't worry about payment, good Lord knows we can spare the children a spot for a few days," Abigail said, holding a hand out to Molly. "Come inside, child. Have you eaten yet? And what about you, Elias? Those wounds on your face look a fright."

"It's just a scratch, Abigail, but thank you," Elias replied.

The older woman raised an eyebrow towards the bloody cloth covering Elias's missing eye, then ushered both children to herself.

William looked at Elias. "I'll come and take a look at those tracks for myself," he said. "If you don't mind."

"Don't mind at all," Elias replied. Truth be told, he was grateful for the more experienced man's help.

◆━━◆

Midday arrived as Elias used the poker to remove the hand from the ashes. It hadn't burned, but the edges had melted inward like a good cheese.

"It's made of metal?" William said in confusion, testing the edge with his finger before lifting it from the floor.

"Is it?" Elias asked, shuddering as the creature's scream sounded yet again in his head. In his memories it sounded too much like a woman in pain.

"It is," William said, holding the hand up to Elias,

who took it carefully. It was heavier than he expected, and still warm from the ashes. Now he could see the six fingers, the extra joint that made the fingers (for lack of a better word) longer than they had a right to be.

"Never seen anything like it," William said, shaking his head.

"This is now three times this beast has haunted my home," Elias said.

"I doubt fire could deter it."

"What do I do about it, William?"

The older man shrugged. "Never seen anything like it," he repeated.

"You've spoken with the natives?"

"They didn't say anything about this." William dropped the claw to the table where it landed with a hard thud. Even the tendons were made of fine metal, longer from where they'd been ripped out of the creature's leg.

"The children can stay with us," William added. "You can too, for a few days."

"This is my home," Elias replied. "Can't leave it, not yet."

Both men understood that the lot had to be inhabited should an inspector visit, else Elias would forfeit his claim on the land.

"God be with you," William said, clapping his hand on Elias's shoulder, then walking back to his horse.

Elias busied himself by putting the ox away, restacking the firewood and nailing the shutters of the window closed, all the while sending suspicious glances towards the woods with his remaining eye.

When he finished the chores there was still a bit of daylight left, so he used a stout branch as a walking stick to work his way along the engorged creek to the clearing where he'd laid Faithful.

The uneven ground made the journey difficult, and Elias wondered if he'd make a mistake.

Finally arriving at the clearing Elias looked up from his footing, only to stumble and finally fall to his knees.

Something had torn open Faithful's grave. The dirt was churned up, the pile of stones he'd placed on top scattered throughout the round clearing.

Crawling across the wet grass Elias reached the frozen wave of dark earth that surrounded her resting place. A massive hole, as if dug by a giant mole, had collapsed in on itself. Despite the rain Elias' gaze found long raking marks through the mud. He pushed himself to his feet, taking in the open grave, the broken cross that had marked it. In a puddle not far from the end of the grave a single shoe sat, soaked and half-submerged. He recognized it; it was made of soft leather, and had survived the journey from New York City to the frontier. He'd pondered saving them for when Molly was old enough, but the thought of burying Faithful without shoes made leaving her seem even more like abandonment.

Elias stumbled in the direction the shoe pointed, stopping himself from entering the woods. He stood, his heels tipped forward, torn between wanting to know and fearing the truth. Practicality won out, and he turned back towards the homestead. The sun was sinking, and he had less than an hour until nightfall.

Branches rubbed together, leaves rustling.

A voice — or perhaps it was nothing more than the wind through the trees, all breathy and hoarse — hissed behind him. "Eeeeeeehhhhh."

Elias froze.

"Ehhhhhhliassssss."

He turned slowly. A shape stood under the shadows of the tree.

"Who's there?" he demanded. "Show yourself."

It jerked forward, clicking softly in the darkness as it moved like a broken clock. Standing on two legs it was almost as tall as him, and torn, matted hair hid its face.

"What in God's name are you?" Elias shouted.

"Ehhhliasss," it said again, stepping closer to the light without entering it. Parts of it reflected the afternoon sun, as if it were a dirty mirror.

"That's my name," Elias replied, stepping back. The cuts to his face, which had swollen throughout the day, throbbed as the creature lurched forward once more. Its long arms hung unevenly near its knees, and the lopsided head tipped to one side.

"Ehlias." Now it stepped into the light, and Elias stumbled back. A shining skull was half covered by grayed, rotting flesh, and he recognized the dirty fabric of the torn dress it wore.

"Faithful?" he said, his voice barely escaping his mouth.

"Elias." One of the arms reached for him across the torn ground. A hand, three claws facing forward and three facing back, beckoned him.

"Begone, demon!" Elias tried to scream, but his command came out a whisper. He could see where his axe had torn away Faithful's hair, exposing the gray skull.

"Elias," the beast said, its voice scratching across sharp gravel.

"No!" he said, finally finding strength in his words. "Get away from me, devil!"

He turned and ran for the cabin, vertigo making the ground sway. In his doorway he turned back. The creature wearing Faithful's face was just steps behind him.

"Elias, please," it said, blocking his attempt to close the door with a wrist that ended in nothing. Abandoning the effort Elias reached for the axe — only to realize he'd left it out at the wood pile. The door thudded gently against the wall as the creature stepped into the room, the smell of rot and the click of misfiring clockworks filling the dark space.

"You're not Faithful!" Elias cried, his back hitting the pantry shelves and knocking the carved dishes to the floor.

"No. Not Faithful." It lifted its separated hand off the table and stared at the strange appendage. Through gaps in the dress, Elias could see where metal struts extended upward like eaves on a home. Curves of pipe connected several organ-like sacks here and there until the skirt of the dress hid where the legs met the torso.

"Not Faithful," the creature repeated. "So cold, she

was, when we found her."

"What do you mean?" Elias's fingers searched for a weapon, finding Faithful's wooden rolling pin and gripping behind his back.

"I was cold, no sparks." When it spoke, he could see one of the sack-like organs inflating and deflating. "She was cold, no sparks." It moved towards him and Elias scrambled backwards, keeping his back to the wall and pinning himself in an inescapable corner. "It was cold, few sparks. Such a distance through the stars."

The creature stopped, looking down at the hand it was holding, then carefully hooked its fingers through one of the holes in the dress, bringing the edges together. It looked back up at him, something glinting in the gaps where Faithful's eyes should have shown.

"It had come so far between the stars and been buried so long. She had also come far, beneath the stars and been buried. We became I." It stopped advancing on him, its voice became stronger, as though remembering how. It looked at him. "Faithful is here. I am here." The remaining hand reached up and adjusted the skin across its otherwise hidden face.

"She's come home. Elias, where are the children?"

His mouth opened and closed. He couldn't tell this *thing* where his children were. What if it went after them when it finished with him?

"What are you?" he demanded, holding the rolling pin out in front of him.

"I've explained myself," it replied, pausing in the

middle of the cabin, the fading sunlight filling the hollows of its mangled face. "But you are human, and perhaps do not understand." It reached for him. "Faithful has come home, Elias. Welcome her."

Elias swung the rolling pin, knocking the creature's hand away. "You are not Faithful."

"Part of me was once Faithful." It reached up to touch the rotted face.

He lunged, his fingers tangling in the dirty hair and yanking as he darted to the other side of the small cabin. Continuing his momentum he threw the handful of hair and skin into the coals, willing the fire to burn it. The hair was dry enough that it took at once, filling his nostrils with an awful stench.

The unholy shriek he'd become familiar with bounced off the close walls of the cabin. A metal hand raked his back, dragging him away from the fireplace, and it reached into the flames with an empty wrist. Elias didn't waste the moment. He fled through the cabin door, his feet sliding in the dirt as he ran to the woodpile.

Axe in hand he turned back toward the cabin, where the spreading light from the fire fell across a smooth, shining, almost featureless face.

"What have you done to me?" the specter asked, its voice rising in a shriek as it held the melted and charred remains in its one hand.

Elias didn't speak. Instead he charged towards it and swung the axe, metal clanging on metal. The thing caught the axe just below the blade, all six fingers wrapping around the worn wood. Man and creature were caught, the wooden handle between them. Elias pulled back, trying to yank his weapon free, and he didn't see the handless wrist until it connected with his gut. He fell back, the wind knocked from him as he struggled to keep his feet. The specter tossed the axe, shifting its grip lower onto the handle, and then flung it over its head where it stuck fast in the roof's peak.

When the specter spoke again there was a different tone to its voice. It made Elias's heart ache with loss and longing, even as the words chilled him. "Elias, run! It's angry now, and I can't stop it. Run!"

The voice was at once familiar and urgent. Elias obeyed, turning and bolting into the fields past the animal's shelter. With the harvest in there was nowhere to hide, just an open field full of holes and cut vegetation.

He heard the rustle before the specter struck his back, six points of pain tearing from his waist up to his shoulders as it threw him into the soft earth. It leapt over him, landing on its feet and good arm, the shortened limb held against its chest.

"Why?" it demanded, this voice different from either before. "She wanted to come back to you. She *insisted*." It straightened up, legs spread wide as they folded unnaturally. It had torn off the dress, leaving only its sleeves behind. Elias could see the gaps in its chest, the misshapen organs where it all came together and the junction where the unnaturally long legs met the body.

Wrapping his fingers around one of the rocks that

had been exposed in the harvest, Elias pushed his legs underneath him and climbed to his feet. He'd just gotten up when the creature moved again, this time catching him across the cheek and knocking him back. The rock fell from his gasp as the hand caught him around the throat, tightening and lifting him. Elias gasped, unable to breathe through the specter's grip as his feet left the ground. He clawed at the hand, his fingers finding the exposed tendons. He chose one at random, yanking as hard as he could until it ripped out of the creature's arm. His other hand had already found another tendon, and he pulled that out too. The creature howled, tightening its grip as it shook him like a dog. Elias's legs swung as his fingers found yet another thread to remove.

The crushing grip opened, and he fell to the ground in a gasping heap. Its foot caught him on the nose, sending blood spattering. Another kick followed it, striking him on the breastbone. Elias crawled back, and he knew there was no chance of getting up and running.

A foot struck him, this time in the side, and he pinned it to his ribs with his elbow. Six long toes tore into his flesh as he grabbed just above the knee, then wrapped his hands around the upper thigh. A hand, and the empty wrist, beat down on him as he chose one of the visible organs at random. It was cool and smooth in his hands; He found the narrow neck where it connected to something else, and he pulled.

The beating on his head and shoulders became even more frantic, and with both hands around the organ Elias threw himself backward. It gave. The flesh splintered in his hands like glass, sending something slick and skin-burning to the ground. The creature leapt away, its useless wrists clawing at the hole in its midsection.

Elias pressed his advantage, lunging through its frantic arms to grab another organ. This one was warm, and shook in his fingers. He yanked again, but this time the creature pushed toward him, knocking them both onto Elias's back. Its body weighed less than he'd expected, so Elias brought his foot up and kicked as hard as he could. The organ broke, cutting his fingers and sending bits and pieces of hot metal raining down on him.

The creature thrashed, its motions jerking like a clock winding down.

Elias threw it off, fighting his way to his feet. It jerked once more, the movement slowing and slowing. The axe was out of reach on the roof, but by the time Elias returned with the hand scythe the specter lay still. He kicked it twice, then used the scythe and his bleeding hands to work the head from the shoulders. He carried this to the open grave, burying it as deeply as he could. William found him the next day, sitting in the doorway to the cabin.

Elias burned with fever for two days before he passed away.

❖—○—❖

Having found the remains of Faithful's grave William buried him far from the cursed clearing. Instead, Elias was laid to rest next to William and Abigail's oldest daughter.

The creature's body refused to be burned, so William and his sons broke it into pieces. They were too practical to hide valuable materials in the woods, which meant several of the larger pieces went into adding onto the barn, or a roof repair, until soon the creature was scattered across three or four homesteads. The men who'd seen it never spoke of it again, and nothing ever grew in the corner of the field where they had found its body.

"Such a shame." Abigail would say when Molly was older.

"The wolves in these parts are awful," William said in the spring to the family that moved into the Ober's cabin.

"Do you think it's safe?" the woman asked, looking anxiously at her husband.

William shrugged. "Just don't be digging in that clearing yonder, the round one."

"Why not?" the man asked.

William scratched his beard, thinking about the axe thrown up onto the peak of the roof, the metal hand with six fingers, the corpse of the creature that had killed Elias and the wounds it had left him with.

"Didn't seem to work too good for the last family, is all," he finally said, before putting his hat back on and going home. He had two more mouths to feed, but at least he had more animals to do so with.

M. A. HOYLER
ABOUT THE AUTHOR

M. A. Hoyler has been involved with her local historical society for many years and writes fantasy and horror stories set in her hometown. She has a dark modern fantasy trilogy in the works and will be featured in an upcoming volume of the Agents of the Abyss stories. Find her online at https://justahoyler.weebly.com/.

Three Balloons
Chris Lilienthal

The heavy clouds rolled in just in time to spoil any view of the springtime super-moon. Somewhere, up beyond the swirl of moisture and ice crystals, a full moon was rising bigger and brighter than usual. It was a phenomenon that always awed Ted — the larger-than-life moon just above the tree line ushering in the mysterious night. He longed for it now as he piled newly-cut brushwood on the woodpile.

He was cleaning up from the after-dinner chores —wood splitting, bush trimming, and a little mulching. He had nearly five acres of property to maintain, and he found it was best to do so in stages. Most evenings after dinner this is where he could be found, gassing up his chainsaw or raking cedar mulch around bushes and flower beds. Katrina stayed inside, and that was fine with Ted. He wouldn't have known what to say to her anyway.

The dark set in quickly beneath the cloud cover. Ted was collecting his rake and a few small yard tools when he noticed three silvery shadows slowly dropping from the clouds. They looked like small, misshapen spaceships gracefully floating down from the ether onto a muddy patch of land close to where the backyard descended into forest.

Ted gazed back at the yellow lights around the deck, the inviting glow of his study just inside. Curiosity, though, drew him back to the yard and the mysterious objects that had fallen from heaven. Where had they come from, and why had they dropped from the sky just now? He leaned his rake against the shed door, retrieved his searchlight, and rapped on top of Bradley's doghouse. "Come on, boy," he said. "Let's go see what we got."

The pair trod across the yard, Ted's light leading their way. As they got closer the objects came into focus. Two silver mylar balloons were fluttering in the gentle breeze by the edge of the forest. The first balloon was curvy, shaped like a rain cloud with a frowny face painted on one side in a thin, pink line. "Missing You" was printed on the other side. The second balloon hovered not far from the first. This one was heart-shaped and outlined in dark red, and on both sides was printed "My Heart Burns For You."

Ted yanked both balloons by their red ribbons, bringing them closer to get a better look in the dim light. They felt heavier than he expected.

Ted shined his light toward the forest, which stood tall and wild in the dusk. A chorus of cheeping frogs sang from the banks of the creek down the hill, and Ted squinted. He thought he had seen three objects drop down from the clouds, but if there was a third he couldn't find it now. Venturing closer to the forest's edge he felt queasy, a pang of nausea falling over him all at once. He grabbed hold of an Osage orange tree to steady himself. As he grabbed it Bradley galloped past him, barking fiercely and rushing into the wood.

"BRADLEY!" Ted shouted, but the dog ignored him, his growls receding into the darkness. Ted sighed and jogged after him, towing the two balloons behind him.

Shining his light over the trees, he called, "BRADLEY, HERE!" Ted stepped on a large stick, and the crisp crack of it breaking underfoot hit his ears like nails on a chalkboard. Something tightened in his stomach. Then, somewhere in the darkness, Bradley erupted into a fit of howls. Ted shined the light back and forth ahead of him. The dog's cries, sounding pained at first, quickly rose into furious barks.

"BRADLEY, WHERE ARE YOU?" Ted bellowed.

A minute later he found the dog barking up a tall white oak about 50 yards or so into the wood. Ted knelt down and gently scolded him, "Bradley, bad! You don't run off like that!" Bradley stopped barking, but maintained his attention up the tree. Ted looked up to see the third silver mylar balloon trapped in some low-hanging branches. It was easy to miss in the thickness of the tree and the darkness of the evening. Standing on tiptoes Ted was just able to grip it and untangle the red ribbon, which was caught around small branches and notches in the tree.

Ted added the third balloon to his collection. It was

shaped, strangely, like a tombstone; it was grayer than the other two, and even its surface appeared ragged and weathered. Somebody had painted "RIP" on both sides of the balloon in bright red paint.

The balloon made Ted feel uneasy, especially being hidden in the forest as he was. He called to Bradley to follow him, and the two headed back to the house.

To his surprise Katrina was sitting on the couch in his study, waiting for him.

"We need to talk," she said. Then noticing the balloons floating around his head, she asked, "What are those?"

"Balloons," Ted said. "I found them in the yard. They kind of dropped out of nowhere."

"'RIP,'" Katrina said, reading the red lettering on the tombstone mylar. "Jesus, are they funeral balloons?"

"I don't know," he said, wondering if funeral balloons were even a thing.

"Well, do me a favor," she said. "Get them the Hell out of the house."

Ted awoke on the recliner in his study. He had a book open on his chest, providing him with an excuse for sleeping there rather than in his own bed with his wife. He simply fell asleep while reading; it was a rather unnecessary excuse. Katrina and he had an unspoken agreement that this is how it would be, for the time being. But having the book open on his chest, the excuse so close at hand, made Ted feel less vulnerable while he slept.

The quick patter of feet on hardwood is what woke him, and Ted wondered if it had been a dream. He was a deep sleeper who rarely woke in the wee hours, and certainly not to the small sounds of the night. Katrina slept much more lightly, waking to every creaking door hinge and shift in the old farmhouse's foundation. If the footsteps were real it was probably Katrina in the kitchen, getting a glass of water or a cup of tea. Ted quietly closed the recliner's leg rest and sat upright, waiting for confirmation of movement in the kitchen or a tea kettle on the stove. He heard neither. What he did hear were footsteps, louder and more frantic now, like a child lost in a funhouse. The sound echoed throughout the house, upstairs and downstairs alike. He could hear furniture moving, picture frames being knocked over, and papers rustling as someone ran roughshod over everything.

Outside his study the hallway to the kitchen was lit up with moonlight pouring in from a window at the far end. The super-moon had arrived after all, illuminating the cloudless, midnight sky. Whatever front had rolled in at dusk had clearly moved on its merry way.

Ted stood at the end of the hallway, mesmerized by the brilliant moon filling the window frame. It shimmered and pulsated, as close as it could be to the window without bumping up against the glass. It almost seemed to want to pass through and come into the house for a look around, and the more he looked at it the more the sight of it unnerved Ted. The super-moon was big, but it wasn't supposed to be that big.

The hurried footsteps returned. He could hear them approaching from behind, from the direction of the study. Step-step, step-step, step-step. Deliberate at first, then faster. Now almost running. Whoever it was seemed to be getting both closer, and farther away, with every step. Ted remained paralyzed, his eyes locked on the unnaturally large moon filling the window frame, while the footsteps came and went in a seamless loop.

Ted flinched at the sound of a scream. When he looked out the window again the moon, bright and still quite large, had returned to its distant place in the night sky. He turned to run upstairs.

In the bedroom, Ted found Katrina sitting on the edge of the bed, panting and trembling. She had turned on a light on the nightstand.

"Are you all right?" he asked.

"There was a baby," she said, still breathing heavily. "There was a baby crawling on the ceiling and the walls."

"What?" Ted asked.

"There was a BABY crawling around on the CEILING and the WALLS!" she shouted.

Ted looked up reflexively. "I don't see —"

"Well, obviously, it's gone now," she snapped.

"You must have had a bad dream."

She shook her head. "It was too real. And fast, like a cockroach."

Ted shivered at the thought of a baby-like cockroach crawling all over the walls and ceiling of the bedroom.

"Look," he said after a moment. "Why don't you go splash some water on your face, and I'll go get you a cup of tea. Does that sound all right?" Katrina nodded without making eye contact, and walked slowly into the master bathroom.

Ted had barely gotten out the door when Katrina screamed again.

"What the fuck!" she yelled at him, when he came running back in. She was standing in the bathroom doorway holding the tombstone balloon by its red ribbon. The red-letter "RIP" looked almost drippy now. "Is this some kind of sick joke?" she asked.

"That's one of the balloons that landed in the yard last night," he said.

"Yeah," she said. "Why was it up here in the master bath?"

"I don't know," Ted said. "I didn't put it there. I put all three balloons in the garage after you told me to get them out of the house."

"Well, I didn't put it in there."

"I don't know."

She reached out her hand, and Ted took the balloon from her. He paused a moment, feeling for an itch in his right ear. Katrina's eyes widened, and her mouth dropped open.

"Your ear," she whispered.

He felt something crawling out of his ear canal, pausing a moment on his ear lobe before scurrying down his neck and onto his shirt. Ted swiped at it with both hands, sending it flying onto the carpet. Katrina pulled her legs fully onto the bed, clutching them with both arms and burying her face in her thighs. The cockroach made a break for it, disappearing behind a dresser. Ted watched it dash, and he thought about the baby that Katrina had seen scampering up the wall and onto the ceiling. He couldn't be sure if it was his imagination, but he thought he saw it too.

A baby, too young to walk, cockroach-crawled across the carpet and behind the dresser. It was barely enough time for the image to register with his brain at all, but it was time enough for Ted to see that the baby had six appendages, just like a cockroach. Was it four arms and two legs, or two arms and four legs? Was it all legs? All arms? He couldn't say, but he had seen enough to send him running out of the room and down the stairs, back to the safety of his study at the back of the house.

It was well past dinnertime the next evening when Ted hung up his rake and hoe in the garage. Katrina had not emerged from her bedroom at all that day. Ted had knocked softly on the door to see if she would like any breakfast, but she shooed him away. The same at lunch. He figured she was still angry about the night before, how he had left her alone with the cockroach that somehow popped out of his ear. The truth is he had returned after fleeing the bedroom, but the door was shut and locked, and he could hear Katrina's rhythmic breathing as she slept inside. Ted didn't see the point of rousing her to look for a cockroach that had surely slipped into the hidden crevices of the old farmhouse by then.

First thing in the morning Ted called the exterminator, but the next appointment wasn't for two days. He ate a bowl of oatmeal and attempted some work in his study, but by early afternoon he was outside tending to the raised vegetable beds and the endless tree trimming.

After carving up the remains of a dead Sycamore limb he returned to the garage to put the chainsaw away. Two of the balloons were swaying easily in the breeze from the open door. The third balloon, the tombstone, had dropped to the concrete floor and was inching forward, the red ribbon trailing behind it. It seemed to be making its way to the open door, bit by bit.

Ted knelt down and lifted the balloon up to his ear. He could hear scratching and straining at the mylar nylon from the inside. The balloon was full of something — something alive — and Ted had a pretty good idea what.

He held the balloon over the fire pit and cut it open with his knife. With a quick pop the cockroaches, hundreds of them, fell from the balloon into the flames, screaming as they were consumed. It couldn't have been screaming he heard, could it? Whatever it was, the sound of it sickened Ted. He dropped the entire balloon in, the burning stink of the foil smelled like an electrical fire, and Ted felt even worse. Once the balloon was fully burned up he poured a pitcher of water onto the embers, then went inside.

Katrina was again waiting for him on the couch in his study. "We need to talk," she said.

She was sitting up straight, with her right arm leaning on the back of the couch and her legs sprawled out in front of her. She was still wearing her pajamas, and they were filthy, as if she had fallen down a muddy embankment. Her face was swollen and her eyes blank, her dark hair scattered and greasy.

"Are you feeling okay?" Ted asked.

"We need to talk," she said mechanically.

"You said that last night, but then a moment later you said you had nothing to say to me," Ted responded.

"We need to talk now," Katrina said.

"What do you want to talk about, Katrina?" He spat, anger swelling up in him unexpectedly. "Would you like to talk about me — catalogue your complaints with me, maybe? How it was all my fault what happened?"

She only blinked at him.

"No? Then, let's talk about you. Let's talk about how you stopped going to work, how you stopped eating and calling your friends back, how you haven't lifted a finger around this house in nearly three months."

"Ted?" she said uncertainly, as if she were saying the name for the first time.

"What?" he asked angrily.

Katrina opened her mouth, but said nothing. Leaning forward slightly she began to make retching sounds.

"Are you going to be sick?" Ted asked. Without waiting for a reply he spun around, grabbing a silver ornamental bowl off a nearby table and thrusting it under her chin.

Katrina gagged a few times, and her eyes rolled into the back of her head. Her mouth opened wider and wider, inhuman and grotesque. Ted dropped the bowl and took several steps back. With a guttural cough they let loose: hundreds, maybe thousands, of cockroaches spilled out of Katrina's gaping mouth, landing on her lap, the couch and the floor. A stream of black, scampering insects flew through the air, landing on all six legs and scattering to the far ends of the room.

Ted was frozen for a moment, unable to process what he was seeing. Shaking his head he eyed the doorway to the hall, but the floor was quickly being overtaken by the never-ending brigade of cockroaches pouring out of Katrina's open mouth. He drew on every bit of courage he had to break out of his paralysis and make a mad dash to the open doorway, leaping over the puddle of cockroaches.

"Wa nweed to twalk," he could hear her saying through a full mouth.

Panting, Ted saw the super-moon waiting for him at the end of the hallway. It again filled the window, alive and pulsing.

"Help me," he whispered, but the moon in the window only throbbed like a beating heart — ba bump, ba bump, ba bump.

The frantic footsteps were behind him again, millions of them. Ted turned to see the swarm of cockroaches rushing out of his study, stepping onto each other as they came toward him. He turned into the kitchen and made his way to the sliding glass door, fumbling with the lock and sliding it open.

The two balloons were hovering just outside — the silver rain cloud and the red-trimmed heart. He read their messages automatically: "Missing You" and "My Heart Burns For You." They were as swollen as Katrina's face, and for a moment Ted was happy to see them. Before he could grab them and run both balloons exploded, more or less in synchronization with each other. Cockroaches sailed into his face and hair, poking at his eyes and crawling into his ears and mouth.

By now the cockroaches from the study were on Ted, and the sheer number and weight of them — they were so much heavier than they seemed like they should be — pulled him down onto the deck just outside the sliding door.

Then Katrina was standing over him, holding the six-legged (or was it six-armed?) baby close to her chest, cockroaches still crawling on her face and hair. Ted looked at her helplessly under the weight of the scurrying cockroaches, begging her with his eyes to help him. But she looked past him, beyond the deck and the yard to the glowing night and the living moon high in the sky.

She smiled and said hoarsely, "There's just something about a super-moon, isn't there?"

Chris Lilienthal
About the Author

Chris Lilienthal is a writer and communications professional in Harrisburg, Pennsylvania. He spent more than two decades telling himself stories in his head. In 2020, he started writing them down. "Three Balloons" is his first published story. When he's not writing, Chris enjoys sketching, kayaking, hiking, and reading in the hammock out back. He lives with his wife, two sons, and two dogs. Follow him on Twitter @ChrisLilienthal and on Instagram @ChristopherLilienthal.

Beloved of the Storm
Elizabeth Davis

"Have you ever seen those farmhouses with trailers parked outside while you were flying down the road?" The waitress asked me as she poured my coffee with a solid plop. I blinked away my stray thoughts, and focused on the middle aged women with a uniform only less stained then the peeling linoleum floors and greasy windows of the diner.

"Yeah, I think so," I mumbled as my fork dug through the corn-chip laced chili, remembering the empty roads when I left Tulsa – a city crushed by its own sky – as I continued my trek west. What was supposed to be a romantic trip to the Pacific Ocean had turned into a lonely vacation, undertaken for the nominative guise of self-discovery, but mostly to show that my heart wasn't that broken.

"We call those trailers 'sacrificial lambs', offered for the tornados to eat so they leave the farm houses alone."

I jerked up from my cooling chili and looked up at the prematurely lined face, set into a solemn frown. "What?"

"It's just a joke we tell out-of-towners." Her laughter came too late, and was too short and sharp to be truly convincing.

"Sacrificial lambs – that's a Bible thing, right?" My parents were never religious, which led to a culture shock during my time on the road.

"Yes hun, from the story of Moses and the Ten Plagues. It's why the Iseralites didn't have their firstborns killed. There was also the story of Isaac and Abraham, in which he nearly killed his own son but God gave him a ram in the nick of time. There's even a whole book in the bible just for sacrifices – including sending a goat in the wilderness to carry the sins of the people. That's why it's called a scapegoat." Theology lessons with your coffee; welcome to the Midwest. A strange scent permeated the grease and coffee. Goat? Lamb? But why would they be cooking something so fancy here?

"Okay... I think I'm ready to head out. Can you please bring my check?" I looked back to my grey and orange chili, not wanting this conversation to continue.

"Honey, you don't want to do that."

"Look, I'm not as hungry as I thought – I've eaten all that I can."

"It ain't that, hun." Any further objections were cut off by a wet slap against the windows, which drowned out the rattling of silverware and loud conversation behind me. I looked out the windows, blinking in disbelief. Rain. How could there be rain after a day driving under blue cloudless skies, where the sun beat down on scorched plains, the heat a waiting wall whenever I left the air-conditioned sanctuary of my car?

This time the woman's laughter was genuine. "Storms come up quick around here, but you don't want to be out on the roads in this weather."

I thought of the empty roads, blessing the freedom from police as I sped through American Indian Nations and the United States. Too easily I imagined sliding off those roads, not being found by the oblivious trucks and few other travelers thanks to the thick curtain of rain.

"Why don't you just sit and enjoy your coffee, hun? The storm will pass soon enough." *Good idea,* I decided as I sipped my coffee, pumping up already buzzing nerves as the room was filled with a blinding flash. As I blinked black spots swam in front of my eyes, and rolling thunder shook the windows and settled in my bones. My nerves on edge, I caught snatches of the other conversations around me.

"Shit, that don't look good."

"Yeah, it's going to be a big one."

"If only we still had that trailer park..."

"Too bad it got devoured only a few months ago..."

"It's going to take more than a chicken this time."

A massive man rose from the table, his jaw bearing a jagged scar that contrasted with his t-shirt proclaiming that 'Real Man Love Jesus.' "Minnie," he said in a low tone that rumbled like the thunder.

Her face grew tight. "I don't mean any disrespect, Pastor, but it's still just a storm. We don't know if it's hungry yet," she forced the words through her lips. A hush fell over the diner, leaving only their voices against the pounding rain.

"I need to know if you are true Minnie, that you will do what's right when the time comes by your kin and kith."

Unease coiled up in my stomach, and shook its rattle. Images of the crowd converging on me, tearing me apart - or, maybe even worse, on somebody else...and then I would have stood there in horror, realizing I was coward while the screams echoed through the air, or...I know these images were unreasonable, but they still poured in.

"I'm true, but this ain't time for that kind of talk." Another blinding flash and rolling thunder.

Before the black spots had finished dancing away, I pushed myself out of the chair and stumbled towards the door.

"Where do you think you're going?" Pastor barked after me. All the heads in the diner turned, watching me with unearned intensity entrenched on previously ordinary faces.

"I need to get going." The words staggered off my tongue as I grabbed at the door handle with sweat-slick hands. I had decided to risk the storm, to risk going off the road, to risk being found drowned or crushed, over whatever was going on in this diner.

"Don't give grief, hun. It's still just a storm." All the patrons held their breath, their positions rigid with tense muscles. But none of them raised their tongue against Minnie, or moved as the handle continued to slip in my hands before the door opened.

The roaring wind fought against me, ripping at my shirt and blinding me with hard rain that stung my face. A single sound broke through the rain, the wind, and the thunder: a high-pitched, oscillating siren. As it burrowed into my ears the room exploded. Men and women climbed over booths, chairs and each other to get to me. That coiled fear bit me, sending adrenaline shooting through my veins as I ran outside. Slipping on the pavement I fought my way through the blinding rain and lightning into the parking lot.

The pounding footsteps and shouted curses were drowned out as I slammed into one of the cars. A car alarm now competed with the thunder. Panicked, I pushed the button on my keyfob, listening for the faint car beep over the chaos. Following those pathetic beeps I slid and slammed as the footsteps and deep splashes came closer. Eventually I felt the beep through chrome as I collided again, but relief didn't stop me from shaking as I pulled myself to the driver's door.

A hand grasped mine, wrenching it from the car handle. I looked through the stinging rain into the face of the Pastor. I don't know what I exactly screamed; something between strings of curse words, "Fuck, shit, fucking shit!" and begging, "God no, let go of me, why?" as I twisted in his grasp. Memories from a self-defense class penetrated my brain, and I dropped like a sack of potatoes, knees tearing on the blacktop. I crawled away from the pastor's confused grabs – right into the waiting crowd that had gathered around my car.

Hands grabbed my clothes, arms locked around mine and my legs were hefted up on shoulders. I uselessly struggled as the rain fell down upon us. The air conditioning shocked me as they entered back into the diner, not realizing how cold it had gotten outside. My chattering teeth were only interrupted by racking coughs, which came from the stray mouthfuls of rain I caught during my flailing shouts. The crowd lowered me down onto one of the plastic tabletops, keeping me pinned despite my increasingly weak attempts to fight back and the involuntary shivers that wracked my body.

Was I going to be beheaded or gutted? Left to bleed out while others watched? Or were they just going to beat me, breaking bones until I blacked out from the pain? There was no good death to be found at their hands – that I knew.

Through the flickering fluorescent lights, and lightning, I watched as the crowd parted for the Pastor. He looked down at me with sorrow etched on his hard face.

"Don't worry, we will not be cruel. You serve a greater purpose, and your soul is in the hands of our heavenly father. Minnie?" I could hear her footsteps between bouts of thunder and the siren. Minnie emerged into view, cradling a serrated chef's knife in her hands.

"I'm sorry hun," she told me, forcing herself to look into my face. "I don't expect you to understand, but there was another town called Springfield just 20 or so miles up the road. You would've driven right by it." Despite my fright, confusion bloomed in my mind – there hadn't been a town 20 miles or so up the road. The closest were collapsed ruins and bare foundations – I assumed they had belonged to a booming town gone bust decades ago. "Two years ago, it was eaten by a tornado. We just want to continue, like we always have."

"The Lord smiles upon your compassion, Minnie," the Pastor began, "but it doesn't change the price." He took the knife from her. "The blood shall be a sign for you on the houses where you live, and when I see the blood I will pass over you, and no plague will befall you," he recited as he pushed back my sodden hair and sliced deeply into my scalp.

The sharp pain sent a fresh bout of swears from me, as I felt my forehead throb and blood leak out. The Pastor's fingers caught the stream of blood before it leaked down to my eyes, bringing the soaked fingers up to his forehead. He marked it with my blood, which mixed with rainwater and sweat. The others bowed their heads as they held me down, and the Pastor's fingers dipped down again and again as my blood ran down my face, marking each member of this makeshift congregation in turn. Even Minnie approached him and received his blessing as I tasted my own blood.

"We don't have much time – the storm is hungry for our lamb. Best get this done before it grows too impatient."

The whole crowd moved with a single intent as they picked me up and carried me back out into the storm.

They pinned me against a flickering light post, and I heard a rip as a roll of tape was opened up. The black, leathery tape was thicker than duct tape, and it held me tight despite the rain. It didn't take the mob long to encircle me completely with the tape, pinning my arms to my side and keeping my legs off the ground so I couldn't find any purchase to pull myself away. The pole dug into my back as I struggled, and as the last of the tape snapped away from the roll the crowd left. With difficulty I turned my head, watching as they retreated in the diner and avoiding the windows. I was unsure if that was due to guilt, or worries about broken glass.

The artificial light fell upon me, the sky above as dark as night – it would be hard to believe it was still afternoon, and that only a few hours ago the sun beat down upon me. Looking through the rain and blinding flashes I could see a green sky behind the dark clouds as the rain hardened into hail, and low, blue flashes in the distance indicated snapped power lines.

What alarmed me, more than the small ice balls beating down upon my still-bleeding head, was the roar that filled the air. It was a roar that drowned out thunders, a roar that sounded like a train with no tracks to click underneath it's wheels, like all the rain had formed into a giant waterfall falling down from the sky, like a plane engine roaring next to my ears without the thin layer of metal between us. The clouds were swirling, like water in a drain, and they were coming for me.

My wordless scream was taken away by the wind as it left my mouth. I kept screaming, gulping breaths as the clouds continued turning. As the turning clouds stretched out, snaking through the air, the funnel grew thinner and thinner. I wordlessly prayed that it would go back up, that it would break up, or that it wouldn't touch the ground.

Finally the twisting tail of the thunderstorm touched land.

I could do nothing except pull against tape that refused to yield as the funnel roared closer, changing from a distant, skinny funnel into a vortex that filled my vision. It ripped up pavement and threw around cars and power lines, until my whole vision was just the tornado. My brain refused to register how quickly the tornado came, even as I felt the edge of its wind pull at me, fighting against the tape. And then the tornado was upon me. I flew, light post and all.

I expected to be bounced off the ground, again and again until I died, or that I would be pummeled by flying debris. I remembered learning in science class that tornados didn't actually suck you up as they did in the movies; instead I felt myself pulled away from the light pole, the tape searing my skin as it was ripped off. The light post blew away from me as I was lifted up.

This shouldn't be happening, the rational part of my mind repeated as I tried to breathe through the wind. In a weightless moment I felt something cover my mouth, blowing into my lungs, as it caressed my bruised and bloody body.

It was something more than just clouds, more than just air droplets huddling together. It was more than hot and cold air colliding. It was more than water molecules clinging together, freezing as they drop through the atmosphere. It was more than electrical currents between the air and it's delayed sound.

I know what you're thinking, and it wasn't like that. It wasn't like your pictures of Zeus throwing down thunder, Thor with his hammer or the Four Winds puffing in the corner of a map. I've looked through encyclopedias and the internet, and I haven't found a god imagined by man.

The voice was like thunder that boomed into me. Its rain fell into me, filling me. Its wind lifted me up, its touch frosting my skin as we rose into the sky. Sparks danced across my skin, blooming out to fry the ground before returning back to me, injecting straight into my nerves. I was the sky that stretched over this flat land, with no kin to those that huddled in holes in the ground, trying to hide from my all-encompassing sight. I was the fury that tossed aside cars and buildings like toys that no longer pleased me. I was hunger that roared, rending everything I touched, yet wanting more. I was the blackness that blotted out the sun, which drowned out all, and it was that blackness that was the last thing I remembered.

I woke up in a hospital bed. Over the next couple days, from doctors and what scraps of news I was allowed to watch, I learned that I was found in the rubble, the only survivor of an F-5. Everyone else was dead. Minnie, Pastor, everyone else; the town was smashed. My wounds were minimal, and were more from the rough handling I had gotten before the tornado had found me. The greatest mystery was not just my survival, but my eyes – my clear, blue iris had darkened into a stormy grey. I was released into the waiting arms of the press. I didn't mention anything about being a sacrificial lamb, or what I experienced in the tornado – instead I just smiled and talked about how glad I was to be alive. Eventually a new disaster struck and I was forgotten, along with the destroyed town.

I don't stay long in one place anymore – I get too restless. Too hungry. That's why I'm in Florida today, watching kids in an ice cream shop on their way to the beach. It's a small town filled with primly-kept houses – like little doll houses made with white marzipan - short businesses shaded by palm trees, boasting of their minimal historical significance. There's even a mobile home park. As I waved at the kids, I felt the wind pick up around me. This town looked so delicious, I could just eat it up...

Elizabeth Davis
About the Author

Elizabeth Davis is a second generation writer living in Dayton, Ohio. She lives there with her spouse and two cats - neither of which have been lost to ravenous corn mazes or sleeping serpent gods. She can be found at deadfishbooks.com when she isn't busy creating beautiful nightmares and bizarre adventures. Her work can be found in, Eerie River Publishing Patreon July 2020, Eternal Haunted Summer Summer 2020, and No Safe Distance: Stories from Isolation.

Keep One in the Chamber
T.M. Brown

"Please…" The man begged. Tears ran down his swollen cheeks, the color in his eyes beginning to fade as skin was peeling from his lips. There was no telling how long he'd been walking this lonely stretch of sun-baked road, and several dozen buzzards circled overhead. Claire had seen a lot over the past two and a half years, but even she couldn't help but feel sorry for the poor bastard.

"Come on Mike, just give it to 'em." Lisa was clearly in one of her coddling moods today, since you couldn't always rely on this kind of benevolence from her. She played the part of den mother one day, only to turn around and act like a bat straight outta Hell the next. "What difference is one gonna make, anyway?"

Mike turned and looked toward Claire. She took a long drag from her cigarette and exhaled. "We can spare *one*. What do you have now, sixteen?"

Mike shook his head. A grease-stained bandana held back his long, dark hair. His face was barely visible behind a thick beard. "Fourteen," he replied.

"That'd put ya' at thirteen…" Amelia interjected from the inside the van. Her thin, tattooed arm danged from the passenger side window. Her face remained hidden beneath the brim of an old, gas station sun visor. "That's gotta be some kinda bad luck."

"We could always just…*you know*…" Mike placed his hand on the hilt of his hunting knife. He once again looked Claire in the eyes. He wanted her approval, but she wasn't going to give it to him.

Claire rolled her eyes. "Don't be gross, Mike. Just give the guy what he wants, and let's get the Hell outta here."

Mike spit a wad of phlegm onto the dusty roadway. He turned toward Ernesto. "You got it ready?"

"Yeah," he responded. "We should be good."

Mike turned back toward the pleading man. "You heard the boss. Looks like it's your lucky day, friend."

"Oh...t-thank you…" The wanderer's throat was parched, the words sticking in his throat. "God bless-"

The 5.56 caliber bullet pierced the man's forehead. Its entry and exit were both remarkably clean. The wanderer collapsed to the searing asphalt. It was a good death, especially when so many had not been quite so lucky in these cursed times. It felt good to do *something* to help others — even if it was just to alleviate a little bit of suffering.

Ernesto stepped forward with the makeshift flamethrower. He squeezed the release mechanism, and kerosine sprayed from the nozzle but the flame failed to ignite.

"Shit," he muttered. He looked around the rest of the party and smiled sheepishly.

"Come on man, night ain't waitin'..." Amelia complained from her seat.

Ernesto nodded, relit the wick with his lighter, and tried again. This time fire spouted from the nozzle, and the wanderer's body was engulfed in flame. The dead man's sores popped and hissed as the fluid within boiled away. His sickly skin crackled in the heat. Claire, Mike, Amelia, Ernesto, and Lisa all watched in silence as the man burned. They each waited for the larva to emerge.

The orange flames reflected in Ernesto's cheap aviator glasses. His face was fixed in a self-satisfied smile. *He enjoys this shit way too much. Somebody really needs to take that thing away from him.*

It took longer than usual for the parasite to emerge, and the wanderer's flesh was already blackened when it finally burst forth. The creature tore through his abdomen and screeched in pain. It's soft, semi-translucent flesh had already begun to boil, and its insectoid legs flailed desperately in the air. Partially developed mandibles spread wide in a scream of agony. The larva's lengthy body had already withdrawn inward in a futile attempt at self-preservation, and what had once been a twelve-foot-long worm was now less than a third its original length.

Ernesto stepped forward and began dousing it with more flame. It shrieked, and viscous fluid oozed from its underdeveloped eyes. It withdrew into its death coil and shrunk as the liquid boiled away from its soft body. Ernesto sprayed it again, his smile growing even wider.

"That's enough!" Mike intervened. "It's dead already!" Ernesto released the valve and backed away. The corpse and the parasite continued to burn.

"Are we done playin' good samaritan?"Amelia asked. Her tone was as sharp as a knife's blade. "Feel better about yourselves?"

"I do, *actually*," Lisa replied. "One less of those damn things."

Amelia shrugged. "It woulda' starved to death anyway…God knows there ain't much left for 'em to eat."

Claire took a final drag of her cigarette and flicked the butt into the smoldering heap. Amelia was right about that much at least; There *wasn't* much left these days. She hoped they all starved.

Lisa touched Claire's shoulder gently and directed her attention upward A stymphalian soared through the cloudless, blue sky. It's dozens of wings and thick torso gave it the appearance of an 18th century galleon fused with a grotesque moth. The creature glided slowly and silently through the air. Though it looked small from this distance, its wingspan was as wide as a football field. Stymphalians remained harmless enough, until the sun began to set.

That's when the real trouble began.

The creature was still in the distance, but was following the highway. It would reach them before long. Lisa gave her a knowing glance; They needed to get moving. Claire climbed into the back of the beat-up, old utility van and Lisa followed. Her hands shook, and she considered lighting another cigarette but decided against it. They were running out of tobacco. They were also running out of food, gas, and bullets. Come to think of it, they were running out of just about everything.

✦—◦—✦

Claire remembered the night the stymphalians arrived as clearly as if it were yesterday. The meteor was anticipated to impact just off the Eastern Seaboard, but did not behave as initially expected. It broke into thousands of pieces earlier than it should have, sending a brilliant shower of light streaking across the night sky. Claire watched with the same amazement and relief experienced by billions. Earth's inhabitants would not all be incinerated, swallowed by massive tidal waves, or suffocated by ash. They each celebrated salvation in their own manner beneath the burning sky.

In that last, glorious moment the fate that would soon befall them all had been utterly unthinkable. There was only relief and, for a fleeting moment, hope. On the best nights Claire dreamed of that time. That was the last time that nobody knew what the stymphalians were. There had been so much relief and happiness, but that was all long gone now. The predators had taken everything.

They came in three general varieties. The stymphalians, like the one that now approached from the east, were distant giants. They never touched the ground. They were always in the sky, riding the winds like dark clouds or airships. They were bloated, floating hives for the harvesters that lived inside them. Their harvesters were the most dangerous of their kind.

They did the hunting.

It was the harvesters that sawed through walls, cut metal with their blade-like claws, and carried away screaming families. They reminded Claire of origami. Despite their size they were surprisingly light, and they could fold and unfold their entire bodies as if they were made of little more than paper. They were also relentless predators. Rumors persisted about ways to avoid or combat the harvesters, but each was proven wrong in a violent, savage manner.

There were only two proven ways to avoid them: stay in the sunlight, or keep underground. Deeper was better, and artificial light didn't work—not even the sunlamps. It sounded like a good idea, but people had tried that. It hadn't worked out well for them. If you were lucky they killed you on the spot, and if you were unlucky you were carried back to the stymphalian for storage. If you were particularly unlucky they shoved a tube down your throat and pumped a larva inside you, which is how you ended up like the smouldering wanderer they'd left in the roadway.

That's why you *always* keep one round in the chamber, just in case.

The larva were the third variety. They weren't particularly dangerous, unless they were already inside of you. If they were then you were fucked. They coiled around your spine and injected some sort of stimulant into your brain. It was all designed to keep you feeding the parasite as much and as quickly as possible. They couldn't control you — not entirely — but they could keep you from ending things on your own terms. They could also keep you searching for more food and water until your legs collapsed from under you.

The van struck a pothole and jarred Claire awake. The air conditioner no longer worked, and the only relief from the stifling heat came from the open windows in the front of the van. Even the wind was hot. She looked back through the rearview window in search of the stymphalian, but she didn't see it.

"It's right above us," Lisa said.

"What?" Claire was still struggling to fully reorient herself to her surroundings.

"The stymphalian. It's above us."

Shit.

"Is…is it following us?"

"Looks like it." Lisa's voice was soft today. Claire wondered how she did that — changed her personality from one moment to the next. For as long as Claire could remember, she'd been the same. She both admired and resented her friend's versatility.

"Maybe they're starting to get hungry too?" Lisa smiled. "Shouldn't be a problem. We've still got at least three hours of daylight, and we're almost to town."

Claire hated relocating; It made her nervous. She'd never had to move with so few people, and with so little equipment. The fact that a stymphalian now hovered somewhere above them certainly didn't help ease her nerves. She needed a smoke. Claire opened the pack, eyed the three remaining cigarettes, and closed it back again. She wasn't sure exactly why she did it. She knew exactly how many were left, and it certainly didn't make her feel any better. *Stupid tick.*

She took a deep breath and reassured herself that she had everything she needed for the next couple days: rations, a flashlight, an odd collection of batteries, and a single round loaded in her .357 revolver. They had plenty of water — enough to last them all at least a week. The group also had solar panels and two generators. Fuel was becoming an issue, but they didn't need gas to survive. Not in the short-term, at least.

Amelia looked back from the passenger seat. "That was a waste back there, seriously."

"Yeah, well, sometimes it's the little things in life, ya know?" Ernesto chuckled to himself. He was one of those guys that kept a baby face despite his age. He pretended to shave, but didn't need to. A few wispy hairs sprouted here and there across his otherwise smooth skin.

Claire rested her head back against the window, watching as the desolate landscape slipped slowly by. Barren, undulating hills defined the horizon. Scraggly pines and patches of yucca flanked a small gully that ran parallel to the highway. Some people liked the desert, but Claire had never been one of them. It's one redeeming quality had been the night sky, but nobody would be spending any time gazing up at that in the near future. Sometimes, when she closed her eyes, she could still see the sky burning. Claire hoped to never see the stars again.

She pretended not to notice the shadow that followed in the hills beyond. They all saw it, and acknowledging its presence didn't help anything. The van struck another pothole, and her head slammed against the glass. "Jesus, Mike…" Claire rubbed her head. "Are you aiming for those things or what?"

"We're getting closer to town now. Gettin' to be a bit more traffic." Mike navigated their vehicle through the burnt husks of minivans and overturned tractor trailers. They all looked like they'd been there since the night of the starshower, and they weren't likely to contain anything beyond the charred corpses of their passengers. Still, Claire wouldn't mind taking a look inside if they'd had more time.

Claire didn't notice the bomb until the moment it exploded. There was no warning from Mike or screeching brakes. One moment she was looking out at the remains of a Dodge Ram, and the next the van was on its side, grinding its way across the pavement. The nearby window shattered, and glass shards cut into her face. She was thrown forward and into the back of the passenger side seat. Searing pain shot through her ribs upon impact.

The van finally skidded to a halt.

Claire's ears rang, and her chest ached. Her vision faltered. She tried to stand but was unable. Lisa was beside her, and she had to be alive because Claire could feel her moving. She thought she could hear Lisa speak, but her words were muffled and indecipherable. There were flashes of light, the sound of a nearby explosion, and heat against her exposed skin. The smell of burning flesh followed. It was a scent with which she'd become all too familiar. *Raiders. It had to be. They'd driven right into an ambush.*

A dust-covered figure emerged in the periphery of her view. She couldn't tell whether it was a man or a woman. The raider's face was obscured by ski goggles and a bandana. Whoever it was carried a weathered, double-barrel shotgun. It's barrel had been sawed off right above the forestock. Claire needed to grab her revolver, but found herself incapable of moving. Her body simply didn't respond to her mind's commands. *Was she paralyzed?* Her breathing became erratic.

The raider aimed the shotgun toward where Claire could feel Lisa pressed against her. There were more muffled words, but she couldn't tell if they came from Lisa or the masked figure. She knew exactly where the sound of the gunshot originated from, however. Claire felt something wet and warm splatter against her face. She didn't have to wonder about the liquid's origin either. The raider knelt down beside her and started rifling through Lisa's clothing.

She *needed* to draw her revolver. She had one round in the chamber with this asshole's name written all over it. Was this guy really just going to leave her here for the buzzards? Was she not even worth a single shotgun shell? *Why couldn't she move?* Claire wanted to scream, but a pitiful gasp was all that emerged.

The raider knelt down in front of her and pressed the warm steel of the shotgun's twin barrels against her forehead. A gloved hand proceeded to rummage through her pockets. *Grab the shotgun barrel. Draw the revolver.* She commanded herself. The raider found her pack of cigarettes and examined it. That asshole was sure to be disappointed with its contents. *Grab the shotgun barrel. Draw the revolver.* She repeated in her mind.

This time — utterly without explanation — it worked.

The raider must have been as surprised as she was. Claire grabbed the shotgun barrel, just as she'd imagined doing, and threw it to one side. The masked figure pulled the trigger, but was ever-so-slightly too slow. There was a deafening blast, and Claire could feel her left ear being shredded apart by pellets. She drew the .357 revolver from her belt, shoving the barrel upward into the bandana that covered her attacker's face. When she felt the resistance of steel pressing against flesh she pulled the trigger.

The .357 caliber bullet didn't make a clean exit like the .556. The back of the raider's skull exploded, painting the ceiling of the van. That was supposed to be *her* head. That was supposed to be *her* bullet. She'd saved it for the day everything finally went to complete shit. That day was starting to seem closer and closer at hand.

Not much remained of Lisa's head but a dangling jaw and a spinal column topped with mangled flesh; Everything above the jawline had been peeled back and sprayed across the front console of the van. Her body was still propped up against the back of the driver's side seat. Lisa had deserved a better death, but at least it had been a quick one. Claire climbed out of the van's open passenger door. The metal on the exterior was charred and hot. She lost her grip and collapsed to the asphalt, landing next to smouldering human remains and a ruptured gas tank. It was Ernesto; Of course that idiot would go and get himself blown up.

The scorched asphalt burned her skin, but she couldn't seem to get up. The fall from the van had knocked whatever fight she had remaining out of her. Another dust-covered raider stepped from around the side of the van, this one clearly a man. His leathery, sun-cured skin hung loosely from an imposing frame. He looked as if he'd lost some weight recently. Everyone had. He clutched a tire iron in his oversized fist.

Claire didn't have a hat trick waiting for this one. She could barely move, and her mind was a mess. Her .357 was spent. She should have grabbed the shotgun, but she hadn't. That was the kind of shitty decision making that got you killed. She accepted that. Still, she'd have preferred death by shotgun to a piece of metal.

A shot rang out. Claire couldn't hear much over the ringing in her ears, but she could tell it wasn't as close as the others had been. A small, red mark appeared in the middle of the big man's stained wife-beater. The red expanded rapidly until it ran down his threadbare jeans. He fell to one knee, the tire iron clattering to the pavement. The big man followed shortly thereafter.

Mike approached moments later with his AR-15 at the

ready. Amelia was with him, and Mike took the big man's tire iron. There were words exchanged between Mike and the dying man, but she couldn't make them out. Mike used the tire iron to bash in its owner's face; No doubt he was trying to conserve ammunition — *stingy bastard*. Blood ran across the asphalt.

Amelia tried to speak to her, but Claire still couldn't make out what anyone was saying. The ringing drowned out all but the loudest sounds. Amelia's face was a bit cut up, but she otherwise looked in decent shape. Claire imagined that she looked much worse right now. Amelia's lips tightened. She adjusted her visor and looked back toward Mike. They exchanged words, and Claire could guess pretty well what they were talking about.

They were deciding whether or not to leave her there.

For a brief moment the sky darkened. Claire looked up to see the stymphalian was still circling high overhead. The sun was already beginning its descent, and the shadows of the surrounding hills were beginning to grow. It wouldn't be long before the harvesters issued forth from their bloated hive. She had to stand up, or she was dead. She knew that look in Amelia's eyes. It was the same one she'd given Sara, Michael, and Diego when the party had left them behind. It was the same look she gave children, elderly, and those too sick to assume responsibility for. It was the look of this whole damned world.

Claire rose to her feet. It was painful, but she did it all the same. Amelia eyed her up and down. "I'm fine," Claire said. She couldn't be exactly sure of her volume. "Let's get going." Amelia glanced back toward Mike for approval. He was already stuffing bottles of water, dented cans of corn, and bolt cutters into a bag. Mike glanced toward the sun, the circling stymphalian, and then back at Amelia. He nodded slowly. Claire could just make out Amelia's response.

"Fine."

⊰───⊱

The party's objective was an old copper mine dug into the hills just outside of town. Ernesto had done a recon of the place a couple weeks back, and it had been sealed from the outside with a lock. From what he'd told the group the place should be perfect. It provided easy access to the town and a door that could be sealed to keep the harvesters at bay. The old mines ran deep — far deeper than they'd ever need — and there was even a creek running just outside. It was a shame the dumb bastard wouldn't be around to harvest the fruits of his labor.

That was the light at the end of the tunnel. They would be pressed, however, to make it there before nightfall. Mike and Amelia had elected to follow the gully, rather than the roadway. It was technically a more direct route, and they'd no doubt hoped to lose the stymphalian that tracked them from high above. Unfortunately the sparse, sickly desert vegetation had proven wholly incapable of masking their movement. The terrain was also difficult. Claire's every step was painful, and she struggled to keep up.

She reminded herself that, against all odds, she was still alive. Dying now — after everything she had been through — would be pointless. She *had* to keep going. She adjusted the weight of the shotgun on her shoulder. They had only managed to find three shells on the raiders bodies, but it was more than she'd had at sunrise, so at least there was that. It felt reassuring to carry a one-way ticket off this God-forsaken planet.

The shadows in the lifeless hills were growing long. They reached the outskirts of town just as the sun dipped below the horizon, where all three paused briefly to watch as harvesters began spilling out from the stymphalian. Hundreds swarmed around the beast like flies on a corpse. They wouldn't begin their hunt just yet, but time was certainly running out. Once their eyes adjusted to the world outside of their broodmother's insulating sacks they would descend, like locusts in search of prey. They seemed to grow increasingly ravenous with each passing day. In this blasted landscape Claire could only imagine that their senses would be honed to precision.

Mike removed the old AM/FM radio from his bag and set the dial to 550 kilohertz. There was nothing but static— for now. Once the harvesters began communicating with one another they'd know. The bastards were pitch-black, and damned near impossible to see in the dark, so the radio would be the best indicator they'd have of their arrival. It also seemed to confuse them a bit if they got close enough. Mike and Amelia looked at one another and broke into a run, and Claire did her best to follow.

Claire couldn't keep up for long. Soon Mike and Amelia were nowhere in sight. She couldn't blame them — not entirely. She'd have done the same thing if she was in better condition. The last vestiges of sunlight were beginning to fade, and a dull, orange glow was all that remained of the sun retreating below the horizon. She knew exactly where she was going. They'd gone over the maps a dozen times, and the town seemed empty enough. That, at least, was a good thing. Interactions with strangers were rarely the pleasant affair they had once been.

Darkness fell as Claire hobbled through desolate streets. The stars began to reveal themselves overhead. They were reluctant at first, then brazen, and they were brilliant in the absence of artificial light. Claire had never wanted to see the damned things again in her life. She did her best not to look up—to stay focused on the road—but the cosmic display overhead made the task nearly impossible.

The stars winked out as the swarm of harvesters began their descent.

Claire staggered across the dilapidated, old bridge that led to the mine. She was exhausted, and could scarcely breathe. She couldn't hear much of anything, except for the incessant ringing in her ears. She could still feel, however, and at that moment she felt the bridge shift under her feet. She turned back the way she came and flicked on the maglight she'd taped to the shotgun barrel, but the beam revealed nothing.

She turned it back toward the mine. A pitch-black harvester crouched in front of her—only feet away. Light reflected off the creature's insectoid, compound eyes, giving them the multi-chromatic sheen of a butterfly's wings or an oil slick. The harvester didn't make a sound; It simply lunged forward with his gaping mandibles.

Claire fired the shotgun. The creature recoiled, emitting a piercing shriek. She felt pressure growing behind her eyes. She slid the barrel selector with her thumb and waited to take another shot. The harvester spread its massive, fleshy wings and dove into the gully below. Claire pressed forward with every ounce of her remaining strength, the stars flickering as black silhouettes danced above.

She entered the dusty mineshaft and rushed toward the iron door. It had to have been at least a hundred years old, and she was surprised to find it had been left slightly ajar. The cut lock lay on the ground nearby; Mike and Amelia had clearly been here. Claire didn't have the luxury of contemplating her next move as she squeezed in through the opening and made her way inside.

She pushed the door closed behind her, and the darkness inside became oppressive. She leaned against the old, iron door and waited for her pursuers to wrench it open. She felt nothing. Eventually her breathing steadied, and her heart-rate decreased. All that remained was the ringing, the exhaustion, and the pain.

The beam of light issuing from her flashlight illuminated a long, straight shaft. Cart tracks continued on into the gloom beyond, and dozens of ancillary tunnels branched off to the left and right. Claire shined the beam on objects piled against the doorway. There were rusty chains and dry-rotted crates, which *something* had pushed aside. That's when she noticed the blood. It was streaked across the nearby rock, and in her panic and exhaustion she hadn't taken notice. She hadn't seen what was right around her.

The bolt cutters and the radio lay on the ground near-by. She pointed her shotgun back down the mineshaft and swallowed deeply. There was no movement. She couldn't hear anything, but she was unlikely to either way. Careful to keep her light and shotgun oriented down the mineshaft, Claire knelt down and picked up the blood-spattered radio. She placed it to her ear and listened. The radio emitted an unnatural, high-pitch whine, and she could feel pressure growing behind her eyes.

Claire placed the radio slowly — quietly — back to the ground. The beam of the maglight grew unstable as her hands began to shake. She stepped forward into the mine, careful to ensure each step was as silent as possible. The smaller, ancillary tunnels led off into blackness. Her vision was restricted to a solitary beam of light. Whatever her fears, she had to find the creature that had made its way inside. The light wouldn't last forever. After that…well, she preferred not to think about what came next.

She passed the first set of intersecting tunnels, then the second, then the third. She swore the light was dimming, flickering even. Were the batteries about to die? She could swap them out, but that would mean time spent in the dark. She'd rather wait. It was all in her head anyway, it was all just in her head…

Something damp brushed against her shoulder. She spun around and pulled the trigger. Mike staggered back against the stone, cradling the side of his chest. Blood ran from the wound.

She'd shot him. She'd shot Mike.

Claire gasped, and tried to explain herself. "I-I didn't hear you…You snuck up on me…" Mike pulled his hand away from the wound and examined the blood. He said words that she couldn't understand, and the ringing seemed worse than ever. The single lightsource cast deep shadows, and she couldn't read his lips.

Suddenly mosaic eyes reflected the light, and pitch-black mandibles dug into Mike's flesh. He screamed. That much, at least, she could still hear. It dragged him back into the nearby tunnel while she aimed the shotgun and pulled the trigger, but nothing happened. Only one shell remained, and it was still in her pocket. She jacked open the chamber and the two expended shells ejected. She slid the final shell into place and snapped the chamber shut, but it was already too late. Mike and the harvester were gone, disappearing into the gloom.

For a moment Claire froze. She considered pursuing the creature, but decided against it. Mike had left her behind, and she had to take care of herself. All she had to do was make it until sunrise. Once the sun came up she could return to the crash, where she could get the solar panels and have all the light she needed. She'd find more ammunition, and clear out whatever harvesters still remained within the mines.

She could still make this work.

Claire found the narrowest crevice she could and squeezed her way through. She'd grown thin since the starshower, and could fit into pretty small places. There was a little chamber at the back of the passage where she sat on the cold stone, waiting in the blackness. Her ears rang and her flashlight grew dim, so she turned it off. She could *really* use a cigarette.

She tried replacing the batteries, but they didn't work. After several minutes spent fumbling about in the dark she was in no better situation than when she began. Claire intermittently turned the light back on to see if she was being followed: She was, of course. Harvesters were relentless.

It squeezed its way through the narrow space, dislocating and twisting its bones where necessary. Its approach was slow, but steady. Each time the light reflected in the creature's eyes it was a little closer than it had been the moment before. Claire considered using her last shotgun shell on it — placing the barrel right to the head and pulling the trigger — but she wasn't sure that it would be enough to kill it. Even if it did, its body was blocking the narrow crevice. There would be no escape.

As the harvester neared Claire's chamber she pressed the button to turn the flashlight back on. It didn't work. She tried again — still nothing. She pictured the desperate, fading eyes of the wanderer they'd killed back on the highway. She could still hear the screech of the boiling parasite inside him, and she could smell its bubbling flesh.

That wasn't going to be her.

Claire's hope died with the light. As she recalled the night that the sky burned she placed her mouth around the barrel of the shotgun. It really had been beautiful, even if it was the beginning of the end. Everything since had been nothing more than a horrible dream, and she was ready to wake up.

Claire recalled the stars. She was glad she'd gotten to see them one last time. She liked to imagine that there was someplace out there not so dissimilar from the world she'd once known.

As mandibles pressed against her flesh she squeezed the trigger.

T.M. Brown
About the Author

Trevor Brown, who writes under the pen name T.M. Brown, serves as an officer in the U.S. Army. He currently lives in Colorado Springs, Colorado with his beautiful wife, Anna, and his two dogs, Fry and Zapp. Although Trevor has long held a passion for speculative fiction, he has only recently taken up writing for publication. His preferred genres include horror, strange fiction, and dark fantasy.

T.M. Brown's debut novella 'The Gloam' is currently available on Amazon in both paperback and Kindle formats. He also has a variety of dark fiction under contract with independent publishers including: Black Hare Press, Burial Day Books, Cosmic Horror Monthly, Eerie River Publishing, Kyanite Publishing, Nothing Ever Happens in Fox Hollow, Sinister Smile Press, and Terror Tract.

You can find him on Facebook at https://www.facebook.com/RavenousShadows or on Twitter @TMBrown_Author

The Winged Plague
E.L. Giles

"I miss the sun, Papa. And the blue sky too. I want to play outside, or go to the beach. I loved the beach…" Caleb's voice cracked. Staring outside, his eyes welled with hot tears as he contemplated the raging storm. "It's raining. It's always raining, and I hate it."

Wilson, tired and defeated, let out a sigh. "I know, Son."

What else could be said? There didn't seem to subsist any hope, any end to this perpetual madness. As far as Wilson's eyes could see the black clouds stretched out malignantly beyond the horizon, vomiting poison that flooded continually onto the surface of the earth and wiping out nearly every living thing. And yet this calamity did not overthrow the threat of the things that lived beyond the noxious azure.

A sudden gust of wind hit the wall of the old farmhouse, shaking it and startling the young boy, who stepped away from the window.

"It's just the wind," Wilson said reassuringly. Caleb went back to the window and searched the sky again.

"Are they there, Papa?" Caleb asked, squinting past the gloom. He saw nothing, and heard nothing except the commotion of the storm and the claps of thunder. "I don't see them anywhere. Do you think they are gone?"

Wilson reached for his flashlight and pointed it through the window toward a distant point in their backyard. He turned it on and off repeatedly until a dark, black-winged shape descended with a piercing shriek, flapping its giant wings and propelling raindrops in every direction. It allowed Wilson to clearly distinguish the abominable beast and its luminescent, yellow eyes. The creature charged the beam of light repeatedly, each time more violently, screaming frustratedly when Wilson turned off the light. The creature stayed there for a moment, roaming the area like a rabid jackal. It growled as it approached the farmhouse, as if it understood the trick.

The beasts were growing more intelligent with time, more than Wilson had expected.

"Don't move," Wilson murmured.

The beast sniffed and advanced surreptitiously, looking from one side to the other before it finally gave up and sprang into the misty sky. A tremor of fear went up Wilson's spine. Neither of them dared move for quite some time, until Caleb couldn't resist the urge to seek comfort in his father's arms.

"Everything will be okay, Son. I promise."

"You don't know that." Caleb weakly punched his

father's arm before crawling back into his tight embrace. "You can't promise what you don't know! Why are they still there? Why aren't they gone?"

As much as Wilson wanted to utter something encouraging and reassuring, there was nothing he could say. Caleb was right. Nothing was okay, and the beasts never left the sky. Once in a while the rain did pause, but it only allowed the toxic mist to elevate and spread unhindered, propagating more death and disaster.

Feeling weak Wilson released his son. He studied Caleb's eyes, and saw the dread inhabiting his mind. He witnessed the apprehension that took his childish innocence away, as the young boy was neither stupid nor blind. He knew what was coming. He didn't search for the beasts outside without reason; Caleb had seen their rations being depleted, and he was aware of the perilous journey to come. They must go out and seek food, and more than likely a new shelter. Feigning sleep Caleb had often seen his father preparing for their upcoming trek. He had heard Wilson sobbing desperately and praying to God, which he'd never done before all this began.

Caleb stopped counting the nights his father spent outside, clothed in ill-assorted apparel meant to protect him from the rain. He stopped numbering the hours he waited for him, the sheets pulled up to his chin, staring at the door of the farmhouse until his father pushed it open without any noise. He watched his father wash frantically before sinking back into the bed, as if he'd never left, but Caleb knew. He saw the sickness that was slowly getting a grip on his father, diminishing his strength and making him cough and spit blood. All of this weighed on him, but he hid his worry from Wilson.

Instead of dwelling on the challenges of their current situation, Wilson decided to simply smile and wait until after they'd eaten their last morsel of food and drank their last drops before speaking about the bleak journey to come.

Pulling the curtains down Wilson walked over to the table and lit a single candle. He dressed up two worn, porcelain plates with the contents of their last can of tuna. The rain plummeted onto the tin roof like heavy hail, resonating throughout the old farmhouse while they ate their meager rations. They were quite accustomed to the downpour, and paid it no notice. Caleb, after finishing his supper, fell asleep on Wilson's lap, comforted by the bedtime stories his father chanted over the Hellish din. There, in that childlike, dreamy realm, no monsters lived.

Wilson stared into the darkness for the whole night, listening as the rain gradually calmed to a stop. Instantly the acrid smell of death elevated, permeating the air and tickling his nose. It initiated a painful coughing fit, and Caleb's face contorted into a grimace of terror. He opened his drowsy eyes and gazed into the gloom of the waking morning.

"The rain stopped," Wilson said grimly, wiping his lips clean from the blood he knew stained them. "We need to go."

"No…" Caleb released a heart-wrenching sob. "I don't want to go. It's our home! We'll die outside."

"We'll die *here*," Wilson said, brushing his son's greasy hair with his fingers. "We won't go far though. You remember old Wyatt, and his little farm with the green porch and the tiny orchard?"

Caleb nodded, his eyes widening with the memories of sunny days when he'd played hide and seek with Wyatt's grandson. "Yes, the old man with the blind dog, right? We're going to live with them? Is Anthony there too? We could play together. I miss him."

Wilson stared at the floor and, gathering all the courage he had left, shook his head. All the happiness vanished from Caleb's countenance. "No, Caleb. Old Wyatt…and Anthony…they're gone, but we should find plenty of provisions to keep us going for a little while."

"Gone, like dead? How?"

The death of Wyatt's family flashed through Wilson's mind: The flying creature had descended from the abysmal sky, shrieking alarmingly and charging them with such rapidity that Wilson had found himself nailed to the ground, trapped in a sudden lethargy. He could only watch the spectacle of claws and sharp beak, horrified. The family was ravaged — skin, muscle, and sinew torn to pieces — until the old man and his family lay limp on the ground. Not even the fury of the old man's dog, or the power of his double-barrelled Winchester shotgun, could overcome the beast.

"They're dead. That's all."

Wilson got up and set about preparing the heavy tarps he'd converted into rain suits, helping Caleb put his on. He then retrieved the rustic gas masks he'd crafted using plastic bottles, pieces of clean cotton, and activated charcoal. Finally they put on their ski goggles, adjusting them to be as airtight as possible.

"Now listen to me. When we get outside, we can't talk. We can't make any noise, and we'll use the cover of darkness to move. You walk when I do, and you stop when I do. We don't run, we don't make any kind of quick movements. The beasts can't see us unless we're too conspicuous."

"Are they blind, the beasts?"

"Sort of. They see light, and can sense movement, but they can't see what's not moving. I've already placed markers leading to Wyatt's house. You think you can do it?"

Caleb hesitated, and finally nodded. Wilson stopped by the doorframe, studying the world outside and measuring the length of time between each flash of lightning. When he felt reassured enough he went out, followed by Caleb. Taking advantage of the darkness they crossed the dismantled porch and stepped down into the cratered yard, approaching the contorted tree where Wilson had placed the first locator — a piece of red tape around the trunk. They waited there for the next flash to appear, and then fade, before daring to venture through the yard to the next locator.

All around them deep puddles, rotten carcasses, and debris of every kind littered the scarred ground. Quickly the thick, miasmatic cloud elevated up to a few inches above the ground, though it was too heavy to rise higher than calf height. It covered almost everything, but Wilson had already memorized the many obstacles scattering their path. He knew where to step, and where not to. The vile smell was becoming prominent as it burned in Wilson's weak lungs, making him more and more dizzy. He fought the impulse to cough as they stopped and waited again for the next flash of lightning to die, then continued on their way.

Their advance was laborious and tedious for Wilson, as every step demanded more strength than he had thought he possessed. After the fourth locator they stopped for a longer period of time, Wilson trying to catch some of his lost air. He felt his son wriggling restlessly and growing more and more worried. Caleb pulled his father's hand and led him across the yard while the beasts roared close above them, fighting each other and whipping the air with their giant wings. Caleb avoided giving the ominous noise any attention.

They were about midway between two locators, Wyatt's domain almost in sight ahead of them beyond the line of putrescent gas, when a series of violent thunderclaps tore through the sky. Wilson stumbled over the carcass of a horse he hadn't seen, and he rolled under a giant pine tree whose needles had faded to a strange shade somewhere between orange and brown.

"Papa, are you okay?" Caleb ran to his father, who pulled him down and clasped a hand over his mouth.

Wilson was attempting to raise himself into a sitting

position when a sharp pain flared up his left leg — an extruding rib bone of the dead horse had pierced his flesh. A growl exited his mouth, too fast for him to hold it back. He gritted his teeth, killing the succeeding grunts as he pressed a hand against the gaping wound on his thigh. Wilson's distress didn't go unnoticed. An ear-splitting, bestial scream awakened Wilson's most raw and primitive survival instincts. One of the monsters descended and hovered over their heads, circling the area in the manner of a detestable vulture.

Wilson placed one arm around his son's trembling shoulder, pulling his head against his chest and pressing tightly. They stood absolutely still, partly dissimulated under the cover of fog. They held their breath, fighting back sobs and tamping down their fright. Wilson's heart beat in his ears, and all he could hear was the annoying whoosh of blood. Often the winged beast came into sight, screaming and creating within Wilson an unprecedented level of panic and terror. Another beast then came unto sight, then another. One of them landed atop a tree nearby, perching there menacingly. Through the branches, and the misty clouds of gas, Wilson noticed the beast's yellow eyes scanning the ground. Instantly Wilson closed his eyes and prayed the monster hadn't seen them.

"Keep your eyes closed," Wilson murmured slowly. "Do not draw their attention."

Wilson's weak brain worked furiously, searching for any possible escape from this deadly trap. He found none, and now that the rain was coming back every hope seemed to have died.

The wait was excruciating. Waiting for death, knowing it was coming but not knowing exactly when it would strike, was unbearable. The rain unexpectedly came back, intensifying with each minute. Cold permeated the air, and the raindrops turned into hail that pummeled painfully against the exposed parts of Wilson's body. He felt his son trembling more violently and, very slowly, moved to cover him with his own body, exposing his back to the elements…and the rabid beasts. Wilson resisted the agony, fighting the drowsiness and the urge to simply let go of life. The poisoned water worked its way into Wilson's system at an alarming pace, making his wound ache unbearably as it insinuated itself into every layer of tissue.

"Everything will be alright, Son," Wilson murmured into Caleb's ear. The young boy sobbed. "Shh, calm down. You're safe. They won't hurt you."

The barking and snarling of a distant dog elevated against the thundering storm, snatching the beasts' attention. Wilson twisted his head and noticed that the one perched on the tree had already sprung away into the air, followed closely by the two others who roared and tried to overtake it. Each was desperate to be the first to sink its awful beak into the poor canine.

Wilson didn't think twice. Feeling a surge of adrenaline-induced strength he took his son in his arms and bounded to his feet, heedless of his wound. He began to run away from the beasts, straight toward old Wyatt's farm. There existed no torment greater than his pain, and Wilson used all the will he had to not fall into the unfathomable abyss of madness.

"We're almost there," said Wilson, glimpsing the rustic house during a short, bright thunderclap. But the poison had already invaded Wilson's system, stiffening his muscles. They refused to obey anymore, and during his abrupt fall Wilson used what was left of his reflexes to protect his son.

"Papa. Papa, wake up! They're coming! Hurry!" Caleb shook his father, panicked at the sight of the creatures that were now departing from the limp body of the dog, unsatiated. "Papa, please, why don't you wake up?"

The wailing of the beasts echoed across the field. Caleb desperately pulled his father, trying to get him to safety.

"Please wake up!"

Wilson opened his heavy eyes, deciphering nothing other than dark, blurry outlines. He took off his mask, but his sight didn't come back. He raised a trembling hand and pulled Caleb's ear closer to his mouth.

"Run."

Wilson pushed his son away. There was no pain more harrowing than forcing his son to go off alone, making him run away into the wild in a world where men were destined for extinction. Wilson successfully rolled onto his back, and with his elbows he weakly pushed his torso up. The creatures were getting closer, their outlines cutting against the stormy sky. He inhaled as deeply as his failing lungs permitted, and screamed at the beasts to come his way.

The flapping intensified, and he continued drawing them his way.

"I love you, Son," Wilson said, letting the words escape his nearly paralyzed lips. Wilson twisted his head and squinted, but no one stood by his side. Caleb had disappeared into the overgrown ferns and wild herbs. He was probably headed toward Wyatt's house. Wilson focused on this thought as the beasts descended upon him, letting go of himself with a sense of peace he wouldn't have believed possible.

Eric Labrie Giles
About the Author

Eric Labrie Giles is a former musician and music composer who diverted into writing some years ago. He specializes mainly in dark stories, science-fiction, dystopian, weird, cosmic and horror stuffs. He loves stories with a thick ambiance over action-packed book. Algernon Blackwood, Ray Bradbury and Frank Belknap Long stand among his favorite authors, alongside with H.P. Lovecraft, Ambrose Bierce and so many other. In 2019 and 2020, Eric has seen over forty of his short stories and drabbles published through many best-selling themed anthologies. Later this year, Eric plans releasing the last instalment of his BIRDMAN PROJECT series. After that, he will start working on some new story ideas that have patiently waited in a corner of his brain for some times now.

Facebook: www.facebook.com/elgilesauthor
Website: www.elgilesauthor.com

Rainfall
Marie McWilliams

I remember the day it came so vividly, its memory etched inside my mind to be replayed nightly in all of its horror. The sky was heavy and dark. Black clouds had gathered, threatening to unleash their load at any moment. You could smell that it would rain soon, and there was something else carried on the breeze, something metallic that was dismissed as quickly as it was identified.

My mother had phoned from work, telling me to bring in the sheets from the washing line before the heavens opened, and my little brother Mark was in the yard practicing with his new BMX bike - a gift for his eighth birthday. I yelled for him to give me a hand, but he pretended not to hear and carried on. I wanted to be mad at him, but the way he stuck his tongue out as he concentrated on going up and down the step was far too adorable. I felt the pang of irritation fade as quickly as it came.

I struggled with the basket, dragging it inside and abandoning it at the back door. My brother's head appeared from behind the curtain, his attention suddenly and coincidentally away from his bike just as the chores were done.

"Can I practice out front, on the street?"

"I don't know. Cars can come through here pretty quick sometimes, and it's going to rain any moment."

"I know, but the high curbs outside the house would be way better to practice on. I'll be super, super careful, I promise. Please? Pretty please?"

"Fine, but you have to come in as soon as it starts to rain, okay?"

"Okay!"

I know I should have said no. God, I wish I had said no. I think about that moment so often, reliving it over and over again. If I had said no, would he have lived? He might have carried on playing out in the yard anyway, where it was supposed to be safer, but maybe he would have come inside. Maybe he would have gotten angry with me, the way he so often did, yelling about a lack of fairness before slamming his bedroom door. Maybe that two-letter word would have saved his life, but this is something I'll never know and something I'll never forgive myself for. *Why didn't I just say no?*

I plonked myself on the sofa near the front window so I could keep an eye on him, somehow feeling like this was enough to keep him safe. It wasn't. I was flicking through my social media, my friend's updates mixed in with adverts for face cream and clothing brands. All of that stuff had seemed so important before, *before*. It was his scream that brought me instantly back into the real world.

I've never heard anyone make sounds like that before. It was so desperate, so ferocious. A scream of true, agonising pain. I sprang up just in time to see him fold over onto the pavement outside, becoming silent and too-still as rain continued to fall. I ran, yanking the front door open, and the smell hit me immediately. It smelled like burned flesh, like bacon left under the grill too long, but there was something else. It was that same metallic scent again, except stronger and more pungent. Everything seemed warmer somehow, like walking into a tropical plant house or like steam rushing at me as I opened a pan lid, except the stench in the air wasn't mom's casserole.

I retched as soon as it hit me, dry-heaving at the doorstep, my eyes watering and causing everything to blur. As I gagged and heaved on all fours I saw steam rising from everything beyond the porch, and I realised that everything around me looked wrong beyond the blurring effect of my tears. My car's red paint seemed to be running, the tires slowly releasing air from melted edges as plants and grass died before my eyes. The whole world looked like a watercolour with too much water added, like a Salvador Dali painting come to life.

I couldn't understand it at first, and it didn't register what these signs could have meant as I dragged myself up. I stumbled towards Mark's prone frame, the smell becoming more over powering with each and every step. I felt my shoes growing heavy, sticky, and I looked down to realize the rubber soles were melting. I should have understood then, but my mind, perhaps out of shock or denial, was unwilling to register these clear and present signs. I refused to accept that Mark might not be okay, and I had convinced myself he must have merely fallen and hit his head, or that he was playing dead. I tried to believe it was just a trick against his gullible, big sister, but as soon as I saw his face I knew he was dead. *His face.*

I've never felt pain like that before; It was a sudden rush of grief and agony as I realized my baby brother was gone forever. Maybe I screamed, or maybe I just wept. I remember a noise coming from my body which I'd never made before, a wail of pure grief. He barely looked like Mark anymore. His skin was blistered and peeling, exposing raw, red flesh. The acrid smell of chemicals and cooked flesh overwhelmed me, and I vomited. His clothes were gone in parts, or melted into his flesh, and he was twisted and contorted, his hands balled into tight fists. The only part that remained was his eyes.

He had been wearing his New York Yankees baseball hat like he always did, regardless of the weather or occasion. The top of the hat was singed and melted amongst tufts of burned hair and exposed, raw scalp, but the peak, while damaged on top, had protected the upper part of his face. His eyes were wide with pain and fear. I had teased him so many times about that hat, saying he must sleep and shower in it or that it was like a toddler carrying around a safety blanket.

These memories stabbed at me now like daggers, and I realized I had been mean to him so many times. I had said such cruel things, words I could never take back. When was the last time I had told him I loved him? I couldn't remember; Maybe never. That wasn't the kind of things that brothers and sisters said to one another, not at this age. I knew, even in that moment, that I would regret it for the rest of my life.

I don't know how long I stood there like that. I wanted to look away, to stop seeing the horror before me, but I couldn't. Part of me thought it was some kind of elaborate joke, that things would be fine again, that he'd get up and yell "Surprise!" as I scolded him through tears of anger and relief. But that's not how life works; Not then, and certainly not now. I wanted to hold him, but I couldn't bring myself to touch the raw, blistered flesh that once was my brother.

I thought I could hear a slight sizzling sound and at first, believing it to be my brother's deformed body continuing to cook and melt, then I felt the bile begin to rise in my throat once again. Before I could vomit I felt searing, hot pain on the bottoms of my feet, and I realized too late that the same rainfall that had done this to Mark was laying on the ground as normal rain would. I had stood long enough for it to burn through my soles and reach my now-exposed feet.

I screamed and ran for the house, each step sending more heat and pain through me before I threw myself into the house. I kicked off what was left of my shoes and dragged myself to the downstairs bathroom, forcing them under cold water for as long as I could stand it. It felt like a chemical burn, like something acidic stripping whatever it touched. My feet were red, raw and blistered, but I was alive - unlike Mark. I lay there, weeping while I prayed I would wake up from this nightmare. I was unable to get Mark's body out of my mind.

I must have passed out from the pain, because when I awoke it was dark outside. My first thought had been my mother. She should have been home by then. Had she been outside when this terrible horror was unleashed from the sky? I reassessed my feet: They weren't as bad as I initially thought, and if I kept them clean and dry I would recover. I grabbed some aloe Mom had for sunburns from under the sink and lathered it on, a mixture of pain and relief washing over me. I used the hand towels as makeshift bandages and hobbled out into the hall.

The front door lay open, and for a split second I thought perhaps Mom had come home, but I quickly remembered that I had left it that way in my panic. I checked the driveway anyway and saw her car was still missing, which made sense; If she had returned she would have found me and comforted me. I couldn't bring myself to turn and look at the fallen figure to my left, so I simply closed the door.

I limped to the landline on the hall table, but there was no dial tone. I assumed the acid rain, or whatever it was, must have damaged the lines. I wobbled towards the sofa and grabbed my mobile phone. There was no signal, no internet, nothing. I went numb as I noticed the distinct lack of people. There was no sound except for distant sirens. Where were the Police? An ambulance? Anyone? My brother's corpse, among countless others, lay on the streets outside. I grabbed the remote and turned on the TV, but found nothing except static and 'Channel off air' messages. What the Hell was going on?

I forced myself to make the painful walk to the attic room where my mom had her paint studio. There was an old, dial radio she listened to while she worked. I remember how she would sing out loud to music, often off key or out of tune, but she never cared. She just liked to sing, and I missed the sound of her voice. I sat on the floor and twisted the dial. There was nothing except static at first, but eventually I heard a weak voice. I found the channel, and the man's voice was suddenly sharp and loud in the eerie silence of my house.

"....where emergency procedures are now being implemented and help provided. I repeat, this is Captain Mark Walters broadcasting to you on the emergency channel from Sanford Army Base. I cannot explain what is happening, but I can provide you with what little information we have so far, as well as evacuation procedures. The rain, which fell at approximately 13:00 hours today on March 31st of 2020, was some kind of chemical rain. The origin is unknown; However, its destructive abilities are clear. Do not venture out of doors if it appears to be raining. The substance is capable of burning flesh and causing significant harm. The secondary reaction is even more baffling. The ,bodies of those exposed have somehow become reanimated, and appear to be extremely dangerous. If you have family or friends who were tragically killed by this phenomenon do NOT, I repeat DO NOT, approach their bodies. If they come to you you must strike them down immediately or they WILL kill you. Whatever reaction the rain has produced they have become savage and homicidal, and cannot be reasoned with. I know how this sounds, but it is the truth. We are fortifying the base, and eliminating any contaminated from within the compound. We encourage all residents to grab whatever provisions they can and immediately make their way to Sanford Army Base now, where emergency procedures are being implemented and help is provided. I repeat, this is Captain Mark Walters…."

The voice continued, repeating its warnings on a loop, but I had stopped listening. The world seemed to be falling away somehow. *This can't be happening, it makes no sense.* Things like that don't happen in real life, or so I thought. I switched the radio off and climbed on top of my mother's work table, forcing open the sky-light window. The frame and rubber seal were warped and twisted from exposure to the rain, and the smell of melted plastic was overpowering.

I peered out across the once-lively neighbourhood. There was more than one set of sirens now, and I could just see blue lights come and go quickly a couple of streets away. In the distance I saw smoke rising, the grey, thick cloud distinct from the clear navy of the sky, and I knew something big was on fire. I could hear yelling too, as well as distant screams and the panicked barking of a dog. I realized that the disembodied voice of Captain Mark Walters had been speaking the truth, and I knew suddenly, and with great clarity, that my mom, just like my brother, was dead. Or at least what made them *them* was dead. I imagined them, disfigured and broken, stumbling through the streets like something from a George Romero Movie; Attacking anyone they came across. I felt tears falling fast and free. *I'm alone. I'm alone.*

I wept for a while, sitting on that floor and clutching the radio as if it was a teddy bear. Everything had seemed so surreal, a nightmare come to life. It was the noise that snapped me out of my despair. Not a bang or thump exactly, more like the sound of something dragging. I slowly stood, tip-toeing my way to the landing and peering down the stairs. I could see the front door lazily swinging in the breeze, the noise of the draft excluder scraping slowly against the hardwood floor. *Didn't I close that?*

I never would have considered myself as the type of person with good instincts, as I had dated enough bums in my day to realize that my gut was out of whack, but I remember a sense of impending dread so clearly. I knew, despite my inner voice attempting to state otherwise, that I had closed the door. I knew there was someone down there, or *something.* I grabbed the baseball bat from Mark's sports bag, discarded haphazardly on his messy bedroom floor, and continued downstairs as quietly as I could.

Not only could I sense a presence in my home, another being unwelcome and unwanted, but I knew where it was. Something in me screamed to check the kitchen, that the intruder was in there. Perhaps I had heard other sounds, or audible queues so slight I only picked them up in my subconscious, or perhaps I knew even then that this was no intruder at all. Maybe I knew this was a boy coming back home, a boy who, out of habit, always went straight to the kitchen to drink the last of the orange juice or fill up on snacks before dinner.

I used the bat to push open the door and saw him standing there. *Mark.* Even without the exposed, oozing blisters and melted flesh I could see something was very wrong. The way he stood, hunched over with limbs hanging, he looked like a grotesque marionette puppet before its strings were pulled. And his eyes, *his eyes...* What were once hazelnut brown with flecks of grey were now filmy and white, and, worst of all, they were looking directly at me.

"Mark?"

I don't know what I had expected. Did I think he would respond? Laugh heartily at a practical joke well done, at his gullible sister? Even after the radio transmission, what that soldier had said, I held out a small sliver of hope that Mark was still in there. But the thing that used to be my brother simply let out a gargled, choking noise before lurching towards me. I backed away, the bat raised before me in a pathetic, hand-shaking attempt at showing strength.

"Mark...please."

That same noise came out of his throat, and this time I realized that congealed blood and other body fluids were leaking from a hole in his throat every time he, no *it,* made this audible effort. Mark was dead; It was obvious, painfully so, but seeing and believing are two completely different things. I knew I had to hit him, to stop him before he got too close. I've seen zombie movies; I've been the girl yelling at the television set, begging the character on screen to do something. 'Fight, shoot, run, anything! Don't just stand there, mouth agape!' But that's exactly what I did. This is my brother, or at least it was. This act, this final act, will mean he's really gone, that he's really dead and that I, in more than one way, caused it.

I was almost at the front window, with only a few feet of floor space left before being backed into a corner. I swung. God help me, I swung. The first swing was a good one, and made contact with his right temple. Where I had expected to hear a thud I heard a squelching noise, like someone dropping an over-ripe melon. He stumbled, but remained standing, so I hit him again and again and *again*. Even when he was still, and it was obvious that the threat was gone, I kept hitting, kept pounding chunks of moist, red lumps into the shag carpeting. I kept hitting him until I fell to the ground. I was exhausted, weeping and scream-ing aloud. *What have I done?*

I sat there, among the gore and goo. I just sat there, holding the bat in my lap, rocking back and forth and crying until I had no more tears to shed and my throat was hoarse and painful. Then I pulled myself together. I grabbed my backpack, doing my best to pack for the apoc-alypse. I put in food and bottled water, a knife and my bat for protection. I added some photos plus clean clothes, and then I left. I just *left.* Even if this had turned out to be a momentary blip, something humanity could recover from, I knew I could never go back to that house. *Never again.*

It wasn't just a blip. The rain came again and again, picking survivors off just as quickly as the things it created. This wasn't a local weather event, it was worldwide. This was the end times. There was no government, no emergency response, just looting and chaos. I made it to Sanford Army Base, a lot of us did, and this is our world now. We just *survive.* That's all we can do. There are dozens of theories about the rain, of course: Aliens, government and military experiments gone wrong, biological warfare, even God punishing us.

I don't think about what caused it, not anymore.

I just think about my brother and my mom, gone forever. I think about my new family, an odd and eclectic mix of people trying to hold it together against the rain, other people and the apocalypse. But, most of all, I think about the changes to my body, the changes that started from my feet up. I think about my eyes lightening, about my inability to feel physical pain, about my ever-growing strength that's far beyond what someone my age and size should be capable of. I wonder if I'm becoming like the others, like my brother, and I wonder if one day I'll stop speaking and simply begin attacking anyone within arm's reach.

Will I become the threat, the monster? Or am I changing into something new, something different altogether?

MARIE MCWILLIAMS
ABOUT THE AUTHOR

Marie McWilliams is a crime and horror writer from Northern Ireland. Her work has been published in various magazines and subscription boxes and her debut novel 'Broken Mirrors' is available on Amazon now. Marie is an avid online influencer with a large Bookstagram following (Instagram for book nerds) and a growing YouTube channel where she shares her love of horror fiction and all things spooky. Check her out below:

Instagram (@bookishmarie):
https://www.instagram.com/bookishmarie/?hl=en
You Tube (Marie McWilliams):
https://m.youtube.com/channel/UCj6gAjgPxaZ5AGUl-j4ALwzw#
Twitter (@MarieMcWblog):
https://mobile.twitter.com/mariemcwblog?lang=en
Blog: www.mariemcwilliams.com

Enjoyed the Book?

Indie Authors live for reviews and recommendations from their readers. Please take a few moments and review this collection on Amazon or Goodreads.

Don't Miss Out!

Looking for a FREE BOOK?

Sign up for Eerie River Publishing's monthly newsletter and get **Darkness Reclaimed** as our thank you gift!

Sign up for our newsletter
https://mailchi.mp/71e45b6d5880/welcomebook

Here at Eerie River Publishing, we are focused on providing paid writing opportunities for all indie authors. Outside of our limited drabble collections we put out each year, every single written piece that we publish -including short stories featured in this collection have been paid for.

Becoming an exclusive Patreon member gives you a chance to be a part of the action as well as giving you creative content every single month, no matter the tier. Free eBooks, monthly short stories and even paperbacks before they are released.

https://www.patreon.com/EerieRiverPub